Villani's Chronicle / Being Selections from the First Nine Books of the Croniche Fiorentine of Giovanni Villani

Giovanni Villani

INTRODUCTION

§ 1. *The Text.*

This book of selections is not intended as a contribution to the study of Villani, but as an aid to the study of Dante. The text of Villani is well known to be in a very unsatisfactory condition, and no attempt at a critical treatment of it has been made. The Florence edition of 1823, in eight volumes, has been almost invariably followed. Here and there the Editor has silently adopted an emendation that obviously gives the sense intended, and on p. 277 has inserted in brackets an acute suggestion made by Mr. A.J. Butler. In a few cases, by far the most important of which occurs on p. 450, passages which appear in some but not in all of the MSS. and editions of Villani are inserted in square brackets.

§ 2. *The References.*

It is probable that many more references to Dante's works might advantageously have been inserted in the margin had they occurred to our minds; and we shall be glad to have our attention called to any important omissions.

As a rule we have aimed at giving a reference to any passage in Dante's works on which the text has a direct bearing, or towards the discussion of which it furnishes materials, without intending thereby necessarily to commit ourselves to any special interpretation of the passage in Dante referred to.

But in some instances such a reference would, in our opinion, distinctly tend to the perpetuation of error. In such cases we have purposely abstained from appearing to bring a passage of Villani into relation with a passage of Dante with which we believe it to have no connection. For instance, to have given a reference to the *Vita Nuova* § 41, 1-11, on p. 320 would have appeared to us so distinct and dangerous a *suggestio falsi* that we have felt compelled to abstain from it even at the risk of being charged with a *suppressio veri* by those who do not agree with us.

§ 3. *The Principle of Selection.*

Our aim has been to translate all the passages from the first nine books of Villani's Chronicles which are likely to be of direct interest and value to the student of Dante.[1] A few chapters have been inserted not for their own sakes but because they are necessary for the understanding of other chapters that bear directly on Dante. When a chapter contains anything to our purpose, we have usually translated the whole of it. Where this is not the case the omissions are invariably indicated by stars * * * * * *. We have given the headings of all the chapters we have not translated, so that the reader may have in his hand the continuous thread of Villani's narrative, and may have some idea of the character of the omitted portions. By these means we hope we have minimised, though we do not flatter ourselves that we have removed, the objections which are legitimately urged against volumes of selections.

The nature of the interest which the Dante student will find in these selections will vary as he goes through the volume.

The early portions, up to the end of Book III., are interesting not so much for the direct elucidation of special passages in Dante as for the assistance they give us in realizing the atmosphere through which he and his contemporaries regarded their own past; and their habitual confusion of legend and history.

From Book IV. on into Book VIII. our interest centres more and more on the specific contents of Villani's Chronicle. Here he becomes the best of all commentators upon one phase of Dante's many-sided genius; for he gives us the material upon which Dante's judgments are passed, and enables us to know the men and see the events he judges as he himself knew and saw them. Chapter after chapter reads like a continuous commentary on *Purg.* vi. 127-151; and there is hardly a sentence that does not lighten and is not lightened by some passage in the *Comedy.* Readers who have been accustomed to weary themselves in attempts to digest and remember historical notes (into which extracts from Villani, torn from their native haunts, have been driven up for instant slaughter, as in battue shooting) will

5

find it a relief to have the story of the battles and revolutions of Florence, as Dante saw and felt it, continuously set before them—even though it be, for the present, in the partial and therefore mutilated form of "selections."

When we come to the later portions of Book VIII. and the first part of Book IX. the interest again changes. To the events after 1300 Dante's chief work contains comparatively few and scattered allusions; but as the direct connection with his writings becomes less marked the connection with his biography becomes more intimate. As we study the tangled period of Florentine politics that coincides with Dante's active political life (about 1300 a.d.), the ill-concerted and feeble attempts of the exiles to regain a footing in their city, and later on the splendid but futile enterprise of Henry, we seem to find the very fibres of Dante's life woven into the texture of the history. The dream of the *De Monarchia* was dreamed by Henry as well as by Dante; but as we read the detail of his failure it is borne in upon us that he not only did fail but must fail, for his ideal was incapable of realization. Italy was not ready for him, and had she been ready she would not have needed him.

Finally, the last pages of our volume, which cover selections from the portion of Book IX., extending from the death of Henry to the death of Dante himself, are for the most part inserted for a very special reason, as to which some little detail is necessary. Strangely enough they derive their importance not from any interest Dante may have taken in the events they record, but from the fact that he did not take enough interest in them to satisfy one of his most ardent admirers. The editions of Dante's collected works include a correspondence in Latin hexameters between Johannes de Virgilio and Dante. Now in the poem that opens this correspondence Johannes refers to Statius and to Lethe in a manner that proves beyond all doubt that the whole of the *Purgatorio* as well as the *Inferno* was in his hands. But he alludes to the *Paradiso*—the poem of the "super-solar" realms which is to complete the record of the "lower" ones—as not yet having appeared. It therefore becomes a matter of extreme interest to the Dante student to learn the date of this poem. Now one of the considerations that led Johannes to address Dante was the hope of inducing him to choose a contemporary subject for a Latin poem and so write something worthy of himself and of studious readers! With this object he suggests a number of subjects:—

"Dic age quo petiit Jovis armiger astra volatu:
Dic age quos flores, quæ lilia fregit arator:
Dic Phrygias damas laceratos dente molosso:
Dic Ligurum montes, et classes Parthenopæas."　　"Come! tell thou of the
flight by which Jove's armour-bearer (the Imperial Eagle = Henry VII.)
sought the stars. Come! tell thou of the flowers and lilies (of Florence)
crushed by the ploughman (Uguccione da Faggiuola). Tell of the Phrygian
does (the Paduans) torn by the mastiff's (Can Grande's) tooth. Tell of the
Ligurian mountains (the Genoese) and the Parthenopæan fleets (of Robert of
Naples)."

The correctness and security of the interpretation of this passage will
not be doubted by any one accustomed to the pedantic allusiveness of the
age; and it is moreover guaranteed by the annotator of the Laurentian MS.,
thought by many to be Boccaccio himself. It will be seen, therefore, from the
study of the concluding pages of this volume, that when Johannes addressed
Dante (after the appearance of the *Inferno* and the *Purgatorio*, but before that
of the *Paradiso*) Henry VII. had died (a.d. 1313), Can Grande had defeated the
Paduans (a.d. 1314 and 1317), Uguccione had defeated the Florentines (a.d.
1315), and Robert had collected his fleet to relieve Genoa (February, 1319). It
also seems highly probable that Can Grande had not yet suffered his reverses
at the siege of Padua (August, 1320). This is perhaps the one unassailable
datum for the chronology of Dante's works, and we have therefore included
in our selections so much as was needed to establish it. Our readers will
perhaps forgive us for having then left the fate of Genoa hanging in the
balance, for as Villani says: "Who could write the unbroken history of the
dire siege of Genoa, and the marvellous exploits achieved by the exiles and
their allies? Verily, it is the opinion of the wise that the siege of Troy itself, in
comparison therewith, shewed no greater and more continuous battling, both
by sea and land."

§ 4. *The Historical Value of Villani's Chronicle.*

An adequate edition of Villani would have to examine his statements in detail, and, where necessary, to correct them. Such a task, however, would be alike beyond our powers, and foreign to our immediate purpose. These selections are intended to illustrate the text of Dante; and for that purpose it is of more consequence to know what were the "horrible crimes" of which Dante supposed Manfred to be guilty, than to enquire whether or no he was really guilty of them. To know whether Constance was fifty-two, or only thirty, when she married Henry VI., and whether he took her from a convent or a palace is of less immediate consequence to the student of Dante than to be acquainted with the Guelf tradition as to these circumstances.

At the same time, the reader may reasonably ask for some guidance as to the point at which the authentic history of Florence disengages itself from the legend, and, further, as to the general degree of reliance he is justified in placing on the details supplied by Villani.

On the first point very few words will suffice. There was probably a Fiesolan mart on the site now occupied by Florence from very remote times; but the form of the "ancient circle" carries us back to a Roman camp and a military colony as the origin of the regular city. Beyond this meagre basis the whole story of "Troy, and of Fiesole and Rome," in connection with Florence must be pronounced a myth. The notices of Florence before the opening of the twelfth century are few and meagre, but they suffice to prove that the story of its destruction by Totila, and rebuilding by Charlemagne, is without foundation; and of all the reported conquests of Fiesole that of 1125 is the first that we can regard as historical.

The history of Florence is almost a blank until about 1115 a.d., the date of the death of the Countess Matilda.

With respect to the second point, it is impossible to give so brief or conclusive an answer. Villani is as valuable to the historian as he is delightful to the general reader. He is a keen observer, and has a quick eye for the salient and essential features of what he observes. When dealing with his own times, and with events immediately connected with Florence, he is a

8

trustworthy witness, but minute accuracy is never his strong point; and in dealing with distant times and places he is hopelessly unreliable.

The English reader will readily detect his confusions in Book VII., § 39, where at one time Richard of Cornwall, and at another Henry III., is called king of England; and Henry of Cornwall and Edward I. are regarded indifferently as sons of Richard or sons of Henry III., but are always said to be brothers instead of cousins.

Here there is little danger of the reader being misled, but it is otherwise in such a case as that of Robert Guiscard and the house of Tancred in Book IV., § 19. By way of putting the reader on his guard, we will go into this exceptionally bad, but by no means solitary, instance of Villani's inaccuracies.

Tancred, of the castle of Hauteville (near Coutances, in Normandy), had twelve sons, ten of whom sought their fortunes in southern Italy and Sicily. Four of these were successively Counts of Apulia, the last of the four being Robert Guiscard. He was followed by his son Roger, and his grandson William, who died childless. Another of the sons of Tancred was Roger, who became Count of Sicily. He was succeeded by his son Roger II., who possessed himself of the Apulian domains of his relative William, on the decease of the latter. Roger now had himself proclaimed King of Sicily by the anti-pope Anaclete, and united Sicily and Naples under his sway. He was followed by his son William (the Bad), and his grandson William (the Good), on whose death, without issue, Henry VI., who married Roger's daughter Constance, claimed the succession in the right of his wife. (*L'Art de Vérifier les Dates.*)

The most important of these relations may be set forth thus:

Tancred of Hauteville   Robert Guiscard
Count of Apulia Roger I.
Count of Sicily   Roger Roger II.
King of Sicily   William   William
the Bad Constance = Henry VI.   William
the Good

Let the reader construct the family tree from the data in Villani, and compare it with the one given above. He will find that Villani, to begin with, makes Robert Guiscard a younger son of the Duke of Normandy, then makes his younger brother, Roger I., into his son (occasionally confounding him with Roger II.); and, finally, ignores William the Bad, and makes William the Good the brother of Constance. His details as to the pretender Tancred are equally inaccurate. These must suffice as specimens; but they are specimens not only of a special class of mistake, but of a style of work against which the reader must be constantly on his guard if he intends to make use of any detailed dates or relations, or even if he wishes to make sure that the Pope or other actor named in any connection is really the right one.

So, too, even well within historical times, Villani is prone to the epic simplification of events. His account of the negociations of Farinata with Manfred, and of the battle of Montaperti for instance, represents the Florentine legend or tradition rather than the history of the events. These events are conceived with the vividness, simplicity and picturesque preponderance of personality which make them easy to see, but impossible to reconstruct in a rationally convincing form.

To enter into further detail under this head would be to transgress the limits we have set ourselves.

The settled conviction of both Villani and Dante that a difference of race underlay the civil wars of Florence, rests upon a truth obscurely though powerfully felt by them.

We have seen that the legend of Fiesole and Florence, upon which they rest their case, is without historical foundation; but the conflict of races was there none the less. And as it is here that modern historians find the key to the history of Florence, our readers will probably be glad to have set before them a brief account of the general conceptions in the light of which modern scholars would have us read the naive and ingenuous records of Villani.

The numerous Teutonic invasions and incursions which had swept over northern and central Italy, from Odoacer to Charlemagne, had established a powerful territorial nobility. They constituted a dominating class, military in their habits, accustomed to the exercise and the abuse of the simpler functions of government, accepting certain feudal traditions, but owning no practical allegiance to any power that was not in a position instantly to enforce it. Their effective organization was based on the clan system, and the informal family council was omnipotent within the limits of the clan. They were without capacity or desire for any large and enduring social organization. Their combinations were temporary, and for military purposes; and internecine family feuds were a permanent factor in their lives. Their laws were based on the "Barbarian" codes, but the influence of Roman law was increasingly felt by them.

In the cities it is probable that the old municipal organization had never wholly died out, though it had no formal recognition. The citizens were sometimes allowed to live "under their own law," and sometimes not; but the tradition of the Roman law was never lost. Nominally the cities were under the jurisdiction of some territorial magnate, or a nominee of the Emperor, but practically they enjoyed various degrees of independence. Their effective organization would depend upon their special circumstances, but in such a case as that of Florence would be based on the trade guilds.

In Florence a number of the Teutonic nobles had settled in the city; but it owed its importance to its trade. The city-dwelling nobles kept up their clan life, and fortified their houses; but in other respects they had become partially assimilated in feeling, and even in habits and occupations, to the mercantile community in which they lived. They filled the posts of military and civil administration, and were conscious of a strong unity of interest with the people.

Under the vigorous and beneficent rule in Tuscany of the great Countess Matilda (1076-1115) Florence was able quietly to consolidate and extend her power without raising any thorny questions of formal jurisdiction. But on the death of Matilda, when the Church and the Empire equally claimed the succession and were equally unable efficiently to assert their claims, it was inevitable that an attempt should be made to establish the *de facto* supremacy of Florence over Fiesole and the whole outlying district upon a firmer and more formal basis. It was equally inevitable that the attempt should be resisted.

Within Florence, as we have seen, there was a heterogeneous, but as yet fairly united citizenship. The germs of organization consisted on the side of the nobles in the clans and the Tower-clubs, and on the side of the people in the Trade-guilds. The Tower-clubs were associations each of which possessed a fortified tower in the city, which was maintained at the common expense of the associates, and with which their houses communicated. Of the Trade-guilds we shall speak briefly hereafter.

In the surrounding country the territorial nobility watched the growing power and prosperity of Florence with jealousy, stoutly resisted her claims to jurisdiction over them and their demesnes, and made use of their command of the great commercial highways to exact regular or irregular tolls, even when they did not frankly plunder the merchants.

Obviously two struggles must result from this situation. The city as a whole was vitally concerned in clearing the commercial routes and rendering the territorial nobility harmless; but within the city two parties, who may almost be regarded as two nations, contended for the mastery.

With respect to the collective struggle of Florence against her foes, which entered on its active phase early in the twelfth century, on the death of

12

Matilda in 1115, it may be said in brief that it was carried on with a vigour and success, subject only to brief and few reverses, during the whole period with which we are concerned. But this very success in external enterprises emphasized and embittered the internal factions. These had been serious from the first. The Uberti and other ruling families resisted the growing influence of the people; and the vicissitudes of the struggle may be traced at the end of the twelfth and beginning of the thirteenth centuries in the alternation of the various forms of the supreme magistracy. But it was part of the policy of the victorious Florentines to compel the nobles they had reduced to submission to live at least for a part of the year in the city; and thus while the merchant people of Florence was increasing in wealth and power, the nobles in the city were in their turn constantly recruited by rich and turbulent members of their own caste, who were ready to support them in their attempt to retain the government in their hands. Thus the more successful Florence was in her external undertakings the greater was the tension within.

The forces arrayed against each other gradually assumed a provisional organization in ever-increasing independence of each other. The old senate or council and the popular assembly of all the citizens were transformed or sank into the background, and the Podestà, or foreign magistrate appointed for a year, with his lesser and greater council of citizens, was the supreme authority from 1207 onwards. This marked a momentary triumph of the nobles. But the people asserted themselves once again, and elected a Captain of the People, also a foreigner, with a lesser and greater council of citizens, who did not dispute the formal and representative supremacy of the Podestà, but was in reality coordinate with him. On this the Podestà naturally became the head of the nobles as the Captain was head of the people; and there rose that spectacle, so strange to us but so familiar to mediæval Italy, of two bodies of citizens, each with its own constitution and magistracy, encamped within the same walls. The Podestà was the head of the "Commonwealth," and the Captain the head of the "People." There was, it is true, for the most part a show of some central and coordinating power, nominally supreme over these independent and often hostile magistrates, such as the body of Ancients. But this central government had little effective power.

13

To understand the course of Florentine history, however, we must turn back for a moment to the informal internal organization of the two bodies thus opposed to each other. The struggle is between the military and territorial aristocracy on the one hand, and the mercantile democracy of the city on the other; and we have seen that the clan system and the Tower-clubs were the germ cells of the one order, and the Craft-guilds those of the other. Now the Craft-guilds were obviously capable of supporting a higher form of political development than could ever come out of the rival system. The officers of the Florentine Crafts were compelled to exercise all the higher functions of government. They preserved a strict discipline within their own jurisdiction—(and the aggregation of the trades in certain streets and districts made that jurisdiction roughly correspond to local divisions)—they had to coordinate their industries one with another, and regulate their complicated relations one with another, and they sent their representatives to all the great trading cities of the world, where they had to conduct such delicate and important negociations that they became the most skilful diplomatists in Italy. Indeed, the training of ambassadors may almost be considered as a Florentine industry! Add to this the vast financial concerns which they had to conduct, and it will readily be seen that as statesmen the merchants of Florence must eventually prove more than a match for their military rivals and opponents. The merchant people was the progressive and constructive element in Florentine society.

Accordingly the constitutional history of Florence resolves itself into a progressive, though chequered, advance of the people against the nobles (or, as they were afterwards called, the magnates) along two lines. In the first place, they had to make the *de facto* trade organization of the city into its *de jure* constitution—a movement which culminated in 1282 in the formal recognition of the Priors of the Crafts as the supreme magistrates of Florence. And, in the second place, they must attempt to bring the magnates effectively within the control of the laws and constitution of the mercantile community, which they systematically and recklessly defied as long as they were in a position to do so. The magnates behaved like brigands, and the people replied by practically making them outlaws. They gradually excluded them from all share of the government, they endeavoured to make the

14

Podestà personally responsible for keeping them in order, they organized a militia of trade bands that could fly to arms and barricade the streets, or lay siege to the fortified houses of the magnates at a moment's notice; and finally, in 1293, they passed the celebrated "Ordinances of Justice" connected with the name of Giano della Bella, by which when a magnate murdered a popolano his whole clan was held directly responsible (the presumption being that the murder had been ordered in a family council), and "public report" vouched for by two witnesses was sufficient evidence for a conviction.

It is this struggle for the supremacy of the mercantile democracy and the Roman Law over the military aristocracy with its "barbarian" traditions, that lies at the back of the Guelf and Ghibelline troubles of the thirteenth century. The papal and imperial principles that are usually associated with the names enter only in a very secondary way into the conflict. In truth neither the popes nor the emperors had any sympathy with the real objects of either party, though they were ready enough to seek their advantage in alliances with them. And in their turn the magnates and merchants of Florence were equally determined to be practically independent of Pope and Emperor alike. Nevertheless the magnates could look nowhere else than to the Emperor when they wanted material support or moral sanction for their claims to power; and it was only in the magnates that the Emperor in his turn could hope to find instruments or allies in his attempt to assert his power over the cities. In like manner the Pope, naturally jealous of a strong territorial power, encouraged and fostered the cities in their resistance to imperial pretensions, while he and the merchant bankers of Florence were indispensable to each other in the way of business.

We have now some insight into the essential motives of Florentine history in the thirteenth century. But another step is needed before we can understand the form which the factions took. It would be a fatal error to suppose that the Ghibellines were soldiers and the Guelfs merchants, and that as each faction triumphed in turn Florence expelled her merchants and became a military encampment, or expelled her soldiers and became a commercial emporium. Such a course of events would be absolutely impossible. The truth is, that the main part of the faction fighting and banishing was done on both sides by the magnates themselves. The industrial community went on its way, sometimes under grievous exactions, sometimes under a friendly Government, always subject to the insolence and violence of the magnates, though in varying degree, but always there, and always pursuing its business occupations. It came about thus. We have seen that in the twelfth century the nobles within Florence were on the whole fairly conscious of having common cause with the merchants, but that the very success of her external undertakings brought into the city a more turbulent and hostile order of nobility. On the other side, rich and powerful merchants pushed their way up into recognition as magnates, while retaining their pecuniary interest in commerce. Thus in the thirteenth century the body of magnates itself became divided, not only into clans, but into factions. It always seemed worth while for some of them to strengthen their alliances with the territorial magnates, the open foes of the city, in order to strengthen their hold on the city itself; and it always seemed worth while for others to identify themselves more or less sincerely with the demands of the people in order to have their support in wrenching from their fellow magnates a larger share of the common spoil. It was here that the absence of any uniting principle or constructive purpose amongst the magnates told with fatal effect. Indeed their house was so divided against itself that the people would probably have had little difficulty in getting rid of them altogether, had they not been conscious of requiring a body of fighting men for service in their constant wars. The knights were at a certain disadvantage in a street fight in Florence, but the merchant statesmen knew well enough that they could not do without them on a battle-field.

We can now understand the Guelf and Ghibelline struggles of the thirteenth century. The Buondelmonte incident of 1215, which both Dante and Villani regard as the cause of these conflicts, was of course only their occasion. The conclusive victory of one party could only mean the reappearance within its ranks of the old factions under new names. For if the faction opposed to the people won a temporary victory, they would be unable to hold their own permanently against the superior discipline, wealth, and constructive genius of their subjects; whereas if it was the champions of the people who had expelled their rivals and seized the plunder, they would be in no hurry to give up to the merchants the power they had won in their

16

name. They would regard themselves as entitled to a gratitude not distinguishable from submission, and would have their own definition of the degree of influence and power which was now their due. Thus what had been the people's party among the magnates would aspire, when victorious, to be the masters of the people, and gradually another people's party would form itself within their ranks. The wonder is not that no reconciliations were permanent, but that Cardinal Latino's reconciliation of 1279 lasted, at least ostensibly, so long as till 1300.

Obviously, if no new forces came upon the field, the only issue from this general situation must be in the conclusive triumph, not of the people's faction amongst the magnates, but of the attempt to break down the opposition of all the magnates to the citizen law, and the successful absorption of them into the commercial community. In the "Ordinances of Justice" and the further measures contemplated by Giano della Bella the requirements of this solution were formulated. Had they been successfully carried out, the magnates as an independent order would have been extinguished. Accordingly from 1293 onwards the fight raged round the Ordinances of Justice. No party, even among the magnates, dared openly to seek their repeal; but while some supported them in their integrity with more or less loyalty, others desired to modify them, or attempted to disembowel them by manipulating the elections and securing magistrates who would not carry them out. This was the origin of the Black and White factions. The Blacks were for circumventing the Ordinances, while the Whites were for carrying them out and extending their principles.

It will be seen at once how false an impression is given when it is said that the Whites were moderate Guelfs, inclining to Ghibellinism, and the Blacks extreme Guelfs. The truth is that the terms of Ghibelline and Guelf had by this time lost all real political meaning, but in so far as Guelfism in Florence had ever represented a principle it was the Whites and not the Blacks that were its heirs. But the magnates of Florence at the beginning of the fourteenth century administered large funds that had accrued from the confiscation of Ghibelline estates; they had fought against the Ghibellines at the Battle of Campaldino in 1289, and they made a boast of being Guelf of the Guelfs. Whatever party of them was in the supremacy, therefore, was

17

prone to accuse those in opposition of Ghibellinism simply because they were in opposition. This was what the victorious Blacks did. Their alliance with Pope Boniface VIII., who wished to make use of them for his ambitious purposes, lent some colour to their claim. Moreover, the remnants of the old Ghibelline party in the city or its territory naturally sought the alliance of the Whites as soon as they were in pronounced hostility to the ruling Guelfs. Thus arose the confusion that has perpetuated itself in the current conception of the Whites as "moderates," or Ghibellinizing Guelfs, a conception which stands in plain contradiction with the most significant facts of the case.

During the closing period of Dante's life the politics of Florence became more tangled than ever. Every vestige of principle seems to disappear, and personal ambitions and hatreds to become more unbridled than ever. The active interference of the Pope and the Royal house of France, followed by the withdrawal of the Papal Court to Avignon, the invasion of Italy by Henry VII., and the rise of such leaders as Can Grande, Uguccione da Faggiuola, and Castruccio, introduced new forces. We dimly perceive, too, that the mercantile democracy of Florence is becoming a mercantile aristocracy with elements of disturbance beneath it in the excluded or oppressed minor arts. In a word, just before the movement that has been steadily proceeding from 1115 to 1300 reaches its natural goal, the conditions of the problem change, the history enters upon a new phase, the far-off preparation for the Medici begins, and the problem ceases to have any direct and intimate connection with the study of Dante.

§ 6. *Dante's Politics.*

Enough has been said to show the reader how very imperfect an idea is given of Dante's politics when it is said that he was at first a Guelf but became a Ghibelline.

We have seen that the political party, for his connection with which he was exiled, was heir to the best Guelf traditions. His own writings show that the maintenance of peace was his idea of the supreme function of Government. The extreme severity of his judgments upon thieving and upon false coining is characteristic of the citizen of the greatest commercial city of the world. In all this, if we must use the misleading words, he is more Guelf than Ghibelline. It is true that he constantly opposed the influence of Boniface VIII. in the affairs of Florence, but Boniface was a disturbing and reactionary force that opposed the legitimate development of the Guelf policy of the Florentine democracy. It is true that he is a passionate advocate of an ideal Empire, and that he looks to the Emperor to heal the wounds of Italy, but the more carefully his writings are studied the more clear does it become that what he seeks in the Emperor is not a champion of Teutonic feudalism and supporter of the territorial nobility, but a power that will make Roman Law run all through Italy, and will hold the turbulent nobles in check. The Empire and the Emperor mean to Dante justice and peace secured by the enforcement of Roman Law. Whatever this is, it is not the Ghibellinism of Farinata or the Ubaldini. It is true, however—and here if anywhere Dante is open to the charge of temporary desertion of his principles—that after his exile he, together with other Whites, entered into a league with the Ubaldini, the most obstinate of the traditional foes of the commercial community of Florence. This was a desperate act, which, however reprehensible or deplorable, cannot be taken as indicating the deliberate adoption of a policy in contradiction to the whole tenor of his life and thought. We may well suppose that the sense of the hollow and indeed dishonourable nature of such an alliance was one of the considerations that induced him to sever himself from the exiles and "make a party for himself."

Lastly, he was an enthusiastic admirer of Henry VII., and he even

19

goaded him on to the attack of Florence. But Henry himself, who came to Italy with the sanction of the Pope, came with the earnest desire to heal and soothe. The Ghibellines proper felt that they had more to fear than to hope from him.

We cannot say, then, that Dante's politics changed. Nor can we define his position by calling him a Guelf or a Ghibelline, or both. His political ideals were his own. They were the outcome of his life and thought, intensely personal, as was all else about him. They cannot be labelled, but must be studied in his life and in his works.

If we are to use the current terms at all, we shall perhaps come nearest to the truth by saying that Dante was a Guelf in his aims, but that he approximated to the traditions if not to the practices of the Ghibellines in the means by which he hoped to see them realized.

SELECTIONS FROM THE CHRONICLES OF VILLANI

NOTES AND WARNINGS

The marginal references are to the divisions and lines of Moore's "Oxford Dante."

* * * * indicates a passage omitted in the translation; . . . indicates a hiatus in the Italian text.

Villani makes the year begin on March 25th. Thus 1300 is still running till March 25th, 1301. For instance, Bk. VII., § 9, gives the last day of February, 1265, as the date of the Battle of Benevento. By our reckoning this is the February of 1266. So too the Reconciliation of the Florentines by the Cardinal Latino, Bk. VII., § 56, took place by our reckoning in February, 1279, and the death of Charles of Anjou, Bk. VII., § 95, on January 7th, 1285, etc.

The Kingdom = The Kingdom of Apulia. The Duchy = The Duchy of Spoleto. The March = The March of Ancona. The Principality = [?] The Principality of Tarento. San Miniato = San Miniato al Tedesco, in the Arno Valley, West of Empoli. Nocera = Nocera of the Saracens near Naples, not the Nocera of *Paradiso* xi. 48. The Duomo or Cathedral = What is now known as the Baptistery.   Master, M., Messer, all represent the Italian Messer.

"Popolo" is translated "people" except where it means "the Democracy" as a form of government. It is there given untranslated. [∵ If this rule is ever departed from, it is through inadvertency.]

The "popolari" or "popolani" are members of the "popolo" or people, sometimes opposed to the "Nobili," or old Nobility of birth, and sometimes to the "Grandi," or Magnates, the new nobility of wealth and status.

To be "placed under bounds" appears to mean banishment or

confinement, under the form of a prohibition to cross certain stated "bounds."

The "Black" Cerchi are merely a branch of the Cerchi family: they were "Whites" politically.

Villani was well acquainted with Dante's works, and evidently regarded him as an authority. Therefore it must not be taken for granted, without further thought, that in every case of agreement Villani's testimony is an *independent* confirmation of Dante.

CHRONICLE
OF JOHN VILLANI

BOOK I.

This book is called the New Chronicle, in which many past things are treated of, and especially the root and origins of the city of Florence; then all the changes through which it has passed and shall pass in the course of time: begun to be compiled in the year of the Incarnation of Jesus Christ, 1300. Here begins the preface and the First Book.

§ 1.—Forasmuch as among our Florentine ancestors, few and ill-arranged memorials are to be found of the past doings of our city of Florence, either by the fault of their negligence or by reason that at the time that Totila, the scourge of God, destroyed it, their writings were lost, I, John, citizen of Florence, considering the nobility and greatness of our city at our present times, hold it meet to recount and make memorial of the root and origins of so famous a city, and of its adverse and happy changes and of past happenings; not because I feel myself sufficient for such a work, but to give occasion to our successors not to be negligent in preserving records of the notable things which shall happen in the times after us, and to give example to those who shall come after, of changes, and things come to pass, and their reasons and causes; to the end that they may exercise themselves in practising virtues, and shunning vices, and enduring adversities with a strong soul, to the good and stability of our republic. And, therefore, I will furnish a faithful narrative in this book in plain vernacular, in order that the ignorant and unlettered may draw thence profit and delight; and if in any part there should be defect, I leave it to the correction of the wiser. And first we will say whence were the origins of our said city, following on for as long a time as God shall grant us grace; and not without much toil shall I labour to extract and recover from the most ancient and diverse books, and chronicles, and authors, the acts and doings of the Florentines, compiling them herein; and first the origin of the ancient city of Fiesole, the destruction whereof was the cause and beginning of our city of Florence. And because our origin starts from very long ago, it seems to us necessary to our treatise to recount briefly other ancient stories; and it will be delightful and useful to our citizens now and to come, and will encourage them in virtue and in great actions to consider how they are descended from noble ancestors and from folk of worth, such as were the ancient and worthy Trojans, and valiant and noble Romans. And to the end our work may be more praiseworthy and good, I beseech the aid of our Lord Jesus Christ, in whose name every work has a good beginning, continuance and end.

§ 2.—*How through the confusion of the Tower of Babel the world began to be inhabited.*

We find in the Bible histories, and in those of the Assyrians, that Nimrod the giant was the first king, or ruler, and assembler of the gatherings of the peoples, that he by his power and success ruled over all the families of the sons of Noah, which were seventy-two in number, to wit, twenty-seven of the issue of Shem the first-born son of Noah, and thirty of Ham the second son of Noah, and fifteen of Japhet the third son of Noah. This Nimrod was the son of Cush, which was the son of Ham, the second son of Noah, and of his pride and strength he thought to rival God, saying that God was Lord of Heaven, and he of Earth; and to the end that God might no longer be able to hurt him by a flood of water, as He had done in the first age, he ordained the building of the marvellous work of the Tower of Babel; wherefore God, to confound the said pride, suddenly sent confusion upon all mankind, which were at work upon the said tower; and where **Inf. xxxi. 12-18, 46-81. Par. xxvi. 124-126. De Vulg. El. i. 6: 49-61 and i. 7. Purg. xii. 34-36.** all were speaking one language (to wit, Hebrew), it was changed into seventy-two divers languages, so that they could not understand one another's speech. And by reason of this, the work of the said tower had of necessity to be abandoned, which was so large that it measured eighty miles round, and it was already 4,000 paces high, and 1,000 paces thick, and each pace is three of our feet. And afterwards this tower remained for the walls of the great city of Babylon, which is in Chaldæa, and the name Babylon is as much as to say "confusion"; and therein by the said Nimrod and his descendants, were first adored the idols of the false gods. The said tower, or wall of Babylon, was begun 700 years after the Flood, and there were 2,354 years from the beginning of the world to the confusion of the Tower of Babel. And we find that they were 107 years working at it; and men lived long in those times. And note, that during this long life, having many wives, they had many sons and descendants, and multiplied into a great people, albeit disordered and without law. Of the said city of Babylon the first king which began to make wars was Ninus, son of Belus, descended from Asshur, son of Shem, which Ninus built the great city **Inf. v. 52-60. De Mon. ii. 9: 22 sqq.** of Nineveh; and then after him reigned Semiramis, his wife, in Babylon, which was the most cruel and dissolute woman in the world, and she was in the time of Abraham.

§ 3.—*How the world was divided into three parts, and of the first called Asia.*
§ 4.—*Of the second part of the world called Africa, and its boundaries.*
§ 5.—*Of the third part of the world called Europe, and its boundaries.*

* * * * This Europe was first inhabited by the descendants of Japhet, the third son of Noah, as we shall make mention hereafter in our treatise; and also according to Escodio, master in history, Noah in person, with Janus his son, which he begat after the Flood, came into this part of Europe into the region of Italy, and there ended his life; and Janus abode there, and from him were descended great lords and peoples, and he did many things in Italy.

§ 6.—*How King Atlas, born in the fifth degree from Japhet, son of Noah, first came into Europe.*
§ 7.—*How King Atlas first built the city of Fiesole.*

* * * * This Atlas, with Electra his wife, and many followers, by omens and the counsel of Apollinus his astrologer and master, arrived in Italy in the country of Tuscany, which was entirely uninhabited by **De Vulg. El. i. 8: 11-13.** human beings, and searching by the aid of astronomy through all the confines of Europe for the most healthy and best situated place which could be chosen by him, he took up his abode on the mount of Fiesole, which seemed to him strong in position and well situated. And upon that rock he began and built the city of Fiesole, by the counsel of the said Apollinus, who found out by astronomical arts that Fiesole **Inf. xv. 61-63. Par. xv. 126.** was in the best and most healthy place that there was in the said third part of the world called Europe. Since it is well-nigh midway between the two seas which

encircle Italy, to wit, the sea of Rome and Pisa, which Scripture calls the Mediterranean, and the Adriatic Sea or Gulf, which to-day is called the Gulf of Venice, and, by reason of the said seas, and by the mountains which surround it, better and more healthy winds prevail there than in other places, and also by reason of the stars which rule over that place. And the said city was founded during the ascendant of such a sign and planet, that it gives more sprightliness and strength to all its inhabitants than any other part of Europe; and the nearer one ascends to the summit of the mountain, the more healthy and better it is. And in the said city there was a bath, which was called the Royal Bath, and which cured many sicknesses; and into the said city there came by a marvellous conduit from the mountains above Fiesole, the finest and most wholesome spring waters, of which the city had great abundance. And Atlas had the said city walled with strongest walls, wondrous in their masonry and their thickness, and with great and strong towers; and there was a fortress upon the summit of the mountain, of the greatest beauty and strength, where dwelt the said king, as is still shown and may be seen by the foundations of the said walls, and by the strong and healthy site. The said city of Fiesole multiplied and increased in inhabitants in a short time, so that it ruled over the surrounding country to a great distance. And note that it was the first city built in the said third division of the world called Europe, and therefore it was named "*Fia Sola*" [it shall be alone], to wit, *first*, with no other inhabited city in that said division.

§ 8.—*How Atlas had three sons, Italus and Dardanus and Sicanus.*

Atlas, king of Fiesole, after that he had built the said city, begat by Electra his wife three sons: the first was called Italus, and from his name the kingdom of Italy was named, and he was lord and king thereof; the second son was named Dardanus, which was the first rider to ride a horse with saddle and bridle. Some have written that Dardanus was son to Jove, king of Crete, and son to Saturn, as has been afore mentioned; but this was not true, forasmuch as Jove abode in Greece, and his descendants were kings and lords thereof, and were always the enemies of the Trojans; but Dardanus came from Italy, and was son to Atlas, as the history will make mention. And Virgil the poet confirms it in his book of the *Æneid*, when the gods said to Æneas that he should seek the country of Italy, whence had come his

26

forefathers which had built Troy; and this was true. The third son of **De Mon. ii. 3: 67, 68.** Atlas was named Sicanus, that is in our parlance Sezzaio [last], which had a most beautiful daughter called Candanzia. This Sicanus went into the island of Sicily, and was the first inhabitant thereof, and from **De Vulg. El. i. 10: 39-85.** his name the island was at the first called Sicania, and by diversity of vernacular of the inhabitants it is now called by them Sicilia, and by us Italians Cicilia. This Sicanus built in Sicily the city of Saragosa, and made it chief of the realm whereof he was king, and his descendants after him for a very long time, as is told in the history of the Sicilians, and by Virgil in the *Æneid*.

§ 9.—*How Italus and Dardanus came to agree which should succeed to the city of Fiesole and the kingdom of Italy.*

When King Atlas had died in the city of Fiesole, Italus and Dardanus his sons were left rulers after him; and each of them being a lord of great courage, and both being worthy in themselves to reign over the kingdom of Italy, they came to this agreement together, to go with their sacrifices to sacrifice to their great god Mars, whom they worshipped; and when they had offered sacrifice they asked whether of them twain ought to abide lord in Fiesole, and whether ought to go and conquer other countries and realms. From the which idol they received answer, either by divine revelation or by device of the devil, that Dardanus should go and conquer other lands and countries, and Italus should remain in Fiesole and in the country of Italy. To which commandment and answer they gave such effect that Italus abode as ruler, and he begat great rulers which after him governed not only the city of Fiesole and the country round about, but well-nigh all Italy, and they built many cities there; and the said city of Fiesole rose into great power and lordship, until the great city of Rome reached her state and lordship. And thereafter, for all the great power of Rome, yet was the city of Fiesole continually at war with and rebelling against it, until at last it was destroyed by the Romans, as this faithful history shall hereafter record. At present we will cease speaking of the Fiesolans and will return to their history in due time and place, and we will now go on to tell how Dardanus departed from Fiesole, and was the first builder of the great city of Troy, and the ancestor of the kings of the Trojans and also of the Romans.

27

§ 10.—*How Dardanus came to Phrygia and built the city of Dardania, which was afterwards the great Troy.*

Dardanus, as he was commanded by the answer of their god, departed from Fiesole with Apollinus, master and astrologer of his father, and with Candanzia his niece, and with a great following of his people, and came into the parts of Asia to the province which was called Phrygia [Frigia], from the name of Friga, of the descendants of Japhet, which was the first inhabitant thereof; which province of Phrygia is beyond Greece, after the islands of Archipelago are passed, on the mainland, which to-day is ruled by the Turks and is called Turkey. In that country the said Dardanus by the counsel and arts of the said Apollinus began to build, and made a city upon the shores of the said Grecian sea, which he called after his own name Dardania, and this was 3,200 years from the creation of the world. And it was called Dardania so long as Dardanus lived, or his sons.

§ 11.—*How Dardanus had a son which was named Tritamus, which was the father of Trojus, after whose name the city of Troy was so called.*

Now this Dardanus had a son which was called Tritamus, and Tritamus begat Trojus and Torajus; but Trojus was the wiser and the more valorous, and because of his excellence he became lord and king of the said city and of the country round about; and he had great war with Tantalus, king of Greece, son of Saturn, king of Crete, of whom we made mention. And then, after the death of the said Trojus, by reason of the goodness and wisdom and worth which had reigned in him, it pleased his son and the men of his city that the said city should always be called Troy after his name; and the chief and principal gate of the city, in memory of Dardanus, retained the name which the city had at the first, to wit Dardania.

§ 12.—*Of the kings which were in Troy; and how Troy was destroyed* **Cf. Convivio iv. 14: 131-154. Purg. xii. 61-63. Inf. xxx. 13-15, 98, 113, 114.** *the first time in the time of the King Laomedon.* § 13.—*How the good King Priam rebuilt the city of Troy.* § 14.—*How Troy was destroyed by the Greeks.* § 15.—*How the Greeks which departed from the siege of Troy well-nigh all came to ill.* § 16.—*How Helenus, son of King Priam, with the sons of Hector, departed from Troy.*

§ 17.—*How Antenor and the young Priam, having departed from Troy, built the city of Venice, and that of Padua.*

Another band departed from the said destruction, to wit Antenor, who was one of the greatest lords of Troy, and was brother of Priam, and **Inf. xxxii. 88. Purg. v. 75.** son of the King Laomedon, who was much accused of betraying Troy, and Æneas was privy to it, according to Dares; but Virgil makes him quite innocent of this. This Antenor, with Priam the younger, son of King Priam, a little child, escaped from the destruction of Troy with a great following of people to the number of 12,000, and faring over the sea with a great fleet arrived in the country where to-day is Venice, the great city, and they settled themselves in those little surrounding islands, to the end they might be free and beyond reach of any other jurisdiction and government, and became the first inhabitants of those rocks; whence increasing later, the great city of **Inf. xxxii. 88.** Venice was founded, which at first was called Antenora, from the said Antenor. And afterwards the said Antenor departed thence and came to dwell on the mainland, where to-day is Padua, the great city, and he **Purg. v. 75.** was its first inhabitant and builder, and he gave it the name of Padua, because it was among paduli [marshes], and by reason of the river Po, which flowed hard by and was called Pado. The said Antenor remained and died in Padua, and within our own times his body has been discovered there, and his tomb engraved with letters which bear witness that it is the body of Antenor, and this his tomb has been renewed by the Paduans and may be seen to-day in Padua.

§ 18.—*How Priam III. was king in Germany, and his descendants kings of France.* § 19.—*How Pharamond was the first king of France, and his descendants after him.* § 20.—*How the second Pepin, father of Charles the Great, was king of France.*

§ 21.—*How Æneas departed from Troy and came to Carthage in Africa.*

Æneas again departed from the said destruction of Troy with Anchises, his father, and with Ascanius, his son, born of Creusa, daughter of the great King Priam, with a following of 3,300 men of the best people of Troy, and they embarked upon twenty-two ships. This Æneas was of the royal race of the Trojans, in this wise: for Ansaracus, son of **De Mon. ii. 3: 62.** Trojus and brother of Ilius, of whom mention was made in the beginning, begat Danaus, and Danaus begat Anchises, and Anchises begat Æneas. This Æneas was a lord of great worth, wise and of great prowess, and very beautiful in person. When he departed from Troy with his following, with great lamentation, having lost Creusa, his wife, in the assault of the Greeks, he went first to the island of Ortygia, and made sacrifice to Apollo, the god of the sun, or rather idol, asking him for counsel and answer whither he should go; from the which he had answer and commandment to go into the land and country of Italy **De Mon. ii. 3: 77-84.** (whence at the first had come Dardanus and his forefathers to Troy), and to enter into Italy by the harbour or mouth of the river of Albola; and he said to him by the said oracle, that after many travails by sea, and battles in the said land of Italy, he should gain **Epist. vii. (3) 62, 63.** a wife and great lordship, and from his race should arise mighty kings and emperors, which should do very great and notable things. When Æneas heard this he was much encouraged by the fair response and promise, and straightway he put to sea with his following and ships, and voyaging long time he met with many adventures, and came to many countries, and first to the country of Macedonia, where already were Helenus and the wife and son of Hector; and after their sorrowful meeting, remembering the ruin of Troy, they departed. And sailing over divers seas, now forwards, now backwards, now crossways, as being ignorant of the country of Italy, not having with them any great masters or pilots of the sea which could guide them, so that they sailed almost whithersoever fortune or the sea winds might lead them, at last they came to the island of Sicily which the poets called Trinacria, and landed where to-day is the city of Trapali, in which Anchises, his father, by reason of his great toils and his old age, **Par. xix. 131, 132.** passed from this life, and in the said place was buried after their manner with great solemnities. And after the great mourning made by Æneas over his dear father, they departed thence to go into Italy; and by stress of storm the said ships were divided, and part held one way, and part another. And one of the said ships, with all on board, was lost in the sea, and the others came to the shores of Africa (neither knowing ought of the other), where the noble city of Carthage was a-building by the powerful and beautiful Queen Dido which had come thither from Sidonia, which is now called Suri [Tyre]; and the said Æneas and Ascanius, his son, and all his following in the twenty-one ships which came to that port, were received by the said queen with **Par. viii. 9.** great honour; above all, because the said queen was taken with great love for Æneas so soon as she beheld him, in such wise that Æneas for her sake abode there long time in such delight that he did not remember the commandment of the gods that he should go into Italy; and by a dream or vision, it was told him by the said gods that he should **Inf. v. 61, 62. Par. ix. 97, 98. Cf. De Monarchia ii. 3: 102-108. Convivio iv. 26: 59-70. Canzon. xii. 35, 36.** no longer abide in Africa. For the which thing suddenly with his following and ships he departed from Carthage; and therefore the said Queen Dido by reason of her passionate love slew herself with the sword of the said Æneas. And those who desire to know this story more fully may read it in the First and Second Books of the *Æneid*, written by the great poet Virgil.

§ 22.—*How Æneas came into Italy.*

When Æneas had departed from Africa, he again landed in Sicily, where he had buried his father Anchises, and in that place celebrated the anniversary of his father with great games and sacrifices; and they **Conv. iv. 26: 96.** received great honour from Acestes, then king of Sicily, by reason of the ancient kinship with the Trojans, who were descendants of Sicanus of Fiesole. Then he departed from Sicily, and came into Italy, to the Gulf of Baiæ, which to-day is called Mare Morto, to the headland of Miseno, very near where to-day is Naples; in which country there were **Inf. ii. 13-15.** many and great woods and forests, and Æneas, going through them, was led by the appointed guide, the Erythræan Sibyl, to behold Hell and the pains that are therein, and afterwards Limbo; and, according to what is related by Virgil in the Sixth Book of the *Æneid*, he there **Par. xv. 25-30.** found and recognised the shades, or soul-images of his father, Anchises, and of Dido, and of many other departed souls. And by his said father were shown to him, or signified in a vision, all his descendants and their lordship, and they which were to build the great city of Rome. And it is said by many, that the place where he was led by the wise Sibyl was through the weird caverns of Monte Barbaro, which is above Pozzuolo, and which still to-day are strange and fearful to behold; and others believe and hold that, either by divine power or by magic arts, this was shown to Æneas in a vision of the **Inf. ii. 13-27.** spirit, to signify to him the great things which were to issue and come forth from his descendants. But however that may be, when he issued forth from Hell, he departed, and entered into a ship, and, following the shores until he came to the mouth of the river Tiber or Albola, he entered it, and came to shore, and by signs and auguries perceived that he had arrived in the country of Italy, which had been promised him by the gods; and with great festival and rejoicing they brought their labours by sea to an end, and began to build for themselves habitations, and to fortify themselves with ditches and palisades of the wood of their ships. And this place afterwards became the city of Ostia; and these fortifications they built for fear of the country people, who, fearing them as strange folk and unused to their customs, held them as foes, and fought many battles against the Trojans to drive them from the country, in all of which the Trojans were victorious.

§ 23.—*How the King Latinus ruled over Italy, and how Æneas had his daughter to wife, and all his kingdom.*

In this country (whereof the capital was Laurentia, the remains of which may still be traced near to where Terracina now stands), the **Inf. xiv. 94-96. Par. xxii. 145, 146.** King Latinus reigned, which was of the seed of King Saturn, who came from Crete when he was driven thence by Jove his son, as we made mention afore. And this Saturn came into the country of Rome, which was then ruled by Janus of the seed of Noah; but the inhabitants were then very ignorant, and lived like beasts on fruits and acorns, and dwelt in caves of the earth. This Saturn, wise in learning and in **Cf. Par. xxi. 25-27.** manners, by his wisdom and counsel led the people to live like men, and caused them to cultivate lands, and plant vineyards, and build houses, and enclose towns and cities; and the said Saturn was the first

32

to build the city of Sutri, called Saturna, and it was so called after his name; and in that country, by his care, grain was first sown, wherefore the dwellers therein held him for a god; and Janus himself, which was lord thereof, made him his partner, and gave him a share in the kingdom. This Saturn reigned thirty-four years in Italy, and after him reigned Picus his son thirty-one years; and after Picus reigned Faunus his son twenty-nine years, and was slain by his people. The two sons of Faunus were Lavinus and Latinus. This Lavinus built the city of Lavina. And Lavinus reigned but a short time; and when he was dead the kingdom was left to Latinus, which changed the name of the city of Lavina to Laurentia, because on the chief tower thereof there grew a great laurel tree. The said Latinus reigned thirty-two years, and was very wise; and he much bettered the Latin tongue. This **Inf. iv. 125, 126. Purg. xvii. 34-39.** King Latinus had only one most beautiful daughter called Lavinia, who by her mother had been promised in marriage to a king of Tuscany, named Turnus, of the city of Ardea, now Cortona. Tuscany was the name of the country and province, because there were the first sacrifices offered to the gods, with the fumes of incense called *tuscio*. Æneas having arrived in the country, sought peace with the King Latinus, and that he might dwell there; by the said Latinus he was received graciously, and not only had leave of him to inhabit the country, but also had the promise of his daughter Lavinia to wife, since the command of the gods was that they should marry her to a stranger, and not to a man of the country. For which cause, and to secure the heritage of King Latinus, great battles arose, for a long time, between Æneas and Turnus and them of Laurentia, and the said Turnus **Par. vi. 35, 36. Inf. i. 107, iv. 124. Purg. xvii. 34-39. Inf. i. 108. Par. vi. 3. De Monarchia ii. 3: 108-117.** slew in battle the great and strong giant, Pallas, son of Evander, king of the seven hills, where to-day is Rome, who had come in aid of Æneas; and on the same account died, by the hand of Æneas, the virgin Camilla, who was marvellous in arms. In the end, Æneas, being victor in the last battle, and Turnus being slain by his hand, took Lavinia to wife, who loved Æneas much, and Æneas her; and he had the half of the kingdom of King Latinus. And, after the death of King Latinus, who lived but a short time longer, Æneas was lord over all.

§ 24.—*How Julius Ascanius, son of Æneas, was king after him, and of the kings and lords who descended from him.* § 25.—*How Silvius,* **Inf. ii. 13.** *second son of Æneas, was king after Ascanius, and how from him descended the kings of the Latins, of Alba, and of Rome.* § 26.—*How Romulus and Remus founded the city of Rome.* § 27.—*How Numa* **Par. vi. 40-42. Convivio iv. 5: 80-97.** *Pompilius was king of the Romans after the death of Romulus.* § 28.—*How there were in Rome seven kings one after the other down to Tarquin, and how in his time they lost the lordship.*

§ 29.—*How Rome was ruled for a long time by the government of the consuls and senators, until Julius Cæsar became Emperor.*

After that the kings had been driven out, and the government of Rome was left to the consuls and senators, the said King Tarquin and his son, with the aid of King Porsenna of Tuscany, who reigned in the city of Chiusi [Clusium], made great war upon the Romans, but in the end the victory remained with the Romans. And afterwards the Republic of Rome was ruled and governed for 450 years by consuls and senators, and at times by dictators, whose authority endured for five years; and they were, so to speak, emperors, for that which they commanded must of necessity be done; and other divers offices, such as tribunes of the people, and prætors, and censors, and chiliarchs. And in this time there were in Rome many changes, and wars, and battles, not only with their neighbours, but with all the nations of the world; the which Romans by force of arms, and virtue and the wisdom of good citizens, ruled over well-nigh all the provinces and realms and dominions in the world, and gained sovereignty over them, and made them tributary, with the greatest battles, and with slaughter of many nations of the world, and of the Romans themselves, in divers times, well-nigh innumerable to relate. And also among the citizens themselves, by reason of envy against the rulers, and strifes between magnates and them of the people; and on the cessation of foreign wars, there arose much fighting and slaughter ofttimes among the citizens; and, in addition to this, from time to time intolerable pestilences arose among the Romans. And this government endured until the great battles of Julius Cæsar against Pompey, and then against his sons, in which Cæsar was victorious; then the said Cæsar did away with the office of consuls and of dictators, and he first was called Emperor. And after him **Par. vi. 79-81. Convivio iv. 5: 16-29. De Monarchia ii. 9: 99-105; and ii. 12. Epist. vii. (3) 64-73.** Octavianus Augustus, who ruled in peace, after many

34

battles, over the whole world, at the time of the birth of Jesus Christ, 700 years after the foundation of Rome; and thus it is seen that Rome was governed by kings for 254 years, and by consuls 450 years, as we have aforesaid, and it is told more at length by Titus Livius and many other authors. But note that the great power of the Romans was not alone in themselves, save in so far that they were at the head and leaders; but first all the Tuscans and then all the Italians followed them in their wars and in their battles, and were all called Romans. But we will now leave the order of the history of the Romans and of the Emperors, save in so far as it shall pertain to our matter, returning to our subject of the building of Florence, which we promised to narrate. And we have made this long exordium, forasmuch as it was necessary to show how the origin of the Roman builders of Florence (as hereafter will be narrated) was derived from the noble Trojans; and the origin and beginning of the Trojans was from Dardanus, son of Atlas, of the city of Fiesole, as we have briefly recounted; and afterwards from the descendants of the noble Romans, and of the Fiesolans, by the force of the Romans a people was founded called Florentines.

§ 30.—*How a conspiracy was formed in Rome by Catiline and his followers.*
680 a.u.c.

At the time when Rome was still ruled by the government of consuls, in the year 680 from the foundation of the said city, Mark Tully Cicero and Caius Antony being consuls, and Rome in great and happy state and lordship, Catiline, a very noble citizen, descended by birth from the royal house of Tarquin, being a man of dissolute life but brave and daring in arms and a fine orator, but not wise, being envious of the good and rich and wise men who ruled the city, their lordship not being pleasing to him, formed a conspiracy with many other nobles and other followers disposed to evil-doing, and purposed to slay the consuls and part of the senators, and to destroy their office, and to overrun the city, robbing and setting fire to many parts thereof, and to make himself ruler thereof; and this he would have done had it not been warded off by the wit and foresight of the wise consul, Mark Tully. So he defended the city from such ruin, and found out the said conspiracy and treason; but because of the greatness and power of the **Convivio iv. 5:**

172-176. said Catiline, and because Tully was a new citizen in Rome, his father having come from Capua or from some other town of the Campagna, he did not dare to have Catiline seized or to bring him to justice, as his misdeeds required; but by his great wit and fine speech he caused him to depart from the city; but many of his fellow-conspirators and companions, from among the greatest citizens, and even of the order of senators, who abode still in Rome after Catiline's departure, he caused to be seized, and to be strangled in prison, so that they died, as the great scholar, Sallust, relates in due order.

§ 31.—*How Catiline caused the city of Fiesole to rebel against the city of Rome.*

Catiline having departed from Rome, with part of his followers came into Tuscany, where Manlius, one of his principal fellow-conspirators, who was captain, had gathered his people in the ancient city of Fiesole, and Catiline being come thither, he caused the said city to rebel against the lordship of the Romans, assembling all the rebels and exiles from Rome and from many other provinces, with lewd folk disposed for war and for ill-doing, and he began fierce war with the Romans. The Romans, hearing this, decreed that Caius Antony, the consul, and Publius Petreius, with an army of horse and many foot, should march into Tuscany against the city of Fiesole and against Catiline; and they sent by them letters and messengers to Quintus Metellus, who was returning from France with a great host of the Romans, that he should likewise come with his force from the other side to the siege of Fiesole, and to pursue Catiline and his followers.

§ 32.—*How Catiline and his followers were discomfited by the Romans in the plain of Piceno.*

Now when Catiline heard that the Romans were coming to besiege him in the city of Fiesole, and that Antony and Petreius were already with their host in the plain of Fiesole, upon the bank of the river Arno, and how that Metellus was already in Lombardy with his host of three legions which were coming from France, and the succour which he was expecting from his allies which had remained in Rome had failed him, he took counsel not to shut himself up in the city of Fiesole, but to go into France; and therefore he departed from that city with his people and with a lord of Fiesole who was called Fiesolanus, and he had his horses' shoes reversed, to the end that when

36

they departed the hoofprints of the horses might show as if folk had entered into Fiesole, and not sallied forth thence, to cause the Romans to tarry near the city, that he might depart thence the more safely. And having departed by night, to avoid Metellus, he did not hold the direct road through the mountains which we call the Alps of Bologna, but took the plain by the side of the mountains, and came where to-day is the city of Pistoia, in the place called Campo Piceno, that was below where to-day is the fortress of Piteccio, purposing to cross the Apennine mountains by that way, and descend thence into Lombardy; but Antony and Petreius, hearing of his departure, straightway followed after him with their host along the plain, so that they overtook him in the said place, and Metellus, on the other side, set guards at the passes of the mountains, to the end he might not pass thereby. Catiline, seeing himself to be thus straitened, and that he could not avoid the battle, gave himself and his followers to the chances of combat with great courage and boldness, in the which battle there was great slaughter of Romans from the city and of rebel Romans and of Fiesolans; at the end of which fierce battle Catiline was defeated and slain in that place of Piceno with all his followers; and the field remained to the Romans, but with such dolorous victory that the said two consuls, with twenty horse, who alone escaped, did not care to return to Rome. The which thing could not gain credence with the Romans till the senators sent thither to learn the truth; and, this known, there was the greatest sorrow thereat in Rome. And he who desires to see this history more fully, let him read the book of Sallust called *Catilinarius*. The injured and wounded of Catiline's people who had escaped death in the battle, albeit they were but few, withdrew where is to-day the city of Pistoia, and there in vile habitations became the first inhabitants thereof, whilst their wounds were healing. And afterwards, by reason of the good situation and fruitful soil, the inhabitants thereof increased, which afterwards built the city of Pistoia, and by reason of the great mortality and pestilence which was near that place, both of their people and of the Romans, they gave it the name of Pistoia; and therefore it is not to be marvelled at if the Pistoians have been and are a fierce and cruel people in war among themselves and against others, being descended from the race of Catiline and from the remnants of such people as his, discomfited and wounded in battle.

§ 33.—*How Metellus with his troops made war upon the Fiesolans.*

After that Metellus, who was in Lombardy near the mountains of the Apennine Alps in the country of Modena, heard of the defeat and death of Catiline, straightway he came with his host to the place where the battle had been, and having seen the slain, through amazement at the strange and great mortality he was afeared, marvelling within himself as at a thing impossible. But afterwards he and his followers equally despoiled the camp of the Romans from the city and that of the enemy, seizing that which they found there; and this done he came towards Fiesole to besiege the city. The Fiesolans vigorously took to arms, and sallied forth from the city to the plain, fighting with Metellus and with his host, and by force thrust him back, and drove him to the other side of the Arno with great hurt to his people, who with his followers encamped upon the hills, or upon the banks of the river; the Fiesolans with their host drew off from the other bank of the river Arno towards Fiesole.

§ 34.—*How Metellus and Fiorinus discomfited the Fiesolans.*

The night following, Metellus ordered and commanded that part of his host should pass the river Arno, at a distance from the host of the Fiesolans, and should place themselves in ambush between the city of Fiesole and the host of the Fiesolans, and of that company he made captain Fiorinus, a noble citizen of Rome of the race of the Fracchi or Floracchi, who was his prætor, which is as much as to say marshal of his host; and Fiorinus, as he was commanded by the consul, so he did. In the morning, at the break of day, Metellus armed with all his people passing over the river Arno, began the battle against the Fiesolans, and the Fiesolans, vigorously defending the ford of the river, sustained the battle in the river Arno. Fiorinus, who was with his people in ambush, when he saw the battle begun, sallied forth boldly in the rear of the Fiesolans, who were fighting in the river against Metellus. The Fiesolans, surprised by the ambush, seeing themselves suddenly assailed by Fiorinus in the rear and by Metellus in front, put to confusion, threw down their arms and fled discomfited towards the city of Fiesole, wherefore many of them were slain and taken.

§ 35.—*How the Romans besieged Fiesole the first time, and how Fiorinus was slain.*

The Fiesolans being discomfited and driven back from the shores of Arno, Fiorinus the prætor, with the host of the Romans, encamped beyond the river Arno towards Fiesole, where were two little villages, one of which was called Villa Arnina, and the other Camarte [Casa Martis], that is campo or *Domus Martis*, where the Fiesolans on a certain day in the week held a market in all commodities for their towns and the region round about. The consul made a decree with Fiorinus that no one should sell or buy bread or wine or other things which might be of use to the troops save in the field where Fiorinus was stationed. After this the consul Quintus Metellus sent incontinent to Rome that they should send him men-at-arms to besiege the city of Fiesole, for the which cause the senators made a decree that Julius Cæsar, and Cicero, and Macrinus, with several legions of soldiers, should come to the siege and destruction of Fiesole; which, being come, besieged the said city. Cæsar encamped on the hill which rose above the city; Macrinus on the next hill or mountain, and Cicero on the other side; and thus they remained for six years besieging the said city, having through long siege and through hunger almost destroyed it. And likewise those in the host, by reason of the long sojourn and their many privations being diminished and enfeebled, departed from the siege, and returned to Rome, save Fiorinus, who remained at the siege with his followers in the plain where he had at first encamped, and surrounded himself with moats and palisades, after the manner of ramparts, or fortifications, and kept the Fiesolans in great straits; and thus he warred upon them long time, till his folk felt secure, and held their foes for nought. Then the Fiesolans having recovered breath somewhat, and mindful of the ill which Fiorinus had done and was doing to them, suddenly, and as if in despair, advanced by night with ladders and with engines to attack the camp or fortification of Fiorinus, and he and his people with but few guards and while they slept, not being on their guard against the Fiesolans, were surprised; and Fiorinus and his wife and his children were slain, and all his host in that place well-nigh destroyed, for few thereof escaped; and the said fortress and ramparts were destroyed, and burnt and done away with by the Fiesolans.

§ 36.—*How, because of the death of Fiorinus, the Romans returned to the siege of Fiesole.*

39

When the news was known at Rome, the consuls and senators and all the commonwealth being grieved at the misadventure which had befallen the good leader Fiorinus, straightway took counsel that this should be avenged, and that a very great host should return once more to destroy the city of Fiesole, for the which were chosen these leaders: Count Rainaldus, Cicero, Teberinus Macrinus, Albinus, Gneus Pompey, Cæsar, and Camertino Sezio, Conte Tudedino, that is Count of Todi, which was with Julius Cæsar, and of his chivalry. This man pitched his camp near to Camarti, nearly where to-day is Florence; Cæsar pitched his camp upon the hill which rose above the city, which is to-day called Mount Cecero, but formerly was called Mount Cæsar, after his name, or after the name of Cicero; but rather it is held to be after Cæsar, inasmuch as he was the greatest leader in the host. Rainaldus pitched his camp upon the hill over against the city on the other side of the Mugnone, and after his name it is so called until this day; Macrinus encamped on the hill still called after him; Camertinus in the region which is still called Camerata after his name. And all the other aforesaid lords, each one for himself pitched his camp around the city, some on the hills and some in the plain; but no other than these aforesaid have left their names to be a memorial of them. These lords, with their followers in great numbers, both horse and foot, besieging the city, arrayed and prepared themselves to make yet greater war upon the city than at the first; but by reason of the strength of the city the Romans wrought in vain, and many of them being dead by reason of the long siege and excessive toil, those great lords and consuls and senators well-nigh all returned to Rome; only Cæsar with his followers abode still at the siege. And during that sojourn he commanded his soldiers to go to the village of Camarti, nigh to the river Arno, and there to build a council house wherein he might hold his council, and might leave it for a memorial of himself. This building in our vernacular we have named Parlagio [Parliament house]. And it was round and was right marvellously vaulted, and had an open space in the midst; and then began seats in steps all around; and from step to step, built upon, vaulting, they rose, widening up to the very top, and the height thereof was more than sixty cubits, and it had two doors; and therein assembled the people to hold council, and from grade to grade the folk were seated, the most noble above, and then descending according to the

40

dignity of the people; and it was so fashioned that all in the Parliament might see one another by face, and that all might hear distinctly that which one was saying; and it held commodiously an infinite multitude of people, and its name, rightly speaking, was Parlatorio [speaking place]. This was afterwards destroyed in the time of Totila, but in our days the foundations may yet be seen, and part of the vaulting near to the church of S. Simone in Florence, and reaching to the beginning of the square of Santa Croce; and part of the palaces of the Peruzzi are built thereupon, and the street which is called Anguillaia, which goes to Santa Croce, goes almost through the midst of the said Parliament house.

§ 37.—*How the city of Fiesole surrendered itself to the Romans and was destroyed and laid waste.*

Circ. 72 b.c.

Fiesole having been besieged as aforesaid the second time, and the city being much wasted and afflicted both by reason of hunger and also because their aqueducts had been cut off and destroyed, the city surrendered to Cæsar and to the Romans at the end of two years and four months and six days (for so long had the siege lasted), on condition that any which desired to leave the city might go in safety. The city was taken by the Romans, and despoiled of all its wealth, and **Par. vi. 53, 54. xv. 124-126.** was destroyed by Cæsar, and laid waste to the foundations; and this was about seventy-two years before the birth of Christ.

§ 38.—*How the city of Florence was first built.*

After the city of Fiesole was destroyed, Cæsar with his armies descended to the plain on the banks of the river Arno, where Fiorinus and his followers had been slain by the Fiesolans, and in this place began to build a city, in order that Fiesole should never be rebuilt; and he dismissed the Latin horseman whom he had with him, enriched with the spoils of Fiesole; and these Latins were called Tudertines. Cæsar, then, having fixed the boundaries of the city, and included two places called Camarti and Villa Arnina [of the Arno], purposed to call it Cæsaræa from his own name. But when the Roman senate heard this, they would not suffer Cæsar to call it after his name, but they made a decree and order that the other chief noble

41

Romans who had taken part in the siege of Fiesole should go and build the new city together with Cæsar, and afterwards populate it; and that whichever of the builders had first completed his share of the work should call it after his own name, or howso else it pleased him.

Then Macrinus, Albinus, Gneus Pompey, and Marcius, furnished with materials and workmen, came from Rome to the city which Cæsar was building, and agreed with Cæsar to divide the work after this manner: that Albinus undertook to pave all the city, which was a noble work and gave beauty and charm to the city, and to this day fragments of the work are found, in digging, especially in the sesto of Santo Piero Scheraggio, and in Porta San Piero, and in Porta del Duomo, where it shows that the ancient city was. Macrinus caused the water to be brought in conduits and aqueducts, bringing it from a distance of seven miles from the city, to the end the city might have abundance of good water to drink and to cleanse the city; and this conduit was carried from the river called Marina at the foot of Montemorello, gathering to itself all the springs above Sesto and Quinto and Colonnata. And in Florence the said springs came to a head at a great palace which was called "caput aquæ," but afterwards in our speech it was called Capaccia, and the remains can be seen in the Terma until this day. And note that the ancients, for health's sake, used to drink spring waters brought in by conduits, forasmuch as they were purer and more wholesome than water from wells; seeing that few, indeed very few, drank wine, but the most part water from conduits, but not from wells; and as yet there were very few vines. Gneus Pompey caused the walls of the city to be built of burnt bricks, and upon the walls of the city he built many round towers, and the space between one tower and the other was twenty cubits, and it was so that the towers were of great beauty and strength. Concerning the size and circuit of the city we can find no chronicle which makes mention thereof; save that when Totila, the scourge of God, destroyed it, history records that it was very great. Marcius, the other Roman lord, caused the Capitol to be built after the fashion of Rome, that is to say the palace, or master fortress of the city, and this was of marvellous beauty; into which the water of the river Arno came by a hollowed and vaulted passage, and returned into the Arno underground; and the city, at every festival, was cleansed by the outpouring of this duct. This

Capitol stood where to-day is the piazza which is called the Mercato Vecchio, over against the church which is called S. Maria, in Campidoglio. This seems to be the best supported opinion; but some say that it was where **Inf. xxiii. 107, 108.** the place is now called the Guardingo [citadel]; beside the Piazza di Popolo (so called from the Priors' Palace), which was another fortress. Guardingo was the name afterwards given to the remains of the walls and arches after the destruction by Totila, where the bad quarter was. And the said lords each strove to be in advance of the work of the others. And at one same time the whole was completed, so that to none of them was the favour granted of naming the city according to his desire, but by many it was at first called "Little Rome." Others called it Floria, because Fiorinus, who was the first builder in that spot, had there died, he being the *fiore* [flower] of warlike deeds and of chivalry, and because in the country and fields around where the city was built there always grew flowers and lilies. Afterwards the greater part of the inhabitants consented to call it Floria, as being built among flowers, that is, amongst many delights. And of a surety it was, inasmuch as it was peopled by the best of **70 b.c.** Rome, and the most capable, sent by the senate in due proportion from each division of Rome, chosen by lot from the inhabitants; and they admitted among their number those Fiesolans which desired there to dwell and abide. But afterwards it was, through long use of the vulgar tongue, called Fiorenza, that is "flowery sword." And we find that it was built in the year 682, after the building of Rome and seventy years before the birth of our Lord Jesus Christ. And note that it is **Inf. xv. 73-78. Par. xv. 124-126.** not to be wondered at that the Florentines are always at war and strife among themselves, being born and descended from two peoples so contrary and hostile and different in habits as were the noble Romans in their virtue and the rude Fiesolans fierce in war.

§ 39.—*How Cæsar departed from Florence, and went to Rome, and was made consul to go against the French.*

After that the city of Florence was built and peopled, Julius Cæsar being angered because he, having been the first builder thereof, and having had the victory over the city of Fiesole, had nevertheless not been permitted to call the city after his name, departed therefrom and returned to Rome, and for his zeal and valour was elected consul and sent against the French, where he abode ten years whilst he was conquering France and England and Germany; and when he returned victorious to Rome his triumph was refused him, because he had transgressed the decree (made by Pompey the consul, and by the senate, through envy, under colour of virtue), that no one was to continue in any command for more than five years. The which Cæsar returning with his army of French and Germans from beyond the Alps, Italians, Pisans, Pirates, Pistoians, and also Florentines, his fellow-citizens, brought footmen and horsemen and slingers with him to begin a civil war, because his triumph had been refused him, but moreover that he might be lord of Rome as he had desired long time. So he fought against Pompey and the senate of Rome. And after the great battle between **Par. vi. 65. Epist. v. (3) 47-49.** Cæsar and Pompey, well-nigh all the combatants were slain in Emathia, to wit Thessaly in Greece, as may fully be read in Lucan the poet, by whoso desires to know the history. And after that Cæsar had gained the victory over Pompey, and over many kings and peoples who were helping those Romans who were his enemies, he returned to Rome, and so became the first Emperor of Rome, which is as much as to say commander over **Par. vi. 73-81. Convivio iv. 5: 16-79. De Mon. ii. 9: 99-105; and ii. 12. Epist. vii. (3) 64-73.** all. And after him came Octavianus Augustus, his nephew and adopted son, who was reigning when Christ was born, and after many victories ruled over all the world in peace; and thenceforward Rome was under imperial government, and held under its jurisdiction and that of the Empire all the whole world.

§ 40.—*Of the ensign of the Romans and of the Emperors, and how from them it came to the city of Florence and other cities.*
De Mon. ii. 4: 30-41.

In the time of Numa Pompilius by a divine miracle there fell from heaven into Rome a vermilion-coloured shield, for the which cause and augury the Romans took that ensign for their arms, and afterwards added S.P.Q.R. in letters of gold, signifying Senate of the People of Rome; the same ensign they gave to all the cities which they built, to wit, vermilion. Thus did they to Perugia, and to Florence, and to Pisa; but the Florentines, because of the name of Fiorinus and of the city, charged it with the white lily; and the

44

Perugians sometimes with the white griffin; and Viterbo kept the red field, and the Orvietans charged it with the white eagle. It is true that the Roman lords, consuls and dictators, after that the eagle appeared as an augury over **Par. xix. 101, 102. De Mon. ii. 11: 23. Purg. x. 80. Par. vi. 32, 100.** the Tarpeian rock, to wit, over the treasure chamber of the Capitol, as Titus Livius makes mention, added the eagle to their arms on the ensign; and we find that the consul Marius in the battle of the Cimbri had on his ensigns the silver eagle, and a similar ensign was borne by Catiline when he was defeated by Antonius in the parts about Pistoia, as Sallust relates. And the great Pompey bore the azure field and silver eagle, and Julius Cæsar bore the vermilion field and golden eagle, as Lucan makes mention in verse, saying,

Signa pares aquilas, et pila minantia pilis.

But afterwards Octavianus Augustus, his nephew and successor, changed it, and bore the golden field and the eagle natural, to wit, in black colour, signifying the supremacy of the Empire, for like as the eagle **Par. xx. 8, 31, 32. Inf. iv. 95, 96. Purg. ix. 30.** surpasses every other bird, and sees more clearly than any other creature, and flies as high as the heaven of the hemisphere of fire, so the Empire ought to be above every other temporal sovereignty. And after Octavianus all the Roman emperors have borne it in like manner; but Constantine, and after him all the other Greek emperors, retained the ensign of Julius Cæsar, to wit, the vermilion field and golden **Ep. vi. (3) 79-85.** eagle, but with two heads. We will leave speaking of the ensigns of the Roman commonwealth and of the Emperors, and we will return to our subject concerning the doings of the city of Florence.

§ 41.—*How the city of Florence became the Treasure-House of the Romans and the Empire.*

§ 42.—*How the Temple of Mars, which is now called the Duomo of S. Giovanni, was built in Florence.*

After that Cæsar and Pompey, and Macrinus and Albinus and Marcius, Roman nobles and builders of the new city of Florence, had returned to Rome, their labours being completed, the city began to increase and multiply both in Romans and Fiesolans who had settled as its inhabitants, and in a short time it became a fine city for those times; for the emperors and

45

senate of Rome advanced it to the best of their power, much like another little Rome. Its citizens, being in prosperous state, determined to build in the said city a marvellous temple in honour of the god Mars, by reason of the victory which the Romans had had over the city of Fiesole; and they sent to the senate of Rome to send them the best and most skilful masters that were in Rome, and this was done. And they caused to be brought white and black marbles and columns from many distant places by sea, and then by the Arno; they brought stone and columns from Fiesole, and founded and built the said temple in the place anciently called Camarti, and where the Fiesolans held their market. Very noble and beautiful they built it with eight sides, and when it had been built with great diligence, they dedicated it to the god Mars, who was the god of the Romans, and they had his effigy carved in marble in the likeness of an armed cavalier on horseback; they placed him on a marble pillar in the midst of that temple, and held him in great reverence, and adored him as their god so long as paganism continued in Florence. And we find that the said temple was begun during the reign of Octavianus Augustus, and that it was built under the ascendant of such a constellation that it will continue almost to eternity; and this we find written in a certain place engraved within the space of the said temple.

§ 43.—*Tells how the province of Tuscany lies.* § 44.—*Concerning the might and lordship possessed by the province of Tuscany before Rome came into power.* § 45.—*These are the bishoprics of the cities of Tuscany.* § 46.—*Of the city of Perugia.* § 47.—*Of the city of Arezzo.* § 48.—*Of the city of Pisa.* § 49.—*Of the city of Lucca.*

§ 50.—*Of the city of Luni.*
Par. xvi. 73.

The city of Luni, which is now destroyed, was very ancient, and we find from the stones of Troy, that from the city of Luni there went a fleet and soldiers in aid of the Greeks against the Trojans; afterwards it was destroyed by soldiers from beyond the mountains, by reason of a lady, the wife of a lord, who, when on the way to Rome, was adulterously seduced in this city of Luni, wherefore, as the said lord returned, he destroyed the city by force, and to-day the country is desert and unhealthy. And note that of old the coasts were much inhabited, and albeit inland there were few cities, and few inhabitants, yet in Maremma and Maretima, towards Rome on the coast of the Campagna, there were many cities and many inhabitants, which to-day are consumed and brought to nought by reason of the corruption **Purg. xiii. 152.** of the air: for there was the great city of Populonia, and Soana, and Talamone, and Grosseto, and Civitaveglia, and Mascona, and Lansedonia, which were with their troops at the siege of Troy; and in Campagna, Baia, Pompeia, Cumina, and Laurenza, and Albania. And the cause why to-day these cities of the coast are almost without inhabitants and unhealthy, and also why Rome is less healthy, is said by the great masters of astronomy to be because of the movement of the eighth sphere of heaven, which in every hundred years moves one degree **Vita Nuova § 2. Convivio ii. 15.** towards the North Pole, and thus it will move 15° in 1,500 years, and afterwards will turn back in like manner, if it be the pleasure of God that the world shall endure so long; and by the said change of the heaven is changed the quality of the earth and of the air, and where it was inhabited and healthy, it now is without inhabitants and unhealthy, and also the converse. And furthermore, we see that in the course of nature all things in the world change, and rise and diminish, as Christ said with His mouth that nothing here abides.

§§ 51-56.—*Of Viterbo, Orvieto, Cortona, Chiusi, Volterra, and Siena.*

§ 57.—*The story returns to the doings of the city of Florence, and how S. Miniato there suffered martyrdom under Decius, the Emperor.*

Now that we have briefly made some mention of our neighbouring cities in Tuscany, we will return to our subject and tell of our city of Florence. As we recounted before, the said city was ruled long time under the government and lordship of the emperors of Rome, and ofttimes the emperors came to sojourn in Florence when they were journeying into Lombardy, and into Germany, and into France to conquer provinces. And we find that Decius, the Emperor, in the first year of his reign, which was in the year of Christ 270, was in Florence, the **270 a.d.** treasure-house and chancelry of the Empire, sojourning there for his pleasure; and the said Decius cruelly persecuted the Christians wheresoever he could hear of them or find them, and he heard tell how the blessed Saint Miniato was living as a hermit near to Florence, with his disciples and companions, in a wood which was called Arisbotto of Florence, behind the place where now stands his

47

church, above the city of Florence. This blessed Miniato was first-born son to the king of Armenia, and having left his kingdom for the faith of Christ, to do penance and to be far away from his kingdom, he went over seas to gain pardon at Rome, and then betook himself to the said wood, which was in those days wild and solitary, forasmuch as the city of Florence did not extend and was not settled beyond Arno, but was all on this side; save only there was one bridge across the Arno, not however where the bridges now are. And it is said by many that it was the ancient bridge of the Fiesolans which led from Girone to Candegghi, and this was the ancient and direct road and way from Rome to Fiesole, and to go into Lombardy and across the mountains. The said Emperor Decius caused the said blessed Miniato to be taken, as his story narrates. Great gifts and rewards were offered him as to a king's son, to the end he should deny Christ; and he, constant and firm in the faith, would have none of his gifts, but endured divers martyrdoms: in the end the said Decius caused him to be beheaded where now stands the church of Santa Candida alla Croce al Gorgo; and many faithful followers of Christ received martyrdom at that place. And when the head of the blessed Miniato had been cut off, by a miracle of Christ, with his hands he set it again upon his trunk, and on his feet passed over Arno, and went up to the hill where now stands his church, where at that time was a little oratory in the name of the blessed Peter the Apostle, where many bodies of holy martyrs were buried; and when S. Miniato was come to that place, he gave up soul to Christ, and his body was there secretly buried by the Christians; the which place, by reason of the merits of the blessed S. Miniato, was devoutly venerated by the Florentines after that they were become Christians, and a little church was built there in his honour. But the great and noble church of marble which is there now in our times, we find to have been built later by the zeal of the venerable Father Alibrando, **1013 a.d.** bishop and citizen of Florence, in the year of Christ 1013, begun on the 26th day of the month of April by the commandment and authority of the catholic and holy Emperor Henry II. of Bavaria, and of his wife the holy Empress Gunegonda, which was reigning in those times; and they presented and endowed the said church with many rich possessions in Florence and in the country, for the good of their souls, and caused the said church to be repaired and rebuilt of marbles, as it is now; and they

48

caused the body of the blessed Miniato to be translated to the altar which is beneath the vaulting of the said church, with much reverence and solemnity by the said bishop and the clergy of Florence, with all the people, both men and women, of the city of Florence; but afterwards the said church was completed by the commonwealth of Florence, and the stone steps were made which lead **Purg. xii. 100-105.** down by the hill; and the consuls of the art of the Calimala were put in charge of the said work of S. Miniato, and were to protect it.

§ 58.—*How S. Crescius and his companions suffered martyrdom in the district of Florence.*

§ 59.—*Of Constantine the Emperor, and his descendants, and the changes which came thereof in Italy.*

We find that our city of Florence remained under the government of the Roman Empire for about 350 years after its first foundation, observing pagan ways, and worshipping idols, albeit there were many Christians, after the fashion whereof I have spoken, but they remained concealed in divers hermitages and caverns without the city, and they which were within did not declare themselves as Christians for fear of the persecutions which the emperors of Rome and their vicars and ministers brought upon the Christians, until the time of the great Constantine, son of Constantine the Emperor, and of Helena his wife, daughter of **Inf. xix. 115-117.** the king of Britain, which was the first Christian emperor, and endowed the Church with all the possessions of Rome, and gave liberty to the Christians in the time of the blessed Pope Sylvester, who **Inf. xxvii. 94, 95.**

320 a.d. baptized him and made him a Christian, cleansing him from leprosy by the power of Christ, and this was in the year of Christ about 320. The said Constantine caused many churches to be built in Rome to the honour of Christ, and having destroyed all the temples of paganism and of the idols, and established Holy Church in her liberty and lordship, **De Mon. iii. 10. Par. vi. 1-3; xx. 55-57.** and having brought the temporal affairs of the Church under due system and order, he departed to Constantinople, which he caused to be thus named, after his own name (for before this it was called Byzantium), and he raised it to great state and lordship, and there he made his seat, leaving here in command of Rome his patricians or censors, that is, vicars, which defended Rome, and fought for her, and for the Empire. After the said Constantine, which reigned more than thirty years, first in command of Rome, and then in command of Constantinople, there were left three sons, Constantine, and Constantius, and Constans, which had war and contentions among themselves, and one of them, to wit, Constantine, was a Christian, and the next, Constantius, was a heretic, and persecuted the Christians by reason of his heresy, which was begun in Constantinople by one named Arius, and this heresy was called Arian, after his name, which spread much error throughout all the world, and throughout the Church of God. These sons of Constantine by their dissensions greatly laid waste the Empire of Rome, and in a sense abandoned it, and henceforward it always seemed as if it were declining, and its sovereignty becoming less; and there began to be two and three emperors at one time, and one would be reigning in Constantinople, and another in the Empire of Rome, and one would be Christian, and another an Arian heretic, persecuting the Christians and the Church, and this endured long time, so that all Italy was infected thereby. Of the other emperors before and after, we shall make no ordered record, save of those which pertain to our subject; but he who desires to find them in order should read the Martinian Chronicle, and therein he will find the emperors and the popes which were in those times set forth in order.

§ 60.—*How the Christian faith first came to Florence.*

At the time that the said great Constantine became a Christian, and gave freedom and sovereignty to the Church, and S. Sylvester, the Pope, was openly established in the papacy in Rome, there spread through Tuscany, and throughout Italy, and afterwards through all the world, the true faith and belief of Jesus Christ. And in our city of Florence, the true faith began to be adopted, and paganism to be abolished, in the time of * * * * who was made bishop of Florence by Pope Sylvester; and from the noble and beautiful temple of the Florentines, of which mention has been made above, the Florentines **Par. xvi. 47, 145, 146.** removed their idol, which they called the god Mars, and placed it upon a high tower, by the river Arno, and would not break or destroy it, because in their ancient records they found that the said idol of Mars had been consecrated under the ascendant of such a planet, that if it **Inf. xiii. 143-150.** were broken or set aside in a place of contempt, the

50

city would suffer peril and injury, and undergo great changes. And although the Florentines had lately become Christians, they still observed many pagan customs, and long continued to observe them, and they still stood in awe of their ancient idol of Mars, so little were they perfected as yet in the holy faith; and this done, they consecrated **Par. xvi. 25, 47.**

Par. xvi. 42. their said temple in honour of God and of the blessed S. John the Baptist, and called it the Duomo of S. Giovanni; and they decreed that the feast on the day of his nativity should be celebrated with solemn sacrifices, and that a race should be run for a samite cloak, and this custom has been always observed by the Florentines on that day. And they had baptismal fonts erected in the middle of the temple, where **Inf. xix. 17-20. Par. xv. 134, 135.** people and children were and still are baptized; and on Holy Saturday, when in the said fonts the baptismal water and fire were blessed, they ordered that the said holy fire should be carried through the city after the custom of Jerusalem, so that some one should enter into every house with a lighted torch, for them to kindle their fires from. And from this solemnity came the privilege of the "great torch," which pertained to the house of the Pazzi, from some hundred and seventy years before 1300; because one of their ancestors, named Pazzo, strong and tall in person, bore a larger torch than any other, and was the first to take the sacred fire, and then the others received it from him. The said duomo, after that it had been consecrated to Christ, was enlarged by the space where to-day is the choir, and the altar of the blessed John; but at the time that the said duomo was the temple of Mars, this addition had not been made thereto, nor the turret and ball at the summit; and indeed it was open above after the fashion of Santa Maria Ritonda of Rome, to the intent their idol, the god Mars, which was in the midst of the temple, might be open to the sky. But after the second rebuilding of Florence, in the year of Christ 1150, the cupola was built upon columns, and the ball, and the golden cross which is at the top, by the consuls of the Art of Calimala, to which the commonwealth of Florence had committed the charge of the building of the said work in honour of S. John. And by many people which have journeyed through the world it is said to be the most beautiful temple or duomo of any that may be found; and in our times has been completed the work of the histories depicted within in

51

mosaic. And we find, from ancient records, that the figure of the sun carved in mosaic, which says: "*En giro torte sol ciclos, et rotor igne,*" was done by astronomy, and when the sun enters into the sign of Cancer, it shines at mid-day on that place through the opening above, where is the turret.

§ 61.—*Of the coming of the Goths and Vandals into Italy, and how they destroyed the country and besieged the city of Florence in the time of S. Zenobius, bishop of Florence.*

END OF SELECTIONS FROM BOOK I.

BOOK II.

Here begins the Second Book: how the city of Florence was destroyed by Totila, the scourge of God, king of the Goths and Vandals.

440 a.d.§ 1.—In the year of Christ 440, in the time of S. Leo the Pope, and of Theodosius and Valentinian emperors, in the northern parts there was a king of the Vandals and of the Goths, which was called Bela, and surnamed Totila. This man was a barbarian and had no religion, and was cruel in customs and in all things, born of the province of Gothland and Sweden, and in his cruelty he slew his brother and subdued many divers nations of peoples by his might and lordship; and afterwards he was minded to destroy and take away the Empire of the Romans, and lay Rome waste; and thus by his sovereignty he gathered together innumerable people from his own country, and from Sweden and from Gothland, and afterwards from Pannonia, which is Hungary, and from Denmark, to enter into Italy. And when he desired to pass into Italy, he was opposed by the Romans and Burgundians and French, and a great battle was fought against him in the district of Lunina, that is to say of Friuli and Aquilea, with the greatest number of slain that had ever been in any battle, both on one side and on the other; and the king of Burgundy was slain. And Totila, being discomfited, returned to his own country with the followers which were left to him. But afterwards, desiring to carry out his purpose of destroying the Empire of Rome, he gathered a larger army than before, and came into Italy. And first he laid siege to the city of Aquilea; so it continued three years, and then he took it, and burnt and destroyed it with all the inhabitants; and when he had entered into Italy, after the same manner he destroyed Vicenza, and Brescia, and Bergamo, and Milan, and Ticino, and well-nigh all the cities of Lombardy, save Modena, for the merits of S. Gemignano, which was bishop thereof; for when he was passing through this city with his people, by a divine miracle he did not see it save when he was without the city, and by reason of the miracle he passed it by, and did not destroy it: and he destroyed Bologna and put to martyrdom S. Proculus, bishop of Bologna, and thus he

53

destroyed well-nigh all the cities of Romagna. And afterwards passing through Tuscany he found the city of Florence strong and powerful. Hearing the fame thereof, and how it had been built by the noblest Romans, and was the treasure-house of the Empire and of Rome, and how in this country had been slain Radagasius, king of the Goths, his predecessor, with so great a multitude of Goths, as before has been narrated, he commanded that it should be besieged, and long time he sat before it in vain. And seeing that he could not obtain it by siege, inasmuch as it was very strong in towers and in walls and in many good soldiers, he set about to gain it by deceit and by flattery and by treachery. Now the Florentines had continual war with the city of Pistoia; and Totila ceased laying waste the country around the city, and sent to the Florentines that he desired to be their friend, and in their service would destroy the city of Pistoia, promising and making show of great love, and to give them privileges with very generous covenants. The imprudent Florentines (and for this cause they were ever afterwards **Inf. xv. 67.** called *blind* in the proverb) believed his false flatteries and vain promises; they opened the gates to him, and admitted him and his followers into the city, and lodged him in the Capitol. And when the cruel tyrant was within the city with all his forces, under false seeming he showed love to the citizens, and one day he invited to his council the greatest and most powerful chiefs of the city in great numbers; and when they came to the Capitol, as they passed one by one through an entry, he caused them to be slain and massacred, none perceiving ought of the fate of the other; and afterwards he had them thrown into the ducts of the Capitol, to wit, the conduit of the Arno which flows underground by the Capitol, to the end that no man might know thereof. And thus he put them to death in great numbers, and nought was perceived thereof in the city of Florence save that at the exit from the city where the said aqueduct or conduit issued forth and flowed back into the Arno, the water was seen to be all red and bloody. Then the people perceived the deceit and treachery; but it was in vain and too late, seeing that Totila had armed all his followers; and when he perceived that his cruelty was discovered, he commanded them to overrun the city and slay both great and small, men and women, and from this there was no escape, forasmuch as the city was unarmed and unprepared, and we find that at that time there were in the city

54

of Florence 22,000 men-at-arms, beside the aged and children. When the people of the city perceived that they were come to such sorrow and destruction, they escaped who could, fleeing into the country and hiding themselves in strongholds, and in woods and in caves; but the most part of the citizens were slain, or wounded, or taken, and the city was all despoiled of substance and riches by the said Goths, Vandals, and Hungarians. And after that Totila had thus wasted it of inhabitants and of goods, he commanded that it should be destroyed and burnt, and laid waste, and that there should not remain one stone upon another, and this was done; save that in the west there remained one of the towers which Gneus Pompey had built, and on the north and on the south one of the gates, and within the city near to the gate the "casa" or "domo," which we take to be the duomo of S. Giovanni, called of yore the "casa" [house] of Mars. And verily it never was entirely destroyed, nor shall be destroyed to eternity, save at the day of judgment, even as is written on the cement of the said duomo. And there were also left standing certain lofty towers or temples, indicated in the ancient chronicles by letters of the alphabet, the which we cannot interpret, to wit S, and casa P, and casa F. The city had four gates and six posterns, and there were towers marvellous strong over the gates. And the idol of the god Mars which the Florentines took from the temple and set upon a pillar, then fell into the Arno, and abode there as long as the city remained in ruins. And thus was destroyed the noble city of Florence by the infamous Totila **450 a.d.** on the 28th day of June, in the year of Christ 450, to wit 520 years after its foundation; and in the said city the blessed Maurice, bishop of Florence, was put to death with great torments by the followers of Totila, and his body lies in Santa Reparata.

§ 2.—*How Totila caused the city of Fiesole to be rebuilt.*

After that the city of Florence was destroyed, Totila went into the hill where had been the ancient city of Fiesole, and encamped there with his banners and tents and booths, and commanded that the said city should be rebuilt, and issued a proclamation that whosoever desired to return and dwell there, swearing to him to oppose the Romans, should abide in safety and freedom, and this in order that the city of Florence should never be rebuilt. For the which thing many which were descended from of old from Fiesole, returned to dwell thither, and of the Florentines themselves which had escaped, which did not know where to dwell or whither to go; and thus in a short time the city of Fiesole was restored and rebuilt, and made strong by walls and by inhabitants, and afterwards, as before so now, it continually rebelled against Rome.

§ 3.—*How Totila departed from Fiesole to go towards Rome, and destroyed many cities, and died an evil death.*

§ 4.—*How the Goths remained lords of Italy after the death of Totila.*

* * * * And the King Theodoric held the Empire of Rome for the said Zeno, the Emperor, doing him homage therefor and paying him tribute. **Circ. 470 a.d.** In these times, about the year of Christ 470, while Leo, Emperor of Rome, was reigning in Constantinople, was born in Great Britain, which is now called England, Merlin the prophet (of a virgin, they say, by conception or machination of a devil), which wrought in that country many marvels by necromancy, and ordained the Round Table of Knights Errant in the time when Uther Pendragon reigned in Britain, which was descended from Brutus, grandson of Æneas, the first inhabitant of that land, as afore we made mention; and afterwards the Round Table was **Cf. Inf. xxxii. 62. De Vulg. El. i. 10: 18, 19.** restored by the good King Arthur, his son, which was a lord of great power and valour, and more gracious and knightly than all other lords, and he reigned long time in happy state, as the Romances of the Britons make mention, and whereof the Martinian Chronicle is not silent when treating of those times.

§ 5.—*How the Goths were driven the first time out of Italy, and how they recovered their sovereignty by means of the young Theodoric, their king.* § 6.—*How the Goths were entirely driven out of Italy by Belisarius, patrician of the Romans.* § 7.—*Of the coming of the Lombards into Italy.* § 8.—*Of the beginning of the religion and sect of the Saracens, instituted by Mahomet.* § 9.—*Of the successors of Rotharis, king of the Lombards.*

§ 10.—*How Charles Martel came from France to Italy at the summons of the Church against the Lombards; and of the origin of the city of Siena.*

In the time of the said Eliprando [Liutprand], albeit he was a Christian, yet by reason of avarice, and of desire to usurp the rights of Holy Church, and by the counsel of the emperor of Constantinople, he began war against the Romans and against Pope Gregory III., and came with all his forces to besiege the said Pope in Rome, he by way of Lombardy, and Grimoald, king of the Samnites and of the Apulians, with his troops from Apulia, in the year of Christ 735. For the which **735 a.d.** thing, after a council had been held in Rome, the Church with the Romans sent to France for aid from Charles Martel, which Charles was son to Pepin, a great baron of France, and was of the Twelve Peers, and governed all the realm and the king himself; and the said Charles Martel did likewise, forasmuch as the king which then was, called Chilperic, had the name only, but Charles had the strength and lordship; and he was the son of the sister of Dodon, king of Aquitania, and afterwards was father of the good King Pepin, which was father of Charles the Great, and he had the surname of Martel, because he bore a hammer as his arms. And in truth he was a hammer, forasmuch as by his prowess he struck at all Germany, Saxony, Suabia, Bavaria, and Denmark as far as Norway, at England, Aquitania, and Navarre and Spain, and Burgundy and Provence, and became ruler over them all, and they became his tributaries. Then, at the summons of the said Pope, he passed into Italy as far as Apulia, and freed Rome and the Church from the encroachments of the Lombards. And it is said that at that time, about the year of Christ 740, was the place first inhabited where is **740 a.d.** now the city of Siena, by the aged and sick [non sana] people which came in with Charles Martel, and remained in that place as has been told afore concerning the building of Siena.

§ 11.—*How Eraco [Rachis], the Lombard king of Apulia, returned to obedience to Holy Church.*

§ 12.—*How Telofre [Astolf], king of the Lombards, persecuted Holy Church, and how King Pepin at the summons of Pope Stephen came from France and defeated him, and took him prisoner.*

After King Rachis there succeeded to the realm of Lombardy, and to that of Apulia, Astolf, called in Latin Telofre, brother of the said Rachis. He was a lord of great power, and cruel, and an enemy of Holy Church and of the Romans; and by the counsel of evil and rebellious Romans, he took Tuscany and the valley of Spoleto, and devastated them, and claimed tribute on every man's head; and made a conspiracy with Leo, and Constantine, his son, emperors of Constantinople, and at his request they came to Rome, and together with Telofre they took it, and sacked it, and burnt the churches and holy places, and carried to Constantinople the riches of Rome, and all the images from the churches in Rome, and in contempt of the Pope and of the Church and to the shame of the Christians he burnt them all with fire, and many faithful Christians they destroyed and consumed in Rome and in all Italy. For which thing Pope Stephen II. excommunicated them, and as a punishment for the misdeed took away from the emperor the kingdom of Apulia and of Sicily, and established by a decree that it should pertain to Holy Church for ever. And afterwards, not being able to resist the force of the said tyrants and so much affliction, he went in person into France to Pepin, prince and governor of the French, to require and pray him to come into Italy to defend Holy Church against Telofre, king of the Lombards, and he gave to the said Pepin many privileges and graces, and made and confirmed him king of France, and deposed Childeric, the king which was of the first race, forasmuch as he was a man of no account, and he became a monk. Which Pepin, a **Cf. Purg. xx. 53 and the Commentators.** faithful and loving son of Holy Church, received him with great honour, and afterwards with all his forces with the said Pope Stephen came into Italy, in the year of Christ 755, and fought great battles **755 a.d.** with the said Telofre, king of the Lombards. In the end, by force of arms and of his folk, the said Telofre was overcome and defeated by the good King Pepin, and he obeyed the command of the Pope and of Holy Church, and made all amends, just as he and his cardinals chose to devise; and he left to the Church by compact and privilege the realm of Apulia and of Sicily, and the patrimony of S. Peter. And when the said Pepin was come to Rome with the said Pope, they were received with great honour by the Romans; and the said Pepin was made patrician, that is, vicar of Rome, and father of the Roman Republic. And when Rome and Holy Church were restored to their liberty and good estate, he returned into France, and ended his life with great honour, and Charles the Great, his son, succeeded him as king of France.

§ 13.—*How Desiderius, son of Telofre, began war again with Holy Church, for the which thing Charles the Great passed into Italy, and defeated him, and took away and destroyed the lordship of the Lombards.*

When King Pepin was departed from Italy and was returned to

France, the Church of Rome and the country was in repose and tranquillity for a time, by reason of the covenant which Pepin had made with Telofre, king of Lombardy, and the victory which he had gained over him; but when Telofre was dead, Desiderius, his son, succeeded to him, which was a worse enemy and persecutor of Holy Church than his father, and broke the peace, and leagued himself with Constantine, which was the son of Leo, the emperor of Constantinople, and with his forces began to make war in Apulia, and Desiderius on his side in Tuscany more than ever his father had done at the first. For the which thing Pope **De Mon. iii. (11) 1-6.** Adrian, which was then governing Holy Church, sent into France for Charles the Great, son of Pepin, to come into Italy to defend the Church from the said Desiderius and from his following, the which Charles, king of France, passed into Lombardy in the year of Christ 775, and after many battles and victories gained against Desiderius, **775 a.d.** he besieged him in the city of Pavia, and when he had won the city by siege, he took the said Desiderius captive, and his wife and his sons; save that the eldest son, which was called Algise [Adelchis], fled into Constantinople to the Emperor Constantine, and continued the war. After he had taken Desiderius and his wife and his sons, Charles the Great caused him to swear fealty to Holy Church, and did the like to all the barons and cities of Italy; and when this was done, he sent the said Desiderius and his wife and his sons prisoners into France, and there they all died in prison. And thus was destroyed, by the power of the Franks and of the good Charles the Great, the sovereignty **Par. vi. 94-96.** of the kings of the Lombards, formerly called Longobards, which had endured two hundred and five years in Italy; for never afterwards was there a king in Lombardy. Of a truth there remained the families of the lords and barons and great citizens descended from the Lombards, **Ep. v. (4).** both in Lombardy and in Apulia; and still to-day there are certain gentlemen of ancient lineage whom in common speech we call Lombard Cattani, descended from the said Lombards which had been lords of Italy. Charles the Great, after the said victory, came to Rome, and by the said Adrian and by the Romans was received with great triumph and honour; and as Charles the Great drew nigh to Rome, and beheld the holy city from Montemalo, he alighted from his horse, and reverently **Cf. Par. xv. 110, 111.** entered Rome on foot; and when he came thither, he kissed the gates of the city and of all the churches, and gave rich offerings to every Church. And when he came to Rome he was made patrician of Rome, and he restored the affairs of Holy Church, and of the Romans, and of all Italy, and he restored them to privileges and liberty, having subdued in all parts the forces of the emperor of Constantinople, and of the king of the Lombards, and of their followers, and confirmed the Church in the donation which Pepin, his father, had given to her, and beyond that he endowed the Church with the duchy of Spoleto and of Benevento. And in the kingdom of Apulia he fought many battles against the Lombards and the rebels against Holy Church, and besieged and destroyed the city of Lacedonia, which is in Abruzzi between Aquila and Sermona, and besieged and conquered Tuliverno, the strong fortress at the entrance of Terra di Lavoro. And many other cities of the Kingdom [Apulia] which were held by the rebels against Holy Church, he entirely subdued to his governance. And when he had done this, leaving Rome and all Italy in peaceful condition under his lordship, in happy hour he was minded to attack the Saracens which had taken possession of Provence, and of Navarre, and of Spain, and with the troops of his twelve barons and peers of France, called Paladins, he entirely conquered and destroyed them; and he passed beyond seas at the request of the Emperor Michael of Constantinople and of the Patriarch of Jerusalem, and conquered the Holy Land and Jerusalem, which were **De Mon. iii. 11: 6. Par. xviii. 43.** occupied by the Saracens, and gained for the emperor of Constantinople all the empire of the East which had been occupied by the Saracens and the Turks. And when he returned to Constantinople, albeit the Emperor Michael desired to give him many very great treasures, yet would he take nothing, save the wood of the holy cross and the nail of Christ, which he brought back into France, and which is in Paris to this day. And when he had returned to France, he ruled by his prowess and virtue not only over the realm of France, but all Germany, Provence, Navarre, and Spain, and all Italy.

§ 14.—*Of the progeny of Charles the Great, and of his successors.*

§ 15.—*How Charles the Great, king of France, was made Emperor of Rome.*

When Charles the Great had returned from over seas into France, as we have said, and had subdued Germany, Italy, and Spain, and Provence, the wicked Romans, with the powerful Lombards and Tuscans, rebelled against the Church, and seized Pope Leo III., which was then reigning, at Rome, as he was going to the procession of the Litanies (S. Mark's Day, April 25th), and put out his eyes and slit his tongue, and drave him out of Rome. And as it pleased God, by divine miracle, and because he was innocent and holy, he recovered the sight of his eyes and the power of speech, and went into France to Charles the Great, praying him to come to Rome to restore the Church to her liberty; which Charles, at the request of the said Pope Leo, came together with him to Rome and restored the Pope and the Church to their state and liberty, and took great vengeance against all the rebels and enemies of Holy Church throughout all Italy. For the which thing the said Pope Leo, with his cardinals and general council, with the consent of the Romans, by reason of the virtuous and holy deeds done by the said **Par. vi. 94. De Monarchia iii. 11.** Charles the Great on behalf of Holy Church and of all Christendom, took away the Roman Empire from the Greeks by a decree, and elected the said Charles the Great Emperor of the Romans, as being most worthy of the Empire; and by the said Pope Leo he was consecrated and crowned in Rome, in the year of Christ 801, with great solemnity and honour, **801 a.d.** on Easter Day.

The said Charles reigned with great good fortune fourteen years one month and four days, ruling over all the empire of the West, and the provinces afore named, and also the emperor of Constantinople was under his obedience; and he caused as many abbeys to be built as there are letters in the alphabet, and the name of each one began with a different letter. And he caused his son Louis to be crowned lord over the Empire and the kingdom of France, giving all his treasure to the poor in God's name after this manner; for he left the third part of his treasure (which was infinite) to all the poor Christians seeking alms, and the other two parts he left to all his archbishops of his empire and realm, that they might distribute them amongst their bishops and all the churches and monasteries and hospitals.

******

814 a.d.

And this done, he commended his spirit in holiness to Christ, in the city of Aquisgrana, in Germany, and was there buried with great honour, to wit, at Aix-la-Chapelle. This was in the year of Christ 814, and he lived seventy-two years, and many signs appeared before his death, as we read in the chronicles of the doings of France. This Charles much extended Holy Church, and Christendom both far and near, and was a man of great virtue.

§ 16.—*How, after Charles the Great, Louis, his son, became Emperor.* § 17.—*How the Saracens of Barbary crossed to Italy, and were defeated, and all slain.* § 18.—*Further, how the Saracens crossed to Calabria and to Normandy in France.* § 19.—*How and in whose person the empire and realm of France fell from the progeny of Pepin.* § 20.—*Of the same matter, and of how the lineage of Hugh Capet reigned thereafter.*

§ 21.—*How the city of Florence lay waste and in ruins for 350 years.*

After the destruction of the city of Florence, wrought by Totila, the scourge of God, as has afore been mentioned, it lay thus ruined and deserted about 350 years by reason of the evil state of Rome and of the Empire, which, at first by Goths and Vandals, and afterwards by Lombards and Greeks and Saracens and Hungarians, was persecuted and brought low, as has afore been related. Truly there were, where Florence had been, certain dwellings and inhabitants round about the duomo of S. Giovanni, forasmuch as the Fiesolans held market there one day in the week, and it was called the Campo Marti, as of old, for it had always been the market-place of the Fiesolans, and had borne this name before Florence was built. It came to pass ofttimes, during the years when the city lay waste and in ruins, that the said inhabitants of the borough and of the market-place, with the aid of certain nobles of the country which of old were descended from the first citizens of Florence and of the inhabitants of the villages round about, sought ofttimes to enclose within moats and palisades some part of the city around the Duomo; but they of the city of Fiesole, and their allies, the counts of Mangone, and of Montecarelli, and of Capraia, and of Certaldo, which were all of one lineage with the counts of Santafiore, which were descended from the Lombards, hindered and opposed them, and would not allow them to rebuild; but whatsoever was being built they came in force, and under arms, and caused it to be violently beaten down and destroyed, so that, for this cause and by reason of the adversities which the Romans were enduring, as has afore been related, and because the Fiesolans always held with the Goths, and afterwards with the Lombards, and with all the rebels and enemies of the Empire of Rome and Holy Church, and were so great and powerful in strength that none of their neighbours durst oppose them, they would not suffer the city of Florence to be rebuilt; and in this wise it abode long time, until God put an end to the adversity of the city of Florence, and brought her to the blessing of her restoration, as by us shall be narrated in the following chapter and Third Book.

END OF SELECTIONS FROM BOOK II.

BOOK III.

Goes back somewhat to tell how the city of Florence was rebuilt by the power of Charles the Great and the Romans.

§ 1.—It came to pass, as it pleased God, that in the time of the good Charles the Great, Emperor of Rome and king of France, of whom above we have made a long record, after that he had beaten down the tyrannical pride of the Lombards and Saracens, and of the infidels against Holy Church, and had established Rome and the Empire in good state and in its liberty, as afore we have made mention, certain gentlemen and nobles of the region round about Florence (whereof it is reported that the Giovanni, the Guineldi and the Ridolfi, descended from the ancient noble citizens of the former Florence, were the heads) assembled themselves together with all the inhabitants of the place where Florence had been, and with all other their followers dwelling in the country around Florence, and they ordained to send to Rome ambassadors from the best among them to Charles the Emperor, and to Pope Leo, and to the Romans; and this was done, praying them to remember their daughter, the city of Florence (the which was ruined and destroyed by Goths and Vandals in despite of the Romans), to the end it might be rebuilt, and that it might please them to give a force of men-at-arms to ward off the men of Fiesole and their followers, the enemies of the Romans, who would not let the city of Florence be rebuilt. The which ambassadors were received with honour by the Emperor Charles, and by the Pope, and by the Romans, and their petition accepted graciously and willingly; and straightway the Emperor Charles the Great sent thither his forces of men-at-arms on foot and on horse in great numbers; and the Romans made a decree and command that, as their forefathers had built and peopled of old the city of Florence, so those of the best families in Rome, both of nobles and of people, should go thither to rebuild and to inhabit it; and this was done. With that host of the Emperor Charles the Great and of the Romans there came whatsoever master-craftsmen there were in Rome, the more speedily to build the walls of the city and to strengthen it, and after them there followed much people; and all they who dwelt in the country around Florence, and her exiled citizens in every place, hearing the tidings, gathered themselves to the host of the Romans and of the Emperor to rebuild the city; and when they were come where to-day is our city, they encamped among ancient remains and ruins in booths and in tents. The Fiesolans and their followers, seeing the host of the Emperor and of the Romans so great and powerful, did not venture to fight against them, but keeping within the fortress of their city of Fiesole and in their fortified places around, gave what hindrance they might to the said rebuilding. But their power was nothing against the strength of the Romans, and of the host of the Emperor, and of the assembled descendants of the Florentines; and thus they began to rebuild the city of Florence, not, however, of the size that it had been at the first, but of lesser extent, as hereafter shall be mentioned, to the end it might more speedily be walled and fortified, and there might be a defence like a rampart against the city of Fiesole; and this was the year of Christ **801 a.d.** 801, in the beginning of the month of April. And it is said that the ancients were of opinion that it would not be possible to rebuild it, if first there were not found and drawn from the Arno the marble image, dedicated by the first pagan builders by necromancy to Mars, the which had been in the river Arno from the destruction of Florence unto that time; and being found, it was placed on a pillar by the side **Inf. xiii. 146-150. Par. xvi. 145, 146.** of the said river, where now is the head of the Ponte Vecchio. This we do not affirm nor believe, forasmuch as it seems to us the opinion of pagans and soothsayers, and not to be reasonable, but very foolish, that such a stone should have such effect; but it was commonly said by the ancients, that, if it was disturbed, the city must needs have great disturbances. And it was said also by the ancients, that the Romans, by the counsel of the wise astrologers, at the beginning of the rebuilding of Florence, took the third degree of Aries as the ascendant, the sun being at his meridian altitude, and the planet Mercury in conjunction with the sun, and the planet Mars in favourable aspect to the ascendant, to the end the city might multiply in power of arms and of chivalry, and in folk eager and enterprising in arts and in riches and in merchandise, and should bring forth many children and a great people. And in those times, so they say, the ancient Romans and all the

Tuscans and Italians, albeit they were baptized Christians, still preserved certain remains of the fashions of pagans, and began their undertakings according to the constellations; albeit, this we do not affirm of ourselves, forasmuch as constellations are not of necessity, nor can they constrain the free will of man or the **Purg. xvi. 65-78.** judgment of God, save according to the merits or sins of folk. And yet, in some effects, meseems the influence of the said constellation is revealed, for the city of Florence is ever in great disturbances and plottings and in war, and now victorious and now the contrary, and prone to merchandise and to arts. But our opinion is that the discords and changes of the Florentines are as we said at the beginning of this treatise—our city was populated by two peoples, divers in every habit of life, as were the noble Romans and the cruel and fierce Fiesolans; **Cf. Inf. xv. 73-78.** for the which thing it is no marvel if our city is always subject to wars and changes and dissensions and treacheries.

§ 2.—*Of the form and size in which the city of Florence was rebuilt.*

The rebuilding of the new city of Florence was begun by the Romans, as aforesaid, on a small site and circuit, after the same fashion as Rome, allowing for the smallness of the undertaking; and it began on the side of the sunrise at the gate of S. Piero, which was where were **Par. xv. 112.** after the houses of M. Bellincione Berti, of the Rovignani, a noble and powerful citizen, albeit to-day they have disappeared; the which **Inf. xvi. 37. Par. xvi. 97-99.** houses by inheritance of the Countess Gualdrada, his daughter, and wife to the first Count Guido, passed to the Counts Guidi, her descendants, when they became citizens of Florence, and afterwards they sold them to the Black Cerchi, a Florentine family; and from the said gate ran a borgo as far as S. Piero Maggiore, after the fashion of Rome, and from that gate the walls proceeded as far as the Duomo, on the site where now runs the great road leading to San Giovanni, as far as the Bishop's Palace. And here was another gate, which was called the gate of the Duomo, but there were who called it the Bishop's Gate; and without this gate was built the church of S. Lorenzo, just as in Rome there is S. Lorenzo without the walls; and within that gate is S. Giovanni, like as in Rome, S. Giovanni Laterano. And then proceeding, as at Rome, on that side they made Santa Maria Maggiore; and then from S. Michele Berteldi, as far as the third gate of S. Brancazio [S. Pancras], where are now the houses of the Tornaquinci, and S. Brancazio was without the city and near S. Paolo, just as in Rome, on the other side of the city over against S. Piero, as at Rome. And then from the said gate of S. Brancazio, they followed on where now is the church of Santa Trinita, which was without the walls; and hard by was a postern gate called the Porta Rossa, and down to our own times the road has retained the name. And afterward the walls turned where are now the houses of the Scali along the Via di Terma as far as the gate of Santa Maria, some way past the Mercato Nuovo, and that was the fourth principal gate, the which was over against the houses which now pertain to the Infangati, on one **Par. xvi. 123.** side; and above the said gate was the church of Santa Maria, called Sopra Porta; and afterwards when the said gate was pulled down, the city having increased, the said church was transported to where it now is. And the Borgo di Santo Apostolo was without the city, and also S. Stefano, after the fashion of Rome; and beyond S. Stefano, at the end of the master street of Porta Santa Maria, they made and built a bridge founded on piles of stone in the Arno, which afterwards was called the Ponte Vecchio, and it exists to this day; and was much more narrow than it now is, and was the first bridge which was made in Florence. And from S. Mary's Gate the walls went on as far as the turret of Altafonte, which was at the extremity of a projection of the city, running out to the river Arno, then running on behind the church of S. Piero Scheraggio, which was so called from a ditch or conduit called the Scheraggio, which received almost all the rain-water of the city that flowed into the Arno. And behind the church of S. Piero **Par. xvi. 124-126.** Scheraggio was a postern gate, which was called the Peruzza Gate, and from there the walls went on by the great street as far as the Via del Garbo, where was another postern, and then behind the Badia of **Cf. Par. xv. 97-99.** Florence the walls returned to Porta S. Piero. And within so small a space the new Florence was rebuilt with good walls and frequent towers, with four master gates, to wit, the Porta San Piero, the Porta del Duomo, the Porta San Brancazio, and the Porta Santa Maria, the which were in the form of a cross; and in the midst of the city were S. Andrea, after the fashion of Rome, and Santa Maria in Campidoglio; and what now is the Mercato Vecchio was the Mercato di Campidoglio [Mart of the Capitol], after the fashion of Rome. And the city was divided into

67

quarters, according to the said four gates; but afterwards, when the city increased, it was divided into six sestos, as being a perfect number, for the sesto of Oltrarno was added thereto, as soon as it was inhabited; and when the Porta di Santa Maria was pulled down, the name was dropped, and it was divided by the course of the main street, and on one side was made the sesto of San Piero Scheraggio, and on the other side that of the Borgo; and the three first gates continued to give their name to sestos, as they have done even to our own times. And they gave the sesto of Oltrarno the lead, to go forth with the host with the ensign of the bridge; and then San Piero Scheraggio with the ensign of the carroccio [chariot of war], the which marble carroccio was brought from Fiesole, and stands before the said church of S. Piero; and then Borgo with the ensign of the goat [becco], forasmuch as in that sesto abode all the butchers [beccari], and those of their calling, and they were in those times very prominent in the city; S. Brancazio next with the ensign of the lion's paw [branca], with reference to the name; and the Porta del Duomo next, with the ensign of the cathedral; Porta San Piero last, with the ensign of the keys, and seeing it was the first sesto inhabited in Florence, in the going forth of the host it was placed in the rear guard, forasmuch as in olden time there were always the best knights and men-at-arms of the city in that sesto.

§ 3.—*How Charles the Great came to Florence, and granted privileges to the city, and caused Santo Apostolo to be built.*

After that the new city of Florence had been rebuilt in the small circuit and form, and at the time aforesaid, the captains which were there in the name of the emperor and the commonwealth of Rome ordained that it should be peopled; and as of old at the first building the order went forth at Rome that of the best families of Rome, both of the nobles and the people, some should dwell as citizens in Florence, so was it at the second restoration; and to each one was given rich possessions. And we find in the Chronicles of France, that after the city of Florence was rebuilt after the manner aforesaid, the Emperor Charles the Great, king of France, when he was departed from Rome, and was returning North, abode at Florence, and caused great festival and solemnity to be held on Easter Day of the Resurrection, in the year of **805 a.d.** Christ 805, and made many knights in Florence, and founded the

68

church of Santo Apostolo in the Borgo, and this he richly endowed to the honour of God and of the Holy Apostles; and on his departure from Florence he granted privileges to the city, and declared the commonwealth and citizens of Florence to be free and independent, and for three miles around, without paying any tax or impost, save twenty-six pence yearly per hearth [*i.e.* per family]. And in like manner he enfranchised all the citizens around which desired to return and dwell within the city, and also strangers; for which thing many returned to dwell therein; and in a short time, by reason of the good situation and convenient spot, by reason of the river and of the plain, the said little Florence was well peopled and strong in walls, and in moats full of water. And they ordained that the said city should be ruled and governed after the manner of Rome, to wit, by two Consuls and by a council of 100 senators, and thus it was ruled long time, as hereafter shall be narrated. Verily, the citizens of Florence had for a long time much trouble and war, first from the Fiesolans, which were foes so nigh at hand, and they were ever jealous one of another, and were continually at war together; and afterwards from the coming of the Saracens into Italy in the time of the French emperors, as before has been narrated, which much afflicted the country; and last of all, from the divers disturbances which befell Rome and all Italy alike, from the discords of the Popes and of the Italian emperors, which were continually at war with the Church. For the which thing, the fame of the city of Florence and its power abode by the space of 200 years, without being able to expand or increase beyond its narrow boundaries. But notwithstanding all the war and trouble, it was continually multiplying in inhabitants and in forces, nor did they much regard the war with Fiesole, or the other adversities in Tuscany; for albeit their power and authority extended but little way beyond the city, forasmuch as the country was all full of fortresses, and occupied by nobles and powerful lords which were not under obedience to the city, and some of them held with the city of Fiesole, nevertheless, within the city the citizens were united, and it was strong in position and in walls, and in moats full of water; and within the little city there were in a short time more than 150 towers pertaining to citizens, and each one 120 cubits high, without counting those pertaining to the city; and by reason of the height of the many towers which then were in Florence, it is said, that it showed forth from afar as the most beautiful and proudest city of its small size which could be found; and in this space of time it was very well peopled, and full of palaces and of houses, and great number of inhabitants, as times went. We will now leave for a time the doings of Florence, and will briefly relate concerning the Italian emperors, which were reigning in those times after the French ceased to be emperors; for this is of necessity, seeing that by reason of their lordship many disturbances came to pass in Italy; and afterwards we shall return to our subject.

901 a.d.§ 4.—*How and why the Empire of Rome passed to the Italians.* § 5.—*How Otho I. of Saxony came into Italy at the request of the Church, and did away with the government of the Italian emperors.*

END OF SELECTIONS FROM BOOK III.

BOOK IV.

§ 1.—**955 a.d.***How the election to the Empire of Rome fell to the Germans, and how Otho I. of Saxony was consecrated Emperor.*

§ 2.—*Of the Emperor Otho III., and the Marquis Hugh, which built the Badia at Florence.*

979 a.d.

After the death of Otho II., his son, Otho III., was elected Emperor, and crowned by Pope Gregory V., in the year of Christ 979, and this Otho reigned twenty-four years. After that he was crowned, he went into Apulia on pilgrimage to Mount S. Angelo, and afterwards returned by way of France into Germany, leaving Italy in good and peaceful estate. But when he was returned to Germany, Crescentius, the consul and lord of Rome, drave away the said Gregory from the papacy, and set a Greek therein, which was bishop of Piacenza, and very wise; but when the Emperor Otho heard this he was very wrath, and with his army returned to Italy, and besieged in Rome the said Crescentius and his Pope in the castle of S. Angelo, for therein had they taken refuge; and he took the said castle by siege, and caused Crescentius to be beheaded, and Pope John XVI. to have his eyes put out, and his hands cut off; and he restored his Pope Gregory to his chair, which was his kinsman by race; and leaving Rome and Italy in good estate, he returned to his country of Germany, and there died in prosperity. With the said Otho III. there came into Italy the Marquis Hugh; I take it this must have been the marquis of Brandenburg, forasmuch as there is no other marquisate in Germany. His sojourn in Tuscany liked him so well, and especially our city of Florence, that he caused his wife to come thither, and took up his abode in Florence, as vicar of Otho, the Emperor. It came to pass, as it pleased God, that when he was riding to the chase in the country of Bonsollazzo, he lost sight, in the wood, of all his followers, and came out, as he supposed, at a workshop where iron was wont to be wrought. Here he found men, black and deformed, who, in place of iron, seemed to be tormenting men with fire and with hammer, and he asked what this might be: and they answered and said

71

that these were damned souls, and that to similar pains was condemned the soul of the Marquis Hugh by reason of his worldly life, unless he should repent: who, with great fear, commended himself to the Virgin Mary, and when the vision was ended, he remained so pricked in the spirit, that after his return to Florence, he sold all his patrimony in Germany, and commanded that seven monasteries should be founded: the first was the Badia of Florence, to the honour of S. Mary; the second, that of Bonsollazzo, where he beheld the vision; the third was founded at Arezzo; the fourth at Poggibonizzi; the fifth at the Verruca of Pisa; the sixth at the city of Castello; the last was the one at Settimo; and all these abbeys he richly endowed, and lived afterwards with his wife in holy life, and had no son, and died in the city of Florence, on S. Thomas' Day, in the year of Christ 1006, and was buried with great honour in the Badia of Florence. And whilst the said Hugh was living, he made in Florence many knights of the family of the Giandonati, of the Pulci, of the **Par. xvi. 127-132.** Nerli, of the counts of Gangalandi, and of the family della Bella, which all for love of him, retained and bore his arms, barry, white and red, with divers charges.

§ 3.—*Of the Seven Princes of Germany which have to elect the Emperor.*

§ 4.—*Of the progeny of the Kings of France, which descended from Hugh Capet.*
987 a.d.

Hugh Capet, as we before made mention, the lineage of Charles the Great having failed, was made king of France in the year of Christ 987. This Hugh was duke of Orleans (and by some it is held that his ancestors were all dukes and of high lineage), son of Hugh the Great, and his mother was sister to Otho I. of Germany; but by the more part it is said that his father was a great and rich burgher of Paris, a butcher, or trader in beasts by birth; but by reason of his great riches and possessions, when the duchy of Orleans was vacant, and only a daughter was left, he had her to wife, whence was born the said Hugh **Purg. xx. 49-60.** Capet, which was very wise and of great possessions, and the kingdom of France was wholly governed by him; and when the lineage of Charles the Great failed, as was aforesaid, he was made king, and reigned twenty years.

✳✳✳✳✳✳

§ 5.—**1003 a.d.** *How Henry I. was made Emperor.*

§ 6.—*How in the time of the said Henry, the Florentines took the city of Fiesole, and destroyed it.*

1010 a.d.

In the said times, when the Emperor Henry I. was reigning, the city of Florence was much increased in inhabitants and in power, considering its small circuit, especially by the aid and favour of the Emperor Otho I., and of the second and third Otho, his son and grandson, which always favoured the city of Florence; and as the city of Florence increased, the city of Fiesole continually decreased, they being always at war and enmity together; but by reason of the strong position, and the strength in walls and in towers which the city of Fiesole possessed, in vain did the Florentines labour to overcome it; and albeit they had more inhabitants, and a greater number of friends and allies, yet the Fiesolans were continually warring against them. But when the Florentines perceived that they could not gain it by force, they made a truce with the Fiesolans, and abandoned the war between them; and making one truce after another, they began to grow friendly, and the citizens of one city to sojourn in the other, and to marry together, and to keep but little watch and guard one against the other. The Florentines perceiving that their city of Florence had no power to rise much, whilst they had overhead so strong a fortress as the city of Fiesole, one night secretly and subtly set an ambush of armed men in divers parts of Fiesole. The Fiesolans feeling secure as to the Florentines, and not being on their guard against them, on the morning of their chief festival of S. Romolo, when the gates were open, and the Fiesolans unarmed, the Florentines entered into the city under cover of coming to the festival; and when a good number were within, the other armed Florentines which were in ambush secured the gates of the city; and on a signal made to Florence, as had been arranged, all the host and power of the Florentines came on horse and on foot to the hill, and entered into the city of Fiesole, and traversed it, slaying scarce any man, nor doing any harm, save to those which opposed them. And when the Fiesolans saw themselves to be suddenly

73

and unexpectedly surprised by the Florentines, part of them which were able fled to the fortress, which was very strong, and long time maintained themselves there. The city at the foot of the fortress having been taken and overrun by the Florentines, and the strongholds and they which opposed themselves being likewise taken, the common people surrendered themselves on condition that they should not be slain nor robbed of their goods; the Florentines working their will to destroy the city, and keeping possession of the bishop's palace. Then the Florentines made a covenant, that whosoever desired to leave the city of Fiesole, and come and dwell in Florence, might come safe and sound with all his goods and possessions, or might go to any place which pleased him; for the which thing they came down in great numbers to dwell in Florence, whereof there were and are great families in Florence. Others went to dwell in the region round about where they had farms and possessions. And when this was done, and the city was devoid of inhabitants and goods, the Florentines caused it to be all pulled down and destroyed, all save the bishop's palace and certain other churches, and the fortress, which still held out, and did not surrender under the said conditions. And this was in the year of Christ 1010, and the Florentines and the Fiesolans which became citizens of Florence, took thence all the ornaments and pillars, and all the marble carvings which were there, and the marble war chariot which is in San Piero Scheraggio in Florence.

§ 7.—*How that many Fiesolans came to dwell in Florence, and made one people with the Florentines.*

The city of Fiesole being destroyed save the fortress of the citadel, as has been aforesaid, many Fiesolans came thence to dwell in Florence and made one people with the Florentines, and by reason of their coming it behoved to increase the walls and the circuit of the city of Florence, as hereafter shall be narrated. And to the end the Fiesolans which were come to dwell in Florence might be more faithful and loving with the Florentines, they caused the arms of the said two commonwealths to be borne in common, and made the arms to be dimidiated red and white, as still to our times they are borne upon the Carroccio and in the host of the Florentines. The red was the ancient field which the Florentines had from the Romans, as we afore made mention, and they were wont to bear thereupon the white lily;

and the white was the ancient field of the Fiesolans, bearing an azure moon: but from the said common arms they took away the white lily and the moon, and so had them dimidiated and uncharged; and they made common laws and statutes, living under one government of two citizen consuls, and with the council of the senate, to wit of 100 men, the best of the city, as was the custom given by the Romans to the Florentines. And they increased greatly the city of Florence both in inhabitants and in power through the destruction of the city of **Cf. Par. xvi. 46-48.** Fiesole, and through the Fiesolans which came to dwell in Florence. Nevertheless, they were not a great people in comparison with what they are in our times; forasmuch as the city of Florence was of small extent, as has been narrated, and as may still be seen by tracing the first circuit, and there were hardly the fourth of the inhabitants which there are to-day. The Fiesolans were much diminished, and at the destruction of Fiesole they were much scattered, and some went one way, and some another; but the most part thereof came to Florence. Yet it was a large city for those times; but, from what we find, all the Fiesolans together were not the half which there are now in our days. And note that the Florentines are always in schism, and in factions and in divisions among themselves, which is not to be marvelled at. One cause is by reason of the city being rebuilt, as was told in the chapter concerning its rebuilding, under the lordship and influence of the planet of Mars, which always inspires wars and divisions. The **Cf. Convivio ii. 14: 171-174.** other cause is more certain and natural, that the Florentines are to-day descended from two peoples so diverse in manners, and who ever of old had been enemies, as the Roman people and the people of Fiesole; and this we can see by true experience, and by the divers changes and parties and factions which after the said two peoples had **Inf. xv. 61-78.** been united into one, came to pass in Florence from time to time, as in this book henceforward more fully shall be narrated.

§ 8.—*How the city of Florence increased its circuit, first by moats and palisades, and then by walls.*

After that the Fiesolans were come in great part to dwell in Florence, as aforesaid, the city multiplied in inhabitants and population; and as it increased in suburbs and dwellings, outside the small old city, after a little while it behoved of necessity that the city should increase its circuit, first with moats and palisades; and then in the time of Henry the Emperor they made the walls, to the end the suburbs and outgrowths, by reason of the wars which arose in Tuscany about the matter of the said Henry, might not be taken nor destroyed, and the city more readily besieged by its enemies. Wherefore, at that time, in the year of Christ 1078, as hereafter, in narrating the story of Henry III., shall be mentioned, the Florentines began the new walls, beginning from the east side at the gate of S. Piero Maggiore, the which was somewhat behind the church so called, enclosing the suburb of S. Piero Maggiore and the said church within the new walls, and afterwards, drawing them nearer in on the north side, a little distance from the said suburb, they made an angle at a postern which was called the Albertinelli Gate from a family which dwelt in that place, which was so called; then they drew them on as far as the gate of the Borgo S. Lorenzo [suburb of S. Lawrence] enclosing the said church within the walls; and after this were two posterns, one at the forked way of the Campo Corbolini, and the other the one afterwards called the Porta del Baschiera. Then they ran on as far as the Porta **1078 a.d.** S. Paolo, and then continued as far as the Carraia Gate, where the wall ended, by the Arno; and there afterwards they began and built a bridge which is called the Carraia Bridge from the name of that gate; and then the walls continuing, not however very high, along the bank of the Arno, included what had been without the old walls, to wit the suburb of San Brancazio [S. Pancras], and that of Parione, and that of Santo Apostolo, and of the Porte Sante Marie as far as the Ponte Vecchio; and then afterwards along the bank of Arno as far as the fortress of Altafonte. From this point the walls withdrew somewhat from the bank of Arno, so that there remained a road between, and two postern gates whereby to come at the river; then they went on the same, and took a turn where now are the supports of the Rubaconte Bridge, and there at the turn was a gate called the Oxen Gate, because there without was held the cattle market, and afterwards it was named the gate of Master Ruggieri da Quona, forasmuch as the family of da Quona, when they came to dwell in the city, established themselves near the said gate. Then the walls went on behind S. Jacopo tra le Fosse (so called because it stood on fosses), as far as where to-day is the end of the piazza before the church of the Minor Friars called Santa Croce; and there was a postern which led to the island of Arno; then the walls went on in a straight line without any gate or postern, returning to S. Piero Maggiore whence they began. And thus the new city of Florence on this side the Arno had five gates for the five sesti, one gate to each sesto, and divers posterns, as has been mentioned. In the Oltrarno [district beyond the Arno] were three roads, all three of which started from the Ponte Vecchio on the side beyond Arno. One was and still is called the Borgo Pidiglioso, seeing that it was inhabited by the baser sort. At the head of this was a gate called the Roman Gate, where now are the houses of the Bardi near S. Lucia de' Magnoli across the Ponte Vecchio, and this was the road to Rome, by Fegghine and Arezzo. There were no other walls to the suburb about the road save the backs of the houses against the hill. The second road was that of Santa Felicita, called the Borgo di Piazza, which had a gate where now is the piazza of San Felice, where runs the road to Siena; and the third road was called after S. Jacopo, and had a gate where now are the houses of the Frescobaldi, where ran the road to Pisa. None of the three suburbs lying around these roads of the sesto of Oltrarno had other walls save the said gates, and the backs of the outside houses, which enclosed the suburbs with orchards and gardens within. But after that the Emperor Henry III. marched upon Florence, the Florentines enclosed Oltrarno within walls, beginning at the said gate to Rome, ascending behind the Borgo alla Costa below San Giorgio, and then coming out behind Santa Felicita, enclosing the Borgo di Piazza and the Borgo di San Jacopo, and roughly following the said Borghi. But afterwards the walls of Oltrarno on the hill were made higher as they are now, in the time when the Ghibellines first ruled the city of Florence, as we will make mention in due place and time. We will now leave for a time the doings of Florence, and we will treat of the emperors which were after Henry I., for it is necessary that we should tell of them here in order to continue our history.

§ 9.—*How Conrad I. was made Emperor.*

1015 a.d.

After the death of the Emperor Henry I., Conrad I. was elected and consecrated by Pope Benedict VIII., in the year of Christ 1015. He was of Suabia, and reigned twenty years as emperor, and when he came into Italy,

77

not being able to obtain the lordship of Milan, he laid siege to it, right in the suburbs of the city itself; but as he was assuming the iron crown outside of Milan in a church, while Mass was being sung, there came great thunder and lightning into the church, and some died therefrom; and the Archbishop which was singing Mass at the altar, rose and said to the Emperor Conrad, that he had visibly seen S. Ambrose, which sternly menaced him except he abandoned the siege of Milan; and he, thus admonished, withdrew his host, and made peace with the Milanese. He was a just man, and made many laws, and kept the Empire in peace long time. Yea, and he went into Calabria against the Saracens which were come to lay waste the country, and fought against them, and, with great shedding of Christian blood, he drove them away and overcame them. This Conrad took much delight in sojourning at Florence when he was in Tuscany, and he advanced it greatly, and many citizens of Florence received knighthood from his hand, and were in his service. And to the intent it may be known who were the noble and powerful citizens in those times in the city of Florence, we will briefly make mention thereof.

§ 10.—*Of the nobles which were in the city of Florence in the time of the said Emperor Conrad, and first of those about the Duomo.*
1015 a.d.

As before has been narrated, the first rebuilding of the smaller Florence was according to the division of four quarters, after the four gates; and to the end we may the better describe the noble families and houses which in the said times, after Fiesole had been destroyed, were great and powerful in Florence, we will recount them according to the quarters where they dwelt. And first, they of the **Cf. Par. xvi. 25, xxv. 5.** Porta del Duomo, which was the first fold and abiding place of the rebuilt Florence, and where all the noble citizens of Florence on Sundays gathered and held civil converse around the Duomo, and where were celebrated all the marriages, and peacemakings, and every festival and solemnity of the commonwealth; and next, the Porta San Piero, and then Porta San Brancazio, and Porta Sante Marie. And the Porta del Duomo was inhabited by the family of the Giovanni, and of the Guineldi which were the first to rebuild the city of

78

Florence, whence afterwards were descended many families of nobles in Mugello, and in Valdarno, and in many cities, which now are popolari and almost **Par. xvi. 104.** come to an end. There were the Barucci which dwelt near Santa Maria Maggiore, which are now extinct; the Scali and Palermini were of their lineage. There were also in the said quarter Arrigucci, and Sizi, and **Par. xvi. 108.**

112-114. the family della Tosa: these della Tosa were of one lineage with the Bisdomini, and were patrons and defenders of the bishopric; but one of them departed from his kin of the Porta San Piero, and took to wife a lady called la Tosa, which was the heiress of her family, and hence **Cf. Par. xv. 137, 138.**

Par. xvi. 100. was derived the name. Also there were the della Pressa, which abode among the Chiavaiuoli, gentlemen.

§ 11.—*Concerning the houses of the nobles in the quarter of the Porta San Piero.*

In the quarter of Porta San Piero were the Bisdomini, which, as aforesaid, were the patrons of the bishopric, and the Alberighi, and **Par. xvi. 89.**

94-99.

65. Inf. xvi. 37. Par. xv. 112-114. Par. xvi. 101. Purg. xii. 104, 105. Par. xvi. 105, 93, 104. theirs was the church of Santa Maria Alberighi towards the house of the Donati, and now, nought remains of them; the Rovignani were very great, and dwelt on Porta San Piero (their houses afterwards belonged to the Counts Guidi, and afterwards to the Cerchi), and from them were born all the Counts Guidi, as has afore been told, of the daughter of the good Messer Bellincione Berti; in our days all that family have disappeared; the Galligari, and Chiarmontesi, and Ardinghi, which dwelt in Orto San Michele, were very ancient; and likewise the Giuochi, which now are popolani, which dwelt by Santa Margherita; the Elisei, which likewise are now popolani, who dwell near the Mercato **Cf. 40-42. 121, 122.**

106, 107. 131, 132.

115-120. Vecchio; and in that place dwelt the Caponsacchi, which were Fiesolan magnates; the Donati or Calfucci, which were all one family; but the Calfucci have come to nought; and the della Bella of San Martino have also become popolani; and the family of the Adimari, which were descended from the house of the Cosi, which now dwell in Porta Rossa, and they built Santa

Maria Nipotecosa; and albeit they are now the chief family of that sesto, and of Florence, nevertheless, they were not of the most ancient in those days.

§ 12.—*Of them of the quarter of Porta San Brancazio.*

Par. xvi. 100, 111. Inf. vi. 80, xxviii. 103-111. Par. xvi. 88.

In the quarter of the Porta San Brancazio were very great and potent the house of the Lamberti, descended from German forefathers. The Ughi were most ancient, which built Santa Maria Ughi, and all the hill of Montughi was theirs, but now they are extinct. The Catellini were most ancient, and now there is no record of them. It is said that the family Tieri were of their lineage, descended from a bastard. The **Par. xvi. 103. Par. xvi. 93; Inf. 121-123; Par. xv. 115, 116, xvi. 92.** Pigli were gentlemen and magnates in those times, and the Soldanieri, and the Vecchietti; very ancient were the dell' Arca, and now they are extinct; and the Migliorelli, which now are nought; and the Trinciavelli of Mosciano were very ancient.

§ 13.—*Concerning them of the great quarter of Porta Santa Maria and of San Piero Scheraggio.*

In the quarter of Porta Santa Maria, which is now included in the sesto of San Piero Scheraggio and in that of Borgo, there were many powerful and ancient families. The chief were the Uberti, whose **Par. xvi. 109, 110; Convivio iv. 20; 38-41. Par. xvi. 104. 105. 89.** ancestor was born in Germany and came thence, which dwelt where is now the Piazza of the Priors, and the Palace of the People; the Fifanti, called Bogolesi, dwelt at the side of Porta Santa Maria; and the Galli, Cappiardi, Guidi; and the Filippi, which now have come to nought, were then great and powerful, and dwelt in the Mercato Nuovo. And likewise the Greci, whereto pertained all the Borgo dei Greci, are **89.** now come to an end and extinct, save that there are in Bologna of their lineage; the Ormanni which dwelt where is now the said Palace of **89.** the People, and who are now called Foraboschi. And behind San Piero Scheraggio where are now the houses of the family of the Petri, dwelt they of Pera or Peruzza; and from their name the postern which was there was called the Peruzza Gate. Some say that the Peruzzi of to-day **124-126.**

104.

92, 127, 93.

123.

133.

136-144. were descended from this lineage, but this I do not affirm. The Sacchetti which dwell in the Garbo were very ancient; around the New Market the Bostichi were of note, and the della Sannella, and the Giandonati, and the Infangati. In the Borgo Santo Apostolo the Gualterotti, and the Importuni, which are now popolani, were then magnates. The Bondelmonti were noble and ancient citizens in the country, and Montebuoni was their fortress, and many others in Valdigrieve; first they settled in Oltrarno, and then they betook themselves to the Borgo. The Pulci, and the Counts of Gangalandi, **Par. xv. 115, xvi. 127-132, xv. 97, 98.** Ciuffagni, and Nerli of Oltrarno, were at one time great and powerful, together with the Giandonati, and the della Bella named above; and from the Marquis Hugh which built the Badia of Florence, they took their arms and knighthood, for they were of great account with him.

§ 14.—*How in those times Oltrarno was but little inhabited.* § 15.—*How Henry II. called III. was made Emperor, and the events which* **1040 a.d.**
1056 a.d.
1073 a.d. *were in his time.* § 16.—*How Henry III. was made Emperor, and the events which were in Italy in his time, and how the Court of Rome was in Florence.* § 17.—*How S. John Gualberti, citizen of Florence, and father of the order of Vallombrosa, was canonized.*

§ 18.—*Narration of many things that were in those times.*
1070 a.d.
Inf. xxviii. 13, 14. Par. xviii. 48.

In those times, the year of Christ 1070, there passed into Italy Robert Guiscard, duke of the Normans, the which by his prowess and wit did great things, and wrought in the service of Holy Church against the Emperor Henry III., who was persecuting it, and against the Emperor Alexis, and against the Venetians, as we shall make mention hereafter: for the which thing he was made lord over Sicily and Apulia, with the confirmation of Holy Church; and his descendants after him, down to the time of Henry of Suabia, father of Frederick **iii. 118-120.**

Cf. Purg. xxxiii. 119. II., were kings and lords thereof. And also in those same times was the worthy and wise Countess Matilda, the which reigned in Tuscany and in Lombardy, and was well-nigh sovereign lady over all, and did many great things in her time for Holy Church, so that it seems to me reasonable and fitting to speak of their beginning and of their state, in this our treatise, forasmuch as they were much mixed up with the doings of our city of Florence through the consequences which followed their doings in Tuscany. And first we will tell of Robert Guiscard, and then of the Countess Matilda, and their beginnings and their doings briefly, returning afterwards to our subject and the deeds of our city of Florence, the which by the increase and the doings of the Florentines began to multiply and to extend the fame of Florence throughout the whole world, more than it had been heretofore; and therefore almost by necessity it behoves us in our treatise to narrate more universally henceforward of the Popes and of the Emperors and of the kings, and of many provinces of the world, the events and things which happened in those times, forasmuch as they have much to do with our subject, and because the aforesaid Emperor Henry III. was the beginner of the scandal between the Church and the Empire, and afterwards the Guelfs and Ghibellines, whence arose the parties of the Empire and of the Church in Italy, the which so grew that all Italy was infected thereby and almost all Europe, and many ills and perils, and destructions and changes have followed thereupon to our city and to the whole world, such as following on with our treatise we shall mention in their times. And we will begin now, at the head of every page to mark the year of our Lord, following on in order of time, to the end that the events of past times may be the more easily looked out in our treatise.

§ 19.—*Of Robert Guiscard and his descendants, which were kings of Sicily and of Apulia.*
880-1110 a.d.

Well, then, as was afore made mention, in the time of the Emperor Charles, which is called Charles the Fat, which reigned in the years of our Lord 880 unto 892, the pagan Northmen being come from Norway, passed

82

into Germany and into France, pressing and tormenting the Gauls and the Germans. Charles, with a powerful hand, came against the Northmen, and peace being made and confirmed by matrimony, the king of the Normans was baptised, and received at the sacred font by the said Charles, and in the end, Charles not being able to drive the Normans out of France, granted them a region on the further side of the Seine, called Lada Serena, the which unto this day is called Normandy, because of the said Normans, in the which land, from that time forward, the duke has reigned as king. The first duke, then, was Robert, to whom succeeded his son William, which begat Richard, and Richard begat the second Richard. This Richard begat Richard and Robert Guiscard, the which Robert Guiscard was not duke of Normandy, but brother of Duke Richard. He, according to their usage, forasmuch as he was a younger son, had not the lordship of the duchy, and therefore desiring to make trial of his powers, he came, poor and needy, into Apulia, where at that time one Robert, a native of the country, was duke, to whom Robert Guiscard, coming, was first made his squire and was then knighted by him. Robert Guiscard having come then to this Duke Robert, won many victories with prowess against his enemies, for he was at war with the prince of Salerno; and carrying with him magnificent rewards, he returned into Normandy, bringing back report of the delights and riches of Apulia, having adorned his horses with golden bridles and shod them with silver, in witness of the facts he alleged; by the which thing, having roused many knights, following this emprise through desire of riches and of glory, returning incontinent into Apulia, he took them with him, and gave faithful aid to the duke of Apulia against Godfrey, duke of the Normans; and, not long time after, Robert, duke of Apulia, being nigh unto death, by the will of his barons made him his successor in the duchy, and as he had promised him, he took his daughter to wife the year of Christ 1078. **1078 a.d.** And a little time after, he conquered Alexis, emperor of Constantinople, who had taken possession of Sicily and of part of Calabria, and he conquered the Venetians, and took all the kingdom of Apulia and of Sicily; and albeit he did this in violation of the Roman Church, to which the kingdom of Apulia belonged, and albeit the Countess Matilda made war against Robert Guiscard in the service of Holy Church; nevertheless, in the end, Robert being, of his own will, reconciled with Holy Church, was made lord of the said kingdom; and not long after, Gregory VII., with his cardinals, being besieged by the Emperor Henry IV. in the castle of S. Angelo, Robert came to Rome and drave away by force the said Henry with his Anti-pope which he had made by force, and he freed the Pope and the cardinals from the siege, and replaced the Pope in the Lateran Palace, having severely punished the Romans, who had shown favour to the Emperor Henry and to the Pope whom he had made against Pope Gregory. This Robert Guiscard, duke of Apulia, was once on a hunting excursion, and he followed the quarry into the depth of a wood, his companions not knowing what had become of him, or where he was, or what he was doing; and then Robert, seeing the night approaching, leaving the beast which he was pursuing, sought to return home; and turning, he found in the wood a leper, who importunately asked alms of him; and when he had said I know not what in reply, the leper said again that the anguish he endured availed him nought, yet him were liefer carry any weight or any burden; and when he asked of the leper what he would have, he said, "I desire that you will put me behind you on your horse"; lest abandoned in the wood, peradventure the beasts might devour him. Then Robert cheerfully received him behind him on his horse; and as they rode forward, the leper said to Robert—great baron as he was:—"My hands are so icy cold, that unless I may cherish them against thy flesh, I cannot keep myself on horseback." Then Robert granted the leper to put his hands boldly under his clothing, and comfort his flesh and his members without any fear; and when yet a third time the leper bespoke his pity, he put him upon his saddle, and he, sitting behind him, embraced the leper, and led him to his own chamber and put him into his own bed, and set him in it with right good care to the end he might repose; no one of his household perceiving ought thereof. And when the banquet of supper was spread, having told his wife that he had lodged the leper in his bed, his wife incontinent went to the chamber to know if the poor sufferer would sup. The chamber, albeit there were no perfumes therein, she found as fragrant as if it had been full of sweet-smelling things, such that neither Robert nor his wife had ever known so sweet scents, and the leper, whom they had come thither to seek, they did not find, whereat the husband and the wife marvelled beyond measure at so great a wonder; but with reverence and with fear, both one and the other asked God to reveal to them what this might be. And the following day Christ appeared in a vision to Robert, saying, that it was Himself that He had revealed to him in the form of a leper, to make trial of his piety; and He announced to him that by his wife he should have sons, whereof one should be emperor, the next king, and the third duke. Encouraged by this promise Robert subdued the rebels of Apulia and of Sicily, and acquired lordship over all; and he had five sons: William, who took to wife the daughter of Alexis, the emperor of the Greeks, and was lord and possessor of his empire, but died without children (some say that this was the William which was called Longsword, but many say that this Longsword was not of the lineage of Robert Guiscard, but of the race of the marquises of **Cf. Purg. vii. 133-136.** Montferrat); and the second son of Robert Guiscard was Boagdinos [Boemond], who was at the first duke of Tarentum; the third was Roger, duke of Apulia, which, after the death of his father, was crowned king of Sicily by Pope Honorius II.; the fourth son of Robert Guiscard was Henry, duke of the Normans; the fifth son, Richard Count Cicerat, that is, I suppose, count of Acerra. This Robert Guiscard, after having done many and noble things in Apulia, purposed and desired, by way of devotion, to go to Jerusalem on pilgrimage; and it was told him in a vision that he would die in Jerusalem. Therefore, having commended his kingdom to Roger, his son, he embarked by sea for the voyage to Jerusalem, and arriving in Greece, at the port which was afterwards called after him Port Guiscard, he began to sicken of his malady; and trusting in the revelation which had been made to him, he in no wise feared to die. There was over against the said port an island, to the which, that he might repose and recover his strength, he caused himself to be carried, and after being carried there he grew no **1110 a.d.** better, but rather grievously worse. Then he asked what this island was called, and the mariners answered that of old it was called Jerusalem. Which thing having heard, straightway certified of his death, devoutly he fulfilled all those things which appertain to the salvation of the soul, and died in the grace of God the year of Christ 1110, having reigned in Apulia thirty-three years. These things concerning Robert Guiscard may in part be read in chronicles, and in part I heard them narrated by those who fully knew the history of the kingdom of Apulia.

§ 20.—*Concerning the successors of Robert Guiscard which were kings of Sicily and of Apulia.*

Afterwards, Roger, son of Duke Robert Guiscard, begat the second Roger; and this Roger, after the death of his father, was made king of Sicily, and he begat William, and Constance his sister. This William **Par. iii. 109-120. Purg. iii. 112, 113. Par. xx. 62.** honourably and magnificently ruled the kingdom of Sicily, and he took to wife the daughter of the king of England, and by her he had neither son nor daughter; and when his father Roger was dead, and the sovereignty of the kingdom had passed to William, a prophecy was made known, that Constance, his sister, should rule over the realm of Sicily in destruction and ruin; wherefore King William, having called his friends and wise men, asked counsel of them what he should do with his sister Constance; and it was counselled him by the greater part of them that if he desired the royal sovereignty should be secure, he should cause her to be put to death. But among the others was one named Tancred, duke of Tarentum, which had been nephew to Robert Guiscard through the sister who is thought to have been wife to Bagnamonte [Boemond], prince of Antioch; this man, opposing the counsel of the others, appeased King William, that he should not cause the innocent lady to be put to death; and so it came to pass that the said Constance was preserved from death, and she, not of her own will, but through fear of death, lived in the guise of a nun in a certain convent of nuns. William being dead, the aforesaid Tancred succeeded him in the kingdom, having taken it to himself against the will of the Church of Rome to which pertained the right and property of that kingdom. This Tancred, instructed by natural wit, was very full of learning, and he had a wife more beautiful than the Sibyl, but as many think without breasts, by whom he begat two sons and three daughters: the first was called Roger, which in his father's lifetime was made king, and he died; the second was William the younger, which in his father's lifetime was made king, and after his father was dead he held the kingdom for a time. During these things, Tancred being alive and on the throne, Constance, sister to King William, already perhaps fifty years old, was a nun in her body but not in her mind in the city of Palermo. Discord then having arisen between King Tancred and the archbishop of Palermo, perhaps for this cause, that Tancred was usurping the rights of the Church, the archbishop then thought how he might transfer the kingdom of Sicily to other lordship, and made a secret treaty with the Pope, that Constance should be married to Henry, duke of Suabia, son of the great Frederick; and Henry having **Par. iii. 112-120.** taken to wife her to whom the kingdom seemed to pertain by right, was crowned emperor by Pope Celestine. This Henry, when Tancred was dead, entered into the kingdom of Apulia, and punished many of them which had held with Tancred, and had shown him favour, and which had done injury to Queen Constance, and had done shame to the nobility of her honour. This Constance was the mother—we shall not say of Frederick II. who was long king of the Roman Empire,—but rather of Frederick who brought the said Empire to destruction, as will appear fully in his deeds. When Tancred was dead then, the kingdom passed to his son William, young in years and in wisdom; but Henry having entered the kingdom with his army the year of Christ 1197, made a false truce with **1197 a.d.** the young King William, and having taken him by fraud and secretly into Suabia, few knowing thereof, he sent him into banishment with his sister, and having caused his eyes to be put out, he there kept him under ward till his death. With this William son of Tancred were taken his three sisters, to wit, Alberia, Constance, and Ernadama. When the Emperor Henry was dead, and the young William who had been castrated and whose eyes had been put out was dead also, Philip, duke of Suabia, through the prayers of his wife, which was daughter of the Emperor Manuel of Constantinople, delivered these three daughters of King Tancred from exile and from prison, and let them go free. And Alberia or Aceria had three husbands: the first was Count Walter of Brienne, brother of King John, from whom was born Walteran, count of Joppa, to whom the king of Cyprus gave his daughter in marriage. After Count Walter had been slain by Count Trebaldo [Diephold], the German, Alberia was wedded to Count James of Tricarico, by whom she had Count Simon and the Lady Adalitta; and he being dead, Pope Honorius gave Alberia to wife to Count Tigrimo, count palatine in Tuscany; and for dowry he gave her the region of Lizia and of Mount Scaglioso in the kingdom of Apulia. Constance was the wife of Marchesono [Ziani], doge of Venice. The third sister, who was named Ernadama, had no husband. These were the fortunes of the successors of

87

Robert Guiscard in the kingdom of Sicily and of Apulia, down to Constance, mother of the Emperor Frederick the son of King Henry; and thus it may be seen that Robert Guiscard and his successors ruled over the kingdom of Sicily and of Apulia 120 years. We will now leave the kings of Sicily and of Apulia; and we will relate concerning the wise Countess Matilda.

§ 21.—*Of the Countess Matilda.*

The mother of Countess Matilda is said to have been the daughter of one who reigned as emperor in Constantinople, in whose court was an Italian of distinguished manners and of great race and well nurtured, skilled in arms, expert and endowed with every gift, such as they are in whom noble blood is wont to declare itself illustriously. Now all these things made him to be loved of all men and gave grace to his ways. And he began to turn his eyes upon the emperor's daughter, and was secretly united to her in marriage, and they took such jewels and moneys as they might, and she fled with him into Italy. And they came first to the bishopric of Reggio, in Lombardy. From this lady, then, and from her husband, was born the doughty Countess Matilda. But the father of the lady aforesaid, that is to say the emperor of Constantinople, who had no other daughter, caused great searching to be made, if by any means he might find her; and found she was, by them that were seeking, in the said place; and when they begged of her that she would return to her father, who would marry her again to any prince she might choose, she gave answer that she had chosen to have him she now had above all other, and it were a thing impossible to abandon him and ever be united to another man. And when all this was told again to the emperor, straightway he sent letters and confirmed the marriage, and money without end, with orders to buy fortresses and villages at any price and erect new castles. And they bought in the said place three fortresses, very nigh together, and because of this close neighbourhood, they are commonly called the Tre Castella at Reggio. And not far from the said three fortresses the lady had such a castle built upon a mountain as might never be taken, the which castle was called Canossa, and there the countess afterward founded and endowed a noble convent of nuns. This was in the mountains; but on the plain she built Guastalla and Sulzariani, and she bought land along the Po and built divers monasteries, and divers noble bridges did she make across the rivers of Lombardy. And moreover

Garfagnana and the greater part of the Erignano, and parts of the see of Modena, are said to have been her possessions, and in the Bolognese district the great and spacious towns of Arzellata and Medicina were of her patrimony; and she had many others in Lombardy. And in Tuscany she established fortresses and the turret at Polugiana, within her jurisdiction, and she liberally endowed many noblemen, under fee, and made them her vassals. In divers places she built many monasteries, and endowed many cathedral churches and others. And in the end, when the Countess Matilda's father and mother were dead, and she was their heir, she thought to marry, and having heard of the fame and the person and the other qualities of a native of Suabia, whose name was Guelf, she sent formal messages to him and authorised agents who should establish a contract of marriage between him and her, albeit they were not present in person together, and who should arrange the place where the wedding should take place. The ring was given at the noble castle of the Conti Ginensi, which is now, however, destroyed. And as Guelf approached the said castle, the Countess Matilda went to meet him with a great cavalcade, and there was held the festival of the wedding right joyously. But soon did sadness follow gladness in that the marriage bond was not consummated, by failure of conception, which is expressly declared to be the purpose of marriage.

******

The countess then, in silence, fearing deception and being averse to the other burdens of matrimony, passed her life in chastity even to her death, and giving herself to works of piety she built and endowed many churches and monasteries and hospitals. And once and again she came with a great army and mightily interposed in service of Holy Church and succoured her. Once was against the Normans, who had taken away the duchy of Apulia from the Church by violence, and were laying waste the confines of Campagna. Them did the Countess Matilda, devout daughter of S. Peter that she was, together with Godfrey, duke of Spoleto, drive off as far as to Aquino in the time of Alexander II., Pope of Rome. The second time she fought against the Emperor Henry III. of Bavaria, and overcame him. And yet once again she fought for the Church in Lombardy against Henry IV., his son, and overcame him, in the time of Pope Calixtus II. And she made a will and offered up all her patrimony on the altar of S. Peter, and made the Church of Rome heir of it all. And not long after she died in God, and she is buried in the church of Pisa, which she had largely endowed. It was in the 1115th year of the Nativity that the countess died. We will leave **1115 a.d.** to speak of the Countess Matilda, and will turn back to follow the history of the Emperor Henry III. of Bavaria.

§ 22.—*Again how Henry III. of Bavaria renewed war against the Church.* § 23.—*How the said Emperor Henry besieged the city of* **1080 a.d.** **1089 a.d.** *Florence.* § 24.—*How in these times was the great crusade over seas.* § 25.—*How the Florentines began to increase their territory.* § 26.—*How the Florentines conquered and destroyed the fortress of Prato.* § 27.—*How Henry IV. of Bavaria was elected Emperor, and how* **1107 a.d.** *he persecuted the Church.* § 28.—*How at last the said Emperor Henry IV. returned to obedience to Holy Church.*

§ 29.—*How the Florentines defeated the Vicar of the Emperor Henry IV.* **1113 a.d.**

In the year of Christ 1113 the Florentines marched against Montecasciolo, which was making war upon the city, having been stirred to rebellion by M. Ruberto Tedesco, vicar of the Emperor Henry in Tuscany, who was stationed with his troops in Samminiato del Tedesco, so called because the vicars of the Emperors with their troops of Tedeschi [Germans] were stationed in the said fortress to harry the cities and castles of Tuscany that would not obey the Emperors. And this M. Ruberto was routed and slain by the Florentines, and the fortress taken and destroyed.

§ 30.—*How the city of Florence took fire twice, whence a great part of the city was burnt.* **1115 a.d.**

In the year of Christ 1115, in the month of May, fire broke out in the Borgo Santo Apostolo, and was so great and impetuous that a good part of the city was burnt, to the great hurt of the Florentines. And in that selfsame year died the good Countess Matilda. And after, in the year 1117, fire again broke out in Florence, and of a truth that which **1117 a.d.** was not burnt in the first fire was burnt in the second, whence great hurt befell the Florentines, and not without cause and judgment of God, forasmuch as the city was evilly corrupted by heresy, among others by the sect of the epicureans, through the vice of **Cf. Inf. x. 13-15.** licentiousness and gluttony, and this over so large a part, that the citizens were fighting among themselves for the faith with arms in their hands in many parts of Florence, and this plague endured long time in Florence till the coming of the holy Religions of St. Francis **Par. xi. 35-123. Par. xii. 31-111.** and of St. Dominic, the which Religions through their holy brothers, the charge of this sin of heresy having been committed to them by the Pope, greatly exterminated it in Florence, and in Milan, and in many other cities of Tuscany and of Lombardy in the time of the blessed Peter Martyr, who was martyred by the Paterines in Milan; and afterwards the other inquisitors wrought the like. And in the flames of the said fires in Florence were burnt many books and chronicles which would more fully have preserved the record of past things in our city of Florence, wherefore few are left remaining; for the which thing it has behoved us to collect from other veracious chronicles of divers cities and countries, great part of those things whereof mention has been made in this treatise.

§ 31.—*How the Pisans took Majorca, and the Florentines protected the city of Pisa.*

1117 a.d.

In the year of Christ 1117 the Pisans made a great expedition of galleys and ships against the island of Majorca, which the Saracens held, and when the said armada had departed from Pisa and was already assembled at Vada for the voyage, the commonwealth of Lucca marched upon Pisa to seize the city. Hearing this, the Pisans dared not go forward with their expedition for fear that the Lucchese should take possession of their city; and to draw back from their emprise did not seem for their honour in view of the great outlay and preparation which they had made. Wherefore they took counsel to send their ambassadors to the Florentines, for the two commonwealths in those times were close friends. And they begged them that they would be pleased to protect the city, trusting them as their inmost friends and dear brothers. And on this the Florentines undertook to serve

91

them and to protect their city against the Lucchese and all other. Wherefore the commonwealth of Florence sent thither armed folk in abundance, horse and foot, and encamped two miles outside the city, and in respect for their women they would not enter Pisa, and made a proclamation that whosoever should enter the city should answer for it with his person; and one who did enter was accordingly condemned to be hung. And when the old men who had been left in Pisa prayed the Florentines for love of them to pardon him, they would not. But the Pisans still opposed, and begged that at least they would not put him to death in their territory; whereupon the Florentine army secretly purchased a field from a peasant in the name of the commonwealth of Florence, and thereon they raised the gallows and did the execution to maintain their decree. And when the host of the Pisans returned from the conquest of Majorca they gave great thanks to the Florentines, and asked them what memorial they would have of the conquest—the metal gates, or two columns of porphyry which they had taken and brought from Majorca. The Florentines chose the columns, and the Pisans sent them to Florence covered with scarlet cloth, and some said that before they sent them they put them in the fire for envy. And the said columns are those which stand in front of San Giovanni.

§ 32.—*How the Florentines took and destroyed the fortress of Fiesole.*

1125 a.d.

In the year of Christ 1125, the Florentines came with an army to the fortress of Fiesole, which was still standing and very strong, and it was held by certain gentlemen Cattani, which had been of the city of Fiesole, and thither resorted highwaymen and refugees and evil men, which sometimes infested the roads and country of Florence; and the Florentines carried on the siege so long that for lack of victuals the fortress surrendered, albeit they would never have taken it by storm, and they caused it to be all cast down and destroyed to the foundations, and they made a decree that none should ever dare to build a fortress again at Fiesole.

§ 33.—*From where the miles are measured in the territory of Florence.* § 34.—*How Roger, duke of Apulia, was at war with the* **1125 a.d.** *Church, and afterwards was reconciled with the Pope, and how after that there were two Popes in Rome at one time.* § 35.—*Tells of the* **1147 a.d.** *second crusade over seas.*

§ 36.—*How the Florentines destroyed the fortress of Montebuono.*

1135 a.d.

In the year of Christ 1135 the fortress of Montebuono was standing, which was very strong and pertained to the house of the Bondelmonti, which were Cattani and ancient gentlemen of the country, and from the **Par. xvi. 66.** name of this their castle the house of Bondelmonti took their name; and by reason of its strength, and because the road ran at the foot thereof, therefore they took toll, for the which thing the Florentines did not desire, nor would they have, such a fortress hard by the city; and they went thither with an army in the month of June and took it, on condition that the fortress should be destroyed, and the rest of the possessions should still pertain to the said Cattani, and that they should come and dwell in Florence. And thus the commonwealth of Florence began to grow, and by force, rather than by right, their territory increased, and they subdued to their jurisdiction every noble of the district, and destroyed the fortresses.

§ 37.—*How the Florentines were discomfited at Montedicroce by the* **1147 a.d.** **1154 a.d.** *Counts Guidi.* § 38.—*How they of Prato were discomfited by the Pistoians at Carmignano.*

93

END OF SELECTIONS FROM BOOK IV.

BOOK V.

Here begins the Fifth Book: How Frederick I. of Staufen of Suabia was Emperor of Rome, and of his descendants, and concerning the doings of Florence which were in their times, and of all Italy.

§ 1.—After the death of Conrad of Saxony, king of the Romans, **1154 a.d.**
Epist. vi. (5) 135, 136. Purg. xviii. 119, 120. Cf. Par. iii. 119. Frederick Barbarossa was elected Emperor, called Frederick the Great, or the First, of the house of Suabia, and surnamed of Staufen. This Frederick, when he had received the votes of the electors, proclaimed himself, and then came into Italy, and was crowned at Rome by Pope Adrian IV., in the year of Christ 1154, and reigned 37 years between king of the Romans and Emperor. He was liberal and a man of worth, eloquent and noble, and glorious in all his deeds. At the first he was friendly to Holy Church in the time of the said Pope Adrian, and rebuilt Tivoli, which had been destroyed; but the same day that he was crowned there was a great scuffle and fight between the Romans and his followers in Nero's meadow, where they were waiting for the said Emperor, to the great loss of the Romans; and again within the portico of St. Peter's; and it was all burnt and destroyed, to wit, the part of Rome which is around St. Peter's. And when he returned to Lombardy in the first year of his reign, because the city of Spoleto would not obey him, forasmuch as it pertained to the Church, he brought an army **Epist. vi. (5) 137.** against it, and overcame it, and destroyed it utterly; and through his desire to usurp the rights of the Church, he soon became her enemy: for after the death of Pope Adrian, in the year of Christ 1159, **1159 a.d.** Alexander III., of Siena, was made Pope, who reigned 22 years; and he, to maintain the rights of Holy Church, had great war with the said Emperor Frederick for long time; which Emperor raised up against him four schismatical anti-popes at divers times, one after the other, and three thereof were cardinals. The first was Octavianus, which took the name of Victor; the second, Guy of Cremona, which took the name of Pascal; the third was John of Struma, which took the

95

name of Calixtus; the fourth was called Landone, which took the name of Innocent; whence came great schism and affliction to the Church of God, forasmuch as these Popes by the power of the Emperor Frederick held all the patrimony of St. Peter and the Duchy, so that the said Pope Alexander had no authority. But the said Pope Alexander fought valiantly against them all, and excommunicated them: the which all, one after the other, during his reign, died an evil death. But whilst they were reigning by the power of Frederick, the said true Pope, Alexander, not being able to abide in Rome, went to the French court to King Louis the Pious, which received him graciously. And it is said in France that when the said Pope was coming to Paris secretly with a small company in the guise of a lesser prelate, immediately that he came to St. Maure, near to Paris, albeit they had not had news of the Pope, yet by Divine miracle there rose a voice: "Behold the Pope! behold the Pope!" and the bells began to ring, and the king, with the clergy and the people of Paris, went out to meet him, whence the Pope marvelled greatly, forasmuch as none knew of his coming; and he thanked God, and made himself known to the king and to the people, and began to give the benediction. And afterwards in France the said Pope called a general council in the city of Tours in Touraine, in the which he excommunicated the said Frederick, and deposed him from the Empire, and absolved all his barons from their oaths, and deposed them of the house of Colonna in Rome, that neither they nor their successors should ever be allowed to hold any office in Holy Church, seeing that they all held to the aid and favour of the said Frederick against the Church. And in that council all the kings and lords of the West promised and leagued themselves with Louis, king of France, in aid of the said Pope Alexander and of Holy Church, against the said Frederick, and likewise many cities of Lombardy rebelled against the said Frederick, to wit, Milan, and Cremona, and Piacenza, and held with the Pope and with the Church; for the which thing, when the said Frederick was passing through Lombardy to go into France against King Louis, who was supporting Pope Alexander, and found that the city of **Epist. vi. (5) 136.**

1157 a.d.

Purg. xviii. 119-120. Epist. vi. (5) 135, 136. Milan had rebelled against him, he laid siege thereto, and, after long siege, he took it, in the year of Christ

1157, in the month of March, and destroyed the walls thereof and burnt all the city, and caused the ground to be ploughed and sown with salt; and the bodies of the Three Kings or Magi which came to adore Christ by the guiding of the star, which were in the city of Milan, in three tombs hewn out of porphyry, he caused to be taken from Milan and sent to Cologne, whence all the Lombards were very wrathful. And afterwards, crossing the mountains to destroy the realm of France, with the aid of the king of Bohemia and the king of Dacia—that is, Denmark—he entered into Burgundy; but King Louis of France, with the aid of Henry, king of England, his son-in-law, and with many lords and barons, was ready to oppose him, so that by the grace of God he had no power, nor gained any land there, but through lack of victuals those kings returned to their own countries and Frederick to Italy. And he made war against the Romans, forasmuch as they had come over to the side of the Church and of Pope Alexander; and when the said Romans with their host were in the region of Tusculum, they were defeated by the chancellor of the said Frederick and his German troops in the place called Monte del Porco, and many Romans were taken and slain in such great numbers that cartloads of dead bodies were taken to Rome to be buried, and this defeat is said to have been by reason of the treachery of the Colonnas, which were always with the Emperor and against the Church; wherefore they were by the Pope deprived of all temporal and spiritual benefit; and because of the said defeat the Romans drove the Colonnas away from Rome, and destroyed an ancient and very beautiful fortress pertaining to them, which was called La Gosta, which is said to have been built by Cæsar Augustus, and this was in the year of Christ 1167. **1167 a.d.** And after this the Emperor came to Rome to besiege it and to destroy it, and brought it into great straits. The Romans caused the clergy of Rome to take the heads of St. Peter and of St. Paul and to carry them in procession all through Rome, for the which thing the Romans all took the cross against the Emperor, and the first which took it was M. Matteo Rosso the Elder, of the Orsini family, grandfather to Pope **Cf. Inf. xix. 70.** Nicholas III., and by reason of old age he had abandoned arms, and taken the habit of a penitent; and for this cause he put off the said habit and took his arms again, for which he was much commended, and by reason of this he and his came into favour with the Church, and increased greatly.

After the said M. Matteo, Gianni Buovo, a great citizen of Rome, took the cross, and afterwards all the others with great zeal and desire; for the which thing, when the Emperor heard thereof, either through fear, or rather through a miracle of the blessed Apostles, straightway he departed from the siege of Rome with his followers, and returned to Viterbo, and the city of Rome was set free.

§ 2.—*How Pope Alexander returned from France to Venice, and the Emperor returned to obedience.*

Then, after the said Pope Alexander had been long time in France, by the aid of the kings of France and of England he returned with his court into Italy by sea, and, landing in Sicily, he was devoutly received and favoured by King William, which then was king thereof, and which declared himself faithful to Holy Church, and that he held the island from him; for the which thing the said Pope confirmed him king of Sicily, and gave him Apulia, wherefore the said King William with his fleet bore him company by sea as far as the city of Venice, whither the Pope desired to go for more security, that the Emperor Frederick might not hurt him; and to show favour to the faithful believers in Holy Church in Lombardy, he sojourned in the said city of Venice, and by the Venetians was reverently received and honoured; and by his favour the Milanese rebuilt the city of Milan in the year of **1168 a.d.** Christ 1168. Then, a little while after, the Milanese, with the aid of Piacenza and Cremona, and of the other cities of Lombardy which obeyed Holy Church, built a city in Lombardy, to be a rampart and defence against the city of Pavia, which always was against Milan, and held with the Empire; and since this city was built, to the honour of the said Pope Alexander, and to the end it might be more famous, they called it Alessandria; and afterwards it was surnamed City della Paglia [of Straw], in contempt, by the Pavians; and at the prayer of the Lombards the Pope gave it a bishop, and deposed the bishop of Pavia, and took away from him the dignity of the Pallium and of the Cross, forasmuch as he had always held with the Emperor Frederick against the Church.

§ 3.—*How the Emperor Frederick Barbarossa was reconciled with the Church, and went over seas, and there died.*

The Emperor Frederick, seeing himself much cast down from his state and sovereignty, and that many cities of Lombardy and of Tuscany were rebelling against him and holding with the Church and with Pope Alexander, which had greatly increased in estate by the favour of the kings of France and of England, and of William, king of Sicily, sought to reconcile himself with the Church and with the Pope, to the end he might not wholly lose the honour of the Empire, and he sent a solemn embassy to Venice to Pope Alexander to ask for peace, promising to make all amends to Holy Church, and the Pope graciously hearkened to him, wherefore the said Frederick went to Venice and threw himself at the feet of the said Pope, and asked for mercy. Then the said Pope set his foot upon his neck, and said the verse of the psalter: "*Super aspidem et basiliscum ambulabis, et conculcabis leonem et draconem*" [Ps. xci. 13]; and the Emperor answered, "*Non tibi sed Petro*" [Not to you, but to Peter, was it said], and the Pope answered, "*Ego sum vicarius Petri*" [I am in the place of Peter]; and then he forgave him every offence which he had committed against Holy Church, causing him to restore that which he held from Holy Church; and this he promised and did, under compact that whatsoever should be found held in possession by the Church on that day throughout the Kingdom, should pertain for ever to Holy Church; and it was found that Benivento was so held; and this was the cause why the Church holds as hers the city of Benivento. And this done, he reconciled him with the Romans, and with Manuel, emperor of Constantinople, and with William, king of Sicily, and with the Lombards; and as amends and penance he imposed upon him, and he promised, to go over seas to the succour of the Holy Land, forasmuch as Saladin, the soldan of Babylon, had retaken **Inf. iv. 129.** Jerusalem and many other fortresses held by the Christians; and this he did. Then the said Frederick, having taken the cross in the year of **1188 a.d.** Christ 1188, departed from Germany with an immense host, and went by land through Hungary to Constantinople as far as Armenia [Pisidia]; but when the said Frederick was come into Armenia, it being summer and very hot, as he was bathing for his solace in a little river called the river of Ferro [Iron], he was miserably drowned. And this, it is believed, was the judgment of God by reason of the many persecutions which he had brought upon Holy Church: and he left a son, which was named Henry, whom he had caused to be elected king of the Romans before he passed over seas in the year of

Christ 1186; and when the said Frederick was dead, his wife, with her son and with their followers, albeit many of them died on this voyage, returned from Syria to the West without having gained anything. We will now return to our subject of the doings of Florence and of other things which were in the time when the said Frederick was reigning; but first we will tell of King Philip of France and of King Richard of England, which went over seas to the succour of the Holy Land in this same time.

§ 4.—*How the king of France and the king of England went over seas.* **1170 a.d.**

1174 a.d. § 5.—*How the Florentines defeated the Aretines.* § 6.—*How the first war of the Florentines against the Sienese began.* § 7.—*How the noble and strong castle of Poggibonizzi was first built, and that of Colle of Valdelsa.*

§ 8.—*Of the great fires which were in the city of Florence.* **1177 a.d.**

In the year of Christ 1177, fire broke out in the city of Florence on the 5th day of August, and spread from the foot of the Ponte Vecchio as far as the Mercato Vecchio. And afterwards, in the same year, fire broke out at San Martino del Vescovo, and spread as far as Santa Maria Ughi and to the Duomo of S. Giovanni, with great hurt to the city, and not without the judgment of God, forasmuch as the Florentines had become very proud by reason of the victories they had gotten over their neighbours; and some among them were very ungrateful towards God, and full of other wicked sins. And in this year, because of a great flood of the river Arno, the Ponte Vecchio fell, which also was a sign of future adversities to our city.

§ 9.—*How civil war began in Florence between the Uberti and the government of the Consuls.* **1177 a.d.**

Wherefore in the selfsame year there began in Florence dissension and great war among the citizens, the worst that had ever been in Florence; and this was by reason of too great prosperity and repose, together with pride and ingratitude; forasmuch as the house of the Uberti, which were the most powerful and the greatest citizens of Florence, with their allies, both

100

magnates and popolari, began war against the Consuls (which were the lords and rulers of the commonwealth for a certain time and under certain ordinances), from envy of the Government, which was not to their mind; and the war was so fierce and unnatural that well-nigh every day, or every other day, the citizens fought against one another in divers parts of the city, from district to district, according as the factions were, and as they had fortified their towers, whereof there was great number in the city, in height 100 or 120 cubits. And in those times, by reason of the said war, many towers were newly fortified by the communities of the districts, from the common funds of the neighbourhood, which were called Towers of the Fellowships, and upon them were set engines to shoot forth one at another, and the city was barricaded in many places; and this plague endured more than two years, and many died by reason thereof, and much peril and hurt was brought upon the city; but this war among the citizens became so much of use and wont that one day they would be fighting, and the next day they would be eating and drinking together, and telling tales of one another's valour and prowess in these battles; and at last they ceased fighting, in that it irked them for very weariness, and they made peace, and the Consuls remained in their government; albeit, in the end they begot and then brought forth the accursed factions, which were afterwards in Florence, as hereafter in due time we will make mention.

§ 10.—*How the Florentines took the castle of Montegrossoli.* **1182 a.d.**

1184 a.d. § 11.—*How the Florentines took the castle of Pogna.*

§ 12.—*How the Emperor Frederick I. took their territory from the city of Florence, and many other cities of Tuscany.*

1184 a.d.

In the said year of Christ 1184, the Emperor Frederick I., as he went from Lombardy into Apulia, passed through our city of Florence on the 31st day of July in the said year, and abode there some days; and receiving a complaint from the nobles of the country that the commonwealth of Florence had taken by force and occupied many of their castles and strongholds against the honour of the Empire, he took from the commonwealth of Florence all the whole territory and the lordship thereof up to the walls, and in the territory he set vicars of his own throughout the villages to administer the law and execute justice; and he did the like to all the other cities of Tuscany which had held with the Church when he was at war with Pope Alexander, save that he did not take the territory from the cities of Pisa and of Pistoia, which held with him. And in this year the said Frederick besieged the city of Siena, but did not take it. And these things he did to the said cities of Tuscany, forasmuch as they had not been on his side; so that, albeit he was at peace with the Church and had cried the said Pope mercy, as afore has been narrated, nevertheless, he did not cease from manifesting ill-will against the cities which had obeyed the Church; and thus the city of Florence was left without any territory for four years, until the said Frederick set forth on his voyage over seas, when he was drowned, as afore we have narrated.

§ 13.—*How the Florentines took the cross, and went over seas to conquer Damietta, and therefore recovered their territory.*
1188 a.d.

In the year of Christ 1188, all Christendom being moved to go to the succour of the Holy Land, there came to Florence the archbishop of Ravenna, the Pope's Legate, to preach the cross for the said expedition; and many good people of Florence took the cross from the said archbishop at S. Donato tra le Torri, or at S. Donato a Torri, beyond Rifredi, or the Monastery delle Donne, forasmuch as the said archbishop was of the Order of Citeaux [the Cistercian Order]; and this was on the 2nd day of the month of February in the said year, and the Florentines were in such great numbers that they made up an army in themselves over seas, and they were at the conquest of the city of Damietta, and among the first which took the city, and for an ensign they brought back thence a crimson standard which is still in the church of S. Giovanni; and because of the said devotion and aid given by the Florentines to Holy Church and to Christendom, the jurisdiction over the territory around was restored to the city of Florence by Pope Gregory and by the said Emperor Frederick, to the distance of ten miles around the city of Florence.

§ 14.—*How the Florentines got the arm of the blessed apostle S.* ***1188 a.d.***

102

Philip. § 15.—*How the Pope brought the Pisans and the Genoese to peace, thereby to strengthen the expedition over seas.*

§ 16.—*How Henry of Suabia was made Emperor by the Church, and how Constance, queen of Sicily, was given him to wife.*

Henry of Suabia, son of the great Frederick, as we said before, whilst his father was alive, had been elected king of the Romans; and when he returned from over seas, and had ordered his government in Germany, he passed into Italy and came to Rome at the request of Pope Clement, and was received with honour by the Romans, forasmuch as he restored to them the city of Tusculum and its territory, which had rebelled against the Romans; which city was all destroyed and laid waste by the Romans, and was never afterwards rebuilt. And when the said Henry was come to Rome he found that the said Pope Clement was dead, which had sent for him; and Pope Celestine, a native of Rome, had been elected by the cardinals, so that the said Henry was present at his consecration, which took place on Easter Day of the Resurrection, in April, in the year of Christ 1192; and he lived as Pope six years and **1192 a.d.** eight months and eleven days. And when Celestine had become Pope, on the second day after his consecration, he crowned the said Henry emperor. And before the said Henry departed from Germany, the Church was at variance with Tancred, king of Sicily and of Apulia (son to the other Tancred, which was sister's son to Robert Guiscard, as we made mention in the chapter wherein we treated of the said Robert), by reason that he did not, as he should, faithfully pay tribute to the Church, and that he presented bishops and archbishops to benefices at his pleasure to the shame of the Pope and of the Church; wherefore the said Pope Clement treated with the archbishop of Palermo to take away the kingdom of Sicily and Apulia from the said Tancred, and gave order to the said archbishop that Constance, sister of King William and rightful heiress of the realm of Sicily, which was a nun in Palermo, as we afore made mention, and was already more than fifty years old, should leave the convent, and he gave her dispensation that she might return to the world and enter into matrimony; and the said archbishop caused her secretly to depart from Sicily and come to Rome, and the Church gave her to wife to the said Emperor Henry, whence a little **Par. iii. 109-120.** while after was born the Emperor Frederick II., which

103

brought such persecutions upon the Church, as we will tell hereafter in treating of him. And it was not without Divine occasioning and judgment that such a baneful heir must needs be the issue, being born of a holy nun, and she more than fifty-two years old, when it is almost impossible for a woman to bear a child; so that he was born of two contradictions—against spiritual laws, and, in a sense, against natural laws. And we find, when the Empress Constance was pregnant with Frederick, there was doubt in Sicily and throughout all the realm of Apulia whether, by reason of her advanced age, she could be pregnant; for the which thing, when the time came for her to be delivered, a pavilion was erected on the piazza at Palermo, and a proclamation was put forth that any lady who desired might go and see her, and many went thither and saw her, and therefore the doubt came to an end.

§ 17.—*How the Emperor Henry conquered the kingdom of Apulia.* **1196 a.d.**
1200 a.d.
1203 a.d.
1192 a.d.
1197 a.d.
1198 a.d. § 18.—*How the Emperor Henry rebelled against the Church, and persecuted it, and how he died.* § 19.—*How Otho IV. of Saxony was elected Emperor.* § 20.—*How the whole orb of the sun was eclipsed.* § 21.—*How they of Samminiato destroyed their whole city by their discords.* § 22.—*How the Florentines bought Montegrossoli.* § 23.—*How Innocent III. was made Pope.*

§ 24.—*How the Order of the Minor Friars began.*

In the time of the said Pope Innocent began the holy Order of the Minor Friars, the founder whereof was the blessed Francis, born in the **Par. xi. 43-117.** city of Assisi in the Duchy, and by this Pope the said Order was accepted and approved with privilege, forasmuch as it was altogether founded on humility, and love, and poverty, following in all things the holy gospel of Christ, and shunning all human delights. And the said Pope saw in a vision S. Francis supporting the Church of the Lateran upon his shoulders, as he afterwards, after the same manner, beheld S. Dominic, the which vision was a figure and prophecy how by them should be supported Holy Church and the faith of Christ.

§ 25.—*How the Order of the Preaching Friars began.*

And still in the time of the said Pope, after the same manner began the Order of the Preaching Friars, the founder whereof was the blessed **Par. xi. 118-123; xii. 46-105.** Dominic, born in Spain. But in this Pope's time it was not confirmed, albeit in a vision it seemed to the said Pope that the Church of the Lateran was falling upon him, and the blessed Dominic sustained it on his shoulders. And by reason of this vision he purposed to confirm it, but death overtook him, and his successor, Pope Honorius, afterwards confirmed it the year of Christ 1216. The visions of the aforesaid **1216 a.d.** Innocent, concerning S. Francis and S. Dominic, were true, for the Church of God was falling through many errors and many licentious sins, not fearing God; and the said blessed Dominic, through his holy learning and preaching, corrected it, and was the first exterminator of heretics therefrom; and the blessed Francis, through his humility and apostolic life and penitence, corrected the wanton life, and brought back Christians to penitence and to the life of salvation. And truly the Erythræan Sibyl, tracing out these times, prophesied of these two holy Orders, saying that two stars would arise to illuminate the world.

§ 26.—*How the Florentines destroyed the castle of Frondigliano.*
1199 a.d.

In the year of Christ 1199, Count Henry della Tosa and his colleagues, being consuls of the city of Florence, the Florentines laid siege to the fortress of Frondigliano, which had rebelled and was making war upon the commonwealth of Florence, and they took it and destroyed it to the very foundations, and it was never built again. And in the same year the Florentines marched against Simifonte, which was a very **Cf. Par. xvi. 62, 63.** strong place and did not obey the city.

§ 27.—*How they of Samminiato destroyed Sanginiegio, and went back to live on the hill.* § 28.—*How the French and Venetians took Constantinople.* § 29.—*How the Tartars descended from the mountains of Gog and Magog.*

§ 30.—*How the Florentines destroyed the strongholds of Simifonti and of Combiata.*
1202 a.d.

In the year of Christ 1202, when Aldobrandino, of the Barucci of Santa Maria Maggiore (a very ancient family), and his colleagues were consuls in Florence, the Florentines took the stronghold of Simifonti, and destroyed it, and took the hill into possession of the commonwealth, forasmuch as it had been long time at war with the Florentines. And the Florentines gained it by the treachery of a **Cf. Par. xvi. 62, 63.** certain man of Sandonato in Poci, which surrendered a tower, and claimed for this cause that he and his descendants should be free in Florence from all taxes; and this was granted, albeit the said traitor was first slain, in the said tower, by the inhabitants, as it was being attacked. And in the said year the Florentines went with their army against the fortress of Combiata, which was very strong, at the head of the river Marina, towards Mugello, which pertained to Cattani of the country which would not obey the commonwealth and made war against it. And when the said strongholds were destroyed, they made a decree that they should never be rebuilt.

§ 31.—*Destruction of Montelupo, and how the Florentines gained Montemurlo.*
1203 a.d.

In the year of Christ 1203, when Brunellino Brunelli de' Razzanti was consul in Florence with his colleagues, the Florentines destroyed the fortress of Montelupo because it would not obey the commonwealth. And in this same year the Pistoians took the castle of Montemurlo from the Counts Guidi; but a little while after, in September, the Florentines went thither with an army on behalf of the Counts Guidi, and retook it, and gave it back to the Counts Guidi. And afterwards, in 1207, **1207 a.d.** the Florentines made peace between the Pistoians and the Counts Guidi, but afterwards the counts not being well able to defend Montemurlo from the Pistoians, forasmuch as it was too near to them, and they had built over against it the fortress of Montale, the Counts Guidi sold it to the commonwealth of Florence for 5,000 lbs. of small florins, **Par. xvi. 64.** which would now be worth 5,000 golden florins; and this was in the year of Christ 1209, but the Counts of Porciano never would give their **1209 a.d.** word for their share in the sale.

§ 32.—*How the Florentines elected their first Podestà.*
1207 a.d.

106

In the year of Christ 1207, the Florentines chose for the first time a foreign magistrate, for until that time the city had been ruled by the government of citizen consuls, of the greatest and best of the city, with the council of the senate, to wit, of 100 good men; and these consuls, after the manner of Rome, entirely guided and governed the city, and administered law and executed justice; and they remained in office for one year. And there were four consuls so long as the city was divided into quarters, one to each gate; and afterwards there were six, when the city was divided into sesti. But our forefathers did not make mention of the names of all, but of one of them of greatest estate and fame, saying: 'In the time of such a consul and of his colleagues'; but afterwards when the city was increased in inhabitants and in vices, and there came to be more ill-deeds, it was agreed for the good of the commonwealth, to the end the citizens might not have so great a burden of government, and that justice might not miscarry by reason of prayers, or fear, or private malice, or any other cause, that they should invite a gentleman from some other city, who might be **Inf. xxiii. 105-107.** their Podestà for a year, and administer civil justice with his assessors and judges, and carry into execution sentences and penalties on the person. And the first Podestà in Florence was Gualfredotto of Milan, in the said year; and he dwelt in the Bishop's Palace, forasmuch as there was as yet no palace of the commonwealth in Florence. Yet the government of the consuls did not therefore cease, but they reserved to themselves the administration of all other things in the commonwealth. And by the said government the city was ruled until the time of the Primo Popolo in Florence, as hereafter we shall make mention, and then was created the office of the Ancients.

§ 33.—*How the Florentines defeated the Sienese at Montalto.* **1208 a.d.** § 34.—*How the Sienese sued for peace to the Florentines and obtained it.* § 35.—*How Otho IV. was crowned Emperor; and how he became the enemy and persecutor of Holy Church.*

§ 36.—*How during Otho's lifetime Frederick II. of Suabia was elected Emperor by the desire of the Church of Rome.*

The said Otho being the enemy of the Church, and being deposed by the general council of the Empire, the Church arranged with the electors of

Germany that they should elect to be king of the Romans, Frederick, the young king of Sicily, who was in Germany, and he won a great victory against the said Otho; and afterwards the said Otho, returning to his duty, went on crusade to Damietta over seas, and there died, and the election was left to Frederick; and afterwards, in the time of Pope Honorius III., who succeeded to the aforesaid Innocent, the said Frederick of Germany came to Venice, and then by sea into his kingdom of Apulia, and then to Rome; and by the said Pope Honorius and by the Romans he was received with great honour, and crowned Emperor, as hereafter in treating of him we will make mention. We will leave speaking of the Emperor for a time, and will tell of the doings of the Florentines up to the time of his coronation.

§ 37.—*Concerning the death of the old Count Guido, and of his progeny.*
1213 a.d.

In the year of Christ 1213, there died the Count Guido Vecchio, which left behind him five sons; but one died, leaving those who had Poppi as the heirs of his portion, forasmuch as he left no children; and from the other four sons were descended all the Counts Guidi. As to this Count Guido, it is said that in ancient times his forbears were **Par. xvi. 64, 98.** great barons in Germany, which came over with the Emperor Otho I., who gave them the territory of Modigliana in Romagna, and there they remained; and afterwards their descendants, by reason of their power, were lords over almost all Romagna, and made their headquarters in Ravenna, but because of the outrages they wrought on the citizens concerning their wives, and other tyrannies, in a popular tumult they were driven out of Ravenna, pursued, and slain in one day, so that none escaped either small or great, save one young child which was named Guido, the which was at Modigliana at nurse, which was surnamed Guido Besangue [drink-blood], through the disaster of his family, as in the story of the Emperor Otho we before made mention. This Guido was the father of the said Count Guido Vecchio, whence all the Counts Guidi are descended. This Count Guido Vecchio took to wife the daughter of M. Bellincione Berti of the Rovignani, which was the **Par. xv. 112, xvi. 99.** greatest and the most honoured knight in Florence, and his houses which were at Porta San Piero above the Old Gate descended by

108

heritage to the Counts. This lady was named Gualdrada, and he took her for her **Par. xvi. 94-99. Inf. xvi. 37.** beauty and her fair speech, beholding her in S. Reparata, with the other ladies and maidens of Florence. For when the Emperor Otho IV. came to Florence, and saw the fair ladies of the city assembled in Santa Reparata, in his honour, this maiden most pleased the Emperor; and her father saying to the Emperor that he had it in his power to bid her kiss him, the maiden made answer that there was no man living which should kiss her, save he were her husband, for the which speech, the Emperor much commended her; and the said Count Guido being taken with love of her by reason of her graciousness, and by the counsel of the said Otho, the Emperor, took her to wife, not regarding that she was of less noble lineage than he, nor regarding her dowry; whence all the Counts Guidi are born from the said Count and the said lady after this fashion; for, as aforesaid, there were left four sons which were the heirs: the first was named William, from whom was born Count Guido Novello and Count Simon, who were Ghibellines; but by reason of wrongs which Count Simon endured of Guido Novello, his brother, concerning his heritage, he became a Guelf and entered into league with the **Cf. Epistolæ Dant. Allig. adscriptæ, i.-iii.**

Inf. xvi. 34-39. Inf. xxx. 73-78. Cf. Epist. ii. Cf. Purg. xiv. 43-45. Guelfs of Florence; and from this Simon was born Count Guido of Battifolle; the second son was named Roger, from whom were born Count Guido Guerra and Count Salvatico, and these held the side of the Guelfs; the third was named Guido of Romena, whence are descended the family of Romena, which have been both Guelfs and Ghibellines; the fourth was Count Tegrimo, whence are the family of Porciano, which were always Ghibellines. The aforesaid Emperor Otho gave said Count Guido the lordship of Casentino. We have spoken at such length of the said Count Guido (albeit in another place we have treated of the beginning of his race), forasmuch as he was a man of worth, and from him are descended all the Counts Guidi, and because his descendants were afterwards much mixed up with the doings of the Florentines, as in due time we will make mention.

§ 38.—*How the parties of the Guelfs and Ghibellines arose in Florence.*
1215 a.d.

In the year of Christ 1215, M. Gherardo Orlandi being Podestà in Florence, one M. Bondelmonte dei Bondelmonti, a noble citizen of Florence, had promised to take to wife a maiden of the house of the **Par. xvi. 136-144.** Amidei, honourable and noble citizens; and afterwards as the said M. Bondelmonte, who was very charming and a good horseman, was riding through the city, a lady of the house of the Donati called to him, reproaching him as to the lady to whom he was betrothed, that she was not beautiful or worthy of him, and saying: "I have kept this my daughter for you;" whom she showed to him, and she was most beautiful; and immediately by the inspiration of the devil he was so taken by her, that he was betrothed and wedded to her, for which thing the kinsfolk of the first betrothed lady, being assembled together, and grieving over the shame which M. Bondelmonte had done to them, were filled with the accursed indignation, whereby the city of Florence was destroyed and divided. For many houses of the nobles swore together to bring shame upon the said M. Bondelmonte, in revenge for these wrongs. And being in council among themselves, after what fashion they should punish him, whether by beating or killing, Mosca de' Lamberti said the **Inf. xxviii. 103-111. Par. xvi. 136-138.** evil word: 'Thing done has an end'; to wit, that he should be slain; and so it was done; for on the morning of Easter of the Resurrection the Amidei of San Stefano assembled in their house, and the said M. Bondelmonte coming from Oltrarno, nobly arrayed in new white apparel, and upon a white palfrey, arriving at the foot of the Ponte Vecchio on **Par. xvi. 145-147.** this side, just at the foot of the pillar where was the statue of Mars, the said M. Bondelmonte was dragged from his horse by Schiatta degli Uberti, and by Mosca Lamberti and Lambertuccio degli Amidei assaulted and smitten, and by Oderigo Fifanti his veins were opened and he was brought to his end; and there was with them one of the counts of Gangalandi. For the which thing the city rose in arms and **Cf. Par. xvi. 128.** tumult; and this death of M. Bondelmonte was the cause and beginning of the accursed parties of Guelfs and Ghibellines in Florence, albeit long before there were factions among the noble citizens and the said parties existed by reason of the strifes and questions between the Church and the Empire; but by reason of the death of the said M. Bondelmonte all the families of the nobles and the other citizens of Florence were divided, and some held with

110

the Bondelmonti, who took the side of the Guelfs, and were its leaders, and some with the Uberti, who were the leaders of the Ghibellines, whence followed much evil and disaster to our city, as hereafter shall be told; and it is believed that it will never have an end, if God do not cut it short. And surely it shows that the enemy of the human race, for the sins of the Florentines, had power in that idol of Mars, which the pagan Florentines of old were wont to worship, that at the foot of his statue such a murder was committed, whence so much evil followed to the city of Florence. The accursed names of the Guelf and Ghibelline parties are said to have arisen first in Germany by reason that two great barons of that country were at war together, and had each a strong castle the one over against the other, and the one had the name of Guelf, and the other of Ghibelline, and the war lasted so long, that all the Germans were divided, and one held to one side, and the other to the other; and the strife even came as far as to the court of Rome, and all the court took part in it, and the one side was called that of Guelf, and the other that of Ghibelline; and so the said names continued in Italy.

§ 39.—*Of the families and the nobles which became Guelfs and Ghibellines in Florence.*

1215 a.d.

By reason of the said division these were the families of the nobles which were at that time and became Guelfs in Florence, counting from sesto to sesto, and likewise the Ghibellines. In the sesto of Oltrarno, of the Guelfs were the Nerli, gentlemen, who dwelt at first **Par. xv. 115.** in the Mercato Vecchio; the family of the Giacoppi, called Rossi, not however of great antiquity of descent, but they were already beginning to be powerful; the Frescobaldi, the Bardi, the Mozzi, but of small beginnings; of the Ghibellines in the sesto of Oltrarno, among the **Par. xvi. 128. Inf. xvii. 62, 63. Par. xvi. 127. 104.** nobles, the counts of Gangalandi, Obriachi, and Mannelli. In the sesto of San Piero Scheraggio, the nobles which were Guelfs were, the house of the Pulci, the Gherardini, the Foraboschi, the Bagnesi, the Guidalotti, the Sacchetti, the Manieri, and they of Quona, fellows to them of Volognano, the Lucardesi, the Chiaramontesi, the Compiobbesi, **Purg. xii. 105. Par. xvi. 105. Convivio iv. 20: 38-41. Par. xvi. 104. 123. 136-139. Cf. 109. 110.** the

111

Cavalcanti, but these were descended recently from merchants. In the said sesto of the Ghibellines were, the family of the Uberti, which was the head of the party, the Fifanti, the Infangati, and Amidei, and they of Volognano, and the Malespini, albeit afterwards by reason of the outrages of the Uberti their neighbours, they and many other families of San Piero Scheraggio became Guelfs. In the sesto of the Borgo of the Guelfs were the family of the Bondelmonti, and they **66, 135.**

127. Inf. xvii. 59, 60. were the leaders of the party; the family of the Giandonati, the Gianfigliazzi, the family of the Scali, of the Gualterotti and of the Importuni. Of the Ghibellines of the said sesto, the house of the Scolari which were by origin fellows to the Bondelmonti, the house of **Par. xvi. 133. 105. 93. xv. 115. xvi. 110. 111. 93. 103.** the Guidi, of the Galli and of the Cappiardi. In the sesto of San Brancazio of the Guelfs were the Bostichi, the Tornaquinci, the Vecchietti. Of the Ghibellines of the said sesto were the Lamberti, the Soldanieri, the Cipriani, the Toschi, and the Amieri, and Palermini, and Migliorelli, and Pigli, albeit afterwards some of them became Guelfs. In the sesto of the Porte del Duomo, of the Guelf party in those times were the Tosinghi, the Arrigucci, the Agli, the Sizii. **108.**

104. Of the Ghibellines of the said sesto were the Barucci, the Cattani of Castiglione and of Cersino, the Agolanti and the Brunelleschi; and afterwards some of them became Guelfs. In the sesto of the Porte San Piero of the Guelf nobles were the Adimari, the Visdomini, the Donati, **115-117. 112-114. 130, 131. 93.**

65, 94-96.

121.

104. 101. the Pazzi, the della Bella, the Ardinghi, and the Tedaldi which were called della Vitella, and already the Cerchi began to rise in condition, albeit they were merchants; of the Ghibellines of the said sesto were the Caponsacchi, the Lisei, the Abati, the Tedaldini, the Giuochi, the Galigari. And many other families of honourable citizens and popolani held some with one side, and some with the other, and they changed with the times in mind and in party, which would be too long a matter to relate. And for the said cause the accursed parties first began in Florence, albeit before that there had been a division secretly among the noble citizens, whereof some loved the rule of the Church and some that of the Empire; nevertheless they were all agreed as to the state and well-being of the commonwealth.

§ 40.—*How the city of Damietta was taken by the Christians, and afterwards lost.*

§ 41.—*How the Florentines caused the dwellers in the country around to swear fealty to the city, and how the new Carraia Bridge was begun.*

1218 a.d.

In the year of Christ 1218, when Otto da Mandella of Milan was Podestà of Florence, the Florentines caused all the dwellers in the country around to swear fealty to the commonwealth, seeing that before that time the greater part had obeyed the rule of the Counts Guidi, and of them of Mangone, and of them of Capraia, and of Certaldo, and of many **Inf. xxxii. 56, 57.** Cattani which had taken possession of the lands by privileges and some by force of the emperors. And in this year the building of the bastions of the Carraia Bridge was begun.

§ 42.—*How the Florentines took Mortennana, and completed the new* **1220** *a.d. bridge called Carraia.*

END OF SELECTIONS FROM BOOK V.

BOOK VI.

How Frederick II. was consecrated and made Emperor, and the great things which came to pass.

§ 1.—1220 a.d.

Inf. x. 119; xiii. 59, 68, 75; xxiii. 66. Purg. xvi. 117. Par. iii. 120. Convivio iv. Canzone, ver. 21; also cap. 3: 37-44; 10: 6-12. De Vulg. El. i. 12: 20-35. Epist. vi. (5) 126-135. Par. iii. 118-120. In the year of Christ 1220, on the day of St. Cecilia in November, there was crowned and consecrated Emperor at Rome Frederick II., king of Sicily, son of the Emperor Henry of Suabia, and of the Empress Constance, by Pope Honorius III., with great honour. In the beginning he was a friend of the Church, and well might he be, so many benefits and favours had he received from the Church, for through the Church his father Henry had for wife Constance, queen of Sicily, and for dowry the said realm, and the kingdom of Apulia; and when his father was dead, he being left a little child, was cared for and guarded by the Church as by a mother, and also his kingdom was defended, and he was elected king of the Romans against the Emperor Otho IV., and he was afterwards crowned Emperor, as aforesaid. But he, son of ingratitude that he was, not acknowledging Holy Church as a mother, but as a hostile stepmother, in all things was her enemy and persecutor, he and his sons, almost more than his precursors, as hereafter we shall make mention. This Frederick reigned thirty years as Emperor, and was a man of great capacity and of great valour, wise in books, and of natural intelligence, universal in all things; was acquainted with the Latin tongue, and with our vernacular, with German and French, Greek and Arabic, of abounding talents, liberal and courteous in giving, courageous and prudent in arms, and was much feared. And he was dissolute and licentious after divers fashions, and had many concubines and catamites, after the manner of the Saracens, and he sought indulgence in all bodily pleasures, and led an epicurean life, not taking account that there were ever another life; and this was one chief cause why he became the enemy of the clergy and of Holy **Inf. x. 119.** Church. And the other was his greed in taking

114

and sequestrating the revenues of Holy Church, to squander them evilly. And many monasteries and churches he destroyed in his kingdom of Sicily and Apulia, and throughout all Italy, and this, either through his own vices and defects, or by reason of the rulers of Holy Church who could not or **Cf. Purg. xvi. 115-117.** would not deal with him, nor be content that he should have the Imperial rights, wherefore he subdued and smote Holy Church; or because that God permitted it as a Divine judgment, because the rulers of the Church had been the means through whom he became the child of the holy nun, Constance, they not remembering the persecutions which Henry, his father, and Frederick, his grandfather, had caused Holy Church to endure. This Frederick did many noteworthy things in his time, and raised in all the chief cities of Sicily and of Apulia, strong and rich fortresses which are still standing, and built the fortress of Capovana, in Naples, and the towers and gate upon the bridge over the river of Volturno at Capua, the which are very marvellous; and he made the park for sport on the marsh of Foggia in Apulia, and made the hunting park near Gravina and Amalfi in the mountains. In winter he abode at Foggia, and in summer in the mountains, for the delights of the chase. And many other noteworthy things he caused to be made, as the castle of Prato, and the fortress of Samminiato, and many other things, as we shall make mention hereafter. And he had two sons by his first wife, Henry and Conrad, whom he caused each one during his lifetime to be elected king of the Romans; and by the daughter of King John of Jerusalem he had King Giordano, and by others he had King Frederick (from whom are descended the lineage of those who are called of Antioch), King Enzo and King Manfred, who were great enemies to Holy Church; and during his life he and his sons lived and ruled with much earthly splendour; but in the end he and his sons because of their sins came to an ill end, and their line was extinguished, as we shall make mention hereafter.

§ 2.—*Of the cause why war broke out between the Florentines and the Pisans.*
§ 3.—*How the Pisans were routed by the Florentines at* **1222 a.d.**

1224 a.d. *Casteldelbosco.* § 4.—*How the Florentines marched against Fegghine, and built l'Ancisa.*

§ 5.—*How the Florentines led an army against Pistoia, and laid waste the country round about.*

In the year of Christ 1228, when M. Andrea of Perugia was Podestà of Florence, the Florentines led an army against Pistoia with the Carroccio, and this was because the Pistoians were making war against Montemurlo, and ill-treating it; and the said host laid waste the country round about the city up to the suburbs, and destroyed the towers of Montefiore which were very strong; and the fortress of Carmignano surrendered to the commonwealth of Florence. And note that upon the rock of Carmignano there was a tower seventy cubits high, and thereupon two arms in marble, whereof the hands were 'making the **Cf. Inf. xxv. 1-3.** figs' at Florence; wherefore the artificers of Florence, to express contempt for money or ought else offered to them, were wont to say: "I can't see it, for the fortress of Carmignano is in the way." And the Pistoians hereupon agreed to whatever terms the Florentines might devise, and caused the said fortress of Carmignano to be destroyed.

§ 6.—*How the Sienese renewed the war with the Florentines on account* **1229 a.d.**

1232 a.d.

1233 a.d.

1234 a.d.

1235 a.d. *of Montepulciano.* § 7.—*Of a great miracle that came to pass in S. Ambrogio in Florence, concerning the body of Christ.* § 8.—*Yet again of the war of the Florentines with the Sienese.* § 9.—*Of the conflagration in Florence.* § 10.—*Yet again of the war with Siena.* § 11.—*The same.* § 12.—*Of the conflagration in Florence.* § 13.—*How peace was made between the Florentines and the Sienese.*

§ 14.—*How the Emperor Frederick came to enmity with the Church.*

After that Frederick II. was crowned by Pope Honorius, as we have aforesaid, in the beginning he was the friend of the Church, but a little time after, through his pride and avarice, he began to usurp the rights of the Church throughout all his Empire, and in the realm of Sicily and Apulia, appointing bishops and archbishops and other prelates, and driving away those sent by the Pope, and raising imposts and taxes from the clergy, doing shame to Holy Church; for the which thing by the said Pope Honorius, which had crowned him, he was cited, and admonished that he should leave to Holy Church her rights, and render the dues. But the Emperor perceived himself to be great in power and estate, alike through the force of the Germans and through that of the realm of Sicily, and that he was lord over sea and land, and was feared by all the rulers of Christendom, and also by the Saracens, and was buttressed around by the sons which he had of his first wife, daughter of the landgrave of Germany, to wit Henry and Conrad, the which Henry he had caused to be crowned in Germany king of the Romans, and Conrad was duke of Suabia, and Frederick of Antioch, his first natural son, he made king, and Enzo, his natural son, was king of Sardinia, and Manfred prince of Taranto; wherefore he would not yield obedience to the Church, but rather was he obstinate, living after the fashion of the world, in all bodily delights. For the which thing by the said Pope Honorius he was excommunicated the year of Christ 1220, and did not for that reason cease from persecuting the **1220 a.d.** Church, but so much the more usurped its rights, and so remained the enemy of the Church and of the Pope Honorius as long as he lived. The which Pope passed from this life the year of Christ 1226, and after **1226 a.d.** him was made Pope Gregory IX., born at Alagna in the Campagna, the which reigned as pope fourteen years; the which Pope Gregory had a great war with the Emperor Frederick, forasmuch as the Emperor would in no wise relinquish the rights and jurisdiction of Holy Church, but rather the more usurped them; and many churches of the kingdom he caused to be pulled down and deserted, laying heavy imposts upon the clergy and the churches; and whereas there were certain Saracens in the mountains of Trapali in Sicily, the Emperor, that he might be the more secure in the island, and might keep them at a distance from the Saracens of Barbary, and also to the end that by them he might keep in fear his subjects in Apulia, by wit and promises drew them from those mountains, and put them in Apulia in an ancient deserted city, which of old was in league with the Romans, and was destroyed by the Samnites, to wit by those of Benivento, the which city was then called Licera, and now is called Nocera, and they were more than 20,000 men-at-arms; and that city they rebuilt very strong; the which ofttimes overran the places of Apulia to lay them waste. And when the said Emperor Frederick was at war with the Church, he caused them to **Cf. De Vulg. El. i. 10: 50, 63. i. 11: 20. i. 13: 31. Par. xi. 53.** come

117

into the duchy of Spoleto, and besieged at that time the city of Assisi, and did great harm to Holy Church; for the which thing the said Pope Gregory confirmed against him the sentence given by Pope Honorius his predecessor, and again gave sentence of excommunication against him, the year of Christ 1230. **1230 a.d.**

§ 15.—*How peace was made between Pope Gregory and the Emperor* **1233 a.d.** *Frederick.* § 16.—*How the Church ordered a crusade over seas, whereof the Emperor Frederick was captain, and how, after the expedition had set forth, he turned back.* § 17.—*How the Emperor* **1234 a.d.**

1236 a.d. *Frederick passed over seas, and made peace with the Soldan, and recovered Jerusalem, against the will of the Church.* § 18.—*How the Emperor returned from over seas because the Kingdom had rebelled against him, and how he began war again with the Church.* § 19.—*How* **1237 a.d.**

1239 a.d.

1240 a.d. *the Emperor Frederick caused the Pisans to capture at sea the prelates of the Church which were coming to the council.* § 20.—*How the Milanese were discomfited by the Emperor.* § 21.—*How the Emperor Frederick besieged and took the city of Faenza.*

§ 22.—*How the Emperor laid hold of King Henry, his son.*

In these same times (albeit it had begun before) Henry Sciancato [the Lame], the first-born of the said Emperor Frederick, who had had him chosen king of the Romans by the electors of Germany as aforesaid, perceiving that the Emperor his father was doing all he might against Holy Church, and feeling the same heavy upon his conscience, time and again reproved his father, for that he was doing ill; whereat the Emperor set himself against him, and neither loving him nor dealing with him as with a son, raised up false accusers who testified that the said Henry had it in his mind to rebel against him as concerning his Empire, at the request of the Church. On the which plea (were it true or false) he seized his said son, King Henry, and two sons of his, little lads, and sent them into Apulia, into prison severally; and there he put him to death by starvation in great torment, and **Purg. iii. 121.** afterward Manfred put his sons to death. The Emperor sent to Germany, and again had Conrad, his second son, elected king of the Romans in succession to himself; and this was the year of Christ 1236. Then after a certain time the Emperor put out the eyes of that wise man **1236 a.d.**

Inf. xiii. 31-108. Master Piero dalle Vigne, the famous poet, accusing him of treason, but this came about through envy of his great estate. And thereon the said M. Piero soon suffered himself to die of grief in prison, and there were who said that he himself took away his own life.

§ 23.—*How the war began between Pope Innocent IV. and the Emperor Frederick.*

1241 a.d.

It came to pass afterwards, as it pleased God, that there was elected Pope Messer Ottobuono dal Fiesco, of the counts of Lavagna of Genoa, **Cf. Purg. xix. 100-102.** the which was cardinal, and was made Pope as being the greatest friend and confidant whom the Emperor Frederick had in Holy Church, to the end there might be peace between the Church and him; and he was called Pope Innocent IV., and this was the year of Christ 1241, and he reigned as Pope eleven years, and added to the Church many cardinals from divers countries of Christendom. And when he was elected Pope, the tidings were brought to the Emperor Frederick with great rejoicing, knowing that he was his great friend and protector. But the Emperor, when he heard it, was greatly disturbed, whence his barons marvelled much, and he said: "Marvel not; for this election will be of much hurt to us; for he was our friend when cardinal, and now he will be our enemy as Pope;" and so it came to pass, for when the said Pope was consecrated, he demanded back from the Emperor the lands and jurisdictions which he held of the Church, as to which request the Emperor held him some time in treaty as to an agreement, but all was vanity and deception. In the end, the said Pope seeing himself to have been led about by deceitful words, to the hurt and shame of himself and of Holy Church, became more an enemy of the Emperor Frederick than his predecessors had been; and seeing that the power of the Emperor was so great that he ruled tyrannously over almost the whole of Italy, and that the roads were all taken and guarded by his guards, so that none could come to the court of Rome without his will and license, the said Pope seeing himself in the said manner thus besieged, sent secret orders to his kinsfolk at Genoa, and caused twenty galleys to be armed, and straightway caused them to come to Rome, and thereupon embarked with all his cardinals and with all his

119

court, and immediately caused himself to be conveyed to his city of Genoa without any opposition; and having tarried some time in Genoa, he came to Lyons on the Rhone, by the way of Provence; and this was the year of Christ 1241.

§ 24.—*Of the sentence which Pope Innocent pronounced at the council of Lyons-on-Rhone, upon the Emperor Frederick.*

1245 a.d.

When Pope Innocent was at Lyons, he called a general council in the said place, and invited from throughout the whole world bishops and archbishops and other prelates, who all came thither; and there came to see him as far as the monastery of Crugni [Clugny] in Burgundy the good King Louis of France, and afterwards he came as far as to the council at Lyons, where he offered himself and his realm to the service of the said Pope and of Holy Church against the Emperor Frederick, and against all the enemies of Holy Church; and then he took the cross to go over seas. And when King Louis was gone the Pope enacted sundry things in the said council to the good of Christendom, and canonized sundry saints, as the Martinian Chronicle makes mention where it treats of him. And this done, the Pope summoned the said Frederick to the said council, as to a neutral place, to excuse himself of thirteen articles proved against him of things done against the faith of Christ, and against Holy Church; the which Emperor would not there appear, but sent thither his ambassadors and representatives—the bishop of Freneborgo [Freiburg] in Germany, and Brother Hugh, master of the mansion of S. Mary of the Germans, and the wise clerk and master Piero dalle Vigne of the Kingdom, who, making **Inf. xiii. 55-78.** excuses for the Emperor that he was not able to come by reason of sickness and suffering in his person, prayed the said Pope and his brethren to pardon him, and averred that he would cry the Pope mercy, and would restore that which he had seized of the Church; and they offered, if the Pope would pardon him, that he would bind himself so to frame it that within one year the soldan of the Saracens should render up to his command the Holy Land over seas. And the said Pope, hearing the endless excuses and vain offers of the Emperor, demanded of the said ambassadors if they had an authentic mandate for this,

120

whereon they produced a full authorization, under the golden seal of the said Emperor, to promise and undertake it all. And when the Pope had it in his hand, in full council, the said ambassadors being present, he denounced Frederick on all the said thirteen criminal articles, and to confirm it said: "Judge, faithful Christians, whether Frederick betrays Holy Church and all Christendom or no: for according to his mandate he offers within one year to make the soldan restore the Holy Land, very clearly showing that the soldan holds it through him, to the shame of all Christians." And this said and declared, he caused the process against the said Emperor to be published; and condemned him and excommunicated him as a heretic and persecutor of Holy Church, laying to his charge many foul crimes proved against him; and he deprived him of the lordship of the Empire, and of the realm of Sicily, and of that of Jerusalem, absolving from all fealty and oaths all his barons and subjects, excommunicating whoever should obey him, or should give him aid or favour, or further should call him Emperor or king. And the said sentence was passed at the said council at Lyons on the Rhone, the year of Christ 1245, the 17th of July. The principal causes why Frederick was condemned were four: first, forasmuch as when the Church invested him with the realm of Sicily and of Apulia, and afterwards with the Empire, he swore to the Church before his barons, and before the Emperor Baldwin of Constantinople, and before all the court of Rome, to defend Holy Church in all her honours and rights against all men, and to pay the rightful tribute, and to restore all the possessions and jurisdictions of Holy Church, of the which things he had done the contrary, and was perjured, and treacherous, and had vilely and wrongfully defamed Pope Gregory IX. and his cardinals by his letters throughout the whole world. The second thing was, that he broke the peace made by him with the Church, not remembering the pardons granted to him by withdrawal of the excommunications, and with respect to all the misdeeds done by him against Holy Church; and in that peace he had sworn and promised never to injure those who had been with the Church against him; but he had done quite the contrary, seeing that he had scattered them all, either by death or by exile, them and their families, taking away their possessions, and had not restored either to the Templars or to the Hospitallers their mansions which he had occupied, the which by the articles

121

of the peace he had promised to restore and give back; and by force he had kept vacant eleven archbishoprics, with many bishoprics and abbeys in the Empire and in the Kingdom, not suffering those who were duly elected by the Pope to hold or to till them; doing violence and extortions on sacred persons, constraining them to appear and plead before his bailiffs and secular lords. The third cause was the sacrilege he had done, when by the galleys of Pisa, and by his son King Enzo, he had taken the cardinals and many prelates at sea, as we afore told, and caused some to be drowned in the sea, and kept some dying in cruel and harsh prisons. The fourth cause was, because he was found and convicted in many articles of heresy in the faith; and certainly he was no Christian Catholic, living always more after his delight and pleasure than according to reason or just law; and in fellowship with the Saracens. Likewise he used the Church and her offices but little or not at all, and did no alms; so that not without great and evident causes he was deposed and condemned; and albeit he did much injury and persecution to Holy Church after that he was condemned, yet in a short time every honour and state and power and greatness God took from him, and showed him His wrath, as we shall make mention hereafter. And because many have made question, who was to blame in the quarrel, whether the Church or the Emperor, hearing his excuses in his letters, therefore to this I make answer and say, that manifestly not by one divine miracle but by many was it shown that the Emperor was to blame, as God showed by open and visible judgments in His wrath upon Frederick and his seed.

§ 25.—*How the Pope and the Church caused a new Emperor to be elected in place of Frederick, the deposed Emperor.*

1245 a.d.

The said Frederick being deposed and condemned, as has been afore said, the Pope sent word to the electors of Germany who elect the king of the Romans, that they should without delay make a new choice for the Empire; and this was done, for they elected William, count of Holland and landgrave, a valiant lord, to whom the Church gave her support, causing a great part of Germany to rebel, and gave indulgence and pardon as if they were going over seas, to whoever should be against the said Frederick;

whence in Germany there was great war between the said elected King William of Holland and King Conrad, son of the said Frederick; but the war endured but a short time, for the said King William died, the year of Christ . . . and the said Conrad reigned in Germany, whom his father Frederick the Emperor had caused to be elected king, as we shall make mention. From this sentence Frederick appealed to the successor of Pope Innocent, and sent his letters and messengers throughout all Christendom, complaining of the said sentence, and setting forth how iniquitous it was, as appears by his epistle written by the said Messer Picro dalle Vigne, which begins, after the salutation: "Although we believe, that words of the already current tidings, etc." But considering the real facts as to the process, and as to the deeds of Frederick against the Church, and as to his dissolute and uncatholic life, he was guilty and deserving of the deposition, for the reasons set forth in the said process; and afterwards for the deeds done by the said Frederick after his deposition; for if before he was and had been cruel and persecuting to Holy Church and to the believers in Tuscany and in Lombardy, afterwards he was much more so, as long as he lived, as hereafter we shall make mention. We will now leave for a time the story of the doings of Frederick, and turn back to where we left off telling of the doings of Florence and of the other noteworthy events which came to pass in those days throughout the whole world; returning afterwards to the doings and to the end of the said Frederick and of his sons.

§ 26.—*We will tell an incident in the affairs of Florence.*
1237 a.d.

The year of Christ 1237, Messer Rubaconte da Mandello of Milan being Podestà of Florence, the new bridge was made in Florence, and he laid the first stone with his own hand, and threw the first trowelful of mortar, and from the name of the said Podestà the bridge was named **Cf. Purg. xii. 102.** Rubaconte. And during his government all the roads in Florence were paved; for before there was but little paving, save in certain particular places, master streets being paved with bricks; and through this convenience and work the city of Florence became more clean, and more beautiful, and more healthy.

§ 27.—*How and when there was a total eclipse of the sun.* § 28.—*Of* **1238**

123

§ 33.—*How the Guelf party was first driven from Florence by the Ghibellines and the forces of the Emperor Frederick.*

1248 a.d.

In the said times when Frederick was in Lombardy, having been deposed from the title of Emperor by Pope Innocent, as we have said, in so far as he could he sought to destroy in Tuscany and in Lombardy the faithful followers of Holy Church, in all the cities where he had power. And first he began to demand hostages from all the cities of Tuscany, and took them from both Ghibellines and Guelfs, and sent them to Samminiato del Tedesco; but when this was done, he released the Ghibellines and retained the Guelfs, which were afterwards abandoned as poor prisoners, and abode long time in Samminiato as beggars. And forasmuch as our city of Florence in those times was not among the least notable and powerful of Italy, he desired especially to vent his spleen against it, and to increase the accursed parties of the Guelfs and Ghibellines, which had begun long time before through the death of M. Bondelmonte, and before, as we have already shown. But albeit ever since this the said parties had continued among the nobles of Florence (who were also ever and again at war among themselves by reason of their private enmities), and albeit they were divided into the said parties, each holding with his own, they which were called the Guelfs loving the side of the Pope and of Holy Church, and they which were called the Ghibellines loving and favouring the Emperor and his allies, nevertheless, the people and commonwealth had been maintained in unity to the well-being and honour, and good estate of the republic. But now the said Emperor sent ambassadors and letters to the family of the Uberti, which were heads of his party, and their allies which were called Ghibellines, inviting them to drive their enemies, which were called Guelfs, from the city, and offering them aid of his horsemen; and this caused the Uberti to begin dissension and civil strife in Florence, whence the city began to be disordered, and the nobles and all the people to be divided, some holding to one party, and some to the other; and in divers parts of the city there was **Par. xvi. 109, 110.** fighting long time. Among the other places, the chief was at the houses of the Uberti, which were where the great palace of the people now is. They gathered there with their allies, and fought against the Guelfs of the sesto of San Piero Scheraggio, whereof were leaders the family dal Bagno, called Bagnesi, and the Pulci, and the Guidalotti, **127.** and all the allies of the Guelfs of that sesto; and also the Guelfs of Oltrarno passing over the mill-dams, came to succour them when they were attacked by the Uberti. The second place of combat was in the Porte San Piero, where the leaders of the Ghibellines were the Tedaldini, forasmuch as they had the strongest dwellings in palaces and towers, and with them held the Caponsacchi, the Lisei, the Giuochi **121, 104, 101, 112-114, 115-117.** and Abati, and Galigari, and the fighting was against the house of the Donati, and the Visdomini, and Pazzi, and Adimari. And the third place of combat was in Porte del Duomo, at the tower of Messer Lancia of the Cattani of Castiglione, and of Cersino, to whom belonged the heads of the Ghibellines, with the Agolanti and Brunelleschi, and many popolari of their party, against the Tosinghi, Agli and Arrigucci. And the **108.** fourth combat and battle was in San Brancazio, whereof the leaders for the Ghibellines were the Lamberti, and Toschi, Amieri, Cipriani, and **110, 111.** Migliorelli, with many followers of the Popolo, against the Tornaquinci, and Vecchietti, and Pigli, albeit part of the Pigli were Ghibellines. And the Ghibellines drew up in San Brancazio at the tower of the Scarafaggio [Scarabæus] of the Soldanieri, and from that tower an arrow struck M. Rustico Marignolli in the face (who was bearing the Guelf standard, to wit, a crimson lily on a white field), whence he **Cf. Par. xvi. 151-154.** died; and the very day that the Guelfs were expelled, and before they departed, they came in arms to bury him in San Lorenzo; and when the Guelfs were departed, the canons of San Lorenzo carried away the body, to the end that the Ghibellines might not unbury it and do it outrage, forasmuch as he was a great leader of the Guelf party. And the next force of the Ghibellines was in the Borgo, whereof the leaders were **93, 66, 140-144, 127, 93.** the Scolari, and Soldanieri, and Guidi, against the Bondelmonti, Giandonati, Bostichi and Cavalcanti,

Scali and Gianfigliazzi. In Oltrarno it was the Ubbriachi and the Mannelli (and there were no other nobles of renown, but families of the popolari) against the Rossi and the Nerli. Thus it came to pass that the said frays endured **Par. xv. 115.** long time, and there was fighting at barricades from street to street, and from one tower to another (for there were many in Florence in these times, 100 cubits and more in height), and with mangonels and other engines they fought together by day and by night. And in the midst of this strife and fighting the Emperor Frederick sent into Florence King Frederick, his bastard son, with 1,600 horsemen of his German followers. When the Ghibellines heard that they were nigh unto Florence, they took courage fighting with more force and boldness against the Guelfs, which had no allies, nor were expecting any succour, forasmuch as the Church was at Lyons on the Rhone beyond the mountains, and the power of Frederick was beyond measure great in all parts of Italy. And on this occasion the Ghibellines used a device of war; for at the house of the Uberti the greater part of the Ghibelline forces assembled, and when the fight began at the places of battle set forth above, they went in a mass to oppose the Guelfs, and in this wise they overcame them well nigh in every part of the city, save in their own neighbourhood against the barricades of the Guidalotti and the Bagnesi, which endured more stoutly; and to that place the Guelfs repaired, and all the forces of the Ghibellines against them. At last, the Guelfs saw themselves to be hard pressed, and heard that Frederick's knights were already in Florence (King Frederick having already entered with his followers on Sunday morning), yet they held out until the following Wednesday. Then, not being able longer to resist the forces of the Ghibellines, they abandoned the defence, and departed from the city on the night of S. Mary Candlemas in the year **Cf. Inf. x. 48.** of Christ 1248. When the Guelf party were driven from Florence, the nobles of that party withdrew, some of them to the fortress of Montevarchi in Valdarno, and some to the fortress of Capraia; and Pelago, and Ristonchio, and Magnale, up to Cascia, were held by the Guelfs, and were called the League; and therein they made war against the city and the territory around Florence. Other popolani of that party repaired to their farms and to their friends in the country. The Ghibellines which remained masters in Florence, with the forces and the horsemen of the Emperor

Frederick, changed the ruling of the city after their mind, and caused thirty-six fortresses of the Guelfs to be destroyed, palaces and great towers, among the which the most noble was that of the Tosinghi upon the Mercato Vecchio, called the Palace, 90 cubits high, built with marble columns, and a tower thereto 130 cubits. Also the Ghibellines attempted a yet more impious deed, forasmuch as the Guelfs resorted much to the church of S. Giovanni, and all the good people assembled there on Sunday morning, and there they solemnized marriages; and when the Ghibellines came to destroy the towers of the Guelfs, there was one among them very great and beautiful, which was upon the piazza of S. Giovanni, at the entrance of the street of the Adimari, and it was called the tower of the Guardamorto, forasmuch as of old all the good folk which died were buried at S. Giovanni; and the Ghibellines, purposing to rase to the ground the said tower, caused it to be propped up in such wise that when the fire was applied to the props it should fall upon the church of S. Giovanni; and this was done. But as it pleased God, by reverence and miracle of the blessed John, the tower, which was 120 cubits high, showed manifestly, when it came to fall, that it would avoid the holy church, and turned and fell directly upon the piazza, wherefore all the Florentines marvelled and the popolo rejoiced greatly. And note, that since the city of Florence had been rebuilt, not one house had been destroyed, and the said accursed destruction thereof was then begun by the Ghibellines. And they ordained that of the Emperor Frederick's followers there should remain 1,800 German horsemen in their pay, whereof Count Giordano was captain. It came to pass that in the same year when the Guelfs were driven from Florence, they which were at Montevarchi were attacked by the German troops which were in garrison in the fortress of Gangareta in the market place of the said Montevarchi, and there was a fierce battle of but few people, as far as the Arno, between the Guelf refugees from Florence, and the Germans. In the end the Germans were discomfited, and a great part thereof slain and taken prisoners, and this was in the year of Christ 1248.

§ 34.—*How the host of the Emperor Frederick was defeated by the Parmesans, and by the Pope's legate.*

1248 a.d.

At this time the Emperor Frederick was laying siege to the city of Parma in Lombardy, because they had rebelled against his lordship and held with the Church; and within Parma was the Pope's legate with mounted men-at-arms sent by the Church to aid them. Frederick was without the city, with all his forces and with the Lombards, and abode there many months, and had sworn never to depart thence until he should have taken it; and for this reason he had made a camp over against the said city of Parma, after the manner of another town, with moats and palisades and towers, and houses roofed and walled, to which he gave the name of Vittoria; and by the said siege he had much straitened the city of Parma, and it was so poorly furnished with victuals, that they could hold out but a short while longer, and this the Emperor knew well by his spies; and for the said cause he held them for folk well-nigh vanquished, and troubled himself little about them. It came to pass, as it pleased God, that one day the Emperor was taking his pleasure in the chase, with birds and with dogs, going forth from Vittoria with certain of his barons and servants; and the **Epist. vi. (5) 127-135.** citizens of Parma, having learnt this from their spies, as folk reckless, or rather desperate, all sallied forth from Parma in arms, foot and horse together, and vigorously attacked the said camp of Vittoria in divers parts. The Emperor's soldiers, unprepared and in disorder, with insufficient guards (as they who took little thought of their enemies), seeing themselves thus suddenly and fiercely attacked, and being unable to defend themselves in the absence of their lord, were all put to flight and discomfiture, albeit there were three times as many horse and foot as there were in Parma; in which defeat many of them were taken or slain, and the Emperor himself, when he heard the news, fled with great shame to Cremona; and the Parmesans took the said camp, wherein they found great store of muniments of war, and victual, and vessels of silver, and all the treasure which the Emperor had in Lombardy, and the crown of the said Emperor, which the Parmesans still have in the sacristy of their bishop's palace; whereby they were all enriched. And when they had spoiled the said place of its booty, they set fire thereto, and destroyed it utterly, to the end there might be no trace of it, whether as city or as camp, for ever. And this was the first Tuesday in February, in the year of Christ 1248.

§ 35.—*How the Guelf refugees from Florence were taken in the fortress of*

128

Capraia.
1248 a.d.

A short time afterwards the Emperor departed from Lombardy, leaving there his natural son Enzo, king of Sardinia, with many horsemen, as his vicar-general over the Lombard League, and came into Tuscany, and found that the Ghibelline party which was ruling the city of Florence had laid siege in the month of March to the fortress of Capraia, wherein were the leaders of the chief families of Guelf nobles exiled from Florence. And when the Emperor came into Tuscany, he would not enter into the city of Florence, nor ever had entered therein, but was ware of it, for by soothsayers or by the saying of some demon or prophecy, he had discovered that he should die in Firenze, wherefore he feared greatly. Nevertheless, he came to the army, and went to sojourn in the castle of Fucecchio, and left the greater part of his followers at the siege of Capraia, which stronghold being straitly besieged, and having scanty provisions, was not able to hold out **1249 a.d.** longer; and the besieged held counsel about coming to parley, and they would have been granted any liberal terms which they desired; but a certain shoemaker, an exile from Florence, which had been a leading Ancient, not being invited to the said council, came to the gate very wrathful, and cried to the host that the town could hold out no longer, for the which thing the host would not consent to treat, wherefore they within, as dead men, surrendered themselves to the mercy of the Emperor. And this was in the month of May, in the year of Christ 1249. And the captains of the said Guelfs were Count Ridolfo of Capraia, and M. Rinieri Zingane of the Bondelmonti. And when they came to Fucecchio to the Emperor, he took them all with him prisoners to Apulia; and afterwards, by reason of letters and ambassadors sent to him by the Ghibellines of Florence, he put out the eyes of all which belonged to the great noble families in Florence, and then drowned them in the sea, save M. Rinieri Zingane, because he found him so wise and great of soul that he would not put him to death, but he put out his eyes, who afterwards ended his life as a monk in the island of Montecristo. And the aforesaid shoemaker was spared by the besiegers; and when the Guelfs had returned to Florence, he also returned thither, and being recognised in the parliament, at the outcry

129

of the people he was stoned, and vilely dragged along the ground by the children, and thrown into the moats.

§ 36.—*How King Louis of France was routed and taken prisoner by the* **1250 a.d.** *Saracens at la Monsura in Egypt.* § 37.—*How King Enzo, son of the Emperor Frederick, was routed and taken prisoner by the Bolognese.* § 38.—*How certain Ghibellines of Florence were discomfited in the village of Fegghine by the Guelf refugees.*

§ 39.—*How the Primo Popolo was formed in Florence to be a defence against the violence and attacks of the Ghibellines.*

1250 a.d.

When the said host came back to Florence there was great contention amongst the citizens, inasmuch as the Ghibellines, who ruled the land, crushed the people with insupportable burdens, taxes, and imposts; and with little to show for it, for the Guelfs were already established up and down in the territory of Florence, holding many fortresses and making war upon the city. And besides all this, they of the house of the Uberti and all the other Ghibelline nobles tyrannized over the people with ruthless extortion and violence and outrage. Wherefore the good citizens of Florence, tumultuously gathering together, assembled themselves at the church of San Firenze; but not daring to remain there, because of the power of the Uberti, they went and took their stand at the church of the Minor Friars at Santa Croce, and remaining there under arms they dared not to return to their homes, lest when they had laid down their arms they should be broken by the Uberti and the other nobles and condemned by the magistrates. So they went under arms to the houses of the Anchioni of San Lorenzo, which were very strong, and there, still under arms, they forcibly elected thirty-six corporals of the people, and took away the rule from the Podestà, which was then in Florence, and removed all the officials. And this done, with no further conflict they ordained and created a popular government with certain new ordinances and statutes. They elected captain of the people M. Uberto da Lucca, and he was the first captain of Florence, and they elected twelve Ancients of the people, two for each sesto, to guide the people and counsel the said captain, and they were to meet in the houses of the Badia over the gate which goes to Santa Margherita, and to return to their own homes to eat

130

and sleep; and this was done on the twentieth day of October, the year of Christ 1250. And on this day the said captain distributed twenty standards amongst the people, giving them to certain corporals divided according to companies of arms and districts, including sundry parishes, in order that when need were every man should arm himself and draw to the standard of his company, and then with the said standards draw to the said captain of the people. And they had a bell made which the said captain kept in the Lion's Tower. And the chief standard of the people, which was the captain's, was dimidiated white and red.

******

§ 40.—*Of the ensigns of war which were borne by the commonwealth of Florence.*
§ 41.—*How the Emperor Frederick died at Firenzuola in Apulia.*
1250 a.d.

In the said year 1250, the Emperor Frederick being in Apulia, in the city of Firenzuola, at the entrance to the Abruzzi, fell grievously sick, and for all his augury he knew not how to take heed; for he had learned that he must die in Firenze, wherefore, as aforesaid, never would he set foot in Firenze, neither in Faenza; yet ill did he interpret the lying word of the demon, for he was bidden beware lest he should die in Firenze, and he took no heed of Firenzuola. It came to pass that, his malady increasing upon him, there being with him one of his bastard sons, named Manfred, which was desirous of having the treasure of Frederick, his father, and the lordship of the kingdom and of Sicily, and fearing that Frederick might recover him of that sickness, or leave a testament, the said Manfred made a league with his private chamberlain, and promising him many gifts and great **Cf. Purg. iii. 121.** lordship, covered the mouth of Frederick with a bolster and so stifled him, and after the said manner the said Frederick died, deposed from the Empire, and excommunicated by Holy Church, without repentance or sacrament of Holy Church. And by this may we note the word which Christ said in the Gospel: "Ye shall die in your sins," for so it came to pass with Frederick, which was such an enemy to Holy Church, who brought his wife and King Henry, his son, to death, and saw himself discomfited, and his son Enzo

131

taken, and himself, by his son Manfred, vilely slain, and without repentance; and this was the day of S. Lucy in December, the said year 1250. And him dead, the said Manfred became guardian of the realm and of all the treasure, and caused the body of Frederick to be brought and buried with honour in the church of Monreale above the city of Palermo in Sicily, and at his burying he desired to write many words of his greatness and power and the mighty deeds done by him; but one Trottano, a clerk, made these brief verses, the which were very pleasing to Manfred and to the other barons, and he caused them to be engraven on the said sepulchre, the which said:—

Si probitas, sensus, virtutum gratia, census

Nobilitas orti, possent resistere morti,

Non foret extinctus Federicus, qui jacet intus.[3]   And note, that at the time when the Emperor Frederick died, he had sent into Tuscany for all the hostages of the Guelfs to cause them to be put to death; and on the way to Apulia, when they were in Maremma, they heard news of the death of Frederick, and the guards, for fear, abandoned them, who escaped to Campiglia, and thence returned to Florence and to the other cities of Tuscany, very poor and in great need.

§ 42.—*How the Popolo of Florence peaceably restored the Guelfs to Florence.*

1250 a.d.

The same night that the Emperor Frederick died, the Podestà who ruled for him in Florence, died also, who was named Messer Rinieri di Montemerlo; for, as he slept in his bed, there fell upon him of the vaulting from the roof of the chamber, which was in the house of the Abati. And this was a sure sign that in the city of Florence his lordship was to be ended, and this came to pass very soon; for the common people having risen in Florence against the violence and outrages of the Ghibelline nobles, as we have said, and tidings coming to Florence of the death of the said Frederick, a few days after, the people of Florence recalled and restored to Florence the party of the Guelfs who had been banished thence, causing them to make peace with **Cf. Inf. x. 49, 50.** the Ghibellines, and this was the seventh day of January, year of Christ 1250.

§ 43.—*How at the time of the said Popolo the Florentines discomfited the men of Pistoia, and afterwards banished certain families of the Ghibellines from Florence.*
1251 a.d.

Greatly did the party for the Church and the Guelf party rejoice throughout all Italy at the death of the Emperor; and the party for the Empire, and the Ghibellines were brought low, inasmuch as Pope Innocent returned from beyond the mountains with his court to Rome, bringing aid to the faithful followers of the Church. It came to pass that in the month of July, in the year of Christ 1251, the people and commonwealth of Florence gathered a host against the city of Pistoia, which had rebelled against them, and fought with the said inhabitants of Pistoia, and discomfited them at Mount Robolini with great loss in slain and prisoners of the men of Pistoia. And at that time Messer Uberto da Mandella of Milan was Podestà of Florence. And because the government of the Popolo was not pleasing to the greater part of the Ghibelline families in Florence, forasmuch as it seemed to them that they favoured the Guelfs more than was pleasing to them, and as in past times they were used to do violence, and to be tyrannical, relying on the Emperor, therefore they were even now unwilling to follow the people and the commonwealth on the said expedition against Pistoia, rather did they

133

both in word and in deed oppose it through factious hatred; forasmuch as Pistoia was ruled in those days by the Ghibelline party; whereby was caused so great mistrust, that when the host returned victorious from Pistoia, the said Ghibelline families in Florence were banished and sent forth from the city by the people of Florence, the said month of July, 1251. And the heads of the Ghibellines in Florence being banished, the people and the Guelfs who remained in the lordship of Florence, changed the arms of the commonwealth of Florence; and whereas of old they bore the field red and the lily white, they now made on the contrary the field white and **Par. xvi. 151-154.** the lily red; and the Ghibellines retained the former standard, but the ancient standard of the commonwealth dimidiated white and red, to wit, the standard that went with the host upon the carroccio, never was changed. We will leave for a while the doings of the Florentines, and we will tell somewhat of the coming of King Conrad, son of the Emperor Frederick.

§ 44.—*How King Conrad, son of Frederick the Emperor, came from Germany into Apulia, and had the lordship over the realm of Sicily, and how he died.*
1251 a.d.

When King Conrad of Germany heard of the death of the Emperor Frederick, his father, he prepared with a great company to pass into Apulia and Sicily, to take possession of the said Kingdom, of the which Manfred, his bastard brother, had become vicar-general, and was ruling it altogether, save only the cities of Naples and of Capua, the which had rebelled after the death of Frederick, and were returned to obedience to the Church; as also many cities of Lombardy and Tuscany, on occasion of the death of the said Frederick, had changed their government and returned to the obedience of the Church. The said Conrad would not adventure himself to come by land, but being arrived in the Trevisan March, he caused a great fleet to be equipped by the Venetians, and from thence by sea with all his people came to Apulia the year of Christ 1251. And albeit Manfred was wrath at his coming, forasmuch as he had purposed to be lord of the said kingdom, he made a great welcome to Conrad, his brother, rendering him much honour and reverence, and when he was in Apulia he led a host against the city of Naples, the which before had been five times attacked and besieged by

134

Manfred, prince of Salerno, and he had not been able to conquer it; but Conrad, with his great host after a long siege, gained the city by surrender, on condition that he should neither slay the defenders nor dismantle the place. But Conrad did not abide by the pact, but so soon as he was in Naples he caused the walls and all the fortresses of Naples to be destroyed; and the like did he to the city of Capua, which had rebelled; and in a short space he had restored all the Kingdom to his lordship, casting down every rebel, or whosoever was a friend or follower of Holy Church; and not only the laity but the monks and holy persons he caused to die by torments, robbing the churches, and subduing whosoever was not in obedience to him, and appointing to benefices, as if he were Pope; so that if Frederick, his **1252 a.d.** father, was a persecutor of Holy Church, this Conrad, if he had lived longer, would have been worse; but as it pleased God, a little time after, he was smitten with a grievous sickness, but not mortal, and as he was being tended by leeches and physicians, Manfred, his brother, to remain in power, caused the said leeches for money and **Cf. Purg. iii. 121.** great promises to poison him by a clyster. By such a judgment of God, by his brother's deed, of such a death did he die without repentance and excommunicated, the year of Christ 1252. And he left behind him in Germany a young son who was named Conradino, whose mother was daughter to the duke of Bavaria.

§ 45.—*How Manfred, natural son of Frederick, took the lordship of the kingdom of Sicily and of Apulia, and caused himself to be crowned.* **1252 a.d.**

Conrad, called king of Germany, being dead, Manfred remained lord and governor of Sicily and of the Kingdom, albeit through the death of Conrad, some cities of the Kingdom rebelled, and Pope Innocent IV., with a great host of the Church, entered into the Kingdom to regain the lands which Manfred was holding against the will of the Church, and under sentence of excommunication; and when the said host of the Church had entered into the Kingdom, all the cities and villages as far as Naples surrendered themselves to the said Pope; but he had sojourned but a short time in Naples ere he fell sick, and passed from this life the year of Christ 1252, and was buried in the city of Naples. Wherefore by the death of the said Pope, and by the vacancy which the Church had after him, which for more than two years abode without pastors, Manfred regained all the Kingdom, and his strength increased greatly both far and near; and with great care he allied himself with all the cities of Italy which were Ghibelline and faithful to the Empire, and aided them by his German knights, making a **1254 a.d.** league and alliance with them in Tuscany and in Lombardy. And when the said Manfred saw himself in glory and state, he thought to have himself made king of Sicily and of Apulia, and to the end this might come to pass, he sought for the friendship of the greatest barons of the Kingdom, with monies and gifts and promises and offices. And knowing that King Conrad, his brother, had left a son named Conradino, the which was by law the rightful heir to the realm of Sicily, and was in Germany under the guardianship of his mother, he devised guileful practices whereby to become king; wherefore he gathered together all the barons of the Kingdom, and took counsel with them what should be done with the lordship, forasmuch as he had received tidings that his nephew Conradino was grievously sick, and could never rule over a realm; wherefore it was counselled by his barons that he should send his ambassadors into Germany to learn of the state of Conradino, and if he were dead or ill; and meanwhile they counselled that Manfred should be made king. To this Manfred agreed, seeing it was he which had falsely arranged it all, and he sent the said ambassadors to Conradino and to his mother with rich presents and great offers. The which ambassadors being come to Suabia, found the boy whom his mother guarded most carefully, and with him she kept many other boys of gentle birth clothed in his garments; and when the said ambassadors asked for Conradino, his mother being in dread of Manfred, showed to them one of the said children, and they with rich presents, offered him gifts and reverence, among the which gifts were poisoned comfits from Apulia, and the boy having eaten of them, straightway died. **Purg. iii. 121.**

1255 a.d. They, believing Conradino to be dead by poison, departed from Germany, and when they had returned to Venice, they caused sails of black cloth to be made to their galley and all the rigging to be black, and they were attired in black, and when they were come into Apulia, they made a show of great grief, as they had been instructed by Manfred. And having reported to Manfred, and to the German barons, and to those of the Kingdom how

Conradino was dead, and Manfred having made show of deep affliction, by the call of his friends and of all the people (as he had arranged), he was elected king of Sicily and of Apulia, and at Monreale, in Sicily, caused himself to be crowned, the year of Christ 1255.

§ 46.—*Of the war between Pope Alexander and King Manfred.*
1255 a.d.

After the death of Pope Innocent, and the vacancy which followed, there was elected Pope Alexander IV., born in the city of Alagna, in Campagna, the year of Christ 1255, and he sat on the papal throne seven years, and certain months and days. The which Pope Alexander, hearing how Manfred had caused himself to be crowned king of Sicily against the will of Holy Church, by the said Pope Manfred was required to abandon the lordship of the Kingdom and of Sicily, the which he would neither hearken to, nor obey; for the which thing the said Pope first excommunicated and deprived him, and then sent against him Otho, the cardinal legate, with a great host of the Church, and he took many places on the coasts of Apulia; to wit, the city of Sipanto, and Mount Santagnolo, and Barletta and Bari, as far as Otranto in Calabria; but afterwards the said host, by reason of the death of the said legate, returned with labour lost, and Manfred took back and regained all, and **1256 a.d.** this was the year of Christ 1256. The said King Manfred was son of a beautiful lady, of the family of the Marquises of Lancia in Lombardy, of whom the Emperor Frederick was enamoured, and he was beautiful in **Purg. iii. 107.** person, and, like his father, but even more, dissolute in every fashion; a musician he was, and singer, and loved to see around him buffoons and minstrels, and beautiful concubines, and was always clad in green raiment; very liberal was he, and courteous, and gracious, so **Cf. De V.E. i. 12, 21 sqq.** that he was much loved and in great favour; but all his way of life was epicurean, caring neither for God nor the saints, but only for bodily delights. An enemy he was to Holy Church, and to priests and monks, occupying the churches as his father had done, and was a very rich lord, alike from the treasure bequeathed to him by the Emperor and by King Conrad, his brother, and from his kingdom, which was rich and fruitful; and, for all the wars that he had with the Church, he kept it in good state so long

137

as he lived, so that he increased much in riches and in power by sea and by land. For wife he took the daughter of the despot of Romagna, by whom he had sons and daughters. The arms which he took and bore were those of the Empire, save where the Emperor, his father, bore the gold field and the black eagle, he bore the silver field and the black eagle. This Manfred caused the city of Sipanto in Apulia to be destroyed, forasmuch as through the marshes around it was not healthy, and it had no harbour; and by its citizens, at two miles distance upon the rock, and in a place where there might be a good harbour, he caused a city to be founded, which after his name was called Manfredonia, the which has now the best harbour that there is between Venice and Brindisi. And of that city was Manfred Bonetta, count chamberlain of the said King Manfred, a delightsome man, a musician and singer, who caused the great bell of Manfredonia to be made in his memory, the which is the largest that can be found for size, and because of its size cannot be rung. We will now leave speaking of Manfred until fit place and time, and will return where we left off in our subject, namely to the doings of Florence and of Tuscany and of Lombardy, albeit they were much mixed up with the doings of the said King Manfred in many things.

§ 47.—*How the Florentines discomfited the Ubaldini in Mugello.* **1251 a.d.** § 48.—*How the Florentines took Montaia and routed the troops of the Sienese and the Pisans.* § 49.—*How the Florentines took Tizzano and* **1252 a.d.** *then routed the Pisans at Pontadera, the Pisans having routed the Lucchese.*

§ 50.—*How the bridge Santa Trinita was built.*

In this time, the city of Florence being in happy state under the rule of the Popolo, a bridge was built over the Arno from Santa Trinita to the house of the Frescobaldi in Oltrarno, and in this the zeal of Lamberto Frescobaldi helped much, which was a noted Ancient in the Popolo, and he and his had come to great state and riches.

§ 51.—*How the Florentines took the fortress of Fegghine.* **1252 a.d. Cf. Par. xvi. 50.**

§ 52.—*How the Sienese were routed by the Florentines at Montalcino.*

§ 53.—*How the golden florins were first made in Florence.* **1252 a.d.**

The host of the Florentines having returned, and being at rest after the victories aforesaid, the city increased greatly in state and in riches and lordship and in great quietness; for the which thing the merchants of Florence, for the honour of the commonwealth, ordained with the people and commonwealth that golden coins should be struck at Florence; and they promised to furnish the gold, for before the custom was to strike silver coins of 12 pence the piece. And then began the good coins of gold, 24 carats fine, the which are called golden florins, and each was worth 20 soldi. And this was in the time of the said M. Filippo degli Ugoni of Brescia, in the month of November, the year of Christ 1252. The which florins weighed eight to the ounce, and on one side was the stamp of the lily and on the other of S. John. By **Cf. Par. xviii. 133-136.** reason of the said new money of the golden florin there fell out a pretty story, and worth narrating. The said new florins having begun to circulate through the world, they were carried to Tunis in Barbary; and being brought before the king of Tunis, which was a worthy and wise lord, they pleased him much, and he caused them to be tried; and finding them to be of fine gold, he much commended them, and having caused his interpreters to interpret the imprint and legend on the florin, he found that it said: S. John the Baptist, and on the side of the lily, Florence. Perceiving it to be Christian money, he sent to the Pisan merchants who were then free of the city and were much with the king (and even the Florentines traded in Tunis through the Pisans), and asked them what manner of city among Christians was this Florence which made the said florins. The Pisans answered spitefully through envy, saying: "They are our inland Arabs": which is to say, "our mountain rustics." Then answered the king wisely: "It does not seem to me the money of Arabs. O you Pisans, what manner of golden money is yours?" Then were they confused, and knew not how to answer. He asked if there were among them any one from Florence, and there was found there a merchant from Oltrarno, by name Pera Balducci, discreet and wise. The king asked him of the state and condition of Florence, whom the Pisans called their Arabs; the which answered wisely, showing the power and magnificence of Florence, and how Pisa in comparison was neither in power nor in inhabitants the half of Florence, and that they had no golden money, and that the florin was the fruit of many victories gained by the Florentines

139

over them. For the which cause the Pisans were shamed, and the king, by reason of the florin and by the words of our wise fellow-citizen, made the Florentines free of the city, and allowed them a place of habitation and a church in Tunis, and he gave them the same privileges as the Pisans. And this we knew to be true from the said Pera, a man worthy of faith, for we were among his colleagues in the office of prior.

§ 54.—*How the Florentines marched upon Pistoia and took it, and then* **1253 a.d.** *upon Siena and took many of their fortresses.*

§ 55.—*How the Florentines marched against Siena, and the Sienese came to terms with them, and there was peace between them.*
1254 a.d.

The next year, 1254, Messer Guiscardo da Pietrasanta, of Milan, being Podestà of Florence, the Florentines marched against the city of Siena and encamped against the castle of Montereggioni and laid siege to it, **Cf. Inf. xxxi. 40, 41.** and of a surety they would have taken it, for the German garrison was in treaty to surrender it for 50,000 lire of 20 soldi to the gold florin; and in one single night the Ancients found twenty citizens each of whom offered a thousand of them, without counting smaller sums, so well disposed for the good of the commonwealth were the citizens of those days. But the Sienese, for fear of losing Montereggioni, agreed to the terms of the Florentines, and peace was made between them and the Sienese, and they completely surrendered the castle of Montalcino to the Florentines.

§ 56.—*How the Florentines seized the fortress of Poggibonizzi and that of Mortennana.* § 57.—*How the Florentines routed them of Volterra and took their city in the fight.* § 58.—*How the* **1254 a.d.** *Florentines marched against Pisa, and the Pisans submitted to their terms.* § 59.—*How the great Khan of the Tartars became a Christian, and sent his army, under his own brother, against the Saracens of Syria.* § 60.—*How the first war arose between the Genoese and the* **1260 a.d.**
1256 a.d. *Venetians.* § 61.—*How the Count Guido Guerra expelled the Ghibelline party from Arezzo, and how the Florentines reinstated it.* § 62.—*How the Pisans broke the peace, and how the Florentines routed them at the bridge over the Serchio.* § 63.—*How the Florentines destroyed the castle of Poggibonizzi the first time.* § 64.—*Incident telling of a great miracle concerning the body of Christ which came to pass in the city of Paris.*

140

§ 65.—*How the Popolo of Florence drave out the Ghibellines for the first time from Florence, and the reason why.*

1258 a.d.

In the year of Christ 1258, when Messer Jacopo Bernardi di Porco was Podestà of Florence, at the end of the month of July they of the house of the Uberti, with their Ghibelline allies, incited thereto by Manfred, purposed to break up the Popolo of Florence, forasmuch as it seemed to them to lean towards the Guelf party. When the said plot was discovered by the Popolo, and they who had made it were summoned and cited to appear before the magistrates, they would not appear nor come before them, but the staff of the Podestà were grievously wounded and smitten by them; for the which thing the people ran to arms, and ran in fury to the houses of the Uberti, where is now the piazza of the palace of the people and of the priors, and there they slew Schiattuzzo degli Uberti and many of the followers and retainers of the Uberti, and they took Uberto Caini degli Uberti and Mangia degli Infangati, which when they had confessed the conspiracy in parliament were beheaded in Orto San Michele; and the rest of the family of the Uberti, with many other Ghibelline families, left Florence. The names of the Ghibelline families of renown which left Florence were these: the Uberti, the Fifanti, the Guidi, the Amidei, the Lamberti, the Scolari, and part of the Abati, Caponsacchi, Migliorelli, Soldanieri, **Par. xvi.** Infangati, Ubriachi, Tedaldini, Galigari, the della Pressa, Amieri, they of Cersino, the Razzanti, and many other houses and families of the popolari and of decayed magnates, which cannot all be named, and other families of nobles in the country; and they went to Siena, which was governed in the Ghibelline interest, and was hostile to the Florentines; and their palaces and strongholds were destroyed, whereof there were many, and with the stones thereof they built the walls of San Giorgio Oltrarno, which the Popolo of Florence caused to be begun in those times by reason of the war with the Sienese. And afterwards, in the following September of the said year, the Popolo of Florence seized the abbot of Vallombrosa, which was a gentleman of the lords of **Inf. xxxii. 118, 119.** Beccheria of Pavia in Lombardy, for they had been told that at the petition of the Ghibelline refugees from Florence he was plotting treason;

141

and this by torture they made him confess, and wickedly in the piazza of Santo Apollinare by the outcry of the people they beheaded him, not regarding his dignity nor his holy orders; for the which thing the commonwealth of Florence and the Florentines were excommunicated by the Pope; and from the commonwealth of Pavia, whence came the said abbot, and from his kinsfolk, the Florentines which passed through Lombardy received much hurt and molestation. And truly it was said that the holy man was not guilty, albeit by his lineage he was a distinguished Ghibelline. For the which sin, and for many other deeds done by the wicked people, it was said by many wise men that God by Divine judgment permitted vengeance to come upon the said people in the battle and defeat of Montaperti, as hereafter we shall make mention. The said Popolo of Florence which ruled the city in these times was very proud and of high and great enterprises, and in many things was very arrogant; but one thing their rulers had, they were very loyal and true to the commonwealth, and when one which was an Ancient took and sent to his villa a grating which had belonged to the lion's den, and was now lying about in the mud of the piazza of S. Giovanni, he was condemned therefor to a fine of 1,000 lire for embezzling the goods of the commonwealth.

§ 66.—*How the Aretines took and destroyed Cortona.* § 67.—*How the* **1259 a.d.**

Cf. Inf. xxii. 40-60. *Florentines took and destroyed the castle of Gressa.* § 68.—*How the people of Florence took the castles of Vernia and of Mangona.*

§ 69.—*Incidents of the doings that were in Florence at the time of the Popolo.*

In the time of the said Popolo in Florence it came to pass that there was presented to the commonwealth a very fine and strong lion, the which was in a den in the piazza of San Giovanni. It came to pass that by lack of care on the part of the keeper, the said lion escaped from its den, running through the streets, whence all the city was moved with fear. It came to a stand at Orto San Michele, and there caught hold of a boy and held him between its paws. The mother, whose only child he was, and not born till after his father's death, on hearing what had chanced, ran up to the lion in desperation, shrieking aloud and with dishevelled hair, and snatched the child from between its paws, and the lion did no hurt either to the woman or to the child, but only gazed steadfastly and kept still. Now the question was what was the cause of this, whether the nobility of the nature of the lion, or that fortune preserved the life of the said child, to the end he might avenge his father, the which he did, and was afterwards called Orlanduccio of the lion, of Calfette. And note, that at the time of the said Popolo, and before and afterwards for a long time, the citizens of Florence lived soberly, and on coarse food, and with **Par. xv. 97-99.** little spending, and in manners and graces were in many respects coarse and rude; and both they and their wives were clad in coarse garments, and many wore skins without lining, and caps on their heads, **Par. xv. 112, 113.** and all wore leather boots on their feet, and the Florentine ladies wore boots without ornaments, and the greatest were contented with one **Par. xv. 101.**

Par. xv. 102, 103. close-fitting gown of scarlet serge or camlet, girt with a leathern girdle after the ancient fashion, with a hooded cloak lined with miniver, which hood they wore on their head; and the common women were clad in coarse green cambric after the same fashion; and 100 lire was the common dowry for wives, and 200 or 300 lire was, in those times, held to be excessive; and the most of the maidens were twenty or more **Par. xv. 103-105.** years old before they were wedded. After such habits and plain customs then lived the Florentines, but they were true and trustworthy to one another and to their commonwealth, and with their simple life and poverty they did greater and more virtuous things than are done in our times with more luxury and with more riches.

§ 70.—*How Paleologus, emperor of the Greeks, took Constantinople* **1259 a.d.** **1260 a.d.** *from the French and the Venetians.* § 71.—*Of a very sore battle which was between the king of Hungary and the king of Bohemia.*

§ 72.—*How the great tyrant, Ezzelino da Romano, was defeated by the Cremonese and died in prison.*

1260 a.d.
Inf. xii. 109, 110. Par. ix. 25-30.

In the said year 1260, Ezzelino of Romano, which is a Trevisan castle, was defeated and wounded and taken prisoner by the Marquis Pallavicino, and by the Cremonese in the country around Milan, near to the bridge of

143

Casciano over the river Adda, as he was on his way to seize Milan, having with him more than 1,500 horsemen; from the which wounds he died in prison, and was buried with honour in the village of Solcino. He knew by augury that he should die in a village of the country of Padua, which was called Basciano, and he would not enter therein; and when he felt himself wounded he asked what the place was called, and they answered, "Casciano"; then he said, "Casciano and Basciano are all the same," and he gave himself up for dead. This Ezzelino was the most cruel and redoubtable tyrant that ever was among Christians, and ruled by his force and tyranny (being by birth a gentleman of the house of Romano), long time the Trevisan March and the city of Padua, and a great part of Lombardy; and he brought to an end a very great part of the citizens of Padua, and blinded great numbers of the best and most noble, taking their possessions, and sending them begging through the world, and many others he put to death by divers sufferings and torments, and burnt at one time 11,000 Paduans; and by reason of their innocent blood, by miracle, no grass grew there again for evermore. And under semblance of a rugged and cruel justice he did much evil, and was a great scourge in his time in the Trevisan March and in Lombardy, to punish them for the sin of ingratitude. At last, as it pleased God, by less powerful men than his own he was vilely defeated and slain, and all his followers were dispersed and his family and his rule came to nought.

§ 73.—*How both the king of Castille and Richard, earl of Cornwall, were elected king of the Romans.*

1260 a.d.

Now some time before the said year, by reason of discord among the electors of the Empire, two Emperors had been elected; one party (that is to say, three of the electors) choosing Alfonso, king of Spain, and the other party of the electors choosing Richard, earl of Cornwall, and brother to the king of England; and because the realm of Bohemia was in discord, and there were two which claimed to be king thereof, each one gave his voice to his own party. And for many years there had been this discord between the two pretenders, but the Church of Rome gave more favour to Alfonso of Spain, to the end that he might, with his forces, come and beat down the pride and

144

lordship of Manfred; for the which cause the Guelfs of Florence sent him ambassadors, to encourage his coming, promising him great succour, to the end he might favour the Guelf party. And the ambassador was Ser Brunetto Latini, a **Inf. xv. 23-120.** man of great wisdom and authority; but before the embassage was ended the Florentines were defeated at Montaperti, and King Manfred gained great vigour and state throughout Italy, and the power of the Church was much abased, for the which thing Alfonso of Spain abandoned the enterprise of the Empire, and neither did Richard of England follow it up.

§ 74.—*How the Ghibelline refugees from Florence, sent into Apulia to King Manfred for succour.*
1260 a.d.

In these times the Ghibelline refugees from Florence (who being in the city of Siena were ill-supported against the Florentines by the Sienese, forasmuch as they had no forces to bring against their host) took counsel amongst themselves to send their ambassadors into Apulia, to King Manfred, for succour. And when they were come thither, albeit they were of the best and chiefest of the band, much time elapsed, and Manfred did not dispatch their affair, nor give audience to their request, by reason of the manifold businesses he had to do. And when at last they had a mind to depart, and took their leave of him very ill-content, Manfred promised them 100 German horsemen for their aid. Whereon the said ambassadors were troubled at this his first offer, and were minded to make their reply in the way of refusing so sorry an aid, for they were ashamed to return to Siena, inasmuch as they had hoped for more than 1,500 horsemen. But hereon Messer Farinata degli Uberti said, "Be not dismayed, neither refuse **Inf. x. 32.** any aid of his, be it never so small. Let us have grace of him to send his standard with them, and when it be come to Siena we will set it in such a place that he must needs send us further succour." And so it came to pass; and following the wise counsel of the knight, they accepted Manfred's offer, praying him as a grace to give his own standard to their captain, and so he did. And when they returned to Siena with so poor an aid, great scorn was made thereof by the Sienese, and great dismay came upon the Florentine refugees, which had

145

looked for aid and support from Manfred beyond measure greater.

§ 75.—*How the commonwealth and people of Florence led a great host up to the gates of Siena with the carroccio.*

1260 a.d.

It happened in the year of Christ 1260, in the month of May, that the people and commonwealth of Florence gathered a general host against the city of Siena and led thither the carroccio. And note, that the carroccio, which was led by the commonwealth and people of Florence, was a chariot on four wheels, all painted red, and two tall red masts stood up together thereupon, whereon was fastened and waved the great standard of the arms of the commune, which was dimidiated white and red, and still may be seen to-day in S. Giovanni. And it was drawn by a great pair of oxen covered with red cloth, which were set apart solely for this, and belonged to the Hospitallers of Pinti, and he who drove them was a freeman of the commonwealth. This carroccio was used by our forefathers in triumphs and solemnities, and when they went out with the host, the neighbouring counts and knights brought it from the armoury of S. Giovanni and conducted it to the piazza of the Mercato Nuovo, and having halted by a landmark, which is still there, in the form of a stone carved like a chariot, they committed it to the keeping of the people, and it was led by popolani in the expeditions of war, and to guard it were chosen the best and strongest and most virtuous among the foot soldiers of the popolani, and round it gathered all the force of the people. And when the host was to be assembled, a month before the time when they were to set forth, a bell was hung upon the arch of Porte Sante Marie, which was at the head of the Mercato Nuovo, and there was rung by day and by night without ceasing. And this they did in their pride, to give opportunity to the enemy, against whom the host should go forth, to prepare themselves. And some called it Martinella, and some the Asses' Bell. And when the Florentine host went forth, they took down the bell from the arch and put it into a wooden tower upon a car, and the sound thereof guided the host. By these two pomps of the carroccio and of the bell was maintained the lordly pride of the people of old and of our forefathers in their expeditions. We will leave this and will turn to the Florentines, how they

146

made war against the Sienese, and took the castle of Vicchio, and that of Mezzano, and Casciole, which pertained to the Sienese, and encamped themselves against Siena, hard by the entrance gate by the monastery of S. Petronella; and there they had brought to them, upon a knoll which could be seen from the city, a tower wherein they kept their bell; and in contempt of the Sienese, and as a record of their victory, they filled it with earth and planted an olive tree in it, the which, until our own days, was still there. It fell out at that siege that one day the Florentine refugees gave a feast to Manfred's German soldiers, and having plied them with wine till they were drunk, in the uproar they incited them to arm themselves and mount on horseback to assail the host of the Florentines, promising them large gifts and double pay; and this was done craftily by the wise, in pursuance of the counsel of Farinata degli Uberti which he had given in Apulia. The Germans, beside themselves and hot with wine, sallied forth from Siena and vigorously assailed the camp of the Florentines, and because they were unprepared and off their guard, holding as nought the force of the enemy, the Germans, albeit they were but few folk, did great hurt to the host in that assault, and many of the people and of the horsemen made a sorry show in that sudden assault, and fled in terror, supposing that the assailants were more in number. But in the end, perceiving their error, they took to arms, and defended themselves against the Germans, and of all those who sallied forth from Siena not one escaped alive, for they were all slain and beaten down, and the standard was taken and dragged through the camp and carried to Florence; and this done, shortly afterwards the Florentine host returned to Florence.

§ 76.—*How King Manfred sent Count Giordano with 800 Germans to succour the Sienese and the Ghibelline refugees from Florence.*
1260 a.d.

The Sienese and the Florentine refugees, perceiving how ill the Florentines had fared in the assault of so small a number of German horsemen, considered that if they had a greater number thereof, they would be victorious in the war. Immediately they provided themselves with money, procuring from the company of the Salimbeni, which were merchants of those days, 20,000 florins of gold, and gave them in pledge the fortress of

147

Tentennana and several more castles of the commonwealth, and sent their ambassadors again into Apulia with the said money to King Manfred, saying how his few German followers by their great vigour and valour had undertaken to assail the whole host of the Florentines, and had turned a great part thereof to flight; but if they had been more, they would have had the victory; but by reason of their small number, they had all been left upon the field, and his standard had been dragged about and insulted in the camp and in Florence and round about. And beside this they plied the best reasons they knew to move Manfred, who, having heard the tidings, was wrath, and with the money of the Sienese, who paid half the charges for three months, and at his own cost, sent into Tuscany Count Giordano, his marshal, with 800 German horsemen, to go with the said ambassadors; who reached Siena in the end of July, the year of Christ 1260, and by the Sienese were received with great rejoicing, and they and all the Ghibellines of Tuscany drew thence great vigour and courage. And when they were come to Siena, immediately the Sienese sent forth their host against the castle of Montalcino, which was under the commands of the commonwealth of Florence, and sent for aid to the Pisans and to all the Ghibellines of Tuscany, so that, what with the horsemen of Siena and the Florentine refugees, and the Germans and their allies, there were found 1,800 horsemen in Siena, whereof the greater part were Germans.

§ 77.—*How the Ghibelline refugees from Florence prepared to deceive the commonwealth and people of Florence, and cause them to be betrayed.*
1260 a.d.

The Florentine refugees, by whose embassy and deed King Manfred had sent Count Giordano with 800 German horsemen, thought within themselves that they had done nothing if they could not draw the Florentines out into the field, inasmuch as the aforesaid Germans were not paid save for three months, and already more than one month and a half of this had passed, since their coming, nor had they more money wherewith to pay them, nor did they look for any from Manfred; and should the time for which they had been paid pass by without having done aught, they would return into Apulia, to the great peril of the state. They reasoned that this could not be

148

contrived without skill and subtlety of war, which business was committed to M. Farinata degli Uberti and M. Gherardo Ciccia de' Lamberti. These subtly chose out two wise minor friars as their messengers to the people of Florence, and first caused them to confer with nine of the most powerful men of Siena, who made endless show to the said friars that the government of Messer Provenzano Salvani was displeasing to them, who was the greatest of the citizens of Siena, and that they would willingly yield **Purg. xi. 109-142.** up the city to the Florentines in return for 10,000 florins of gold, and that they were to come with a great host, under guise of fortifying Montalcino, as far as the river Arbia; and then they with their own forces, and with those of their followers, would give up to the Florentines the gate of Santo Vito, which is on the road to Arezzo. The friars, under this deceit and treachery, came to Florence with letters and seals from the aforesaid, and were brought before the Ancients of the people, and proposed to them means whereby they might do great things for the honour of the people and commonwealth of Florence; but the thing was so secret that it must under oath be revealed to but few. Then the Ancients chose from among themselves Spedito di Porte San Piero, a man of great vigour and boldness, and one of the principal leaders of the people, and with him Messer Gianni Calcagni, of Vacchereccia; and when they had sworn upon the altar, the friars unfolded the said plot, and showed the said letters. The said two Ancients, who showed more eagerness than judgment, gave faith to the plot; and immediately the said 10,000 golden florins were procured, and were deposited, and a council was assembled of magnates and people, and they represented that of necessity it behoved to send a host to Siena to strengthen Montalcino, greater than the one sent in May last to Santa Petronella. The nobles of the great Guelf houses of Florence, and Count Guido Guerra, which was with them, not knowing of the pretended plot, and knowing more of war than the popolani did, being aware of the new body of German troops which was come to Siena, and of the sorry show which the people made at Santa Petronella when the hundred Germans attacked them, considered the enterprise not to be without great peril. And also esteeming the citizens to be divided in mind, and ill disposed to raise another host, they gave wise counsel, that it were best that the host should not go forth at present, for the reasons aforesaid; and

149

also they showed how for little cost Montalcino could be fortified, and how the men of Orvieto were prepared to fortify it, and alleged that the said Germans had pay only for three months, and had already served for half the time, and by giving them play enough, without raising a host, shortly they would be scattered, and would return into Apulia; and the Sienese and the Florentine refugees would be left in worse plight than they were before. And the spokesman for them all was M. Tegghiaio Aldobrandi degli Adimari, a wise knight and valiant in arms, and of great **Inf. vi. 79. xvi. 40-42.** authority, and he counselled the better course in full. His counsel ended, the aforesaid Spedito, the Ancient, a very presumptuous man, rudely replied, bidding him to look to his breeches if he was afraid; and M. Tegghiaio replied that at the pinch he would not dare to follow him into the battle where he would lead; and these words ended, next uprose M. Cece de Gherardini to say the same that Messer Tegghiaio had said. The Ancients commanded him not to speak, and the penalty was 100 pounds if any one held forth contrary to the command of the Ancients. The knight was willing to pay it, so that he might oppose the going; but the Ancients would not have it, rather they made the penalty double; again he desired to pay, and so it reached 300 pounds; and when he yet wanted to speak and to pay, the command was that his head should be forfeit; and there it stopped. But, through the proud and heedless people, the worse counsel won the day, that the said host should proceed immediately and without delay.

§ 78.—*How the Florentines raised an army to fortify Montalcino, and were discomfited by Count Giordano and by the Sienese at Montaperti.*
1260 a.d.

The people of Florence having taken the ill resolve to raise an army, craved assistance from their friends, which came with foot soldiers and with horse, from Lucca, and Bologna, and Pistoia, and Prato, and Volterra, and Samminiato, and Sangimignano, and from Colle di Valdelsa, which were in league with the commonwealth and people of Florence; and in Florence there were 800 horsemen of the citizens and more than 500 mercenaries. And the said people being assembled in Florence, the host set forth in the end of August, and for pomp and display they led out the carroccio, and a bell, which they called Martinella, on a car with a wooden tower on wheels, and there went out nearly all the people with the banners of the guilds, and there did not remain a house or a family in Florence which went not forth on foot or on horseback, at least one for each house, and for some two or more, according to their power. And when they found themselves in the territory of Siena, at the place agreed upon, on the river Arbia, at the place called Montaperti, with the men of Perugia and of Orvieto, which there joined with the Florentines, there were gathered together more than 3,000 horse and more than 30,000 foot. And whilst the host of the Florentines was thus preparing, the aforesaid framers of the plot, which were in Siena, in order that it might be the more fully accomplished, sent to Florence certain other friars to hatch treason with certain Ghibelline magnates and popolani which had not been exiled from Florence, and would therefore have to join the general muster of the army. With these, then, they plotted that when they were drawn up for battle, they should from divers quarters flee from their companies, and repair to their own party, to confound the Florentine army. And this plot they made because they seemed to themselves to be but few in comparison with the Florentines; and so it was done.

Now it happened that when the said host was on the hills of Montaperti, those sage Ancients who were leading the host, and had managed the negotiations, were awaiting the opening of the promised gate by the traitors from within. A magnate from among the people, a Florentine from the gate of S. Piero, which was a Ghibelline, and was named Razzante, having heard something of the expectation of the Florentine host, was commissioned by consent of the Ghibellines in the camp which were meditating the treason, to enter Siena; whereupon he fled on horseback from the camp to make known to the Florentine refugees how the city of Siena was to be betrayed, and how the Florentines were well equipped, and with great strength of horse and foot, and to urge those within not to advise battle. And when he was come unto Siena, and these things had been disclosed to the said M. Farinata and M. Gherardo, the plotters, they said thus to him: "Thou wilt slay us, if thou spreadest this news throughout Siena, inasmuch as fear will fall upon every man, but we desire that thou shouldest say the contrary; for if we do not fight while we have these Germans we are dead men, and shall never return to Florence, and for us death and defeat would be better than to crawl about the world any longer:" and their counsel was to try the fortune of battle. Razzante, instructed by these two aforesaid, determined and promised to speak thus; and with a garland on his head, on horseback with the said two, showing great gladness, he came to the parliament to the palace where were all the people of Siena and the Germans and other allies; and then, with a joyful countenance, he told great news from the Ghibelline party and the traitors in camp, how the host was ill-ordered and ill-led, and disunited, and that if they attacked them boldly, they would certainly be discomfited. And Razzante having made his false report, at the cry of the people they all moved to arms, calling out: "Battle, battle." The Germans demanded a promise of double pay, and this was given them; and their troop led the attack from the gate of San Vito, which was to have been given over to the Florentines; and the other horse and foot sallied out after them. When those among the host which were expecting that the gate should be given to them saw the Germans and the other horse and foot sally forth towards them from Siena in battle array, they marvelled greatly, and were sore dismayed, seeing their sudden approach and unlooked-for attack; and they were the more dismayed that many Ghibellines who were in the host, both on horse and foot, beholding the enemy's troops approaching, fled from divers quarters, as the treason had been ordered; and among them were the della Pressa and they of the Abati, and many others. But the Florentines and their allies did not on this account neglect to array their troops, and await the battle; and when the German troop violently charged the troop of Florentine horse (where was the standard of the cavalry of the commonwealth, which was borne by M. Jacopo del Nacca, a man of great valour, of the house of the Pazzi in Florence), that traitor of a M. Bocca degli Abati, which **Inf. xxxii. 78-111.** was in his troop and near to him, struck the said M. Jacopo with his sword, and cut off the hand with which he held the standard, and immediately he died. And this done, the horsemen and people, beholding the standard fallen, and that there were traitors among them, and that they were so strongly assailed by the Germans, in a short time were put to flight. But because the horsemen of Florence first perceived the treason, there were but thirty-six men of name of the cavalry slain and taken. But the great mortality

152

and capture was of the foot soldiers of Florence, and of Lucca, and of Orvieto, because they shut themselves up in the castle of Montaperti, and were all taken; but more than 2,500 of them were left dead upon the field, and more than **Inf. x. 85-87.** 1,500 were taken captive of the best of the people of Florence, from every house, and of Lucca, and of the other allies which were in the said battle. And thus was abased the arrogance of the ungrateful and proud people of Florence. And this was on a Tuesday, the 4th day of September, in the year of Christ 1260; and there was left the carroccio and the bell called Martinella, with an untold amount of booty, of the baggage pertaining to the Florentines and their allies. And thus was routed and destroyed the ancient Popolo of Florence, which had continued in so many victories and in great lordship and state for ten years.

§ 79.—*How the Guelfs of Florence, after the said discomfiture, departed from Florence and went to Lucca.*

1260 a.d.

The news of the grievous discomfiture being come to Florence, and the miserable fugitives returning therefrom, there arose so great a lamentation both of men and of women in Florence that it reached unto the heavens, forasmuch as there was not a house in Florence, small or great, whereof there was not one slain or taken; and from Lucca, and from the territory there were a great number, and from Orvieto. For the which thing the heads of the Guelfs, both nobles and popolari, which had returned from the defeat, and those which were in Florence, were dismayed and fearful, and feared lest the exiles should come from Siena with the German troops, perceiving that the rebel Ghibellines and those under bounds which were absent from the city were beginning to return thereto. Wherefore the Guelfs, without being banished or driven out, went forth with their families, weeping, from Florence, and betook themselves to Lucca on Thursday, the 13th day of September, **Cf. Inf. x. 48.** in the year of Christ 1260. These were the chief families of the Guelf refugees from Florence: of the sesto of Oltrarno, the Rossi, and the Nerli, and part of the Mannelli, the Bardi, and the Mozzi, and the Frescobaldi; the notable popolani of the said sesto were the Canigiani, Magli, and Macchiavelli, the Belfredelli and the Orciolini, Aglioni, Rinucci, Barbadori, and the Battincenni, and Soderini, and Malduri and Ammirati. Of San Piero Scheraggio, the nobles: Gherardini, Lucardesi, Cavalcanti, Bagnesi, Pulci, Guidalotti, Malispini, Foraboschi, Manieri, they of Quona, Sacchetti, Compiobbesi; the popolani, Magalotti, Mancini, Bucelli, and they of the Antella. Of the sesto of Borgo, the nobles: the Bondelmonti, Scali, Spini, Gianfigliazzi, Giandonati, Bostichi, Altoviti, the Ciampoli, Baldovinetti and others. Of the sesto of San Brancazio, the nobles: Tornaquinci, Vecchietti, and part of the Pigli, Minerbetti, Becchenugi, and Bordoni and others. Of the Porte del Duomo: the Tosinghi, Arrigucci, Agli, Sizii, Marignolli, and Ser Brunetto Latini and his family, and many others. Of the Porte San Piero: Adimari, Pazzi, Visdomini, and part of the Donati. Of the branch of the Scolari there were left della Bella, the Carci, the Ghiberti, the Guidalotti di Balla, the Mazzochi, the Uccellini, Boccatonde; and beside these magnates and popolani of each sesto were put under bounds. And for this departure

154

the Guelfs were much to be blamed, inasmuch as the city of Florence was very strong, and with walls, and with moats full of water, and could well have been defended and held; but the judgment of God in punishing sins must needs hold on its course without hindrance; and to whomsoever God intends ill, from him He takes away wisdom and knowledge. And the Guelfs having departed on Thursday, the Sunday after being the 16th of September, the exiles from Florence which had been at the battle of Montaperti, with Count Giordano and with his German troops, and with the other soldiers of the Ghibellines of Tuscany, enriched by the spoil of the Florentines and of the other Guelfs of Tuscany, entered into the city of Florence without hindrance, and immediately they made Guido Novello of the Counts Guidi, Podestà of Florence for King Manfred, from the first day of the coming January for two years, and his judgment hall was the old palace of the people at Santo Apollinari, the stair of which was on the outer wall. And a little while after he caused the Ghibelline gate to be made, and the road out to be opened; to the intent that by that way, which corresponds with the palace, there might be entrance and exit at need, and he might bring his retainers from Casentino into Florence to guard him and the city. And because it was done in the time of the Ghibellines, the gate and the road took the name of Ghibelline. This Count Guido caused all the citizens which remained in Florence to swear fealty to King Manfred, and by reason of promises made to the Sienese he caused five castles of the territory of Florence which were on their frontier to be destroyed; and there remained in Florence as captain of the host, and vicar-general for King Manfred, the said Count Giordano, with the German troops in the pay of the Florentines, who greatly persecuted the Guelfs in many parts of Tuscany, as we shall make mention hereafter; and took all their goods, and destroyed many palaces and towers pertaining to the Guelfs, and took their goods for the benefit of the commonwealth. The said Count Giordano was a gentleman of Piedmont in Lombardy, and kinsman of the mother of Manfred, and by his prowess, and because he was very faithful to Manfred, and in life and customs as worldly-minded as he, he made him a count, and gave him lands in Apulia, and from small estate raised him to great lordship.

§ 80.—*How the news of the defeat of the Florentines came to the court of the*

Pope, and the prophecy which was made thereupon by Cardinal Bianco.
1260 a.d.

When the news of the aforesaid defeat came to the court of Rome, the Pope and the cardinals who loved the state of Holy Church felt much grief and compassion thereat, alike for the Florentines, and also because thereby the state and power of Manfred, the enemy of the **Inf. x. 120.** Church, would increase; but Cardinal Ottaviano degli Ubaldini, which was a Ghibelline, rejoiced greatly thereat; wherefore Cardinal Bianco, which was a great astrologer and master of necromancy, seeing this, said: if Cardinal Ottaviano knew the future of this war of the Florentines, he would not be rejoicing thus. The college of cardinals prayed him that he would declare himself more openly. Cardinal Bianco would not speak, because to speak of the future seemed to him to be **Cf. Inf. xx. and xxvii. 100-107.** unlawful to his office, but the cardinals so prayed the Pope that he commanded him on his obedience to speak. Having received the said command, he said in brief words: the conquered shall conquer victoriously, and shall not be conquered for ever. This was interpreted to mean that the Guelfs, conquered and driven out of **Cf. Inf. x. 51.** Florence, should victoriously return to power, and should never again lose their state and lordship in Florence.

§ 81.—*How the Ghibellines of Tuscany purposed to destroy the city of Florence, and how M. Farinata degli Uberti defended it.*
1260 a.d.

After the same fashion that the Guelfs of Florence departed, so did those of Prato and of Pistoia, and of Volterra, and of Samminiato, and of San Gimignano, and of many other cities and villages of Tuscany, which all returned to the party of the Ghibellines save the city of Lucca, the which held to the party of the Guelfs for a time, and was a refuge for the Guelfs of Florence, and for the other exiles of Tuscany, the which Guelfs of Florence took their stand in Lucca in the quarter around San Friano; and the loggia in front of San Friano was made by the Florentines. And when the Florentines found themselves in this place, Messer Tegghiaio Aldobrandi, seeing Spedito who had insulted him in the council and bade him look to his breeches, drew

156

himself up and took from his pouch five hundred florins of gold that he had, and showed them to Spedito (who had fled from Florence in great poverty), and said to him reproachfully, "Just look at the state of my breeches! This is what you have brought yourself and me and the rest to, by your rash and overbearing lordship." And Spedito answered, "Then why did you trust us?" We have made mention of these paltry and **Cf. Inf. xxx. 148.** base altercations as a warning, that no citizen, especially if he be a popolano and of small account, when he chances to be in office, should be too bold or presumptuous. At this time the Pisans, the Sienese, and they of Arezzo, with the said Count Giordano, and with the other Ghibelline leaders, caused a council to be held at Empoli, to establish the Ghibelline party in Tuscany, and to form a league; and so it was done. And forasmuch as Count Giordano must needs return into Apulia, to King Manfred, by command of the said Manfred there was proclaimed as his vicar-general and captain of the host in Tuscany, Count Guido Novello of the Counts Guidi of Casentino and of Modigliana, who factiously forsook Count Simone his brother, and Count Guido Guerra his fellow, and all those of his branch of the family which held to the Guelf party; and he was desirous to drive out of Tuscany every Guelf. And at the said council all the neighbouring cities, and the Counts Guidi, and the Counts Alberti, and they of Santafiore, and the Ubaldini, and all the barons around took counsel, **Purg. vi. 111.** and were all of one mind how for the good of the Ghibelline party the city of Florence should be utterly destroyed and reduced to open villages, to the intent there might remain neither renown, nor fame, nor power of its might. To withstand which proposal uprose the valiant and wise knight, Messer Farinata degli Uberti, and in his saying he introduced two ancient proverbs of the street which say: "As the ass has wit, so he munches his rape" [*i.e.*, every one does his business according to his capacity, such as it is], and "Lame goats can go if they meet no wolf" [*i.e.*, any one can get on if there are no difficulties]; and these two proverbs he wove together, saying: "As the ass has wit, lame goats can go; so he munches his rape if they meet no wolf," adroitly turning the vulgar proverbs to examples and comparisons to show the folly of thus speaking, and the great peril and hurt that might follow thereupon; and saying that if there were none other than he, whilst he had life in his body he would defend

157

the **Inf. x. 91-93.** city with sword in hand. Count Giordano perceiving this, and what manner of man and of what authority was Messer Farinata, and his great following, and how the Ghibelline party might be broken up and come to discord, abandoned the idea, and took other counsel, so that by one good man and citizen our city of Florence was saved from so great fury, destruction, and ruin. But afterwards the said people of Florence were ungrateful and forgetful towards the said Messer **Inf. x. 83, 84.** Farinata, and his progeny and descendants, as hereafter we shall make mention. But in despite of the forgetfulness of the ungrateful people, nevertheless we ought to commend and keep in notable memory the good and virtuous citizen, who acted after the fashion of the good Roman Camillus of old, as we are told by Valerius and Titus Livius.

§ 82.—*How Count Guido, the vicar, with the league of the* **1261 a.d.** *Ghibellines of Tuscany, went against Lucca, and took S. Maria a Monte and many fortresses.*

§ 83.—*How the Guelf refugees from Florence sent their ambassadors into Germany to stir up Conradino against Manfred.*

In those times the Guelf refugees from Florence and from the other cities of Tuscany, perceiving themselves to be thus persecuted by the forces of Manfred and of the Ghibellines of Tuscany, and seeing that no lord was rising against the forces of Manfred, and also that the Church had but little power against him, thought within themselves to send their ambassadors into Germany to stir up the little Conradino, offering him much aid and favour, against Manfred, his uncle, who was falsely holding the kingdom of Sicily and of Apulia; and this was done, for from among the chief of the Florentine exiles there went as ambassadors, with those of the commonwealth of Lucca. And the Guelf exiles from Florence were represented by M. Bonaccorso Bellincioni of the Adimari, and M. Simone Donati. And they found Conradino so young a boy that his mother would in no wise consent to let him go from her, albeit with will and with mind she was greatly against Manfred and held him as an enemy and rebel against Conradino. And the said ambassadors, when they returned from Germany, as a token and earnest of the coming of Conradino, caused him to give them his mantle lined with miniver, which being brought to Lucca caused great rejoicing among the

158

Guelfs, and it was shown in S. Friano of Lucca, as if it had been a relic. But the Guelfs of Tuscany did not know the future destiny, how the said Conradino should become their enemy.

§ 84.—*How the Guelf refugees from Florence took Signa, but held it* **1262 a.d.** *Par. xvi. 56. only a short space.* § 85.—*How Count Guido, the vicar, with the Tuscan league and the forces of the Pisans, marched upon Lucca, whereon the Lucchese made their peace, and drave out the Guelf refugees from Lucca.*

§ 86.—*How the Guelf refugees from Florence, and the other exiles of Tuscany, drave out the Ghibellines from Modena and afterwards from Reggio.* **1263 a.d.**

After the miserable Guelfs which had been driven from Florence and from all the cities of Tuscany (whereof none held with the Guelf party) were come into the city of Bologna, they abode there long time in great want and poverty, some receiving pay to serve on foot, and some on horse, and some without pay. It came to pass in those times that the inhabitants of the city of Modena, Guelfs and Ghibellines, came to dissension and civic strife among themselves, as it is the custom of the cities of Lombardy to assemble and fight on the piazza of the commonwealth; and many days they were opposed the one to the other without either side being able to win the victory. It came to pass that the Guelfs sent for succour to Bologna, and especially to the Guelf refugees from Florence, which straightway, as needy folk, and making war for their own behoof, went thither on horse and on foot, as each best could. And when they came to Modena a gate was opened to them by the Guelfs, and they were admitted; and straightway when they were come upon the piazza of Modena, as brave men and used to arms and to war, they attacked the Ghibellines, which could not long endure, but were defeated and slain and driven out of the city, and their houses and their goods spoiled; by reason of which booty the said Guelf refugees from Florence and from the rest of Tuscany were much enriched, and furnished themselves with horses and with arms, whereof they were in great need, and this was in the year of Christ 1263. And whilst they were in Modena, a little while after, in the same manner as in Modena, fighting began in the city of Reggio in Lombardy, between the Guelfs and the Ghibellines; and when the Guelfs of Reggio sent

159

for aid to the Guelf refugees from Florence, which were in Modena, straightway they went thither, and they chose as their captain Messer Forese degli Adimari. And when they were come to Reggio they joined in the battle on the piazza, which endured long time, forasmuch as the Ghibellines of Reggio were very powerful, and among them was one called Caca of Reggio, on whose name wit is spilled in gibes even yet. This man was well-nigh as tall as a giant, and of marvellous strength, and he had an iron club in his hand, and none dared to approach him whom he did not fell to the earth, either slain or maimed, and by him the battle was well-nigh wholly sustained. When the gentlemen in banishment from Florence perceived this, they chose among them twelve of the most valiant, and called them the twelve paladins, which, with daggers in hand, all set upon that valiant man, which, after very brave defence, and beating down many of his enemies, was struck down to the earth and slain upon the piazza; and so soon as the Ghibellines saw their champion on the ground, they took to flight and were discomfited and driven out of Reggio; and if the Guelf refugees from Florence and from the other cities of Tuscany were enriched by the spoil of the Ghibellines of Modena, much more were they enriched by that of the Ghibellines of Reggio; and they all provided themselves with horses, so that in a short time, while they abode in Reggio and in Modena, they numbered more than 400 horsemen, good men-at-arms well mounted, and they came at great need to the succour of Charles, count of Anjou and of Provence, when he came into Apulia against Manfred, as we shall hereafter relate. We will now leave the doings of Florence, and of the Guelf refugees, and turn to the things which came to pass in those times between the Church of Rome and Manfred.

§ 87.—*How Manfred persecuted Pope Urban and the Church with his Saracens of Nocera, and how a crusade was proclaimed against them.*
1261 a.d.

By reason of the discomfiture of the Florentines, and of the other Guelfs of Tuscany at Montaperti, as we have afore said, King Manfred rose to great lordship and state, and all the imperial party in Tuscany and in Lombardy greatly increased in power, and the Church and its devout and faithful followers were much abased in all places. It came to pass that a very

160

little while after, in the said year 1260, Pope Alexander passed from this life in the city of Viterbo, and the Church was vacant without a pastor for five months through the disputings among the cardinals; afterwards they elected Pope Urban IV., of the city of Troyes, of Champagne in France, the which was of low origin, being son of a cobbler, but was a man of worth, and wise. But his election was in this fashion: he was a poor clerk which came to the court of Rome to plead a cause about his Church, which had been taken from him, which brought in twenty pounds tournois a year. The cardinals, by reason of their disputes, locked the doors when they were shut up, and made among themselves a secret decree that the first clerk which knocked at the door should be Pope. As it pleased God this Urban was the first, and where he came to plead for the poor church of twenty pounds tournois revenue, he received the Universal Church, after the ordinances of God, as fixed in the election of the blessed Nicholas. Because the election was miraculous, therefore have we made mention and record thereof. And he was consecrated the year of Christ 1261. Finding the Church much beaten down by the power of Manfred, which was occupying the greater part of Italy, and had stationed the host of his Saracens of Nocera in the lands of the patrimony of S. Peter, the said Urban preached a crusade against them; wherefore many faithful people took the cross and marched in the army against them. For the which cause, the Saracens fled into Apulia, but Manfred did not therefore cease to molest the Pope and the Church in their followers and troops, and he abode now in Sicily and now in Apulia, in great luxury and in great delights, following a worldly and epicurean life, and for his pleasure keeping many concubines, living lasciviously, and it seemed that he cared neither for God nor for the saints. But God, the just Lord, which, through grace, delays His **Cf. Par. xxii. 16-18.** judgments upon sinners to the intent they may bethink them, but in the end does not pardon those who do not turn to Him, presently sent forth His curse and ruin upon Manfred, when he believed himself to be in the height of his state and lordship, as hereafter we shall make mention.

§ 88.—*How the Church of Rome elected Charles of France to be king of Sicily and of Apulia.*

1263 a.d.

The said Pope Urban and the Church being thus brought down by the power of Manfred, and the two Emperors-elect (to wit, the Spaniard and the Englishman) not being in concord nor having power to come into Italy, and Conradino, son of King Conrad, to whom pertained by inheritance the kingdom of Sicily and of Apulia, being so young a boy that he could not as yet come against Manfred, the said Pope, by reason of the importunity of many faithful followers of the Church, the which by Manfred's violence had been driven from their lands, and especially by reason of the Guelf exiles from Florence and from Tuscany who were continually pursuing the court, complaining of their woes at the feet of the Pope, the said Pope Urban called a great council of his cardinals and of many prelates, and made this proposal: seeing the Church was subjugated by Manfred, and since those of his house and lineage had always been enemies and persecutors of Holy Church, not being grateful for many benefits received, if it seemed well to them, he had thought to release Holy Church from bondage and restore her to her state and liberty, and this might be done by summoning Charles, count of Anjou and of Provence, son of the king of France, and brother of the good King Louis, the which was the most capable prince in prowess of arms and in every virtue that there was in his time, and of so powerful a house as that of France, and who might be the champion of Holy Church and king of Sicily and of Apulia, regaining it by force from King Manfred, which was holding it unjustly by force, and was excommunicated and condemned, and was against the will of Holy Church, and as it were a rebel against her; and he trusted so much in the prowess of the said Charles, and of the barons of France, which would follow him, that he did not doubt but that he would oppose Manfred and take from him the lands and all the Kingdom in short time, and would put the Church in great state. To the which counsel all the cardinals and prelates agreed, and they elected the said Charles to be king of Sicily and of Apulia, him and his descendants down to the fourth generation after him, and the election being confirmed, they sent forth the decree; and this was the year of Christ 1263.

§ 89.—*How Charles, count of Anjou and of Provence, accepted the election*

offered him by the Church of Rome to Sicily and to Apulia.
1263 a.d.

When the said invitation was carried to France by the Cardinal Simon of Tours to the said Charles, he took counsel thereupon with King Louis of France and with the count of Artois, and with the count of Alençon, his brother, and with the other great barons of France, and by all he was counselled that in the name of God he should undertake the said emprise in the service of Holy Church, and to bear the dignity of crown and Kingdom. And the King Louis of France, his elder brother, proffered him aid in men and in money, and likewise offers were made to him by all the barons of France. And his lady, which was **Purg. vii. 128.** youngest daughter to the good Count Raymond Berenger, of Provence, through whom he had the heritage of the county of Provence, when she heard of the election of the Count Charles, her husband, to the intent that she might become queen, pledged all her jewels and invited all the bachelors-at-arms of France and of Provence to rally round her standard and to make her queen. And this was largely by reason of the contempt and disdain which a little while before had been shown to her by her three elder sisters, which were all queens, making her sit a degree lower than they, for which cause, with great grief, she had made complaint thereof to Charles, her husband, which answered her: "Be at peace, for I will shortly make thee a greater queen than them;" for which cause she sought after and obtained the best barons of France for her service, and those who did most in the emprise. And thus Charles wrought in his preparations with all solicitude and power, and made answer to the Pope and to the cardinals, by the said cardinal legate, how he had accepted their election, and how, without loss of time, he would come into Italy with a strong arm and great force to defend Holy Church, and against Manfred, to drive him from the lands of Sicily and of Apulia; by the which news the Church and all her followers, and whosoever was on the side of the Guelfs, were much comforted and took great courage. When Manfred heard the news, he furnished himself for defence with men and money, and with the force of the Ghibelline party in Lombardy and in Tuscany, which were of his league and alliance, he enlisted and equipped many more folk than he had

163

before, and caused them to come from Germany for his defence, to the intent the said Charles and his French following might not be able to enter into Italy or to proceed to Rome; and with money and with promises he gathered a great part of the lords and of the cities of Italy under his lordship, and in Lombardy he made vicar the Marquis Pallavicino of Piedmont, his kinsman, which much resembled him in person and in habits. And likewise he caused great defences to be prepared at sea, of armed galleys of his Sicilians and Apulians, and of the Pisans which were in league with him, and they feared but little the coming of the said Charles, whom they called, in contempt, Little Charles. And forasmuch as Manfred thought himself, and was, lord over sea and land, and his Ghibelline party was uppermost and ruled over Tuscany and Lombardy, he held his coming for nought.

§ 90.—*Incident relating to the good Count Raymond of Provence.*

Since in the chapter above we have told of the worthy lady, wife of King Charles and daughter of the good Count Raymond Berenger, of Provence, it is fitting that something should briefly be said of the said count, to whom King Charles was heir. Count Raymond was a lord of gentle lineage, and kin to them of the house of Aragon, and to the family of the count of Toulouse. By inheritance Provence, this side of the Rhone, was his; a wise and courteous lord was he, and of noble state and virtuous, and in his time did honourable deeds, and to his court came all gentle persons of Provence and of France and of Catalonia, by reason of his courtesy and noble estate, and he made many Provençal coblas and canzoni of great worth. There came to his court a certain Romeo [pilgrim], who was returning from S. James', and **Par. vi. 127-142. Vita Nuova, § xli. 34-52.** hearing the goodness of Count Raymond, abode in his court, and was so wise and valorous, and came so much into favour with the count, that he made him master and steward of all that he had; who always continued in virtuous and religious living, and in a short time, by his industry and prudence, increased his master's revenue threefold, maintaining always a great and honourable court. And being at war with the count of Toulouse on the borders of their lands (and the count of Toulouse was the greatest count in the world, and under him he had fourteen counts), by the courtesy of Count Raymond, and by the wisdom of the good Romeo, and by the treasure which he had gathered, he had so many barons and knights that he was victorious in the war, and that with honour. Four daughters had the count, and no male child. By prudence and care the good Romeo first married the eldest for him to the good King Louis of France by giving money with her, saying to the count, "Leave it to me, and do not grudge the cost, for if thou marryest the first well, thou wilt marry all the others the better for the sake of her kinship, and at less cost." And so it came to pass; for straightway the king of England, to be of kin to the king of France, took the second with little money; afterwards his carnal brother, being the king elect of the Romans, after the same manner took the third; the fourth being still to marry, the good Romeo said, "For this one I desire that thou should'st have a brave man for thy son, who may be thine heir,"—and so he did. Finding Charles, count of Anjou, brother of King Louis of France, he said, "Give her to him, for he is like to be the best man in the world," prophesying of him; and this was done. And it came to pass afterwards, through envy, which destroys all good, that the barons of Provence accused the good Romeo that he had managed the count's treasure ill, and they called upon him to give an account; the worthy Romeo said, "Count, I have served thee long while, and raised thy estate from small to great, and for this, through the false counsel of thy people, thou art little grateful: I came to thy court a poor pilgrim, and I have lived virtuously here; give me back my mule, my staff, and my scrip, as I came here, and I renounce thy service." The count would not that he should depart; but for nought that he could do would he remain; and as he came, so he departed, and no one knew whence he came or whither he went. But many held that he was a sainted soul.

§ 91.—*How in these times there appeared a great comet, and what it* **1264 a.d.** *signified.*

END OF SELECTIONS FROM BOOK VI.

BOOK VII.

Here begins the Seventh Book, which treats of the coming of King Charles, and of many changes and events which followed thereupon.

§ 1.—Charles was the second son of Louis le Debonnaire, king of **1264 a.d.**
Inf. xix. 99. Purg. vii. 113, 124, 128, 129; xi. 137; xx. 67-69. France, and grandson of the good King Philip, the blear-eyed, his grandfather, whereof we before made mention, and brother of the good King Louis of France, and of Robert, count of Artois, and of Alfonso, count of Poitou; all these four brothers were the children of Queen Bianca, daughter of the King Alfonso of Spain. The said Charles, count of Anjou, by inheritance from his father, and count of Provence, this side the Rhone, by inheritance through his wife, the daughter of the **Purg. xx. 61-63.** good Count Raymond Berenger, so soon as he was elected king of Sicily and of Apulia by the Pope and by the Church, made preparation of knights and barons to furnish means for his enterprise and expedition into Italy, as we before narrated. But in order that those who come after may have fuller knowledge how this Charles was the first of the kings of Sicily and of Apulia descended from the house of France, we will tell somewhat of his virtues and conditions; and it is very fitting that we should preserve a record of so great a lord, and so great a friend and protector and defender of Holy Church, and of our city of Florence, as we shall make mention hereafter. This Charles was wise, prudent in counsel and valiant in arms, and harsh, and much feared and redoubted by all the kings of the earth, great-hearted and of high purposes, steadfast in carrying out every great undertaking, firm in every adversity, faithful to every promise, speaking little and acting much, scarcely smiling, chaste as a monk, catholic, harsh in judgment, and of a fierce countenance, tall and stalwart in person, **Purg. vii. 113, 124.** olive-coloured, large-nosed, and in kingly majesty he exceeded any other lord, and slept little and woke long, and was wont to say that all the time of sleep was so much lost; liberal was he to knights in arms, but greedy in acquiring land and lordship and money, from whencesoever it came, to

166

furnish means for his enterprises and wars; in jongleurs, minstrels or jesters he never took delight; his arms were those of France, that is an azure field charged with the golden lily, barred with vermilion above; so far they were diverse from the arms of France. This Charles, when he passed into Italy, was forty-six **1265 a.d.** years of age, and he reigned nineteen years in Sicily and Apulia, as we shall make mention hereafter. He had by his wife two sons and several daughters; the first was named Charles II., and was somewhat **Purg. vii. 126.** crippled, and was prince of Capua; and after the first Charles, his father, he became king of Sicily and of Apulia, as we shall make mention hereafter. The second was Philip, who was prince of the Morea in his wife's right; but he died young and without issue, for he ruptured himself in straining a crossbow. We will now leave for a while to speak of the progeny of the good King Charles, and will continue our story of his passing into Italy, and of other things which followed thereupon.

§ 2.—*How the Guelf refugees from Florence took the arms of Pope Clement, and how they joined the French army of Count Charles.*
1265 a.d.

In those times the Guelf refugees from Florence and from the other cities of Tuscany, who were much advantaged by the booty they had made of the cities of Modena and Reggio, whereof we before made mention, hearing that Count Charles was preparing to pass into Italy, gathered all their strength in arms and in horses, each one doing all in his power; and they numbered more than 400 good horsemen of gentle lineage and proved in arms, and they sent their ambassadors to Pope Clement, to the end he might recommend them to Count Charles, King elect of Sicily, and to proffer themselves for the service of Holy Church; which were graciously received by the said Pope, and provided with money and other benefactions; and the said Pope required that for love of him the Guelf party from Florence should always bear his proper arms on their standard and seal, which was, and is, a white field with a vermilion eagle above a green serpent, which they bore and kept henceforward, and down to our present times, though it is true that the Guelfs added afterwards a small vermilion lily above the head of the eagle; and with this banner they departed from Lombardy in company with the

167

French horsemen of Count Charles when they journeyed to Rome, as we shall make mention hereafter; and they were among the best warriors and the most skilled in arms, of all those which King Charles had at the battle against Manfred. We will now leave for the present to speak of the Guelf refugees from Florence, and will tell of the coming of Count Charles and of his followers.

§ 3.—*How Count Charles departed from France, and passed by sea from Provence to Rome.*

1265 a.d.

In the year of Christ 1265, Charles, count of Anjou and of Provence, having collected his barons and knights of France, and money to furnish means for his expedition, and having mustered his troops, left Count Guy of Montfort, captain and leader of 1,500 French horsemen, which were to journey to Rome by way of Lombardy; and having kept the feast of Easter, of the Resurrection of Christ, with King Louis of France and with his other brothers and friends, he straightway departed from Paris with a small company. Without delay he came to Marseilles in Provence, where he had had prepared thirty armed galleys, upon which he embarked with certain barons whom he had brought with him from France, and with certain of his Provençal barons and knights, and put out to sea on his way to Rome in great peril, inasmuch as King Manfred with his forces had armed in Genoa, and in Pisa, and in the Kingdom, more than eighty galleys, which were at sea on guard, to the intent that the said Charles might not be able to pass. But the said Charles, like a bold and courageous lord, prepared to pass without any regard to the lying-in-wait of his enemies, repeating a proverb, or perhaps the saying of a philosopher, that runs: Good care frustrates ill fortune. And this happened to the said Charles at his need; for being with his galleys on the Pisan seas, by tempest of the sea they were dispersed, and Charles with three of his galleys, utterly forespent, arrived at the Pisan port. Hearing this, Count Guido Novello, then vicar in Pisa for King Manfred, armed himself with his German troops to ride to the port and take Count Charles; the Pisans seized their moment, and closed the doors of the city, and ran to arms, and raised a dispute with the vicar, demanding back the fortress of Mutrone, which he

168

was holding for the Lucchese, which was very dear and necessary to them; and this had to be granted before he was able to depart. And on account of the said interval and delay, when Count Guido had departed from Pisa and reached the port, Count Charles, the storm being somewhat abated, had with great care refitted his galleys and put out to sea, having departed but a little time before from the port, so great peril and misfortune being past; and thus, as it pleased God, passing afterwards hard by the fleet of King Manfred, sailing over the high seas, he arrived with his armada safe and sound at the mouth of the Roman Tiber, in the month of May of the said year, the which coming was held to be very marvellous and sudden, and by King Manfred and his people could scarce be believed. Charles having arrived in Rome, was received by the Romans with great honour, inasmuch as they loved not the lordship of Manfred; and immediately he was made senator of Rome by the will of the Pope and the people of Rome. Albeit Pope Clement was in Viterbo, yet he gave him all aid and countenance against Manfred, both spiritual and temporal; but by reason of his mounted troops, which were coming from France by land, and which through the many hindrances prepared by the followers of Manfred in Lombardy, had much difficulty in reaching Rome, as we shall make mention, it behoved Count Charles to abide in Rome, and in Campagna, and in Viterbo throughout that summer, during which sojourn he took counsel and ordered how he might enter the Kingdom with his host.

§ 4.—*How Count Guy of Montfort, with the horse of Count Charles, passed through Lombardy.*

1265 a.d.

Count Guy of Montfort, with the horsemen which Count Charles had left him to lead, and with the countess, wife to the said Charles, and with her knights, departed from France in the month of June of the said year. * * * * * * And they took the way of Burgundy and of Savoy, and crossed the mountains of Monsanese [M. Cenis]; and when they came into the country about Turin and Asti, they were received with honour by **Cf. Purg. vii. 133-136. Conv. iv. 11: 125-127.** the marquis of Monferrato, which was lord over that country, forasmuch as the marquis held with the Church, and was against Manfred; and by his conduct, and with the aid of the Milanese, they set out to pass through Lombardy, from Piedmont as far as Parma, all in arms, and riding in troops, with much difficulty, forasmuch as the Marquis Pallavicino, kinsman of Manfred, with the forces of the Cremonese, and of the other Ghibelline cities of Lombardy which were in league with Manfred, was guarding the passes with more than 3,000 horsemen, some Germans and some Lombards. At last, as it pleased God, albeit the two hosts came very nigh one another at the place called . . . the French passed through without any battle being fought and arrived at the city of Parma. Truly it is said that one Master Buoso, of the house of da **Inf. xxxii. 115, 116.** Duera, of Cremona, for money which he received from the French, gave counsel in such wise that the host of Manfred was not there to contest the pass, as had been arranged, wherefor the people of Cremona afterwards destroyed the said family of da Duera in fury. When the French came to the city of Parma they were graciously received, and the Guelf refugees from Florence and from the other cities of Tuscany, with more than 400 horsemen (whereof they had made captain Count Guido Guerra of the Counts Guidi) went out to meet them as far as the city of Mantua. And when the French met with the Guelf refugees from Florence and from Tuscany, they seemed to them such fine men, and so rich in horses and in arms, that they marvelled greatly, that being in banishment from their cities they could be so nobly accoutred, and their company highly esteemed our exiles. And afterwards they took them round by Lombardy to Bologna, and by Romagna and by the March, and by the Duchy, for they could not pass through Tuscany, forasmuch as it all pertained to the Ghibelline party, and was under the lordship of Manfred; for the which thing they spent long time in their journeying, so that it was not till the beginning of the month of December, in the said year 1265, that they arrived in Rome; and when they were come to the city of Rome, Count Charles was very joyful, and received them with great gladness and honour.

§ 5.—*How King Charles was crowned in Rome king of Sicily, and how he straightway departed with his host to go against King Manfred.*
1265 a.d.

When the mounted troops of Count Charles had reached Rome, he

170

purposed to assume his crown; and on the day of the Epiphany in the said year 1265, by two cardinal legates, despatched by the Pope to Rome, he was consecrated and crowned over the realm of Sicily and Apulia, he and his lady with great honour; and so soon as the festival of his coronation was ended, without any delay he set out with his host by way of the Campagna, towards the kingdom of Apulia, and Campagna; and very soon he had a large part thereof at his command without dispute. King Manfred hearing of their coming, to wit, first of the said Charles, and then of his people, and how through failure of his great host, which was in Lombardy, they had passed onward, was much angered. Immediately he gave all his care to defend the passes of the Kingdom, and at the pass at the bridge at Cepperano he placed the Count Giordano and the count of Caserta, the which were of the house of da Quona, with many followers, both foot and horse; and in San Germano he placed a great part of his German and Apulian barons, and all the Saracens of Nocera with bows and crossbows, and great store of arrows, trusting more in this defence than in any other, by reason of the strong place and the position, which has on the one side high mountains, and on the other marshes and stagnant waters, and was furnished with victuals and with all things necessary for more than two years. King Manfred having fortified the passes, as we have said, sent his ambassadors to King Charles to treat with him concerning a truce or peace; and their embassage being delivered, it was King Charles's will to make answer with his own mouth; and he said in his language, in French: "Allez, et ditez pour moi au sultan de Nocere, aujourdhui je mettrai lui en enfer, ou il mettra moi en paradis;" which was as much as to say: I will have nothing but battle, and in that battle, either he shall slay me, or I him; and this done without delay he set out on his road. It chanced that King Charles having arrived with his host at Fresolone in Campagna, as he was descending towards Cepperano, the said Count Giordano, which was defending that **Cf. Inf. xxviii. 16.** pass, seeing the king's followers coming to pass through, desired to defend the pass; the count of Caserta said that it was better to let some of them pass first so that they might seize them on the other side of the pass without stroke of sword. Count Giordano, when he saw the people increase, again desired to assail them in battle; then the count of Caserta, who was in the plot, said that the battle would be a great risk, seeing that too many of them had passed. Then Count Giordano, seeing the king's followers to be so powerful, abandoned the place and bridge, some say from fear, but more say on account of the pact made by the king with the count of Caserta, inasmuch as he loved not Manfred, who, of his inordinate lust, had forcibly ravished the count of Caserta's wife. Wherefore he held himself to be greatly shamed by him, and sought to avenge himself by this treachery. And to this we give faith, because he and his were among the first who gave themselves up to King Charles; and having left Cepperano, they did not return to the host of King Manfred at San Germano, but abode in their castles.

§ 6.—*How, after King Charles had taken the pass of Cepperano, he stormed the city of San Germano.*

1265 a.d.

When King Charles and his host had taken the pass of Cepperano, they took Aquino without opposition, and they stormed the stronghold of Arci, which is among the strongest in that country; and this done, they encamped the host before San Germano. The inhabitants of the city, by reason of the strength of the place, and because it was well furnished with men and with all things, held the followers of King Charles for nought, and in contempt they insulted the servants which were leading the horses to water, saying vile and shameful things, calling out: "Where is your little Charles?" For which reason the servants of the French began to skirmish, and to fight with those of the city, whereat all the host of the French rose in uproar, and fearing that the camp would be attacked, the French were all suddenly in arms, running towards the city; they within, not being on their guard, were not so quickly all in arms. The French with great fury assailed the city, fighting against it in many places; and those who could find no better protection, dismounting from their horses, took off their saddles, and with them on their heads went along under the walls and towers of the town. The count of Vendôme, with M. John, his brother, and with their standard, which were among the first to arm themselves, followed the grooms of the besieged which had sallied forth to skirmish, and pursuing them, entered the town together with them by a postern which was open to receive them; and this

172

was not without great peril, forasmuch as the gate was well guarded by many armed folk, and of those which followed the count of Vendôme and his brother, some were there slain and wounded, but they by their great courage and strength nevertheless were victorious in the combat around the gate by force of arms, and entered in, and straightway set their standard upon the walls. And among the first which followed them were the Guelf refugees from Florence, whereof Count Guido Guerra was captain, and the ensign was borne by Messer Stoldo Giacoppi de' Rossi; the which Guelfs at the taking of San Germano bore themselves marvellously and like good men, for the which thing the besiegers took heart and courage, and each one entered the city as he best could. The besieged, when they saw the standards of their enemies upon the walls, and the gate taken, fled in great numbers, and few of them remained to defend the town; wherefore King Charles's followers took the town of San Germano by assault, on the 10th day of February, 1265, and it was held to be a very great marvel, by reason of the strength of the town, and rather the work of God than of human strength, forasmuch as there were more than 1,000 horsemen within, and more than 5,000 footmen, among which there were many Saracen archers from Nocera; but by reason of a scuffle which arose the night before, as it pleased God, between the Christians and the Saracens, in the which the Saracens were vanquished, the next day they were not faithful in the defence of the city, and this among others was truly one of the causes why they lost the town of San Germano. Of Manfred's troops many were slain and taken, and the city was all overrun and robbed by the French; and there the king and his host abode some time to take repose and to learn the movements of Manfred.

§ 7.—*How King Manfred went to Benivento, and how he arrayed his troops to fight against King Charles.*

1265 a.d.

King Manfred, having heard the news of the loss of San Germano, and his discomfited troops having returned thence, he was much dismayed, and took counsel what he should do, and he was counselled by the Count Calvagno, and by the Count Giordano, and by the Count Bartolommeo, and by the Count Chamberlain, and by his other barons, to withdraw with all his forces to the city of Benivento, as a stronghold, in order that he might give battle on his own ground, and to the end he might withdraw towards Apulia if need were, and also to oppose the passage of King Charles, forasmuch as by no other way could he enter into the Principality and into Naples, or pass into Apulia save by the way of Benivento; and thus it was done. King Charles, hearing of the going of Manfred to Benivento, immediately departed from San Germano, to pursue him with his host; and he did not take the direct way of Capua, and by Terra di Lavoro, inasmuch as they could not have passed the bridge of Capua by reason of the strength of the towers of the bridge over the river, and the width of the river. But he determined to cross the river Volturno near Tuliverno, where it may be forded, whence he held on by the country of Alifi, and by the rough mountain paths of Beniventana, and without halting, and in great straits for money and victual, he arrived at the hour of noon at the foot of Benivento in the valley over against the city, distant by the space of two miles from the bank of the river Calore which flows at the foot of Benivento. King Manfred seeing the host of King Charles appear, having taken counsel, determined to fight and to sally forth to the field with his mounted troops, to attack the army of King Charles before they should be rested; but in this he did ill, for had he tarried one or two days, King Charles and his host would have perished or been captive without stroke of sword, through lack of provisions for them and for their horses; for the day before they arrived at the foot of Benivento, through want of victual, many of the troops had to feed on cabbages, and their horses on the stalks, without any other bread, or grain for the horses; and they had no more money to spend. Also the people and forces of King Manfred were much dispersed, for M. Conrad of Antioch was in Abruzzi with a following, Count Frederick was in Calabria, the count of Ventimiglia was in Sicily; so that, if he had tarried a while, his forces would have increased; but to whom God intends ill, him He deprives of wisdom. Manfred having sallied forth from Benivento with his followers, passed over the bridge which crosses the said river of Calore into the plain which is called S. Maria della Grandella, to a place called the Pietra a Roseto; here he formed three lines of battle or troops, the first was of Germans, in whom he had much confidence, who numbered fully 1,200 horse, of whom Count Calvagno was the captain; the second was of Tuscans and Lombards, and also of Germans, to the number of 1,000 horse, which was led by Count Giordano; the third, which Manfred led, was of Apulians with the Saracens of Nocera, which was of 1,400 horse, without the foot soldiers and the Saracen bowmen which were in great numbers.

§ 8.—*How King Charles arrayed his troops to fight against King Manfred.*
1265 a.d.

King Charles, seeing Manfred and his troops in the open field, and ranged for combat, took counsel whether he should offer battle on that day or should delay it. The most of his barons counselled him to abide till the coming morning, to repose the horses from the fatigue of the hard travel, and M. Giles le Brun, constable of France, said the contrary, and that by reason of delay the enemy would pluck up heart and courage, and that the means of living might fail them utterly, and that if others of the host did not desire to give battle, he alone, with his lord Robert of Flanders and with his followers, would adventure the chances of the combat, having confidence in God that they should win the victory against the enemies of Holy Church. Seeing this, King Charles gave heed to and accepted his counsel, and through the great desire which he had for the combat, he said with a loud voice to his knights, "Venu est le jour que nous avons tant desiré," and he caused the trumpets to be sounded, and commanded that every man should arm and prepare himself to go forth to battle; and thus in a little time it was done. And he ordered, after the fashion of his enemies, over against them, three principal bands: the first band was of Frenchmen to the number of 1,000 horse, whereof were captains Philip of Montfort and the marshal of Mirapoix; of the second King Charles with Count Guy of Montfort, and with many of his barons and of

175

the queen's knights, and with barons and knights of Provence, and Romans, and of the Campagna, which were about 900 horse; and the royal banners were borne by William, the standard-bearer, a man of great valour; the third was led by Robert, count of Flanders, with his Prefect of the camp, Marshal Giles of France, with Flemings, and men of Brabant, and of Aisne, and Picards, to the number of 700 horse. And besides these troops were the Guelf refugees from Florence, with all the Italians, and they were more than 400 horse, whereof many of the greater houses in Florence received knighthood from the hand of King Charles upon the commencement of the battle; and of these Guelfs of **Inf. xvi. 34-39.** Florence and of Tuscany Guido Guerra was captain, and their banner was borne in that battle by Conrad of Montemagno of Pistoia. And King Manfred seeing the bands formed, asked what folk were in the fourth band, which made a goodly show in arms and in horses and in ornaments and accoutrements: answer was made him that they were the Guelf refugees from Florence and from the other cities of Tuscany. Then did Manfred grieve, saying: "Where is the help that I receive from the Ghibelline party whom I have served so well, and on whom I have expended so much treasure?" And he said: "Those people (that is, the band of Guelfs) cannot lose to-day"; and that was as much as to say that if he gained the victory he would be the friend of the Florentine Guelfs, seeing them to be so faithful to their leader and to their party, and the foe of the Ghibellines.

§ 9.—*Concerning the battle between King Charles and King Manfred, and how King Manfred was discomfited and slain.*
1265 a.d.

The troops of the two kings being set in order on the plain of Grandella, after the aforesaid fashion, and each one of the said leaders having admonished his people to do well, and King Charles having given to his followers the cry, "Ho Knights, Monjoie!" and King Manfred to his, "Ho, Knights, for Suabia!" the bishop of Alzurro as papal legate absolved and blessed all the host of King Charles, remitting sin and penalty, forasmuch as they were fighting in the service of Holy Church. And this done, there began the fierce battle between the two first troops of the Germans and of the

176

French, and the assault of the Germans was so strong that they evilly entreated the French troop, and forced them to give much ground and they themselves took ground. The good King Charles seeing his followers so ill-bestead, did not keep to the order of the battle to defend himself with the second troop, considering that if the first troop of the French, in which he had full confidence, were routed, little hope of safety was there from the others; but immediately with his troop he went to succour the French troop, against that of the Germans, and when the Florentine refugees and their troop beheld King Charles strike into the battle, they followed boldly, and performed marvellous feats of arms that day, always following the person of King Charles; and the same did the good Giles le Brun, constable of France, with Robert of Flanders and his troop; and on the other side Count Giordano fought with his troop, wherefore the battle was fierce and hard, and endured for a long space, no one knowing who was getting the advantage, because the Germans by their valour and strength, smiting with their swords, did much hurt to the French. But suddenly there arose a great cry among the French troops, whosoever it was who began it, saying: "To your daggers! To your daggers! Strike at the horses!" And this was done, by the which thing in a short time the Germans were evilly entreated and much beaten down, and well-nigh turned to flight. King Manfred, who with his troop of Apulians remained ready to succour the host, beholding his followers not able to abide the conflict, exhorted the people of his troop that they should follow him into the battle, but they gave little heed to his word, for the greater part of the barons of Apulia and of the Kingdom, among others the Count Chamberlain, and him of Acerra and him of Caserta, and others, either through cowardice of heart, or seeing that they were coming by the worse, and there are those who say through treachery, as faithless **Cf. Inf. xxviii. 16.** folk, and desirous of a new lord, failed Manfred, abandoning him and fleeing, some towards Abruzzi and some towards the city of Benivento. Manfred, being left with few followers, did as a valiant lord, who would rather die in battle as king than flee with shame; and whilst he was putting on his helmet, a silver eagle which he wore as crest fell down before him on his saddle bow; and he seeing this, was much dismayed, and said to the barons, which were beside him, in Latin: "*Hoc est signum Dei,* for I fastened this crest

177

with my own hand after such a fashion that it should not have been possible for it to fall"; yet for all this he did not give up, but as a valiant lord he took heart, and immediately entered into the battle, without the royal insignia, so as not to be recognised as king, but like any other noble, striking bravely into the thickest of the fight; nevertheless, his followers endured but a little while, for they were already turning; and straightway they were routed and King Manfred slain in **Purg. iii. 118, 119.** the midst of his enemies, it was said by a French esquire, but it was not known for certain. In that battle there was great mortality both on the one side and on the other, but much more among the followers of Manfred; and whilst they were fleeing from the field towards Benivento, they were pursued by the army of King Charles, which followed them as far as the city (for night was already falling), and took the city of Benivento and those who were fleeing. Many chief barons of King Manfred were taken; among the others were taken Count Giordano, and Messer Piero Asino degli Uberti; which two King Charles sent captive to Provence, and there he caused them to die a cruel death in prison. The other Apulian and German barons he kept in prison in divers places in the Kingdom; and a few days after, the wife of the said Manfred, and his children and his sister, who were in Nocera of the Saracens in Apulia, were delivered as prisoners to King Charles, and they afterwards died in his prison. And without doubt there came upon Manfred and his heirs the malediction of God, and right clearly was shown the judgment of God upon him because he was excommunicated, and the enemy and persecutor of Holy Church. At his end, search was made for Manfred for more than three days, and he could not be found, and it was not known if he was slain, or taken, or escaped, because he had not borne royal insignia in the battle; at last he was recognised by one of his own camp-followers by sundry marks on his person, in the midst of the battle-field; and his body being found by the said camp-follower, he threw it across an ass he had and went his way crying, "Who buys Manfred? Who buys Manfred?" And one of the king's barons chastised this fellow and brought the body of Manfred before the king, who caused all the barons which had been taken prisoners to come together, and having asked each one if it was Manfred, they all timidly said Yes. When Count Giordano came, he smote his hands against his face, weeping and crying: "Alas, alas, my lord," wherefor he was commended by the French; and some of the barons prayed the king that he would give Manfred the honour of sepulture; but the king made answer: "*Je le fairois volontiers, s'il ne fût excommunié*"; but forasmuch as he was excommunicated, King Charles would not have him laid in a holy place; but at the foot of the bridge of Benivento he was buried, and upon his grave each one of the host threw a stone; **Purg. iii. 124-132.** whence there arose a great heap of stones. But by some it was said that afterwards, by command of the Pope, the bishop of Cosenza had him taken from that sepulchre, and sent him forth from the Kingdom which was Church land, and he was buried beside the river of Verde [Garigliano], on the borders of the Kingdom and Campagna; this, however, we do not affirm. This battle and defeat was on a Friday, the last day of February, in the year of Christ 1265.

§ 10.—*How King Charles had the lordship of the Kingdom and of Sicily, and how Don Henry of Spain came to him.* § 11.—*How the Saracens of Berber passed into Spain, and how they were there routed.* § 12.—*How the Florentine Ghibellines laid siege to Castelnuovo in* **1266 a.d.** *Valdarno, and how they departed thence worsted.*

§ 13.—*How the Thirty-six were established in Florence, and how the Guilds of Arts were formed and standards given thereto.*

1266 a.d.

When the news came to Florence and to Tuscany of the discomfiture of Manfred, the Ghibellines and the Germans began to be discouraged and to fear in all places; and the Guelf refugees from Florence, which were in rebellion, and those who were under bounds in the territory, and in many places, began to be strengthened and to take heart and courage, and coming nearer to the city, plotted changes and mutations within the city, by compacts with their friends within, which had understanding with them, and they came as far as to the Servi of S. Maria to take counsel, having hope from their people which had been at the victory with King Charles, from whom with his French folk they were expecting aid; wherefore the people of Florence, which were at heart more Guelf than Ghibelline, through the losses they had received, one of his father, another of his son, a third of his brothers, at the defeat of Montaperti, likewise began to take courage, and to murmur and to talk through the city, complaining of the spendings and the outrageous burdens which they endured from Count Guido Novello, and from the others which were ruling the city; whence those which were ruling the city of Florence for the Ghibelline party, hearing in the city the said tumult and murmuring, and fearing lest the people should rebel against them, by a sort of half measure, and to content the people, chose two knights of the Jovial Friars of **Inf. xxiii. 103-108.** Bologna as Podestàs of Florence, of which one was named M. Catalano of the Malavolti, and the other M. Roderigo of Landolo, one held to be of the party of the Guelfs, to wit, M. Catalano, and the other of the party of the Ghibellines. And note that Jovial Friars was the name of the Knights of S. Mary, and they became knights when they took that habit, for they wore a white gown and a grey mantle; and for arms, a white field with a red cross and two stars; and they were bound to defend widows, and children under ward, and to be peace makers; and other ordinances they had, as religious persons. And the said M. Roderigo was the beginner of this Order; but it endured but a short while, for the fact followed the name, to wit, they gave themselves more to joviality than to aught else. These two friars were brought thither by the people of Florence, and they put them in the People's Palace over against the Badia, believing that by virtue of their habit they would be impartial, and would guard the commonwealth from extravagant spendings; the which, albeit in heart they were of diverse parties, under cover of false hypocrisy were at one, more for their own gain than for the public weal; and they ordained thirty-six good men, merchants and artificers of the greatest and best which there were in the city, the which were to give counsel to the said two Podestàs, and were to provide for the spendings of the commonwealth; and of this number were both Guelfs and Ghibellines, popolani and magnates which were to be trusted, which had remained in Florence at the banishment of the Guelfs. And the said thirty-six met together every day to take counsel as to the common well-being of the city, in the shop and court of the consuls of Calimala, which was at the foot of the house of the Cavalcanti in the Mercato Nuovo; the which made many good ordinances for the common weal of the city, among which they decreed that each one of the seven principal Arts in Florence should have a college of consuls, and each should have its ensign and standard, to the intent that, if any one in the city rose with force of arms, they might under their ensigns stand for the defence of the people and of the commonwealth. And the ensigns of the seven greater Arts were these: the judges and notaries, an azure field charged with a large golden star; the merchants of Calimala, to wit, of French cloths, a red field with a golden eagle on a white globe; money changers, a red field sewn with golden florins; wool merchants, a red field charged with a white sheep; physicians and apothecaries, a red field, thereupon S. Mary with her son Christ in her arms; silk merchants and mercers, a white field charged with a red gate, from the title of Porta Sante Marie; furriers, arms vair, and in one corner an Agnus Dei upon an azure field. The next five, following upon the greater arts, were regulated afterwards when the office of Priors of the Arts was created, as in time hereafter we shall make mention; and they had assigned to them after a similar fashion to the seven Arts, standards and arms: to wit, the Baldrigari (that is, retail merchants of Florentine cloths, of stockings, of linen cloths, and hucksters), white and red standard; butchers, a yellow field with a black goat; shoemakers, the transverse stripes, white and black, known as the pezza gagliarda [gallant piece]; workers in stone and in timber, a red field charged with the saw, and the axe, and the hatchet, and the pick-axe; smiths and iron workers, a white field charged with large black pincers.

§ 14.—*How the second Popolo rose in Florence, for the which cause Count Guido Novello, with the Ghibelline leaders, left Florence.*

1266 a.d.

By reason of the said doings in Florence by the said two Podestàs and the Thirty-six, the Ghibelline magnates in Florence, such as the Uberti, the Fifanti, and Lamberti, and Scolari, and the others of the great Ghibelline houses, began to have their factious fears raised, for it seemed to them that the said Thirty-six supported and favoured the Guelf popolani which had remained in Florence, and that every change was against their party. Through this jealousy, and because of the news of the victory of King Charles, Count Guido Novello sent for help to all the neighbouring allies, such as were the Pisans, Sienese, Aretines, Pistoians, and them of Prato, of Volterra, Colle, and Sangimignano, so that with 600 Germans which he had, his horsemen in Florence numbered 1,500. It came to pass that in order to pay the German troops, which were with Count Guido Novello, captain of the league, he required that an impost of 10 per cent. should be levied; and the said Thirty-six sought some other method of finding the money, less burdensome to the people. For this cause, when they delayed some days longer than appeared fitting to the Count and to the other great Ghibellines of Florence, by reason of the suspicion which they felt concerning the ordinances made by the Popolo, the said nobles determined to put the town in an uproar, and destroy the office of the said Thirty-six, with the help of the great body of horse which the vicar had in Florence; and when they were armed, the first that began were the Lamberti, which with their armed troops sallied forth from their houses in Calimala, saying, "Where are these thieving Thirty-six, that we may cut them all in pieces?" which Thirty-six were then taking counsel together in the shop where the consuls of Calimala administered justice, under the house of the Cavalcanti in the Mercato Nuovo. When the Thirty-six heard this they broke up the council, and straightway the town rose in uproar, and the shops were closed, and every man flew to arms. The people all gathered in the wide street of Santa Trinita, and Messer Gianni de' Soldanieri made himself head of **Inf. xxxii. 121.** the people to the end he might rise in estate, not considering the end, that it must bring about loss to the Ghibelline party, and damage to himself, which seems always to have happened in Florence to whomsoever becomes head of the people; and thus armed, at the foot of the house of the Soldanieri, the popolani gathered in very great numbers and put up barricades at the foot of the tower of the Girolami. Count Guido Novello, with all the horsemen and with the Ghibelline magnates of Florence, was in arms and mounted in the piazza of S. Giovanni; and they advanced against the people, and drew up before the barricade on the ruins of the houses of the Tornaquinci, and made some show and attempt at fighting, and some mounted Germans passed within the barricade; the people defended it boldly with crossbows and by hurling missiles from the towers and houses. When the Count saw that they could not dislodge the people, he reversed the banners and returned with all the horsemen to the piazza of S. Giovanni, and then came to the palace on the piazza of S. Apollinari, where were the two Podestàs, M. Catalano and M. Roderigo, the Jovial Friars; the horsemen meanwhile having command of the city from Porte San Piero as far as San Firenze. The Count demanded the keys of the gates of the city to depart from the town; and for fear missiles should be hurled at him from the houses, he had for his safety on one side of him Uberto de' Pucci, and on the other Cerchio dei Cerchi, and behind him Guidingo Savorigi, which were of the said Thirty-six, and among the greatest in the town. The said two friars were crying from the palace, demanding with loud voices that the said Uberto and Cerchio should come to them, to the end they might pray the Count to return to his house and not depart; and they themselves would quiet the people, and see that the soldiers were paid. The Count being in greater suspicion and fear of the people than was called for, would not wait, but would only have the keys of the gate; and this showed that it was more the work of God than any other cause; for that great and puissant body of horse had not been opposed nor driven out, nor dismissed, nor was there any force of enemies against them; for albeit the people were armed and gathered together, this was more from fear than to oppose the Count and his horsemen, and they would soon have been quieted, and have returned to their houses, and laid down their arms. But when the judgment of God is ripe, the occasion is ever at hand. When the Count had gotten the keys, during a great silence, he caused a cry to be made whether all the Germans were there; he was told that they were. Then the same was asked concerning the Pisans, and likewise concerning all the cities of the league; and when he knew that all were there, he gave orders to his standard-bearer to advance with banners, and this was done; and they took the wide road of San Firenze, and behind San Pietro Scheraggio and San Romeo to the old Ox Gate, and when this was opened, the Count, with all his horsemen, sallied forth, and held on by the moats behind San Jacopo, and by the piazza of Santa Croce, where as yet there were no houses, and along the Borgo di Pinti; and there stones were cast upon them; and they turned by Cafaggio, and in the evening went to Prato; and this was on S. Martin's Day, the 11th day of November, in the year of Christ 1266.

§ 15.—*How the Popolo restored the Guelfs to Florence, and how they afterwards drave out the Ghibellines.*

1266 a.d.

183

When Count Guido Novello, with all his horsemen and with many Ghibelline leaders of Florence, reached Prato, they perceived that they had done very foolishly in departing from the city of Florence, without stroke of sword and not driven thence, and they perceived that they had done ill, and took counsel to return to Florence the following morning; and this they did; and they came all armed and in battle array at the hour of tierce to the gate of the Carraia Bridge, where is now the borough of Ognissanti, but there were no houses then; and they demanded that the gate should be opened to them. The people of Florence were in arms, and for fear lest the Count, returning with his horsemen into Florence, might take vengeance upon them and devastate the city, agreed together not to open the gate, but to defend the city, which was very strong, with walls and with moats full of water around the second circle; and when they would have made a dash for the gate, they were shot at and wounded; and there they abode until after noon, and neither by persuasions nor by threats were they allowed to enter in. They returned to Prato gloomy and shamed, and as they were returning, being angry, they attacked the fortress of Capalle, but did not take it. And when they came to Prato they bitterly reproached each other; but after a thing ill-judged, and worse carried out, repentance is in vain. The Florentines which were left reorganized the town, and dismissed the said two Podestàs, the Jovial Friars of Bologna, and sent to Orvieto for aid in soldiers, and for a Podestà and Captain, which Orvietans sent 100 horsemen to guard the city, and M. Ormanno Monaldeschi was Podestà, and another gentleman of Orvieto was the Captain of the People. And by a treaty of peace, the following January the Popolo restored to Florence both Guelfs and Ghibellines, and caused many marriages and alliances to be made between them, among the which these were the chief: that M. Bonaccorso Bellincioni degli Adimari gave for wife to M. Forese, his son, the daughter of Count Guido Novello, and M. Bindo, his brother, took one of the Ubaldini; and M. Cavalcante, of the Cavalcanti, gave **Cf. Inf. x. 58-69, 110, 111. Purg. xi. 97-99.** for wife to his son Guido the daughter of M. Farinata degli Uberti; and M. Simone Donati gave his daughter to M. Azzolino, son of M. Farinata degli Uberti; for the which alliances the other Guelfs of Florence distrusted their loyalty to the party; and for the said **Vita Nuova iii. 96-104; xxiv. 18, 19; xxv. 111-113; xxxi. 21-24;**

184

reason the said peace endured but a little while; for when the said Guelfs had returned to Florence, feeling themselves stronger and emboldened by the victory which they had gained over Manfred, with King Charles, they sent secretly into Apulia to the said King Charles for soldiers, and for a captain, and he sent Count Guy of Montfort, with 800 French horsemen, and he came to Florence on Easter Day of the Resurrection in the year of Christ 1267. And when the Ghibellines heard of his coming, the night before they departed from Florence without stroke of sword, and some went to Siena, and some to Pisa, and to other places. The Florentine Guelfs gave the lordship over the city to King Charles for ten years, and when they sent him their free and full election by solemn embassy, with authority over life and death and in lesser judgments, the king answered that he desired from the Florentines their love and good-will and no other jurisdiction; nevertheless, at the prayer of the commonwealth he accepted it simply, and sent thither year by year his vicars; and he appointed twelve good citizens to rule the city with the vicar. And it may be noted concerning this banishment of the Ghibellines, that it was on the same day, Easter Day of the Resurrection, whereon they had committed the murder of M. Bondelmonte de' Bondelmonti, whence the factions in Florence broke out, and the city was laid waste; and it seemed like a **Cf. Inf. x. 51.** judgment from God, for never afterwards did they return to their estate.

§ 16.—*How, after the Ghibellines had been driven from Florence, the ordinances and councils of the city were reorganized.*
1267 a.d.

When the Guelf party had returned to Florence, and the vicar or Podestà was come from King Charles (the first of them being M. . . .), and after twelve good men had been appointed, as of old the Ancients, to rule the republic, the council was re-made of 100 good men of the people, without whose deliberation no great thing or cost could be carried out; and after any measure had been passed in this council, it was put to the vote in the council of the colleges of consuls of the greater Arts, and the council of the credenza [privy council of the Captain of the People] of eighty. These councillors,

185

which, when united with the general council, numbered 300, were all popolani and Guelfs. After measures had been passed in the said councils, the following day the same proposals were brought before the councils of the Podestà, first before the council of ninety, including both magnates and popolani (and with them associated yet again the colleges of consuls of the Arts), and then before the general council, which was of 300 men of every condition; and these were called the occasional councils; and they had in their gift governorships of fortresses, and dignities, and small and great offices. And this ordered, they appointed revisors, and corrected all statutes and ordinances, and ordered that they should be issued each year. In this manner was ordered the state and course of the commonwealth and of the people of Florence at the return of the Guelfs; and the chancellors of finance were the monks of Settimo and of Ognissanti on alternate half-years.

§ 17.—*How the Guelfs of Florence instituted the Ordinances of the Party.*
1267 a.d.

In these times, when the Ghibellines had been driven out from Florence, the Guelfs which had returned thither being at strife concerning the goods of the Ghibelline rebels, sent their ambassadors to the court, to Pope Urban and to King Charles, to order their affairs, which Pope Urban and King Charles for their estate and peace ordered them in this manner, that the goods should be divided into three parts—one part to be given to the commonwealth, the second to be awarded in compensation to the Guelfs which had been ruined and exiled, the third to be awarded for a certain time to the "Guelf Party"; but afterwards all the said goods fell to the Party, whence they formed a fund, and increased it every day, as a reserve against the day of need of the Party; concerning which fund, when the Cardinal Ottaviano degli Ubaldini heard thereof, he said, "Since the Guelfs of **Cf. Inf. x. 120.** Florence are funding a reserve, the Ghibellines will never return thither." And by the command of the Pope and the king, the said Guelfs made three knights heads of the Party, and called them at first consuls of the knights, and afterwards they called them Captains of the Party, and they held office for two months, the sesti electing them alternately, three and three; and they gathered to their councils in the new church of Santa Maria Sopra Porta, being the most central place in the city, and where there are most Guelf houses around; and their privy council consisted of fourteen, and their larger council of sixty magnates and popolani, by whose vote were elected the Captains of the Party and other officers. And they called three magnates and three popolani Priors of the Party, to whom were committed the order and care of the money of the Party; and also one to hold the seal, and a syndic to prosecute the Ghibellines. And all their secret documents they deposited in the church of the Servi Sancte Marie. After like manner the Ghibelline refugees made ordinances and captains. We have said enough of the Ordinances of the Party, and we will return to the general events, and to other things.

§ 18.—*How the soldan of the Saracens took Antioch.* § 19.—*How the Guelfs of Florence took the castle of Santellero, with many Ghibelline rebels.* § 20.—*How many cities and towns of Tuscany went over to the Guelf party.* § 21.—*How King Charles's marshal advanced upon Siena with the Florentines, and how the king came to Florence and took Poggibonizzi.* § 22.—*How King Charles with the Florentines marched upon the city of Pisa.*

§ 23.—*How the young Conradino, son of King Conrad, came from Germany into Italy against King Charles.*

1267 a.d.

King Charles being in Tuscany, the Ghibelline refugees from Florence formed themselves into a league and company with the Pisans and Sienese, and came to an agreement with Don Henry of Spain, which was Roman senator, and already at enmity with King Charles, his cousin. Therefore, with certain barons of Apulia and Sicily, he made oath and conspiracy to make certain towns in Sicily and in Apulia to rebel, and to send into Germany, and to stir up Conradino, which was the son of Conrad, the son of the Emperor Frederick, to cross into Italy to take away Sicily and the Kingdom from King Charles. And so it was done; for immediately in Apulia there rose in rebellion Nocera of the Saracens, and Aversa in Terra di Lavoro, and many places in Calabria, and almost all in Abruzzi, if we except Aquila, and in Sicily almost all, or a great part of the island of Sicily, if we except Messina and Palermo; and Don Henry caused Rome to rebel, and all

187

Campagna and the country around; and the Pisans and the Sienese and the other Ghibelline cities sent of their money 100,000 golden florins to stir up the said Conradino, who being very young, sixteen years old, set forth from Germany, against his mother's will, who was daughter of the duke of Austria, and who was not willing for him to depart because of his youth. And he came to Verona in the month of February, in the year of Christ 1267, with many barons and good men-at-arms from Germany in his train; and it is said that there followed him as far as Verona nigh upon 10,000 men on horses or ponies, but through lack of means a great part returned to Germany, yet there remained of the best 3,500 German cavalry. And from Verona he passed through Lombardy, and by the way of Pavia he came to the coast of Genoa, and arrived beyond Saona at the shores of Varagine, and there put out to sea, and by means of the forces of the Genoese, with their fleet of twenty-five galleys, came by sea to Pisa, and arrived there in May in 1268, and by the Pisans **1268 a.d.** and by all the Ghibellines of Italy was received with great honour, almost as if he had been Emperor. His cavalry came by land, crossing the mountains of Pontremoli, and arrived at Serrazzano, which was held by the Pisans, and then took the way of the seacoast with an escort as far as Pisa. King Charles, hearing how Conradino was come into Italy, and hearing of the rebellion of his cities in Sicily and Apulia, caused by the treacherous barons of the Kingdom (the most of whom he had released from prison), and by Don Henry of Spain, immediately departed from Tuscany, and by hasty marches came into Apulia, and left in Tuscany M. William di Belselve, his marshal, and with him M. William, the standard-bearer, with 800 French and Provençal horsemen to keep the cities of Tuscany for his party, and to oppose Conradino so that he should not be able to pass. And Pope Clement, hearing of the coming of Conradino, sent to him his messengers and legates, commanding him, under pain of excommunication, not to go forward, nor to oppose King Charles, the champion and vicar of Holy Church. But Conradino did not by reason of this abandon his enterprise, nor would he obey the commands of the Pope, forasmuch as he believed that his cause was just, and that the Kingdom and Sicily were his, and of his patrimony, and therefore he fell under sentence of excommunication from the Church, which he despised and cared little for; but being in Pisa, he collected money and people, and all the Ghibellines and whosoever belonged to the imperial party, gathered themselves to him, whence his force grew greatly. And being in Pisa, his host marched against the city of Lucca, which was held for the party of Holy Church, and within it were the marshal of King Charles with his people, and the legate of the Pope and of the Church, with the forces of the Florentines and of the other Guelfs of Tuscany, and with many who had taken the cross, and through proclamations and indulgences and pardons given by the Pope and by his legates, had come against Conradino; and he remained over against Lucca ten days with his host; and the two hosts met together to fight at Ponterotto, two miles distant from Lucca, but they did not fight, but each one shunned the battle, and they remained one on each side of the Guiscianella; so they returned, the one part to Pisa, and the other to Lucca.

§ 24.—*How the marshal of King Charles was defeated at Ponte a Valle by Conradino's army.*

1268 a.d.

Then Conradino departed with his followers from Pisa, and came to Poggibonizzi, and when the inhabitants thereof heard how Conradino was come to Pisa, they rebelled against King Charles and against the commonwealth of Florence, and sent the keys to Pisa to Conradino. And then from Poggibonizzi he went to Siena, and by the Sienese was received with great honour; and whilst he sojourned in Siena, the marshal of King Charles, which was called, as we have said, M. William di Belselve, with his people, departed from Florence on S. John's Day in June to go to Arezzo to hinder the movements of Conradino; and by the Florentines they were escorted and accompanied as far as Montevarchi; and they desired to accompany him till he should be nigh unto Arezzo, hearing that the journey was like to be disputed, and fearing an ambush in the region round about Arezzo. The said marshal, being beyond measure confident in his people, would have the Florentines accompany him no further, and in front of the cavalcade he set M. William, the standard-bearer, with 300 horsemen well armed and in readiness, and he passed on safe and sound. The marshal, with 500 of his horsemen, not on their guard nor keeping their ranks, and for the

189

most part unarmed, prepared to advance, and when they came to the bridge at Valle which crosses the Arno nigh to Laterino, there sallied forth upon their rear an ambush of the followers of Conradino, which, hearing of the march of the said marshal, had departed from Siena under conduct of the Ubertini and other Ghibelline refugees from Florence; and being come to the said bridge, the French, not being prepared, and without much defence, were defeated and slain, and the greater part were taken, and those which fled towards Valdarno to the region round about Florence were taken and spoiled as if they had been enemies; and the said M. William, the marshal, and M. Amelio di Corbano, and many other barons and knights were taken and brought to Siena to Conradino, and this was the day after the Feast of S. John, the 25th day of the month of June, in the year of Christ 1268. At which defeat and capture the followers of King Charles and all those of the Guelf party were much dismayed, and Conradino and his people increased thereupon in great pride and courage, and held the French almost for naught. And this being heard in the Kingdom, many cities rebelled against King Charles. And at this time King Charles was at the siege of the city of Nocera of the Saracens in Apulia, which had rebelled, to the end that the others on the coast of Apulia, which were all subject to him, might not rebel against him.

§ 25.—*How Conradino entered into Rome, and afterwards with his host passed into the kingdom of Apulia.*
1268 a.d.

Conradino, having sojourned somewhat in Siena, departed to Rome, and by the Romans and by Don Henry, the senator, was received with great honour, as if he had been Emperor, and in Rome he gathered together people and money, and despoiled the treasures of S. Peter and the other churches of Rome to raise monies; and he had in Rome more than 5,000 horsemen, what with Germans and Italians, together with those of the senator, Don Henry, brother of the king of Spain, which had with him full 800 good Spanish horsemen. And Conradino, hearing that King Charles was with his host in Apulia at the city of Nocera, and that many of the cities and barons of the Kingdom had rebelled, and that others were suspected, it seemed to him a convenient time to enter into the Kingdom, and he departed from Rome the 10th day of August, in the year of Christ 1268, with the said Don Henry, and with his company and his barons, and with many Romans; and he did not take the way of Campagna, forasmuch as he knew that the pass of Cepperano was furnished and guarded; wherefore he did not desire to contest it, but took the way of the mountains between the Abruzzi and the Campagna by Valle di Celle, where there was no guard nor garrison; and without any hindrance he passed on and came into the plain of San Valentino in the country of Tagliacozzo.

§ 26.—*How the host of Conradino and that of King Charles met in battle at Tagliacozzo.*

1268 a.d.

King Charles, hearing how Conradino was departed from Rome with his followers to enter into the Kingdom, broke up his camp at Nocera, and with all his people came against Conradino by hasty marches, and at the city of Aquila in Abruzzi awaited his followers. And being at Aquila, he took counsel with the men of the city, exhorting them to be leal and true, and to make provision for the host; whereupon a wise and ancient inhabitant rose and said: "King Charles, take no further counsel, and do not avoid a little toil, to the end thou mayest have continual repose. Delay no longer, but go against the enemy, and let him not gain ground, and we will be leal and true to thee." The king, hearing such sage counsel, without any delay or further parley, departed by the road crossing the mountains, and came close to the host of Conradino in the place and plain of San Valentino, and there was nought between them save the river of . . . King Charles had of his people, between Frenchmen and Provençals and Italians, less than 3,000 cavaliers, and seeing that Conradino had many more people than he, he took the counsel of the good M. Alardo di Valleri, a French knight of great wisdom and prowess, which at that time had arrived in **Inf. xxviii. 17, 18.** Apulia from over seas from the Holy Land, who said to King Charles, if he desired to be victorious it behoved him to use stratagems of war rather than force. King Charles, trusting much in the wisdom of the said M. Alardo, committed to him the entire direction of the host and of the battle, who drew up the

191

king's followers in three troops, and of one he made captain M. Henry of Cosance, tall in person, and a good knight at arms; he was armed with royal insignia in place of the king's person, and led Provençals and Tuscans and Lombards, and men of the Campagna. The second troop was of Frenchmen, whereof were captains M. Jean de Cléry, and M. William, the standard-bearer; and he put the Provençals to guard the bridge over the said river, to the end the host of Conradino might not pass without the disadvantage of combat. King Charles, with the flower of his chivalry and barons, to the number of 800 cavaliers, he placed in ambush behind a little hill in a valley, and with King Charles there remained the said M. Alardo di Valleri, with M. William de Ville, and Arduino, prince of the Morea, a right valiant knight. Conradino, on the other side, formed his followers in three troops, one of Germans, whereof he was captain with the duke of Austria, and with many counts and barons; the second of Italians, whereof he made captain Count Calvagno, with certain Germans; the third was of Spaniards, whereof was captain Don Henry of Spain, their lord. In this array, one host over against the other, the rebel barons of the Kingdom guilefully, in order to cause dismay to King Charles and his followers, caused false ambassadors to come into the camp of Conradino, in full pomp, with keys in their hands, and with large presents, saying that they were sent from the commonwealth of Aquila to give him the keys and the lordship of the city, as his men and faithful subjects, to the end he might deliver them from the tyranny of King Charles. For which cause the host of Conradino and he himself, deeming it to be true, rejoiced greatly; and this being heard in the host of King Charles caused great dismay, forasmuch as they feared to lose the victual which came to them from that side, and also the aid of the men of Aquila. The king himself, hearing this, was seized with so great pangs that in the night season he set forth with a few of the host in his company, and came to Aquila that same night, and causing the guards at the gates to be asked for whom they held the city, they answered, For King Charles: who, having entered in without dismounting from his horse, having exhorted them to good watch, immediately returned to the host, and was there early in the morning: and because of the weariness of going and returning by night from Aquila, King Charles laid him down and slept.

§ 27.—*How Conradino and his people were defeated by King Charles.*

1268 a.d.

Now Conradino and his host were puffed up with the vain hope that Aquila had rebelled against King Charles, and therefore, all drawn up in battle array, they raised their battle cry, and made a vigorous rush to force the passages of the river and engage with King Charles. King Charles, albeit he was reposing, as we have said, hearing the din of the enemy, and how they were in arms and ready for battle, immediately caused his followers to arm and array themselves after the order and fashion whereof we before made mention. And the troop of the Provençals, which was led by M. Henry of Cosance, being at guard on the bridge to hinder the passing of Don Henry of Spain and his people, the Spaniards set themselves to ford the river, which was not very great, and began to enclose the troop of Provençals which were defending the bridge. Conradino and the rest of his host, seeing the Spaniards had crossed, began to pass the river, and with great fury assailed the followers of King Charles, and in a short time had routed and defeated the Provençal troop; and the said M. Henry of Cosance; and the standard of King Charles was beaten down, and M. Henry himself was slain. Don Henry and the Germans, believing they had got King Charles in person, inasmuch as he wore the royal insignia, all fell upon him at once. And the said Provençal troop being routed, they dealt in like fashion with the French and the Italian troop, which was led by M. Jean de Cléry and M. William, the standard-bearer, because the followers of Conradino were two to one against those of King Charles, and very fierce and violent in battle; and the followers of King Charles, seeing themselves thus sore bestead, took to flight, and abandoned the field. The Germans believed themselves victorious, not knowing of King Charles's ambush, and began to scatter themselves over the field, giving their minds to plunder and booty. King Charles was upon the little hill above the valley, where was his troop, with M. Alardo di Valleri, and with Count Guy of Montfort, beholding the battle; and when he saw his people thus routed, first one troop and then the other thus put to flight, he was deadly grieved, and longed even to put in motion his own troop to go to the succour of the others. M. Alardo, which was commander of the host, and wise in war, **Inf. xxviii. 17, 18.** with great temperance and with wise words much restrained the king, saying that for God's sake he should suffer it a while, if he desired the honour of the victory, because he knew the cupidity of the Germans, and how greedy they were for booty; and he must let them break up more from their troops; and when he saw them well scattered, he said to the king: "Let the banners set forth, for now it is time;" and so it was done. And when the said troop sallied forth from the valley, neither Conradino nor his followers believed that they were enemies, but that they were of their own party; and they were not upon their guard; and the king, coming with his followers in close ranks, came straight to where was the troop of Conradino, with the chief among his barons, and there began fierce and violent combat, albeit it endured not long, seeing that the followers of Conradino were faint and weary with fighting, and had not near so many horsemen in battle array as those of the king, forasmuch as the greater part were wandering out of the ranks, some pursuing the enemy and some scattered over the field in search of booty and prisoners; and the troop of Conradino, by reason of the unexpected assault of the enemy, was continually diminishing, and that of King Charles continually increasing, because his first troops, which had been put to flight through the first defeat, recognising the royal standard, joined on to his company, insomuch that in a little while Conradino and his followers were discomfited. And when Conradino perceived that the fortunes of war were against him, by the counsel of his greater barons he took to flight, together with the duke of Austria, and Count Calvagno, and Count Gualferano, and Count Gherardo da Pisa, and many more. M. Alardo di Valleri, seeing the enemy put to flight, cried aloud, praying and entreating the king and the captains of the troop not to set forth either in pursuit of the enemy or other prey, fearing lest the followers of Conradino should gather together, or should sally forth from some ambush, but to abide firm and in order on the field; and so was it done. And this was very fortunate, for Don Henry, with his Spaniards, and other Germans, which had pursued into a valley the Provençals and Italians whom they had first discomfited, and which had not seen King Charles offer battle nor the discomfiture of Conradino, had now gathered his men together, and was returning to the field; and seeing King Charles' troop, he believed them to be Conradino and his following, so that he came down from the hill where he had assembled his men, to come to his allies; and when he drew nigh unto them, he recognised the standards of the enemy, and how much deceived he had been; and he was sore dismayed; but, like the valiant lord he was, he rallied and closed up his troop after such a fashion that King Charles and his followers, which were spent by the toils of the combat, did not venture to strike into Don Henry's troop, and to the end they might not risk the game already won, they abode in array over against one another a good space. The good M. Alardo, seeing this, said to the king that they must needs make the enemy break their ranks in order to rout them; whereon the king bade him act after his mind. Then he took of the best barons of the king's troop from twenty to thirty, and they set forth from the troop, as though they fled for fear, as he had instructed them. The Spaniards, seeing how the standard-bearers of sundry of these lords were wheeling round as though in act to flee, with vain hope began to cry: "They are put to flight," and began to leave their own ranks, desiring to pursue them. King Charles, seeing gaps and openings in the troop of Spaniards, and others on the German side, began boldly to strike among them, and M. Alardo with his men wisely gathered themselves together and returned to the troop. Then was the battle fierce and hard; but the Spaniards were well armed, and by stroke of sword might not be struck to the ground, and continually after their fashion they drew close together. Then began the French to cry out wrathfully, and to take hold of them by the arms and drag them from their horses after the manner of tournaments; and this was done to such good purpose that in a short time they were routed, and defeated, and put to flight, and many of them lay dead on the field. Don Henry, with many of his followers, fled to Monte Cascino, and said that King Charles was defeated. The abbot, which was lord of those lands, knew Don Henry, and judging by divers signs that they were fugitives, caused him and great part of his people to be seized. King Charles, with all his followers, remained upon the field, armed and on horseback, until the night, to the end he might gather together his men, and to be sure of full victory over the enemy; and this defeat was on the vigil of S. Bartholomew, on the 23rd day of August, in the year of Christ 1268. And in that place King Charles afterwards caused a rich abbey to be built for the souls of his men which had been slain; which is called S. Mary of the Victory, in the plain of

Tagliacozzo.

Conradino, with the duke of Austria and with many others, which were fled from the field with him, arrived at the beach towards Rome upon the seashore hard by a place which is called Asturi, which pertained to the Infragnipani, noblemen of Rome; and when they were come thither, they had a pinnace furnished to pass into Sicily, hoping to escape from King Charles; and in Sicily, which had almost all rebelled against the king, to recover state and lordship. They having already embarked unrecognised on the said vessel, one of the said Infragnipani which was in Asturi, seeing that they were in great part Germans, and fine men and of noble aspect, and knowing of the defeat, was minded to gain riches for himself, and therefore he took the said lords prisoners; and having learnt of their conditions, and how Conradino was among them, he led them captive to King Charles, for which cause the king gave him land and lordship at Pilosa, between Naples and Benivento. And when the king had Conradino and those lords in his hands, he took counsel what he should do. At last he was minded to put them to death, and he caused by way of process an inquisition to be made against them, as against traitors to the Crown and enemies of Holy Church, and this was carried out; for on the . . . day were **Purg. xx. 68.** beheaded Conradino, and the duke of Austria, and Count Calvagno, and Count Gualferano, and Count Bartolommeo and two of his sons, and Count Gherardo of the counts of Doneratico of Pisa, on the market place at Naples, beside the stream of water which runs over against the church of the Carmelite friars; and the king would not suffer them to be buried in a sacred place, but under the sand of the market place, forasmuch as they were excommunicate. And thus with Conradino ended the line of the house of Suabia, which was so powerful both in emperors and in kings, as before we have made mention. But certainly we may see, both by reason and by experience, that whosoever rises against Holy Church, and is excommunicate, his end must needs be evil for soul and for body; and therefore the sentence of excommunication of Holy Church, just or unjust, is always to be feared, for very open miracles have come to pass confirming this, as whoso will may read in ancient chronicles; as also by this present chronicle it may be seen with regard to the emperors and lords of past times, which were rebels and persecutors of Holy Church. Yet because of the said judgment King Charles was much blamed by the Pope and by his cardinals, and by all wise men, forasmuch as he had taken Conradino and his followers by chance of battle, and not by treachery, and it would have been better to keep him prisoner than to put him to death. And some said that the Pope assented thereto; but we do not give faith to this, forasmuch as he was held to be a holy man. And it seems that by reason of Conradino's innocence, which was of such tender age to be adjudged to death, God showed forth a miracle against King Charles, for not many years after God sent him great adversities when he thought himself to be in highest state, as hereafter in his history we shall make mention. To the judge which condemned Conradino, Robert, son of the count of Flanders, the king's son-in-law, when he had read the condemnation, gave a sword-thrust, saying that it was not lawful for him to sentence to death so great and noble a man, from which blow the judge died; and it was in the king's presence, and there was never a word said thereof, forasmuch as Robert was very high in the favour of the king, and it seemed to the king and to all the barons that he had acted like a worthy lord. Now Don Henry of Spain was likewise in the king's prison, but forasmuch as he was his cousin by blood, and because the abbot of Monte Cascino, which had brought him prisoner to the king, to the end he might not break his rule, had made a compact with him that he should not be put to death, the king would not condemn him to death, but to perpetual imprisonment, and sent him prisoner to the fortress in the hill Sanctæ Mariæ in Apulia; and many other barons of Apulia and of Abruzzi, which had opposed King Charles and been rebellious against him, he put to death with divers torments.

§ 30.—*How King Charles recovered all the lands in Sicily and in* **1268 a.d.** *Apulia which had rebelled against him.*

§ 31.—*How the Florentines defeated the Sienese at the foot of Colle di Valdelsa.* **1269 a.d.**

In the year of Christ 1269, in the month of June, the Sienese, whereof M. Provenzano Salvani, of Siena, was governor, with Count Guido Novello, with the German and Spanish troops, and with the Ghibelline refugees from

198

Florence and from the other cities of Tuscany, and with the forces of the Pisans, to the number of 1,400 horse and 8,000 foot, marched upon the stronghold of Colle di Valdelsa, which was under the lordship of the Florentines; and this they did because the Florentines had come in May with an army to destroy Poggibonizzi. And when they had encamped at the abbey of Spugnole, and the news was come to Florence on Friday evening, on Saturday morning M. Giambertaldo, vicar of King Charles for the league of Tuscany, departed from Florence with his troops which he then had with him in Florence to wit 400 French horse; and sounding the bell, and being followed by the Guelfs of Florence on horse and on foot, he came with his cavalry to Colle on Sunday evening, and there were about 800 horsemen or less with but few of the people, forasmuch as they could not reach Colle so speedily as the horsemen. It came to pass that on the following Monday morning, the day of S. Barnabas, in June, the Sienese, hearing that the horsemen had come from Florence, broke up their camp near the said abbey and withdrew to a safer place. M. Giambertaldo, seeing the camp in motion, without awaiting more men passed the bridge with his horse and marshalled his troops with the cavalry of Florence and such of the people as had arrived together with them of Colle (who by reason of the sudden coming of the Florentines were not duly arrayed either with captains of the host or with the standard of the commonwealth); and M. Giambertaldo took the standard of the commonwealth of Florence and requested of the horsemen of Florence, amongst whom were representatives of all the Guelf houses, that one of them should take it; but none advanced to take it, whether through cowardice or through jealousy, one of the other; and after they had been a long time in suspense, M. Aldobrandini, of the house of Pazzi, boldly stepped forward and said: "I take it to the honour of God and of the victory of our commonwealth;" wherefore he was much commended for his boldness; and straightway he advanced, and all the horsemen followed him, and struck boldly into the ranks of the Sienese; and albeit it was not held to be very wise and prudent leadership, yet as it pleased God these bold and courageous folk with good success broke up and defeated the Sienese and their allies, which numbered well-nigh twice as many horse and a great number of foot, whereof many were slain and taken; and if on the Florentine side the foot had arrived and had been at the battle, scarce one of the Sienese would have escaped. Count Guido Novello fled, and M. Provenzano Salvani, lord and commander of **Purg. xiii. 115-119.** the host of the Sienese, was taken prisoner; and they cut off his head and carried it through all the camp fixed on a lance. And truly thus was fulfilled the prophecy and revelation made to him by the devil by means of incantation, though he did not understand it; for having invoked him to learn how he would fare in that expedition, he made a lying answer and said, "Thou wilt go and fight; thou goest to conquer not to die in the battle, and thy head shall be the highest in the field;" and he, thinking to have the victory from these words, and thinking he would remain lord over all, did not put the stop in the right place and detect the fraud, where he said, "Thou goest to conquer not, to die," etc. And therefore it is great folly to believe in such counsel as is that of the devil. This M. Provenzano was a great man in Siena in his day after the victory which he gained at Montaperti, and he ruled all the city; and all the Ghibelline party in **Purg. xi. 109-114, 120-123.** Tuscany made him their head, and he was very presumptuous in will. In this battle the said M. Giambertaldo bore himself like a valiant lord in fighting against his enemies, and likewise did his followers and all the Guelfs of Florence, making great slaughter of their enemies to avenge their kinsfolk and friends which were slain at the defeat of Montaperti; and none, or scarce any, did they lead to prison, but put them all to death and to the sword; wherefore the city of Siena, in comparison with the number of its inhabitants, suffered greater loss of its citizens in this defeat than Florence did on the day of Montaperti; and they left on the field all their belongings. For the which thing a little while after, the Florentines restored the Guelf refugees to Siena and drave out the Ghibellines and made peace between one commonwealth and the other, remaining ever after friends and allies. And in this manner ended the war between the Florentines and the Sienese which had endured so long.

§ 32.—*How the Florentines took the castle of Ostina in Valdarno.* **1269 a.d.**

§ 33.—*How the Florentines, serving for the Lucchese, marched upon Pisa.*

§ 34.—*How there was a great flood of waters which carried away the Santa Trinita Bridge and the Carraia Bridge.*

1269 a.d.

200

In the said year 1269, on the night of the first of October, there was so great a flood of rain and waters from heaven, raining down continually for two nights and one day, that all the rivers of Italy increased more than had ever been known before; and the river of Arno overflowed its borders so beyond measure that a great part of the city of Florence became a lake, and this was by reason of much wood which the rivers brought down, which was caught and lay across at the foot of the Santa Trinita Bridge in such wise, that the water of the river was so stopped up that it spread through the city, whence many persons were drowned and many houses ruined. At last so great was the force of the river that it tore down the said bridge of Santa Trinita, and again by the disgorging thereof the rush of the water and of the timber struck and destroyed the Carraia Bridge; and when they were destroyed and cast down the height of the river, which had been kept up by the said retention and damming of the river, went down, and the fulness of the water ceased which had spread through the city.

§ 35.—*How certain rebel nobles in Florence were beheaded.* § 36.—*How the Florentines took the stronghold of Piandimezzo in Valdarno, and how they destroyed Poggibonizzi.*

§ 37.—*-How King Louis of France made an expedition to Tunis, wherein he died.*

1270 a.d.

In the year of Christ 1270 the good King Louis of France, which was a most Christian man, and of good life and works, not only as becomes a man of the world, being king over so great a realm and dominion, but also as becomes a man of religion, ever working for the good of Holy Church and of Christianity, not fearing the great toil and cost which he endured in the expedition over seas when he and his brothers were taken prisoners at Monsura by the Saracens, as we made mention before; set his heart, as it pleased God, on going once more against the Saracens and the enemies of the Christians; and this he carried out with great zeal and preparation, taking the cross and gathering treasure, and calling upon all his barons and knights and good men of his realm. And this done, he set forth from Paris and came

201

into Provence, and from there with a great fleet he set sail from his port of Aigues Mortes in Provence with his three sons, Philip and John and Louis, and with the king of Navarre, his son-in-law, and with all his chief men, counts and dukes and barons of the realm of France, and his friends from without the realm. And on his expedition there afterwards followed him Edward, son of the king of England, with many Englishmen and Scots and Frisians and Germans, more than 5,000 horse; the which army and crusade was an almost innumerable company on horse and on foot, and were reckoned 200,000 fighting men. And believing it to be the better course they determined to go against the kingdom of Tunis, thinking that if it could be taken by the Christians they would be in a very central place whence they could more easily afterwards take the kingdom of Egypt, and could cut off and wholly impede the force of the Saracens in the realm of Ceuta, and also that of Granada. And the said host with their fleet passed over safe and sound and came to the port of the ancient city of Carthage, which is distant from Tunis fifteen miles; the which Carthage, whereof some part had been rebuilt and fortified by the Saracens in defence of the port, was very soon stormed by the Christians. And when the Christians would have entered into the city of Tunis, as it pleased God, by reason of the sins of the Christians, the air of those shores began to be greatly corrupted, and above all in the camp of the Christians, by reason that they were not accustomed to the air, and by reason of their hardships and the excessive crowding of men and of animals, for the which thing there died first John, son of the said King Louis, and then the cardinal of Albano, which was there for the Pope, and afterwards there fell sick and died the said good King Louis with a very great number of counts and of barons; and an innumerable company of the common folk died there. Wherefore Christendom suffered very great loss, and the said host was well-nigh all dispersed, and came well-nigh to naught without stroke of the enemy. And albeit the said King Louis had not had good success in his enterprises against the Saracens, yet in his death he had good success for his soul; and the king of Navarre, which was there present, wrote in his letters to the cardinal of Tusculum that in his infirmity he did not cease to praise God, continually saying this prayer: "Cause us, Lord, to hate the prosperity of the world, and to fear no adversity." Then he prayed for the people which he had brought with him, saying, "Lord, be Thou the Sanctifier and Guardian of Thy people," and the other words which follow in the said prayer. And at last, when he came to die, he lift up his eyes to heaven and said: "Introibo in domum tuam, adorabo ad templum sanctum tuum, et confitebor nomini tuo" [see Ps. v. 7]. And this said he died in Christ. And when his host heard of his death they were greatly troubled, and the Saracens greatly rejoiced; but in this sorrow Philip, his son, was made king of France, and King Charles, brother of the said King Louis, which had sent for him before he died, came from Sicily and arrived in Carthage with a great fleet and with many followers and reinforcements, whence the Christian host regained great vigour, and the Saracens were afraid. And albeit the Saracen host was increased by an innumerable company, for from every place the Arabs were come to succour them, and there were many more of them than of the Christians, yet they never dared to come to a pitched battle with the Christians; but they came with ambushes and with artifices, and did them much hurt; and this was one among others, that the said country is very sandy, and when it is dry there is very much dust; wherefore the Saracens, when the wind was blowing against the Christian host, stationed themselves in great numbers upon the hills where was the said sand, and stirring it up with their horses and with their feet, set it all in motion, and caused much annoyance and vexation to the host; but when water rained down from heaven the said plague ceased, and King Charles with the Christians, having prepared engines of divers fashions both for sea and land, set himself to attack the city of Tunis; and of a truth it is said, if they had gone on, in a short time they would have taken the city by force, or the king of Tunis with his Turks and Arabs would have abandoned it.

§ 38.—*How King Charles concluded a treaty with the king of Tunis, and how the host departed.*

1270 a.d.

The king of Tunis with his Saracens seeing themselves in evil case, and fearing to lose the city and the country round about, sought to make peace with King Charles and with the other lords by free and liberal covenants, to which peace King Charles consented and concluded it in the following manner: first, that all the Christians which were prisoners in Tunis, or in all that realm, should be freed, and that monasteries and churches might be built by the Christians, and therein the sacred office might be celebrated; and that the gospel of Christ might be freely preached by the minor friars and the preaching friars and by other ecclesiastical persons; and whatsoever Saracen should desire to be baptized, and turn to the faith of Christ, might freely be allowed so to do; and all the expenses which the said kings had incurred were to be fully restored to them; and beyond that the king of Tunis was to pay tribute every year to Charles, king of Sicily, of 20,000 golden pistoles; and there were many other articles which it were long to tell. Concerning this peace some said that King Charles and the other lords did for the best, considering their evil state from the pestilential air and the mortality among the Christians; for the king of Navarre, when King Louis was dead, fell sick and departed from the host and died in Sicily, and the cardinal legate of the Pope died; and the Church of Rome in those times had no pastor which could provide for all things, and Philip, the new king of France, desired to depart from the host and return to France with his father's body. Others blamed King Charles, saying that he did it through avarice, to the end he might henceforward, by reason of the said peace, always receive tribute from the king of Tunis for his own special benefit; for if the kingdom of Tunis had been conquered by all the host of the Christians, it would have afterwards pertained in part to the king of France, and to the king of England, and to the king of Navarre, and to the king of Sicily, and to the Church of Rome, and to divers other lords which were at the conquest. And it may have been, both one cause and the other; but however that may have been, when the said treaty was concluded the said host departed from Tunis, and when they came with their fleet to the port of Trapali in Sicily, as it pleased God, so great a storm overtook them while the fleet was in the said port that without any redemption the greater part perished, and one vessel broke the other, and all the belongings of that host were lost, which were of untold worth, and many folk perished there. And it was said by many that this came to pass by reason of the sins of the Christians, and because they had made a covenant with the Saracens through greed of money when they could have overcome and conquered Tunis and the country.

§ 39.—*How Gregory X. was made pope at Viterbo, and how Henry, son of the king of England, there died.*
1272 a.d.

When the said Christian host was come to Sicily, they abode there sometime to recover the sick, and to be refreshed, and to repair their fleet; and those kings and lords were held in much honour by Charles, king of Sicily; and afterwards they departed from Sicily, and King Charles with them, and came into the kingdom of Apulia, and by Calabria to Viterbo, where was the papal court without a Pope, and at Viterbo there tarried the said kings Philip of France, and Charles of Sicily, and Edward, and Henry his brother, sons of the king of England, to see that the cardinals, which were in disunion, should elect a good pastor to reform the papal chair. And since they were not able to agree upon any one of those there present, they elected Pope Gregory X., of Piacenza, which was cardinal legate of Syria in the Holy Land; and when he was elected, and had returned from beyond seas, he was consecrated Pope in the year of Christ 1272. Whilst the aforesaid lords were in Viterbo, there came to pass a scandalous and abominable thing, under the government of King Charles; for Henry, brother of Edward, son of King Richard of England, being in a church at Mass, at the hour when the sacrifice of the body of Christ was being celebrated, Guy, count of Montfort, which was vicar for King **Inf. xii. 118-120.** Charles in Tuscany, having no regard for reverence towards God, nor towards King Charles his lord, stabbed and slew with his own hand the said Henry in revenge for Count Simon of Montfort, his father, slain, through his own fault, by the king of England. And of this it is well to preserve a notable record. When Henry, father of the good Edward, was reigning in England, he was a man of simple life, so that the **Purg. vii. 130-132.** barons held him for nought, wherefore he sent for the said Count Simon, his kinsman, to guide the realm for him, seeing that Edward was but young. This Simon was much feared and dreaded; and when he saw the government of the realm in his hands, as a felon and traitor, he falsely averred that the king had passed certain iniquitous laws against the people, and he put him and Edward in prison in the castle of Dover, and held the realm himself. The queen, . . . Edward's maternal aunt, was desirous of saving

205

him, and knew that Count Simon came every Easter to Dover, and took Edward out of the castle, and made him ride with him; and when he departed he caused him to be again imprisoned with strong and strict guard, that he might not so much as have letters. So the wise queen sent to Dover a wise and beautiful damsel, which knew how to work in jewels, purses, and pouches. And when Edward saw her he loved her, and so wrought with his guards that they brought him the said damsel, and when he would have touched her, she said to him: "I am here for other matters," and she drew forth letters sent him by the queen, advising him as to his deliverance and welfare; and therein she advised him that she was sending him one of our Florentine horse-dealers, which was named Persona Fulberti, with fine steeds, and a small ship equipped with many oars, and advising him what he was to do. Now, after his wont, at Easter, Count Simon came to Dover, and took Edward out of the castle, and while they were trying the steeds of the said dealer, Edward, with the count's permission, mounted the best of them, and galloping round in a wide sweep, at last took to the field and made off, and came to the port and found the bark prepared. Then he left the horse, and embarked, and came to France, and then with aid from the king of France, and Flanders, and Brabant, and Germany, with a great host he passed into England, and fought against Count Simon, and discomfited him, and seized him by the scalp, and had him dragged along the ground, and then hung. Then he set his father free; and when he was dead, then was Edward crowned king of England with great honour. And now we return to our chief subject—how was slain Count Henry, earl of Cornwall, brother of King Edward, in revenge for this, as we said before. The court was greatly disturbed, giving much blame therefor to King Charles, who ought not to have suffered this if he knew thereof, and if he did not know it he ought not to have let it go unavenged. But the said Count Guy, being provided with a company of men-at-arms on horse and on foot, was not content only with having done the said murder; forasmuch as a cavalier asked him what he had done, and he replied, "J'ai fait ma vangeance," and that cavalier said, "Comment? Votre père fût trainé;" and immediately he returned to the church, and took Henry by the hair, and dead as he was, he dragged him vilely without the church; and when he had done the said sacrilege and homicide, he departed from Viterbo, and came safe and sound into Maremma to the lands of Count Rosso, his father-in-law. By reason of the death of the said Henry, Edward, his brother, very wrathful and indignant against King Charles, departed from Viterbo, and came with his followers through Tuscany, and abode in Florence, and knighted many citizens, giving them horses and all knightly accoutrements very nobly, and then he came into England, and set the heart of his said brother in a golden cup upon a pillar at the head of London Bridge **Inf. xii. 120.** over the river Thames, to keep the English in mind of the outrage sustained. For the which thing, Edward, after he became king, was never friendly towards King Charles, nor to his folk. After like manner, Philip, king of France, departed with his folk, and came and dwelt many days in Florence; and when he was come into France, he buried the body of the good King Louis, his father, with great honour, and had himself crowned with great solemnity at Rheims.

§ 40.—*How the Tartars came down into Turkey, and drave thence the* **1270 a.d.**

1271 a.d. *Saracens.* § 41.—*How King Enzo, son of the Emperor Frederick, died in prison at Bologna.*

§ 42.—*How Pope Gregory came with his court to Florence, and caused peace to be made between the Guelfs and Ghibellines.*
1272 a.d.

In the year 1272, Gregory X., of Piacenza, having returned from his mission over seas, was consecrated and crowned Pope, and because of the great affection and desire which he had to succour the Holy Land, and that a general crusade should set forth over seas, therefore so soon as he was made Pope, he called a general council at Lyons-on-Rhone in Burgundy, and by his mandate caused the electors of **Purg. vi. 103-105; vii. 91-96; Convivio iv. 3: 37-42.** the empire of Germany to elect as king of the Romans, Rudolf, count of Friburg, which was a valiant man-at-arms, albeit he was of small possessions; but by his prowess he conquered Suabia and Austria; and the duchy of Austria being vacant, since the duke had been slain with Conradino by King Charles, he made Albert, his son, to be duke. The **Purg. vi. 97-117.**
1273 a.d. aforesaid Pope, the year after his coronation, set forth with his

court from Rome to go to Lyons-on-Rhone to the council which he had summoned, and he entered into Florence with his cardinals, and with King Charles, and with the Emperor Baldwin of Constantinople, which was of the lineage of the chief house of Flanders. This Baldwin was son of Henry, the brother of the first Baldwin, which conquered Constantinople with the Venetians, as we before made mention. And with the Pope, and with King Charles, there came to Florence many other lords and barons, on the 18th day of June, in the year of Christ 1273, and were received with honour by the Florentines. And the situation of Florence being pleasing to the Pope, by reason of the convenience of the water, and the pure air, and that the court found much comfort there, he purposed to abide there, and pass the summer in Florence. And finding that this good city of Florence was being destroyed by reason of the parties (the Ghibellines being now in exile), he determined that they should return to Florence, and should make peace with the Guelfs; and so it came about, and on the 2nd day of July in the said year, the said Pope, with his cardinals, and with King Charles, and with the said Emperor Baldwin, and with all the barons and gentlemen of the court (the people of Florence being assembled on the sands of the Arno hard by the head of the Rubaconte Bridge, great scaffolds of wood having been erected in that place whereon stood the said lords), gave sentence, under pain of excommunication if it were disobeyed, upon the differences between the Guelf and Ghibelline parties, causing the representatives of either party to kiss one another on the mouth, and to make peace, and to give sureties and hostages; and all the castles which the Ghibellines held they gave back into the hands of King Charles, and the Ghibelline hostages went into Maremma under charge of Count Rosso. The which peace endured but a short time, as hereafter we shall make mention. And on that day the said Pope founded the church of San Gregorio, and called it after his own name, which church was built by them of the house of Mozzi, which were merchants for the Pope and for the Church, and in a little time were come to great riches and state; and the said Pope dwelt in their palaces at the head of the Rubaconte Bridge on the further side of Arno, whilst he abode in Florence; and King Charles abode in the garden of the Frescobaldi, and the Emperor Baldwin at the Bishop's Palace. But on the fourth day thereafter, the Pope departed from

208

Florence, and went to sojourn in Mugello with Cardinal Ottaviano, which was of the house of the Ubaldini, who were his hosts, and who did him great honour. At the end of the summer, the Pope departed, and his cardinals and King Charles, and went over the mountains to Lyons-on-Rhone in Burgundy. And the reason why the Pope departed suddenly from Florence was that when he had caused the representatives of the Ghibelline party to come to Florence, and to kiss the representatives of the Guelfs on the mouth in token of peace, and to remain in Florence to complete the treaty of peace, and they returned to the place of their sojourn in the house of the Tebalducci in Orto San Michele, it was told them, whether it were true or false, that King Charles' marshal, on the petition of the great Guelfs would cause them to be hewn in pieces if they did not depart from Florence. And that this was the cause we believe by reason of the virulence of the factions. And straightway they left Florence and departed, and the said peace was broken; wherefore the Pope was sorely disturbed, and departed from Florence, leaving the city under an interdict, and went, as we have said, to Mugello; and for this cause he continued in great wrath against King Charles.

§ 43.—*How Pope Gregory held a council at Lyons on the Rhone.* **1274 a.d.** § 44.—*How the Ghibelline party were expelled from Bologna.* § 45.—*How the judge of Gallura with certain Guelfs was driven out of Pisa.* § 46.—*Of a great miracle which came to pass in Baldacca and* **1275 a.d.** *Mansul [Bagdad and Mosul] over seas.* § 47.—*How Count Ugolino with all the remaining Guelfs was driven out of Pisa.* § 48.—*How the Bolognese were discomfited at the bridge of San Brocolo by the Count of Montefeltro and by the Romagnuoli.* § 49.—*How the Pisans were discomfited by the Lucchese at the stronghold of Asciano.*

§ 50.—*Of the death of Pope Gregory, and of three other Popes after him.* **1275 a.d.**

In the year of Christ 1275, on the eighteenth day of the month of December, when Pope Gregory X. was returning from the council at Lyons-on-Rhone, he arrived in the country of Florence; and forasmuch as the city of Florence was under interdict, and her inhabitants excommunicate, because they had not observed the treaty of peace which he had made between the Guelfs and Ghibellines, as was aforesaid, he was not minded to

209

enter into Florence, but by cunning he was led past the old walls, and some said that he could have done no other, because the river Arno was so swollen by rain that he could not cross the ford, but needs must cross over the Rubaconte Bridge, so that unwittingly, and not being able to do otherwise, he entered into Florence; and whilst he was passing over the bridge, and through the Borgo San Nicolò, he took off the interdict, and passed on, blessing the folk; but so soon as he was without he renewed the interdict, and excommunicated the city afresh, with a wrathful mind repeating that verse of the Psalter which says: "In camo et fræno maxillas eorum constringe" [Ps. xxxiii. 9]; wherefore the Guelfs which were governing Florence were in great doubt and fear. And the said Pope departing from Florence, went to the abbey at Ripole, and from there straightway he departed to Arezzo; and being come to Arezzo, he fell sick, and as it pleased God, he passed from this life on the tenth day of the following month of January, and was buried in Arezzo with great honour; at whose death the Guelfs of Florence rejoiced greatly, by reason of the evil will which the said Pope had towards them. And when the Pope was dead, straightway the cardinals were shut up, and on the twentieth day of the said month of January they proclaimed as Pope, Innocent V. a Burgundian, which had been a preaching friar and then a cardinal; and he lived as Pope until the following June, so that he **1276 a.d.** did little, and died in the city of Viterbo, and was there buried honourably. And after him, on the twelfth day of July, Cardinal Ottobuono dal Fiesco, of the city of Genoa, was elected, which lived as Pope but twenty-nine days, and was called Pope Adrian V., and was **Purg. xix. 98-145.** buried in Rome. And after him, in the month of September following, Cardinal Piero Spagnuolo was elected Pope, which was called Pope John **Par. xii. 134, 135.** XXI., and lived as Pope but eight months and some days; for as he was sleeping in his room at Viterbo the ceiling fell down upon him and he **1277 a.d.** died; and he was buried at Viterbo on the twentieth day of May, 1277; and the chair was vacant six months. And in that same year there was great scarcity of all victuals, and the bushel of wheat was sold for fifteen shillings, of thirty shillings to the florin. And a great and true vision should be noted concerning the death of the said Pope, which was seen by one of our Florentine merchants of the Company of Apothecaries, which was called Berto Forzetti, and it is well that this should be told. The said merchant had a natural infirmity of a wandering fancy, so that often when sleeping he would rise and sit upon his bed, and speak of strange wonders; and there is yet more, for being questioned by those around him as to what he was saying, he would answer rationally, and all the time he was sleeping. It came to pass, on the night when the said Pope died, the said man being in a ship on the high seas, journeying to Acre, rose and cried out, "Alas, alas!" His companions awoke, and asked him what ailed him; he replied: "I see a gigantic man in black with a great club in his hand, and he is about to break down a pillar, above which is a ceiling." And after a little he cried out again, and said: "He has broken it down, and he is dead." He was asked: "Who?" He replied: "The Pope." The said companions wrote down the words, and the night; and when they were come to Acre, a short time after there came to them the news of the death of the said Pope, which came to pass in that same night. And I, the writer, had testimony of this from those merchants which were present with the said man upon the said ship, and heard the said Berto, which were men of great authority, and worthy of belief; and the fame of this spread throughout all our city. Afterwards was elected Pope Nicholas III., of the house of the Orsini of Rome, which **Inf. xix. 69-87.** was called by his proper name, Cardinal Gianni Guatani, which lived as Pope two years and nine months and a half. We have spoken of the **1280 a.d.** aforesaid Popes because four Popes died in sixteen months. We will say no more, at this present time, of the aforesaid Popes, and we will speak of those things which came to pass in their days in Florence and throughout the world.

§ 51.—*How the Florentines and Lucchese defeated the Pisans at the* **1275 a.d. 1276 a.d.**

1277 a.d. *moat called Arnonico.* § 52.—*How the Della Torre of Milan were defeated.* § 53.—*How King Philip of France caused all the Italian money-lenders to be seized.*

§ 54.—*How Nicholas III., of the Orsini, was made Pope, and concerning that which he did in his time.*
1277 a.d.

In the said year, whereof we related somewhat before, M. Gianni Guatani was made Pope, a cardinal, of the house of the Orsini of Rome, which, whilst he was young, as priest and then cardinal, was virtuous and of good life, and it is said that he was virgin in his body; but after he was called Pope Nicholas III. he had great schemes, and through warmth towards his kinsfolk, he undertook many things to make them great, and was among the first, if not the first, of the Popes in whose court simony was openly practised on behalf of his kindred, by the which thing he increased them much in possessions, and in castles, **Inf. xix. 52-84.** and in treasure beyond all the Romans, during the short time that he lived. This Pope made seven Roman cardinals, whereof the most part were his kinsfolk; among others, at the prayer of M. Gianni, head of the house of Colonna, his cousin, he made M. Jacopo della Colonna a cardinal, to the end the Colonnesi might not lend aid to the Annibaldeschi, enemies of the Orsini, but might rather aid these latter; and this was held a great thing; because the Church had deprived all the Colonnesi, and those of their kindred, of any ecclesiastical benefice, since the time of Pope Alexander III., forasmuch as they had held with the Emperor Frederick I. against the Church. Afterwards the said Pope caused the noble and great papal palaces to be built at S. Peter's; then he entered into strife with **Inf. xix. 98, 99.** King Charles by reason that the said Pope had requested King Charles to form an alliance with him by marriage, desiring to give one of his nieces as wife to a nephew of the King's, to which alliance King Charles would not consent, saying, "Albeit he wears red hose, yet is **Cf. Inf. xix. 81.** not his lineage worthy to mate with ours; and his lordship will not be hereditary." For the which thing the Pope's wrath was kindled against him, and he was no longer his friend, but opposed him secretly in all things, and openly made him renounce the office of Roman senator, and of vicar of the Empire, which he held from the Church during the imperial vacancy; and he was much against him in all his undertakings, and for money which it was said he received from Paleologus, he consented, and gave aid and favour to the plot and rebellion in the island of Sicily, as hereafter we shall narrate; and he took from the Church the castle Santangiolo, and gave it to M. Orso, his nephew. Again the said Pope made Rudolf, king of the Romans, invest him, on behalf of the Church, with the county of Romagna, and the city of Bologna, by reason that he was debtor to the Church for the fulfilment of the promise which he had made to Pope Gregory at the council of

212

Lyons-on-Rhone, when he confirmed his election, to wit that he would pass into Italy, and equip the expedition over seas, as we before made mention; which thing he had not done by reason of his other undertakings and wars in Germany. Now this gift to the Church of the privileges of the country of Romagna and the city of Bologna, neither could nor ought to have been made by right; among other reasons, because the said Rudolf had not yet attained to the imperial benediction; but that which the clergy take, they are slow in giving back. So soon as the said Pope held privilege over Romagna, he made Bertoldo degli Orsini, his nephew, count thereof, in the Church's name, and sent him into Romagna with a company of horsemen and men-at-arms, and with him as legate Brother Latino, of Rome, cardinal of Ostia, his nephew, his sister's son, of the family of the Brancaleoni, of which was the chancellor of Rome by inheritance; and this he did to take the lordship out of the hand of Guido di Montefeltro, which held it and ruled there tyrannically; and this was **Inf. xxvii. 67.** done in such wise, that in a short time almost all Romagna came under the Church's rule, but not without war and great cost to the Church, as hereafter we will tell in due place and time.

§ 55.—*How King Rudolf of Germany defeated and slew the king of* **1277 a.d.** *Bohemia.*

§ 56.—*How the Cardinal Latino, by the Pope's command, made peace between the Guelfs and Ghibellines of Florence, and composed all the other feuds in the city.* **1278 a.d.**

In these times the Guelf magnates of Florence—having rest from their wars without, with victory and honour, and fattening upon the goods of the exiled Ghibellines, and through other gains—by reason of pride and envy began to strive among themselves; whence arose in Florence many quarrels and enmities between the citizens, with death and wounds. Among the greater of these was the contest between the house of the Adimari on the one side, which were very great and powerful, and on the other side the Tosinghi, and the house of the Donati, and the Pazzi, all leagued together against the Adimari in such sort that almost all the city was divided, and one held with one side, and one with the other; wherefore the city and the Guelf party were in great peril. For the which thing the commonwealth and the Captains of the Guelf party sent their solemn ambassadors to the court to Pope Nicholas, that he should take counsel, and give aid in making peace among the Guelfs of Florence; if not, the Guelf party would be broken up, and one side would drive out the other. And in like guise the Ghibelline refugees from Florence sent their ambassadors to the said Pope, to pray and entreat him to put into execution the treaty of peace which Pope Gregory IX. had commanded between them and the Guelfs of Florence. For the foregoing reasons the said Pope put forth and confirmed the said treaty, and ordained a mediator and legate, and committed the said questions to the Cardinal Frate Latino which represented the Church in Romagna; a man of great authority and learning, and highly considered by the Pope, who, by command of the Pope, departed from Romagna, and came to Florence with 300 horsemen, in service of the Church, on the eighth day of the month of October, in the year of Christ 1278, and by the Florentines and the clergy was received with great honour and with a procession, the carroccio coming out to meet him, with many jousters; and afterwards the said legate on the day of S. Luke the Evangelist in that same year and month, founded and blest the first stone of the new church of Santa Maria Novella, which pertained to the Order of Preaching Friars, whereof he was a friar; and in that place of the friars he dealt with and ordained generally the treaties of peace between all the Guelf citizens, and between the Guelfs and Ghibellines. And the first was between the Uberti and the Bondelmonti (and it was the third peace between them), save only that the sons of M. Rinieri Zingane de' Bondelmonte would not consent thereto, and were excommunicated by the legate and banished by the commonwealth. But the peace was not set aside on their account; for afterwards the legate very happily concluded it in the month of February following, when the people of Florence were assembled in parliament on the old piazza of the said church, which was all covered with cloths and with great wooden scaffolds, whereon were the said cardinal, and many bishops, and prelates, and clergy, and monks, and the Podestà, and the Captain, and all the counsellors, and the orders of Florence. And at that time a very noble speech was made by the said legate with citation of great and very fine authorities, as behoved the matter, seeing that he was a very dexterous and beautiful preacher; and this done, he caused the representatives ordained by the Guelfs and Ghibellines to kiss one another on the mouth, making peace with great joy among all the citizens, and there were 150 on either side. And in that place, and at that same time, he gave judgment as to the terms and agreements and conditions which were to be observed, both on one side and on the other, confirming the said peace with solemn and authentic documents, and with all due sureties. And from that time forward the Ghibellines and their families were to be allowed to return to Florence; and they did return, and they were free from all sentence of banishment and condemnation; and all the books of condemnation and banishment which were in the chamber were burnt; and the said Ghibellines recovered their goods and possessions, save that to some of the chief leaders, it was commanded for more security of the city that for a certain time they should be under bounds. And when the cardinal legate had done this, he made contracts of peace between single citizens; and the first was that one where had been greatest discord, to wit, between the Adimari, and the Tosinghi, and Donati, and Pazzi, bringing about several marriages between them, and in like manner were all the agreements made in Florence and in the country round about, some willingly, and some by command of the commonwealth, the cardinal having pronounced sentence, with good securities and sureties; by which contracts of peace the said legate won much honour, and well-nigh all of them were observed, and the city of Florence abode thereafter long time in peaceful and good and tranquil state. And the said legate gave and ordained, for the general government of the city, fourteen good men, magnates and popolani, whereof eight were Guelfs and six Ghibellines, and their term of office endured for two months, and there was a certain order in their election; and they assembled in the house of the Badia of Florence, over the gate which goes to Santa Margherita, and returned to their homes to eat and to sleep. And this done, the said Cardinal Latino returned to Romagna to his legation with great honour. We will now leave the affairs of Florence for a while, and we will tell of other things which came to pass in those times, and especially of the revolt of the island of Sicily against King Charles, which was notable and great, and whence afterwards grew much ill; and it was a thing well-nigh marvellous and impossible, and therefore we will treat of it more at

215

large.

1282 a.d.

In the year of Christ 1282, on Easter Monday of the Resurrection, which was the 30th day of March, as had been purposed by M. John of Procita, all the barons and chiefs which had a hand in the plot were in the city of Palermo for Easter, and the inhabitants of Palermo, men and women, going in a body, on horse and on foot, to the festival at Monreale, three miles outside the city (and as those of Palermo went, so also went the Frenchmen, and the captain of King Charles, for their disport), it came to pass, as was purposed by the enemy of God, that a Frenchman in his insolence laid hold of a woman of Palermo to do her villainy; she beginning to cry out, and the people being already sore and all moved with indignation against the French, the retainers of the barons of the island began to defend the woman, whence arose a great battle between the French and the Sicilians, and many were wounded and slain on either side; but those of Palermo came off worst. Straightway, all the people returned in flight to the city, and the men flew to arms, crying, "Death to the French." They gathered **Par. viii. 75.** together in the market place, as had been ordained by the leaders of the plot; and the justiciary, which was for the king, fighting at the castle, was taken and slain, and as many Frenchmen as were in the city were slain in the houses and in the churches, without any mercy. And this done, the said barons departed from Palermo, and each one in his own city and country did the like, slaying all the Frenchmen which were in the island, save that in Messina they delayed some days before rebelling; but through tidings from those in Palermo giving account of their miseries in a fair epistle, and exhorting them to love liberty and freedom and fraternity with them, the men of Messina were so moved to rebellion that they afterwards did the like of what they of Palermo had done against the French, and yet more. And there were slain in Sicily more than 4,000 of them, and no one could save another though he were never so much his friend, no not if he would lay down his life for him; and if he had concealed him, he must needs yield him up or slay him. This plague spread through all the island, whence King Charles and his people received great hurt both in person and in goods. These adverse and evil tidings the Archbishop of Monreale straightway made known to the Pope and to King

217

Charles by his messengers.

1282 a.d.

In the year of Christ 1282, the city of Florence being under government of the order of the fourteen good men as the Cardinal Latino had left it, to wit eight Guelfs and six Ghibellines, as we afore made mention, it seemed to the citizens that this government of fourteen was too numerous and confused; and to the end so many divided hearts might be at one, and, above all, because it was not pleasing to the Guelfs to have the Ghibellines as partners in the government by reason of the events which were come to pass (such as the loss which King Charles had already sustained of the island of Sicily, and the coming into Tuscany of the imperial vicar, and likewise the wars begun in Romagna by the count of Montefeltro on the Ghibelline side), for the safety and welfare of the city of Florence they annulled the said office

218

of the fourteen and created and made a new office and lordship for the government of the said city of Florence, to wit, the Priors of the Arts; the which name, Priors of the Arts, means to say "the first," chosen over the others; and it was taken from the Holy Gospel, where Christ says to His disciples, "Vos estis priores." And this invention and movement began among the consuls and council of the art of Calimala, to which pertained the wisest and most powerful citizens of Florence, and the most numerous following, both magnates and popolani, of those which pursued the calling of merchants, seeing the most part of them greatly loved the Guelf party and Holy Church. And the first priors of the Arts were three, whereof the names were these: Bartolo di M. Jacopo de' Bardi, for the sesto of Oltrarno and for the art of Calimala; Rosso Bacherelli, for the sesto of San Piero Scheraggio, for the art of the exchangers; Salvi del Chiaro Girolami, for the sesto of San Brancazio and for the woollen art. And their office began in the middle of June of the said year, and lasted for two months, unto the middle of August, and thus three priors were to succeed every two months, for the three greater Arts. And they were shut up to give audience (sleeping and eating at the charges of the commonwealth), in the house of the Badia where formerly, as we have aforesaid, the Ancients were wont to assemble in the time of the old Popolo, and afterwards the fourteen. And there were assigned to the said priors six constables and six messengers to summon the citizens; and these priors, with the Captain of the Popolo, had to determine the great and weighty matters of the commonwealth, and to summon and conduct councils and make regulations. And when the office had endured the two months, it was pleasing to the citizens; and for the following two months they proclaimed six, one for each sesto, and added to the said three greater Arts the art of the doctors and apothecaries, and the art of the Porta Santæ Mariæ, and that of the furriers and skin-dressers; and afterwards from time to time all the others were added thereto, to the number of the twelve greater Arts; and there were among them magnates, as well as popolani, great men of good repute and works, and which were artificers or merchants. And thus it went on until the second Popolo was formed in Florence, as hereafter, in due time, we shall relate. From thenceforward there were no magnates among them, but there was added thereto the gonfalonier of justice. And sometimes there were twelve priors, according to the changes in the condition of the city and special occasions that arose; and they were chosen from the number of all the twenty-one Arts, and of those which were not themselves artificers, albeit their forefathers had been artificers. The election to the said office was made by the old priors with the colleges of consuls of the twelve greater Arts, and with certain others which elected the priors for each sesto, by secret votes; and whosoever had most votes the same was made prior; and this election took place in the church of San Piero Scheraggio; and the Captain of the Popolo was stationed over against the said church in the houses which pertained to the Tizzoni. We have said so much of the beginning of this office of the priors, forasmuch as many and great changes followed therefrom to the city of Florence, as hereafter, in due place and time, we shall relate. At present we will leave telling, for a time, of the doings of Florence, and we will tell of other events which came to pass in those times.

§ 80.—*How Pope Martin sent M. Jean d'Appia into Romagna, and how he* **1282 a.d.** *took the city of Faenza and besieged Forlì.*

§ 81.—*How M. Jean d'Appia, count of Romagna, was defeated at Forlì by the count of Montefeltro.*

1282 a.d.

In the said time, when the said M. Jean d'Appia, count of Romagna, was in Faenza, and was making war against the city of Forlì, he dabbled in practices whereby he might gain the said city by treachery; the which practices Count Guido of Montefeltro himself, which was lord of the city, had set in motion and floated, as one that was master both of **Inf. xxvii. 76-78.** plots and of war, and who knew the folly of the French. At last, on the first day of May, in the year of Christ 1282, the said M. Jean came with his forces in the morning very early before day to the city of Forlì, thinking to have it; and as it was ordered by the count of Montefeltro, the entrance to one gate was granted him, which he entered with part of his followers, and part he left without with the orders, if need arose, to succour those within, and if things went against them, to assemble all his forces in a field under a great oak. The French which entered into Forlì rode through the city without meeting any opposition; and the count of Montefeltro, which knew all the plot, had gone forth from the city with his followers; and it was said that this same count of Montefeltro was guided by the augury and counsel of one Guido Bonatti, a roof-maker, who had turned astrologer **Inf. xx. 118.** or the like, and that it was he who prompted his actions; and for this emprise he gave him the standard and said, "Thou hast it at such a pitch, that so long as a rag of it hold, wheresoever thou bearest it thou shalt be victorious." But I more believe that his victories were won by his own wit and mastery of war. And according as he had planned, he charged those without under the tree, and put them to rout. They which had entered in, thinking the city was theirs, had given themselves to plunder and gone into the houses; and as was ordered by the count of Montefeltro, the citizens had taken off the bridles and saddles from the most of their horses; and suddenly the said count, with part of his followers, entered again into Forlì by one of the gates, and overran the city; and part of his horse and foot he left in troops drawn up under the oak, as the French had been. M. Jean d'Appia and his men, seeing themselves thus handled, when they thought they had conquered the city, held themselves for dead and betrayed, and whosoever could recover his horse fled from the city, and came to the tree without, thinking to find friends there; and when they came thither they were taken or slain by their enemies, and likewise they which had remained within the city; wherefore the French and the followers of the Church suffered great discomfiture and loss, **Inf. xxvii. 44.** and there died there many good French knights, and of the Latin leaders, among others, Count Taddeo da Montefeltro, cousin to Count Guido, which by reason of disputes concerning his inheritance held with the Church against the said Count Guido; and there died there Tribaldello de' Manfredi, which had betrayed Faenza, and many others; **Inf. xxxii. 122.** albeit the count of Romagna, M. Jean d'Appia, escaped with certain others from the said discomfiture, and returned to Faenza.

§ 82.—*How Forlì surrendered to the Church, and how there was peace* **1282 a.d.** *in Romagna.* § 83.—*How the king of Armenia with a great company of Tartars was defeated at Cammella [Emesa] in Syria by the soldan of Egypt.* § 84.—*How the war between the Genoese and Pisans began.* § 85.—*How the prince, son of King Charles, with many barons of France and of Provence, came to Florence to march against the Sicilians.* § 86.—*How King Charles and King Peter of Aragon engaged to fight in* **1283 a.d.** *single*

221

*combat at Bordeaux, in Gascony, for the possession of Sicily. § 87.—How on the appointed day, King Peter, of Aragon, failed to appear at Bordeaux, wherefore he was excommunicated and deposed by the **1282 a.d.***

1283 a.d. *Pope. § 88.—How there was in Florence a flood of waters and great scarcity of victuals. § 89.—How a noble court and festival was held in the city of Florence, whereat all were arrayed in white. § 90.—How the Genoese did great hurt to the Pisans returning from Sardinia. § 91.—Still of the doings of the Pisans and the Genoese.* **1284 a.d.** *§ 92.—How the Genoese discomfited the Pisans at Meloria. § 93.—How Charles, prince of Salerno, was defeated and taken prisoner at sea, by Ruggeri di Loria, with the fleet of the Sicilians. § 94.—How King Charles arrived at Naples with his fleet, and then made ready to pass to Sicily.*

§ 95.—How the good King Charles passed from this life at the city of Foggia in Apulia.

1284 a.d.

When King Charles had returned with his host to Brindisi, he disbanded them and returned to Naples to make his arrangements, and to furnish himself with money and with men to go again to Sicily the coming spring. And like one whose anxious mind could not rest, when mid-December was past, he returned into Apulia, to be at Brindisi to hasten on his fleet. When he was at Foggia, in Apulia, as it pleased God, he fell sick of a grievous sickness, and passed from this life on the day following the Epiphany, on the 7th day of January, in the year of Christ 1284. But before he died, with great contrition taking the Body of Christ, he said with great reverence these words: "Sire Dieu, comme je crois vraiment que vous étes mon Sauveur, ainsi je vous prie, que vous ayez merci de mon ame; ainsi comme je fis la prise du royaume de Cicile plus pour servir sainte Eglise que pour mon profit ou autre convoitise, ainsi vous me pardonniez mes péchés;" and a short time **Purg. vii. 113, 124, 128.** after he passed from this life, and his body was brought to Naples; and after great lamentation had been made over his death, he was buried at the archbishop's at Naples with great honour. Concerning this death of King Charles there was a great marvel, for the same day whereon he died, the tidings of his death were published by one Brother Arlotto, a minister of the Minor Friars, and by M. Giardino da

Carmignanola, a teacher in the University; and when this came to the notice of the king of France he sent for them to learn whence they knew it. They said that they knew his nativity, which was under the lordship of Saturn, and by its influence had resulted his exaltations and his adversities; and some said that they knew it by revelation of some spirit, for each of them was a great astrologer and necromancer. This Charles was the most feared and redoubted lord, and the most valiant in arms, and of the most lofty designs, of all the kings of the house of France from Charles the Great to his own day, and the one which most exalted the Church of Rome; and he would have done more if, at the end of his life, fortune had not turned against him. Afterwards there came as guardian and defender of the kingdom, Robert, count of Artois, cousin of the said king, with many French knights, and with the princess, and with the prince's son, grandson to King Charles, which was called after him Charles Martel, and which was some **Par. viii. 31, 49-72; ix. 1.** twelve or thirteen years old. Of King Charles there remained no other heir than Charles II., prince of Salerno, of whom we have made mention. And this Charles was comely in person, and gracious and **Cf. Par. viii. 82, 83; Purg. xx. 79-84.** liberal, and whilst his father was living and afterwards he had many children by the princess, his wife, daughter and heiress of the king of Hungary. The first was the said Charles Martel, which was afterwards king of Hungary; the second was Louis, which became a Minor Friar, and afterwards was bishop of Toulouse; the third was Robert, **Par. viii. 76-84.** duke of Calabria; the fourth was Philip, prince of Taranto; the fifth was Raymond Berenger (count that was to be of Provence); the sixth was John, prince of Morea; the seventh was Peter, count of Eboli.

§ 96.—*How the prince, son to King Charles, was condemned to death by* **1284 a.d.** *the Sicilians, and afterwards was sent prisoner into Catalonia by Queen Constance.* § 97.—*How there was a great flood of waters in Florence, which overwhelmed part of the Poggio de' Magnoli.* § 98.—*How the Florentines, with the Genoese and with the Tuscans, made a league against the Pisans, whereby the Ghibellines were driven out of Pisa.* § 99.—*How the Florentines began the foundation of the gates, to build the new walls of the city.* § 100.—*Of the great events that came to pass among the Tartars of Turigio.* § 101.—*How* **1285 a.d.** *the Saracens took and destroyed Margatto in Syria.* § 102.—*How King Philip of France went with a great army against the king of Aragon.*

§ 103.—*How the king of Aragon was discomfited and wounded by the French, of the which wound he afterwards died.* § 104.—*How the king of France took the city of Gerona, and how his fleet was discomfited at sea.*

§ 105.—*How the king of France departed from Aragon, and died at Perpignan.*
1285 a.d.

King Philip of France, seeing his fortune so changed and adverse, and his fleet, which was bringing victuals to his host, taken and burnt, was overcome with grief and melancholy in such wise that he fell grievously sick with fever and a flux, wherefore his barons took counsel to depart and return to Toulouse, and of necessity they were forced thereto by lack of victuals, and by reason of the adverse season of autumn, and because of the sickness of their king. And thus they departed about the first day of October, carrying their sick king in a litter, and they dispersed with but little order, each one getting away as best he could and most quickly; wherefore, when they were crossing the difficult pass of the Schiuse through the great mountains of Pirris [? the defiles of the great mountains of Pertus], the Aragonese and Catalans which were at the pass, sought to hinder the passing of the litter wherein the king of France lay sick. And when the French saw this, they gave battle in despair to them which were at the pass, to the end they might not take the body of the king, and by force of arms they broke them up and discomfited them, and drave them from the pass; but many of the French common people on foot were taken and slain, and many mules and horses and much baggage destroyed and taken by the Catalans and Aragonese. And a little while after the departure of the king of France and of his host, the king of Aragon received Gerona back on conditions. And when the host of the king of France in guise as if defeated came to Perpignan, as it pleased God, King Philip of France passed from this life on the 6th **Purg. vii. 105.** day of October, in the year of Christ 1285; and in Perpignan the queen of Morea, his wife, with her company made great lamentation and sorrow. And afterwards Philip and Charles, his sons, caused the body to be brought to Paris, and he was buried at S. Denys with his predecessors, with great honour. This enterprise against Aragon was attended with greater loss of men and more cost in horses and money, than the realm of France had almost

224

ever suffered in times past; for afterwards the king which succeeded the said Philip, and the greater part of the barons, were always in debt and ill provided with money. And after the death of King Philip of France, King Philip the Fair, his eldest son, was made king of France, and crowned king in the city **Cf. Purg. vii. 109.** of Rheims, with the Queen Joanna of Navarre, his wife, on the day of the Epiphany next following. And note, that in one year or little **Par. xix. 143-148.** more, as it pleased God, there died four such great lords of Christendom, as were Pope Martin, and the good Charles, king of Sicily and of Apulia, and the valiant King Peter of Aragon, and the powerful King Philip of France, of whom we have made mention. This King Philip was a lord of a great heart, and in his life did high emprises; first, when he went against the king of Spain, and then against the count of Foix, and then against the king of Aragon, with greater forces than ever his predecessor had gathered. We will leave now speaking of the doings beyond the mountains, whereof we have said enough for this time, and we will go back to speak of the doings of our Italy which came to pass in the said time.

§ 106.—*Of the death of Pope Martin IV., and how Honorius de' Savelli* **1285 a.d.**

Purg. xxiv. 20-24.

1286 a.d. *of Rome was made Pope.* § 107.—*How a certain Genoese flotilla was taken by the Pisans.* § 108.—*How Count Guido of Montefeltro, lord of Romagna, surrendered to the Church of Rome.* § 109.—*How Pope Honorius changed the habit of the Carmelite Friars.* § 110.—*How the bishop of Arezzo caused Poggio a Santa Cecilia, in the territory of Siena, to rebel, and how it was recovered.* § 111.—*How there was great scarcity of victual in Italy.* § 112.—*How M. Prezzivalle dal Fiesco came into Tuscany as Imperial Vicar.* § 113.—*How Pope* **1287 a.d.** *Honorius de' Savelli died.*

§ 114.—*Of a notable thing which came to pass in Florence at this time.*
1287 a.d.

In the said year, M. Matteo da Fogliano di Reggio, being Podestà of Florence, had taken and condemned to be beheaded for murder one Totto de' Mazzinghi da Campi, which was a great warrior and leader; and as he was on his way to execution, M. Corso dei Donati with his following would have rescued him from the officers by force; for the which thing the said Podestà caused the great bell to be sounded: wherefore all the good people of Florence armed themselves and assembled at the palace, some on horse and some on foot, crying: "Justice, justice." For the which thing the said Podestà carried out his sentence, but whereas the said Totto should have been beheaded, he caused him to be dragged along the ground, and then hung by the neck, and he condemned to a fine those who had begun the uproar and impeded justice.

1288 a.d.

In the year of Christ 1288, in the month of July, great divisions and factions having arisen in Pisa concerning the government, for of one party Judge Nino di Gallura de' Visconti was head with certain Guelfs, **Purg. viii. 53.** and of another Count Ugolino dei Gherardeschi with another party of the Guelfs, and of a third the Archbishop Ruggeri degli Ubaldini with **Inf. xxxiii. 31-33.** the Lanfranchi, and Gualandi, and Sismondi, with the other Ghibelline houses. And the said Ugolino, in order to gain power, sided with the archbishop and his party, and betrayed Judge Nino, not considering that he was his grandson, his daughter's son; and they ordained that he should be driven out of Pisa with his followers, or taken prisoner. Judge Nino hearing this, and seeing that he was not well able to defend himself, left the city and went to his castle of Calci, and allied himself with the Florentines and Lucchese to make war against Pisa. Count Ugolino, before the departure of Judge Nino, to the end he might hide his treachery when he had planned the banishment of the judge, departed from Pisa, and went to one of his manors in the country, which was called Settimo. When he heard of the departure of Judge Nino, he returned to Pisa with great rejoicing; and the Pisans made him their lord with great rejoicings and festivities; but he abode only a short time in the government, for Fortune turned against him, as it pleased God, because of his treacheries and crimes; for of a truth it was said that he caused Count Anselm of Capraia, his nephew, his sister's son, to be poisoned, from envy, and because he was beloved in Pisa, and he feared lest he might rob him of his state. And that happened to Count Ugolino, which a little while before had been foretold him by a wise and valiant man of affairs, named Marco Lombardo; for when the count was called by all lord of Pisa, and when **Purg. xvi. 46.** he was in greatest state and happiness, he prepared a rich feast on his birthday, and invited thereto his sons and grandsons, and all his lineage and kinsfolk, both men and women, with great pomp in dress and ornaments, and preparations for a great festival. The count taking the said Marco, showed him all his grandeur and possessions, and the preparations for his feast; and this done, he asked him: "Marco, what thinkest thou of all this?" The sage answered and said unto him at once: "You are better prepared for evil fortune than any nobleman of Italy." And the count fearing these words of Marco's, said: "Why?" and Marco answered: "Because the wrath of God is the only thing lacking to you." And of a truth the wrath of God soon came upon him, as it pleased God, because of his treacheries and crimes; for when the archbishop of Pisa and his followers had succeeded in driving out Nino and his party, by the counsel and treachery of Count Ugolino, the forces of the Guelfs were diminished; and then the archbishop took counsel how to betray Count Ugolino, and in a sudden uproar of the people, he was attacked and assaulted at the palace, the archbishop giving the people to understand that he had betrayed Pisa, and given up their fortresses to the Florentines and the Lucchese; and being without any defence, the people having turned against him, he surrendered himself prisoner, and at the said assault one of his bastard sons and one of his grandsons were slain, and Count Ugolino was taken, and two of his sons, and three grandsons, his son's children, and they were put in prison; and his household and followers, and the Visconti and Ubizinghi, Guatani, and all the other Guelf houses were driven out of Pisa. And thus was the traitor betrayed by the traitor; wherefore the Guelf party in Tuscany was greatly cast down, and the Ghibellines greatly exalted because of the said revolution in Pisa, and because of the force of the Ghibellines of Arezzo, and because of the power and victories of Don James of Aragon, and of the Sicilians against the heirs of King Charles.

§ 122.—*How the Lucchese took the castle of Asciano from the Pisans.* **1288 a.d.** § 123.—*How the Pisan mercenaries, coming from Campagna, were routed by the Florentine mercenaries in Maremma.* § 124.—*Of the dash on Latterina made by the Florentines as an attack on Arezzo.* § 125.—*How Prince Charles was released from the prison of the king of Aragon.* § 126.—*Of a great flood of water that was in Florence.* § 127.—*How the Aretines came and laid waste the territory of Florence as far as San Donato in Collina.*

§ 128.—*How the Pisans chose for captain the count of Montefeltro, and how they starved to death Count Ugolino and his sons and grandsons.*
1288 a.d.

In the said year 1288, in the said month of March, the wars in Tuscany between the Guelfs and Ghibellines becoming hot again (by reason of the war begun by the Florentines and Sienese against the Aretines, and by the Florentines and Lucchese against the Pisans), the Pisans chose for their captain of war Count Guido of Montefeltro, giving him wide jurisdiction and lordship; and he passed the boundaries of Piedmont, within which he was confined by his terms of surrender to the Church, and came to Pisa; for the which thing he and his sons and family, and all the commonwealth of Pisa, were excommunicated by the Church of Rome, as rebels and enemies against Holy Church. And when the said count was come to Pisa in the said month of March, the Pisans which had put in prison Count Ugolino and his two sons, and two sons of Count Guelfo, his son, as we before made mention, in a tower on the Piazza degli Anziani, caused the door of the said tower to be locked, and the keys thrown into the Arno, and refused to the said prisoners any food, which in a few days died there of hunger. And albeit first **Inf. xxxiii. 1-90.** the said count demanded with cries to be shriven; yet did they not grant him a friar or priest to confess him. And when all the five dead bodies were taken out of the tower, they were buried without honour; and thenceforward the said prison was called the Tower of Hunger, and will be

228

always. For this cruelty were the Pisans greatly blamed throughout the whole world wherever it was known, not so much by reason of the count, which because of his crimes and treacheries was peradventure worthy of such a death, but by reason of his sons and grandsons which were young and innocent boys; and this sin committed by the Pisans did not go unpunished, as in due time hereafter may be found. We will leave speaking, for a while, of the affairs of Florence and of Tuscany, and will tell of other events which took place in the said times and came to pass through the whole world.

§ 129.—*How the Saracens took Tripoli in Syria.*

§ 130.—*Of the coronation of King Charles II., and how he passed through Florence, and left Messer Amerigo di Nerbona as captain of war for the Florentines.*
1289 a.d.

In the said year, on the 2nd day of May, there came to Florence Prince Charles, son of the great King Charles, which was returning from France after he had been loosed from prison, and was going to the court at Rieti where was the Pope; and he was received by the Florentines with great rejoicing, and the Florentines did him much honour and made him many presents; and having sojourned three days in Florence, he departed on his journey towards Siena. And when he was departed, tidings came to Florence that the troops of Arezzo were making ready to go into the country of Siena to hinder or bring shame upon the said Prince Charles, which had but a small company of men-at-arms. Straightway the Florentines caused the horsemen of the cavalry to ride forth, wherein were all the flower of the best families of Florence, together with mercenaries which were in Florence, and they were in number 800 horse, and 3,000 foot, to accompany the prince; wherefore the prince took in very good part such honourable service, and speedy and unasked succour of so many good men, though it came not to the pinch of need withal; for the Aretines having heard of the riding forth of the Florentines, did not venture to go out against them; but nevertheless the Florentines accompanied the said prince beyond Bricola to the borders of the territory of Siena and of Orvieto. And when the commonwealth of Florence asked of the prince to appoint them a captain of war, and also that he would grant them to carry forth the royal standard with the host, the prince allowed it, and knighted Amerigo di Nerbona, a man very noble, and brave and wise in war, and gave him to them for captain; which M. Amerigo with his company, about 100 mounted men, came to Florence with the said horse; and the prince came to the court, and was honourably received by Pope Nicolas IV. and by his cardinals; and the day of Pentecost following, on the 29th day of May, 1289, in the city of Rome the said Charles was crowned by the said Pope, king of Sicily and of Apulia, with great honour, solemnity and rejoicing, and many favours and grand presents of jewels and of money were made to him by the Church, with subsidies of tithes to aid him in his war in Sicily. And this done, King Charles departed from the court, and went into the Kingdom.

§ 131.—*How the Florentines defeated the Aretines at Certomondo in Casentino.* **1289 a.d.**

In the said year, and month of May, the horsemen of Florence being returned from escorting Prince Charles, with their captain, M. Amerigo di Nerbona, a host was straightway gathered against the city of Arezzo, by reason of outrages received from the Aretines, and the banners of war were given out on the 13th day of May, and the royal standard was borne by M. Gherardo Ventraia de' Tornaquinci; and so soon as they were given to them, they bore them to the abbey at Ripoli, as was their wont, and there they left them under guard, making as though they would march by that road upon the city of Arezzo. And the allies being come and the host being ordered, by secret counsel they purposed to depart by the way of Casentino, and suddenly, the 2nd day of June, the bells sounding a toll, the ever-prosperous host of the Florentines set forth, and they bore the banners which were at Ripoli across the Arno, and held the way of Pontassieve, and encamped to await the gathering of forces on Monte al Pruno; and there were assembled 1,600 horse and 10,000 foot, whereof 600 were citizens with their horses, the best armed and mounted which ever sallied forth from Florence; and 400 mercenaries, together with the following of the Captain, M. Amerigo, in the pay of the Florentines; and of Lucca there were 150 horsemen; and of Prato, 40 horsemen and foot soldiers; of Pistoia, 60 horse and foot; and of Siena, 120 horse; and of Volterra, 40 horse; and of Bologna, their ambassadors with their company; and of Samminiato, and of Sangimignano, and of Colle, men mounted and on foot from each place; and Maghinardo of Susinana, a good and wise captain in war, with his Romagnoli. And the said host being assembled, they descended into the **Inf. xxvii. 49-51. Purg. xiv. 118, 119.** plain of Casentino, devastating the places of Count Guido Novello, who was Podestà of Arezzo. Hearing this, the bishop of Arezzo, with the other captains of the Ghibelline party (for there were many men of name amongst them), determined to come with all their host to Bibbiena, to the end it might not be destroyed; and they were 800 horse and 8,000 foot, very fine men; and many wise captains of war were among them, for they were the flower of the Ghibellines of Tuscany, of the March, and of the Duchy, and of Romagna; and all were men experienced in arms and in war; and they desired to give battle to the Florentines, having no fear, albeit the Florentines were two horsemen to one against them; but they despised them, saying that they adorned themselves like women, and combed their tresses; and they derided them and held them for nought. Truly there was further cause why the Aretines should declare battle against the Florentines, albeit their horsemen were two to one against them; for they were in fear of a plot which the bishop of Arezzo had set on foot with the Florentines, and conducted by M. Marsilio de' Vecchietti, to give over to the Florentines Bibbiena, Civitella, and all the castles of his see, and he to have 5,000 golden florins each year of his life, on the security of the company of the Cerchi. The progress of this plot was interrupted by M. Guiglielmino Pazzo, his nephew, to the end the bishop might not be slain by the Ghibelline leaders; and therefore they hastened the battle, and took thither the said bishop, where he was left dead, together with the rest; and thus was the bishop punished for his treason, who at the same time sought to betray both the Florentines and his own Aretines. And the Florentines, having joyfully received the gage of battle, arrayed themselves; and the two hosts stood over against one another, after more ordered fashion, both on one side and on the other, than ever in any battle before in Italy, in the plain at the foot of Poppi, in the region called Certomondo, for such is the name of the place, and of a church of the Franciscans, which is near there, and in a plain which is called Campaldino; and this was a Saturday morning, the 11th day of June, the day of S. Barnabas the Apostle. M.

231

Amerigo and the other Florentine captains drew up in well-ordered troops, and enrolled 150 forefighters of the best of the host, among the which were twenty new-made knights, who then received their spurs; and M. Vieri de' Cerchi being among the **Cf. Par. xvi. 65, 94-96.** captains, and being lame in his leg, would not therefore desist from being among the forefighters; and since it fell to him to make the selection for his sesto, he would not lay this service upon any who did not desire to be chosen, but chose himself, and his son and nephews; the which thing was counted to him as of great merit; and for his good example and for shame many other noble citizens offered themselves as forefighters. And this done, they flanked them on either side by troops of light-armed infantry, and crossbowmen, and unmounted lancers. Then, behind the forefighters, came the main body, flanked in its turn by footmen, and, behind all, the baggage, so collected as to close up the rear of the main body, outside of which were stationed two hundred horse and foot of the Lucchese and Pistoians and other **Purg. xxiv. 82. Cf. Par. iii. 106, 107.** foreigners, whereof was captain M. Corso Donati, which then was Podestà of Pistoia; and their orders were to take the enemy in flank, should occasion rise. The Aretines on their part ordered their troops wisely, inasmuch as there were, as we have said, good captains of war amongst them; and they appointed many forefighters, to the number of 300, among the which were chosen twelve of the chief leaders, who were called the Twelve Paladins. And each side having given a war-cry to their host, the Florentines, "Ho, knights, Nerbona," and the Aretines, "Ho, knights, San Donato," the forefighters of the Aretines advanced with great courage, and struck spur to smite into the Florentine host; and the rest of their troop followed after, save that Count Guido Novello, which was with a troop of 150 horse to charge in flank, did not adventure himself into the battle, but drew back, and then fled to his castle. And the movement and assault made upon the Florentines by the Aretines, who esteemed themselves to be valiant men-at-arms, was to the end that by their bold attack they might break up the Florentines at the first onset, and put them to flight; and the shock was so great that most of the Florentine forefighters were unhorsed, and the main body was driven back a good space, but they were not therefore confounded nor broken up, but received the enemy with constancy and fortitude; and the wings of infantry on either side, keeping their ranks well, enclosed the enemy, and there was hard fighting for a good space. And M. Corso Donati, who was apart with the men of Lucca and Pistoia, and had been commanded to stand firm, and not to strike under pain of death, when he saw the battle begun, said, like a valiant man: "If we lose, I will die in the battle with my fellow-citizens; and if we conquer, let him that will, come to us at Pistoia to exact the penalty"; and he boldly set his troop in motion, and struck the enemy in flank, and was a great cause of their rout. And this done, as it pleased God, the Florentines had the victory, and the Aretines were routed and discomfited, and between horse and foot more than 1,700 were slain, and more than 2,000 taken, whereof many of the best were smuggled away, some for friendship, some in return for ransom; but there came of them bound to Florence more than 740. Among the dead left on the field were M. Guiglielmino of the Ubertini, bishop of Arezzo, the which was a great warrior, and M. Guiglielmino de' Pazzi of Valdarno and his nephews, the which was the best and the most experienced captain of war that there was in Italy in his time; **Purg. v. 88-129. Inf. xxvii. 68-129.** and there died there Bonconte, son of Count Guido of Montefeltro, and three of the Uberti, and one of the Abati, and two of the Griffoni of Fegghine, and many other Florentine refugees, and Guiderello d'Alessandro of Orvieto, a renowned captain, who bore the imperial standard, and many others. On the side of the Florentines was slain no man of renown save M. Guiglielmo Berardi, bailiff of M. Amerigo da Nerbona, and M. Bindo del Baschiera de' Tosinghi, and Ticci de' Visdomini; but many other citizens and foreigners were wounded. The news of the said victory came to Florence the same day, at the same hour that it took place, for after their meal, the Priors being gone to sleep and repose, after the care and wakefulness of the past night, suddenly there was a knocking on the chamber door, with the cry: "Arise, for the Aretines are discomfited"; and having risen and opened the door, they found no one, and their servants without had heard nothing, wherefore it was held to be a great and notable marvel, inasmuch as no person came from the host with tidings before the hour of vespers. And this was the truth, for I heard it and saw it; and all the Florentines marvelled whence this could be, and awaited the issue in suspense. But when they arrived which came from the host, and reported the tidings in Florence, there was great gladness and rejoicing; and there was good cause, for at the said discomfiture were slain many captains and valiant men of the Ghibelline party, and enemies of the commonwealth of Florence, and there were brought low the arrogance and pride not only of the Aretines, but of the whole Ghibelline party and of the Empire.

§ 132.—*How the Florentines besieged the city of Arezzo, and laid waste the region round about.*

1289 a.d.

After the said victory of the commonwealth over the Aretines, the trumpet was sounded for the return from pursuing the fugitives, and the Florentine host was marshalled upon the field; and this done, they departed to Bibbiena, and took it without any resistance; and having plundered and despoiled it of all its wealth and much booty, they caused the walls and the fortified houses to be destroyed to the foundations, and many other villages round about, and they abode there eight days. Whereas, if on the day following, the Florentine host had ridden upon Arezzo, without doubt they would have taken the city; but during that sojourn they that had escaped from the battle returned thither, and the peasants round about took refuge there, and order was taken for the defence and guard of the city. The host of the Florentines came thither after some days, and laid siege to the city, continually laying waste the region round about, and taking their fortresses, so that they gained them nearly all, some by force, and some on conditions; and the Florentines caused many thereof to be destroyed, but they kept possession of Castiglione of Arezzo, and Montecchio, and Rondine, and Civitella, and Laterina, and Montesansavino. And with the host there went two of the Priors of Florence as inspectors; and the Sienese came in a body, with much force of horse and foot, after the defeat, to regain their lands taken by the Aretines, and they took Lucignano of Arezzo, and Chiusura of Valdichiane, on conditions. And the said Florentine host being at Arezzo, in the old palace of the bishops, for twenty days, they laid **Inf. xxii. 4, 5.**

Cf. Par. xvi. 42. waste all round about them, and they ran their races there on the feast of S. Giovanni, and erected there many engines, and hurled into the city asses with mitres on their heads, in contempt and reproach of their

234

bishop, and raised many wooden towers and other works to attack the city; and a fierce battle ensuing, a great part of the palisade (for there was not then any other wall in that part) was burnt and laid low; and if the captains of the host had made the besiegers fight lustily, they would have taken the city by storm; but where they should have fought, they caused the retreat to be sounded, wherefore they were held in abomination, forasmuch as this was done through greed of gain; for the which cause the people and the combatants, losing heart, were slack in skirmishing and on guard; wherefore the night following they of Arezzo issued forth and set fire to many wooden towers, and burnt them, with many other works. And this done, the Florentines lost hope of taking the city by battle, and the better part of the host departed, leaving the aforesaid strongholds guarded, to the end they might continually harry the city; and the host returned to Florence on the 23rd day of July with great rejoicing and triumph, and there came to meet them the clergy in procession, the men of birth jousting, and the populace with the standards and ensigns of each of the Arts, with its company; and they set a canopy of cloth of gold over the head of M. Amerigo di Nerbona, borne upon pikes by many knights, and likewise over M. Ugolino de' Rossi of Parma, which was then Podestà of Florence. And note that all the expenses of the said host were furnished by our commonwealth by a tax of six and a quarter per cent., which raised more than 36,000 golden florins, so well ordered were then the registers of the city and country; and the other affairs and revenues of the commonwealth were equally well ordered. True it is that after the return of the said host the popolani began to suspect that the magnates, through pride of the said victory, might lay burdens on them beyond accustomed usage; and for this cause the seven greater Arts drew to themselves the five lesser Arts, and made ready among themselves arms, and shields, and certain standards, and this was in a sense a beginning of the Popolo, which afterwards took the form of the Popolo of 1292, as hereafter we shall narrate. From the aforesaid victory the city of Florence was much exalted, and rose to good and happy state, the best which it had seen until these times, and it increased greatly in people and in wealth, for every one was gaining by some merchandise, art, or trade; and it continued in peaceful and tranquil state for many years after, rising every day. And by reason of

235

gladness and well-being, every year, on the first day of May, they formed bands and companies of gentle youths, clad in new raiment, and raised pavilions covered with cloth and silk and with wooden walls, in divers parts of the city; and likewise there were bands of women and of maidens going through the city dancing in ordered fashion, and ladies, by two and two, with instruments, and with garlands of flowers on their heads, continuing in pastimes and joyance, and at feasts and banquets.

§ 133.—*Of a fierce and violent battle between the duke of Brabant* **1289 a.d.** *and the count of Luxemburg.* § 134.—*How Don James came from Sicily into Calabria with his armada, and there received some loss, and afterwards laid siege to Gaeta.* § 135.—*How Charles Martel was* **Par. viii. 64-66.** *crowned king of Hungary.* § 136.—*How they of Chiusi were routed, and the Guelf refugees restored.* § 137.—*How the Lucchese, with the forces of Florence, marched upon the city of Pisa.* § 138.—*Of an expedition that the Florentines made wherein they should have had Arezzo yielded up to them.* § 139.—*Of a great fire that broke out in Florence in the house of the Pegolotti.* § 140.—*How the Florentines and their allies made a third expedition against Arezzo.* § 141.—*How Porto Pisano was taken and laid waste by the Florentines and Genoese and Lucchese.* § 142.—*How the marquis of Montferrat was taken* **Purg. vii. 136. Convivio iv. 11: 126.** *prisoner by them of Alexandria.* § 143.—*Of a great miracle that came to pass in Paris concerning the body of Christ.* § 144.—*How they of Ravenna seized the count of Romagna, who was there to represent the Church.*

§ 145.—*How the soldan of Babylon conquered by force the city of Acre, to the great hurt of the Christians.*

236

1291 a.d.
Cf. Inf. xxvii. 89.

In the year of Christ 1291, in the month of April, the soldan of Babylon [Cairo] of Egypt having first garrisoned and provisioned Syria, traversed the desert and came into the said Syria with his host, and laid siege to the city of Acre, which of old was called in the Scriptures Ptolemais, and now is called Acon in Latin; and the soldan had with him so much people, both foot and horse, that his host stretched over more than twelve miles. But before we tell more of the loss of Acre, we will tell the reason why the soldan came to besiege it, and took it, as it was related to us by trustworthy fellow-citizens of our own, and merchants which were in Acre at that time. It is true that, because the Saracens had in foregoing times taken from the Christians the city of Antioch, and of Tripoli, and of Tyre, and many other towns which the Christians held on the seashore, the city of Acre had greatly increased, both in folk and in power, forasmuch as no other city was held by the Christians in Syria; so that the kings of Jerusalem, and of Cyprus, and the princes of Antioch, and of Tyre, and of Tripoli, and the Orders of the Templars and the Hospitallers, and other Orders, and the Pope's legates, and they which had gone over seas from the kings of France and of England, all gathered at Acre, and there were there seventeen hereditary lordships, which was a great confusion. And at that time there was truce between the Christians and the Saracens, and there were there more than 18,000 pilgrims who had taken the cross; and their pay not being forthcoming, and because they could not get it from the lords and states which had sent them forth, part of them, which were wild and lawless men, scrupled not to break the truce, and to rob and to slay all the Saracens which were in Acre, under the security of the truce, with their merchandise and victuals; and in like manner they went through many villages round about Acre, robbing and slaying the Saracens. For the which thing, the soldan holding himself much aggrieved, sent his ambassadors to Acre to those lords, demanding compensation for the wrongs that had been committed, and that for his honour and the satisfaction of his people, there should be sent to him as prisoners some of the chiefs and leaders of them which had broken the truce, to the end that he

237

might execute justice upon them, the which requests were denied him. Wherefore he came with his army, as we have said, and because of the multitude of his people, by force they filled up part of the moats, which were very deep, and took the outer circle of the walls; and the next circle they caused in part to fall by the aid of mines and engines; and they took the great tower, which was called Accursed, because it had been foretold that by it Acre should be lost. But with all this they could not take the city, for albeit the Saracens broke down the walls by day, by night they were repaired and stopped up with planks, or with sacks of wool and of cotton, and vigorously defended on the day following, by the wise and valiant brother, Guillaume de Beaujeu, master of the Temple, which was captain-general of the war and of the defence of the city, and had, with much prowess and foresight and care, vigorously defended the city. But as it pleased God, and to punish the sins of the inhabitants of Acre, the said master of the Temple, lifting up his right arm in the combat, was shot by a Saracen with a poisoned arrow, which entered into the joints of his cuirass, by the which wound he shortly after died; and because of his death the whole city was moved and put in fear; and by reason of the confusion of so many lords and captains, as we before said, all fell into disorder, and there was discord in the guard and defence of the city; and each one who could gave heed to his own safety, taking refuge in ships and in other vessels which were in the port. For the which cause the Saracens, continuing the attacks by day and by night, entered the city by force and traversed it, robbing everywhere and slaying all who came in their way, and the young men and maidens they carried off as slaves; and there were of slain and prisoners, men, women and children, more than 60,000; and the loss of goods and booty was infinite. And having collected the booty and treasures, and carried away the prisoners out of the city, they broke down the walls and strongholds, and set fire to them, and destroyed all the city, whereby Christendom sustained very great hurt, for by the loss of Acre there remained in the Holy Land no city pertaining to the Christians; and never again was any one of the good trading cities, which are on our sea-shores and borders, worth one-half of its former profit in merchandise and arts; because of the loss of the city and port of Acre, by reason of its good situation right on the brow of our sea, and in the midst of Syria, and well-nigh in the midst of the

238

inhabited world, seventy miles distant from Jerusalem, a magazine and port for all merchandise, both from the East and from the West; and all races of men in the world met there to barter merchandise; and there were interpreters there of all the languages of the world, so that it was like one of the elements of the world. And this disaster was not without the great and just judgment of God, for that city was more full of sinful men and of women of every kind of abandoned vice than any other Christian city. When the sorrowful tidings came to the West, the Pope proclaimed great indulgences and pardons to whosoever should give aid and succour to the Holy Land, sending word to all Christian lords that he purposed a general crusade; and he forbade, under pain of severe judgments and excommunications, that any Christian should go to Alexandria or the land of Egypt with merchandise, or victuals, or wood, or iron, or should give aid and favour there in any wise.

§ 146.—*Of the death of King Rudolf of Germany.*
1291 a.d.

In the said year 1291, King Rudolf of Germany died, but he never attained to the honours of the Empire, because he was always intent upon increasing his state and lordship in Germany, leaving the **Purg. vi. 103-105.** enterprises of Italy that he might increase land and possessions for his sons; who, by his energy and valour, from a small count rose to be Emperor, and gained for himself the duchy of Austria, and a great part of the duchy of Suabia.

§ 147.—*How King Philip of France caused all the Italians to be taken prisoner, and then ransomed.* § 148.—*How the Pisans recaptured the fortress of Pontadera.*

§ 149.—*How the city of Forlì in Romagna was taken by Maghinardo da Susinana.*
1291 a.d.

In the said year all the county of Romagna, being obedient to Holy Church, and under the care of the bishop of Arezzo, which was count thereof for the Pope, Maghinardo da Susinana, with certain nobles and great men of Romagna, took the city of Forlì by theft, and in it they took the

Count Aghinolfo of Romena with his sons, which was brother to the said count bishop of Arezzo; and they besieged the said count bishop in Cesena; whence arose great war in Romagna. The said Maghinardo was a great and wise tyrant, holding many castles between Casentino and Romagna, and having many followers; and he was wise in war and very fortunate in many battles, and in his time did great things. He was a Ghibelline by race and by his works, but with the Florentines he was a Guelf and the enemy of all their enemies, whether **Cf. Inf. xxvii. 49-51.** they were Guelfs or Ghibellines; and in every expedition and battle which the Florentines undertook, whilst he was alive, he was with his people in their service as a captain; and this was because, when his father died, which was called Piero Pagano, a great nobleman, leaving the said Maghinardo, a young child and with many enemies, to wit, the Counts Guidi and the Ubaldini and other lords of Romagna, this said father left him to the care and tutelage of the people and commonwealth of Florence, him and his lands; by the which commonwealth his patrimony was benignly increased and guarded and improved, and for this cause he was grateful and very faithful to the commonwealth of Florence in all its needs.

§ 150.—*How the Florentines took the castle of Ampinana.* **1292 a.d.** § 151.—*How Pope Nicholas, of Ascoli, died.* § 152.—*How the whole city of Noyon, in France, was burnt.* § 153.—*How Adolf was elected king of the Romans.* § 154.—*How the Florentines marched upon the city of Pisa.* § 155.—*Of the miracles which were manifested in Florence by S. Maria d'Orto San Michele.*

END OF SELECTIONS FROM BOOK VII.

BOOK VIII.

Here begins the Eighth Book. It tells how the second Popolo arose in the city of Florence, and of many great changes which by reason thereof came afterwards to pass in Florence, following on with the other events of those times.

§ 1.—In the year of Christ 1292, on the 1st day of February, the city **1292 a.d.** of Florence being in great and powerful state, and prosperous in all things, and the citizens thereof waxing fat and rich, and by reason of excessive tranquillity, which naturally engenders pride and novelties, being envious and arrogant among themselves, many murders, and wounds, and outrages were done by one citizen upon another; and above all the nobles known as magnates and potentates, alike in the country and in the city, wrought upon the people who might not resist them, force and violence both against person and goods, taking possession thereof. For the which thing certain good men, artificers and merchants of Florence, which desired good life, considered how to set a remedy and defence against the said plague, and one of the leaders therein, among others, was a man of worth, an ancient and noble citizen, being one of the popolani, rich and powerful, whose name was Giano della Bella, of **Par. xvi. 131, 132.** the people of S. Martin, with the following and counsel of other wise and powerful popolani. And instituting in Florence an order of judges to correct the statutes and our laws, as by our ordinances the custom was of old to do, they ordained certain laws and statutes, very strong and weighty, against such magnates and men of power as should do wrong or violence against the people; increasing the common penalties in divers ways, and enacting that one member of a family of magnates should be held answerable for the others; and two bearing witness to public fame and report should be held to prove such crimes; and the public accounts should be revised. And these laws they called the Ordinances of Justice. And to the intent they might be maintained and put into execution, it was decreed that beyond the number of six Priors which governed the city, there should be a gonfalonier of justice appointed by the several sesti in succession, changing every two months, as do the Priors. And when the bells were set tolling, the people were to rally to the church of San Piero Scheraggio and give out the banner of justice, which before was not the custom. And they decreed that not one of the Priors should be of the noble houses called magnates; for before this good and true merchants had often been made Priors, albeit they chanced to be of some great and noble house. And the ensign and standard of the said Popolo was decreed to be a white field with a red cross; and there were chosen 1000 citizens, divided according to the sesti, with certain standard-bearers for each region, with fifty footmen to each standard, which were to be armed, each one with hauberk and shield marked with the cross; and they were to assemble at every tumult or summons of the gonfalonier, at the house or at the palace of the Priors, to do execution against the magnates; and afterwards the number of the chosen footmen increased to 2,000, and then to 4,000. And a like order of men-at-arms for the people, with the said ensign, was enrolled in each country and district of Florence, and they were called the Leagues of the People. And the first of the said gonfaloniers was one Baldo de' Ruffoli of the Porte del Duomo; and in his time the standard sallied forth with armed men to destroy the goods of a family named Galli of Porta S. Marie, by reason of a murder which one of them had committed in the kingdom of France on the person of a popolano. This new decree of the people, and change in the State was of much importance to the city of Florence, and had afterwards many and divers consequences both ill and good to our commonwealth, as hereafter in due time we shall make mention. And in this new thing and beginning of the Popolo, the popolani would have been hindered by the power of the magnates but that in those times the said magnates of Florence were in greater broils and discords among themselves than ever before since the Guelfs returned to Florence; and there was great war between the Adimari and the Tosinghi, and between the Rossi and the Tornaquinci, and between the Bardi and the Mozzi, and between the Gherardini and the Manieri, and between the Cavalcanti and the Bondelmonti, and between certain of the Bondelmonti and the Giandonati, and between the Visdomini and the Falconieri, and between the Bostichi and the Foraboschi, and between the Foraboschi and the Malispini, and among the Frescobaldi themselves, and among the family of the Donati themselves,

242

and many other noble houses. [And therefore let not the reader marvel because we have put this event at the head of our book, forasmuch as the most strange events arose from this beginning, and not only to our city of Florence, but to all the region of Italy.]

§ 2.—*How the people of Florence made peace with the Pisans, and many* **1293** **a.d.** *other notable things.* § 3.—*Of a great fire which broke out in Florence in the district of Torcicoda.* § 4.—*How the war began between the king of France and the king of England.*

§ 5.—*How Celestine V. was elected and made Pope, and how he renounced the papacy.*

1294 a.d.

Cf. Inf. iii. 58-60; xxvii. 104, 105.

In the year of Christ 1294, in the month of July, the Church of Rome had been vacant after the death of Pope Nicholas d'Ascoli for more than two years, by reason of the discord of the cardinals, which were divided, each party desiring to make one of themselves Pope. And the cardinals being in Perugia and straitly constrained by the Perugians to elect a Pope, as it pleased God they were agreed not to name one of their own college, and they elected a holy man which was called Brother Peter of Morrone in Abruzzi. This man was a hermit, and of austere life and penitence, and in order to abandon the vanity of the world, after he had ordained many holy monasteries of his Order, he departed as a penitent into the mountain of Morrone, which is above Sermona. He, being elected and brought and crowned Pope, made in the following September, for the reformation of the Church, twelve cardinals, for the most part from beyond the mountains, by the petition and after the counsel of King Charles, king of Sicily and of Apulia. And this done, he departed with the court to Naples, and by King Charles was graciously received and with great honour; but because he was simple and knew no letters, and did not occupy himself willingly with the pomps of the world, the cardinals held him in small esteem, and it seemed to them that they had made an ill choice for the well-being and estate of the Church. The said holy father perceiving this, and not feeling himself sufficient for the government of the Church, as one who more loved the service of God and the weal of his soul

243

than worldly honour, sought every way how he might renounce the papacy. Now, among the other cardinals of the court was one M. Benedetto Guatani d'Alagna, very learned in books, and in the things of the world much practised and sagacious, which had a great desire to attain to the papal dignity; and he had laid plans seeking and striving to obtain it by the aid of King Charles and the cardinals, and already had the promise from them, which afterwards was fulfilled to him. He put it before the holy father, hearing that he was desirous to renounce the papacy, that he should make a new decretal, that for the good of his soul any Pope might renounce the papacy, showing him the example of S. Clement, whom, when S. Peter came to die, he desired should be Pope after him; but he, for the good of his soul, would not have it so, and in his room first S. Linus and then S. Cletus was **Par. xxvii. 41.** Pope. And even as the said cardinal gave counsel, Pope Celestine made the said decretal; and this done, the day of S. Lucy in the following December, in a consistory of all the cardinals, in their presence he took off the crown and papal mantle, and renounced the papacy, and **Cf. Inf. iii. 59, 60.** departed from the court, and returned to his hermit life, and to do his penance. And thus Pope Celestine reigned in the papacy five months and nine days. But afterwards it is said, and was true, that his successor, M. Benedetto Guatani aforesaid (who was afterwards Pope Boniface), caused him to be taken prisoner in the mountains of S. Angiolo in Apulia above Bastia, whither he had withdrawn to do penance; and some say that he would fain have gone into Slavonia, but the other secretly held him in the fortress of Fummone in Campagna in honourable confinement, to the intent that so long as he lived none should be set up as a rival to his own election, forasmuch as many Christians held Celestine to be the right and true Pope, notwithstanding his renunciation, maintaining that such a dignity as was the papacy by no decretal could be renounced; and albeit S. Clement refused the papacy at the first, the faithful nevertheless held him to be father, and it behoved him to be Pope after S. Cletus. But Celestine being held prisoner, as we have said, in Fummone, lived but a short time in the said place; and dying there, he was buried poorly in a little church without Fummone pertaining to the order of his brethren, and put underground more than ten cubits deep, to the end his body might not be found. But during his life, and after his death,

244

God wrought many miracles by him, whence many people held him in great reverence; and a certain time afterwards by the Church of Rome, and by Pope John XXII., he was canonised, and called S. Peter of Morrone, as hereafter in due time we shall make mention.

§ 6.—*How Boniface VIII. was elected and made Pope.*

1294 a.d.

Inf. vi. 69. xix. 52-57, 76-81. xxvii. 70, 85-111.

Purg. xx. 86-90. Par. ix. 136-142. xii. 90. xvii. 49-51. xviii. 118-136. xxvii. 22-27. xxx. 148.

In the said year 1294, Cardinal Benedetto Guatani, having by his wit and sagacity so wrought that Pope Celestine had renounced the papacy, as before in the last chapter we have made mention, followed up his enterprise, and wrought upon the cardinals and the support of King Charles, which had the friendship of many cardinals, specially of the twelve newly elected by Celestine. And while he was pursuing this quest, one evening by night he went secretly with but few companions to King Charles, and said to him: "King, thy Pope Celestine had the will and the means to serve thee in thy Sicilian war, but he had not the knowledge. Now, if thou wilt work with thy friends the cardinals that I may be elected Pope, I shall know, and I shall will, and I shall be able," promising him by his faith and oath to put thereto all the power of the Church. Then the king, trusting in him, promised him and agreed with his twelve cardinals that they should give him their votes; and there being at the election M. Matteo Rosso and M. Jacopo della Colonna, which were the heads of factions among the cardinals, they perceived what was toward, and straightway they too gave him their votes, but the first to do it was M. Matteo Rosso Orsini. And on this wise he was elected Pope in the city of Naples, the vigil of the Nativity of Christ in the said year; and immediately when he was elected, he willed to depart from Naples with his court, and came to Rome, and there caused himself to be crowned with great solemnity and honour in the middle of January. And this done, the first act which he did, hearing that great war was begun between King Philip of France and King Edward of England on the question of Gascony, was to send beyond the mountains two cardinal legates, to the end they might

245

reconcile them together; but they availed little, for the said lords continued in greater war than before. This Pope Boniface was of the city of Alagna, a very noble man of his city, son of M. Lifredi Guatani, a Ghibelline by race, and whilst he was cardinal he was their protector, specially of the Todini; but after he was made Pope he became a strong Guelf, and did much for King Charles in the war in Sicily, albeit it is said by many wise men that he broke up the Guelf party, under cover of showing himself a strong Guelf, as hereafter in his actions may be manifestly seen by him who observes closely. A man of large schemes was he and lordly, and sought for much honour, and well knew how to maintain and advance the rights of the Church, and by reason of his knowledge and power he was much redoubted and feared; he was very rich through making the Church great and his kinsfolk; making no scruple of gain, for he said all was lawfully his which was the Church's. And when he was made Pope he annulled all the assignments of the revenues of vacant benefices made by Pope Celestine, except where one was in possession; and he had his nephew made count of Caserta by King Charles, and two sons of the said nephew, the one count of Fondi, and the other count of Palazzo. He bought the military fortress at Rome, which was the palace of Octavianus the emperor, and caused it to be enlarged and rebuilt at great cost, and other strong and fine castles in Campagna and in Maremma. And always he abode in winter in Rome, and in summer and spring in Rieti or Orvieto, but afterwards the most in Alagna, to make his city great. We will now leave speaking of the said Pope, following from time to time the things which came to pass in other parts of the world, and above all those in Florence, whereof the matter increases much.

§ 7.—*When the foundation of the new church of Santa Croce was begun* **1294** *a.d. in Florence.*

§ 8.—*How the great man of the people, Giano della Bella, was driven out of Florence.*

1294 a.d.

In the said year 1294, in the month of January, when M. Giovanni da Lucino da Como had lately entered upon the office of Podestà of Florence, a cause came for trial before him accusing M. Corso de' Donati, a noble and

246

powerful citizen among the best in Florence, of having slain a popolano, a retainer of his associate M. Simone Galastrone, in a scuffle and fray which they had together, and wherein that retainer was slain; for which M. Corso Donati refused to pay the fine and bade justice take its course, trusting in the favour of the said Podestà, to be granted at the prayers of friends and of the lords; whereas the people of Florence looked that the said Podestà should condemn him; and already the standard of justice had been brought forth to carry the sentence into execution; but he absolved him; for the which thing, when the said declaration of innocence was read from the palace of the Podestà, and M. Simone Galastrone was condemned for having inflicted wounds, the common people cried out: "Death to the Podestà," and sallied forth in haste from the palace, crying, "To arms! to arms! long live the people!" and a great number of the people flew to arms, and especially of the common people, and rushed to the house of Giano della Bella, their chief; and he, it is said, sent them with his brother to the palace of the Priors to follow the gonfalonier of justice; but this they did not do, but came only to the palace of the Podestà, and furiously assaulted the said palace with arms and crossbows, and set fire to the gates and burnt them, and entered in, and seized and scornfully robbed the said Podestà and his staff. But M. Corso in fear of his life fled from the palace over the roofs, for then was it not so walled as it is now. And the tumult displeased the Priors which were very near to the palace of the Podestà, but by reason of the unbridled populace, they were not able to hinder it. But some days after, when the uproar had been quieted, the great men could not rest, in their desire to abase Giano della Bella, forasmuch as he had been among the chiefs and beginners of the Ordinances of Justice, and was moreover desirous further to abase the magnates by taking from the Captains of the Guelf Party the seal and the common fund of the Party (which fund was very great), and to give them to the commonwealth; not that he was not a Guelf and of Guelf stock, but he would fain diminish the power of the magnates. Wherefore the magnates, seeing themselves thus treated, created a faction together with the Council of the College of Judges and of Notaries, which held themselves to be oppressed by him, as we before made mention, and with other popolani grassi, friends and kinsmen of the magnates, which loved not that Giano della

247

Bella should be greater in the commonwealth than they. And they determined to elect a body of stalwart Priors. And this was done, and they were proclaimed earlier than the wonted time. And this done, when they were in office they conferred with the Captain of the People, and set forth a proclamation and inquisition against the said Giano della Bella and his other confederates and followers and those which had been leaders in setting fire to the gates of the Palace, charging them with having set the city in an uproar, and disturbed the peace of the State, and assaulted the Podestà, against the Ordinances of Justice; for the which thing the common people was much disturbed, and went to the house of Giano della Bella, and offered to surround him with arms, to defend him or to attack the city. And his brother bore to Orto San Michele a standard with the arms of the people; but Giano was a wise man, albeit somewhat presumptuous, and when he saw himself betrayed and deceived by the very men which had been with him in making the Popolo, and saw that their force together with that of the magnates was very great, and that the Priors were already assembled under arms at their house, he would not hazard the chances of civil war; and to the end the city might not be ravaged, and for fear of his person, he would not face the court, but withdrew, and departed from Florence on the 5th day of March, hoping that the people might yet restore him to his state; wherefore by the said accusation or notification he was for contumacy condemned in person and banished, and he died in exile in France (for he had affairs to attend to there, and was a partner of the Pazzi); and all his goods were destroyed; and certain other popolani were accused with him; and he was a great loss to our city, and above all to the people, forasmuch as he was the most leal and upright popolano, and lover of the common good, of any man in Florence, and one who gave to the commonwealth and took nothing therefrom. He was presumptuous and desired to avenge his wrongs, and this he did somewhat against the Abati, his neighbours, with the arm of the commonwealth, and, perhaps for the said sins, he was by his own laws, wrongfully and without guilt, judged by the unjust. And note that this is a great example to those citizens which are to come, to beware of desiring to be lords over their fellow-citizens or too ambitious; but to be content with the common citizenship. For the very men which had aided him to rise, through envy

248

betrayed him and plotted to abase him; and it has been seen and experienced truly in Florence in ancient and modern times, that whosoever has become leader of the people and of the masses has been cast down; forasmuch as the ungrateful people never give men their due reward. From this event arose great disturbance and change amongst the people and in the city of Florence, and from that time forward the artificers and common people possessed little power in the commonwealth, but the government remained in the hands of the powerful popolani grassi.

§ 9.—*When the building of the great church of Santa Reparata was* **1294 a.d.** *begun.*

§ 10.—*How M. Gianni di Celona came into Tuscany as Imperial Vicar.*
******

1294 a.d.
Inf. xv. 23-120.

In the said year 1294 there died in Florence a worthy citizen whose name was M. Brunetto Latini, who was a great philosopher, and was a perfect master in rhetoric, understanding both how to speak well and how to write well. And he it was which commented upon the rhetoric of Tully, and made the good and useful book called "The Treasure," and **Inf. xv. 119, 120.** "The Little Treasure," and "The Key to the Treasure," and many other books in philosophy, and concerning vices and virtues. And he was secretary of our commonwealth. He was a worldly man, but we have made mention of him because it was he who was the beginner and master in refining the Florentines and in teaching them how to speak well, and how to guide and rule our republic according to policy.

§ 11.—*How S. Louis, king that was of France, was canonised.* **1294 a.d.**

§ 12.—*How the magnates of Florence raised a tumult in the city to break up the Popolo.*
1295 a.d.

On the 6th day of the month of July of the year 1295, the magnates and great men of the city of Florence, seeing themselves mightily oppressed by the new Ordinances of Justice made by the people—and especially by that ordinance which declares that one kinsman is to be held to account for another, and that two witnesses establish public report—having their own friends in the priorate, gave themselves to breaking down the ordinances of the people. And first they made up their great quarrels amongst themselves, especially between the Adimari and Tosinghi, and between the Mozzi and the Bardi. And this done, on an appointed day, they made a great gathering of folk, and petitioned the Priors to have the said articles amended; whereupon all the people in the city of Florence rose in tumult and rushed to arms; the magnates, on armoured horses themselves, and with their retainers from the country and other troops on foot in great numbers; and one set of them drew up in the piazza of S. Giovanni, over whom M. Forese degli Adimari held the royal ensign; another set assembled at the Piazza a Ponte, whose ensign was held by M. Vanni Mozzi; and a third set in the Mercato Nuovo, whose standard M. Geri Spini held; with intent to overrun the city. The popolani were all in arms, in their ranks, with ensigns and banners, in great numbers; and they barricaded the streets of the city at sundry points to hinder the horsemen from overrunning the place, and they gathered at the palace of the Podestà, and at the house of the Priors, who at that time abode at the house of the Cerchi behind San Brocolo. And the people found themselves in great power and well ordered, with force of arms and folk, and they associated with the Priors, whom they did not trust, a number of the greatest and most powerful and discreet of the popolani of Florence, one for each sesto. Wherefore the magnates had no strength nor power against them, and the people might have overthrown them; but consulting for the best, and to avoid civil battle, by the mediation of certain friars between the better sort of either side, each party disarmed; and the city returned to peace and quiet without any change; the Popolo being left in its state and lordship; save that whereas before the proof of public report was established by two witnesses, it was now laid down that there must be three; and even this was conceded by the Priors against the will of the popolani, and shortly afterwards it was revoked and the old order re-established. But for all that this disturbance was the root and beginning of the dismal and ill estate of the city of Florence which thereafter followed, for thenceforth the magnates never ceased to search for means to beat down the people, to their utmost power; and the leaders of the people sought every way of strengthening the people and abasing the magnates by reinforcing the Ordinances of Justice, and they had the great crossbows taken from the magnates and bought up by the commonwealth; and many families which were not tyrannical nor of any great power they removed from the number of the magnates and added them to the people, to weaken the power of the magnates and increase that of the people; and when the said Priors went out of office they were struck with cudgels behind and had stones flung at them, because they had consented to favour the magnates; and by reason of these disturbances and changes there was a fresh ordering of the people in Florence, whereof the heads were Mancini and Magalotti, Altoviti, Peruzzi, Acciaiuoli, Cerretani and many others.

§ 13.—*How King Charles made peace with King James of Aragon.*
1295 a.d.
Purg. vii. 115-120, iii. 116.

In the year of Christ 1295 the King Alfonso of Aragon died; by the which death Don James, his brother, which had been crowned king of Sicily and held the island, sought to make peace with the Church and with King Charles; and by the hand of Pope Boniface it was done after this manner: that the said Don James should take to wife the daughter of King Charles, and should resign the lordship of Sicily, and should set the hostages free which King Charles had left in Aragon, to wit Robert and Raymond and John, his sons, with other barons and knights of Provence. And the Pope, with King Charles, promised that they would cause Charles of Valois, brother of the king of France, to renounce the claim which Pope Martin IV. had granted him to the kingdom of Aragon; and to the end he might consent thereto, King Charles gave him the county of Anjou, and his daughter to wife. And to order this matter King Charles went into France in person, and when he returned with the compact made, and with his sons whom he had set free from prison, he came to the city of Florence, whither was already come to meet him Charles Martel, his son, king of Hungary, with his company **Cf. Par. viii. 49-75.** of 200 knights with golden spurs, French and Provençal and from the Kingdom, all young men, invested by the king with habits of scarlet and dark green, and all with saddles of one device, with their palfreys adorned with silver and gold, with arms quarterly, bearing golden lilies and surrounded by a bordure of red and silver, which are the arms of Hungary. And they appeared the noblest and richest company a young king ever had with him. And in Florence he abode more than twenty days, awaiting his father, King Charles, and his brothers; and the Florentines did him great honour, and he showed great love to the **Par. viii. 55.** Florentines, wherefore he was in high favour with them all. And when King Charles was come into Florence, and Robert and Raymond and John, his sons, with the marquis of Montferrat, which was to have for wife the daughter of the king, he made many knights in Florence and received much honour and many presents from the Florentines; and then the king with all his sons returned to the papal court and afterwards to Naples. And this done, and after all the articles of the treaty of peace had been fulfilled by the Pope and by King Charles, Don James departed from Sicily and came into Aragon, and was crowned king over the realm; but whosoever may have been in fault, whether the Pope or **Purg. iii. 116, vii. 115-120. Par. xix. 130-135, xx. 61-63; Convivio iv. 6: 180-190. De Vulg. Eloquio i. 12: 15-38.** Don James, King Charles found himself deceived, for when King Charles thought to have the island of Sicily again in quiet, after Don James had departed, Frederick, his next brother, became lord thereof, and caused himself to be crowned king by the Sicilians against the will of the Church by the bishop of Cephalonia; wherefore the Pope was much angered with the king of Aragon, as well as with Frederick his brother, and caused him to be summoned to court, which King James came thither the following year, as hereafter we shall make mention.

§ 14.—*How the Guelf party were driven by force out of Genoa.* **1296 a.d.** § 15.—*The doings of the Tartars of Persia.* § 16.—*How Maghinardo da* **Inf. xxvii. 49-51.** *Susinana defeated the Bolognese and took the city of Imola.* § 17.—*How the people of Florence built the cities and strongholds of Sangiovanni and Castelfranco in Valdarno.* § 18.—*How King James of Aragon came to Rome, and Pope Boniface granted him the island of Sardinia.* § 19.—*How the counts of Flanders and of Bar rebelled against the king of France.* § 20.—*How the count of Artois defeated* **1297 a.d.** *the Flemings at Furnes, and how the king of England passed into Flanders.* § 21.—*How Pope Boniface* *deposed from the cardinalate* M. **1298 a.d.**

Purg. vi. 97. *Jacopo and* M. *Piero della Colonna.* § 22.—*How Albert of Austria defeated and slew Adolf, king of Germany, and how he was elected king of the Romans.*

§ 23.—*How the Colonnesi came to ask pardon of the Pope, and afterwards rebelled a second time.*

1298 a.d.

In the said year, in the month of September, negociations having taken place between Pope Boniface and the Colonnesi, the said Colonnesi, both laymen and clergy, came to Rieti, where the court was, and threw themselves at the feet of the said Pope, asking pardon, who forgave them and absolved them from excommunication, and desired them to surrender the city of Palestrina; and this they did, and he promised to restore them to their state and dignity, which promise he did not fulfil, but caused the said city of Palestrina to be destroyed from the hill and stronghold where it was, and a new city to be built on the plain, to which the name of the Civita Papale was given; and all this false and fraudulent treaty the Pope made by the counsel of the **Inf. xxvii. 67-111.** count of Montefeltro, then a minor friar, when he said the evil word "ample promise and scant fulfilment." The said Colonnesi, finding themselves deceived in that which had been promised to them, and the noble fortress of Palestrina destroyed by the said deceit, before the year was ended rebelled against the Pope and the Church; and the Pope excommunicated them again with heavy sentence; wherefore, fearing lest they should be taken or slain through the persecution of the said Pope, they departed from the city of Rome and were dispersed, some to Sicily, some to France and to other places, concealing themselves in one place after another so as not to be recognised, and to the end no certain abiding-place of theirs might be known, especially M. Jacopo and M. Piero, which had been cardinals; and thus they continued in exile so long as the said Pope lived.

§ 24.—*How the Genoese defeated the Venetians at sea.* § 25.—*Of the great earthquakes that befell in certain cities in Italy.*

§ 26.—*When the palace of the people of Florence was begun, where dwell the Priors.*

1298 a.d.

In the said year 1298, the commonwealth and people of Florence began to build the Palace of the Priors, by reason of the differences between the people and the magnates, forasmuch as the city was always in jealousy and commotion, at the election of the Priors afresh every two months, by reason of the factions which had already begun; and the Priors which ruled the city and all the republic, did not feel themselves secure in their former habitation, which was the house of the White Cerchi behind the church of San Brocolo. And they built the said palace where had formerly been the houses of the Uberti, rebels against Florence, and Ghibellines; and on the site of those houses they made a piazza, so that they might never be rebuilt. And they bought other houses from citizens, such as the Foraboschi, and there built the said palace and the tower of the priors, which was raised upon a tower which was more than fifty cubits high, pertaining to the Foraboschi, and called the Torre della Vacca. And to the end the said palace might not stand upon the ground of the said Uberti, they which had the building of it set it up obliquely; but for all that it was a grave loss not to build it four-square, and further removed from the church of San Piero Scheraggio.

§ 27.—*How peace was made between the commonwealth of Genoa and that* **1299 a.d.** *of Venice.* § 28.—*How peace was made between the commonwealth of Bologna and the marquis of Este and Maghinardo da Sussinana by the Florentines.* § 29.—*How King James of Aragon with Ruggeri di Loria and with the armada of King Charles defeated the Sicilians off Cape Orlando.* § 30.—*How peace was made between the Genoese and Pisans.* § 31.—*When the new walls of the city of Florence were begun again.* § 32.—*How the king of France by his practices got hold of all Flanders, and had the count and his sons in prison.* § 33.—*How the king of France allied himself with King Albert of Germany.* § 34.—*How the prince of Taranto was defeated in Sicily.* § 35.—*How Ghazan, lord of the Tartars, defeated the soldan of the Saracens, and took the Holy Land in Syria.*

§ 36.—*How Pope Boniface VIII. gave pardons to all Christians which should go to Rome, in the year of the jubilee,* 1300.

1300 a.d.

In the year of Christ 1300, according to the birth of Christ, inasmuch as it was held by many that after every hundred years from the nativity of

Christ, the Pope which was reigning at the time granted great indulgences, Pope Boniface VIII., which then occupied the apostolic chair, in reverence for the nativity of Christ, granted **Cf. Purg. ii. 98, 99.** supreme and great indulgence after this manner; that within the whole course of this said year, to whatsoever Roman should visit continuously for thirty days the churches of the Blessed Apostles S. Peter and S. Paul, and to all other people which were not Romans which should do likewise for fifteen days, there should be granted full and entire remission of all their sins, both the guilt and the punishment thereof, they having made or to make confession of the same. And for consolation of the Christian pilgrims, every Friday and every solemn feast day, was shown in S. Peter's the Veronica, the true image of **Par. xxxi. 104-108.** Christ, on the napkin. For the which thing, a great part of the Christians which were living at that time, women as well as men, made the said pilgrimage from distant and divers countries, both from far and near. And it was the most marvellous thing that was ever seen, for throughout the year, without break, there were in Rome, besides the inhabitants of the city, 200,000 pilgrims, not counting those who were coming and going on their journeys; and all were suitably supplied and satisfied with provisions, horses as well as persons, and all was well ordered, and without tumult or strife; and I can bear witness to this, **Inf. xviii. 28-33.** for I was present and saw it. And from the offerings made by the pilgrims much treasure was added to the Church, and all the Romans were enriched by the trade. And I, finding myself on that blessed pilgrimage in the holy city of Rome, beholding the great and ancient things therein, and reading the stories and the great doings of the Romans, written by Virgil, and by Sallust, and by Lucan, and Titus Livius, and Valerius, and Paulus Orosius, and other masters of history, which wrote alike of small things as of great, of the deeds and actions of the Romans, and also of foreign nations throughout the world, myself to preserve memorials and give examples to those which should come after took up their style and design, although as a disciple I was not worthy of such a work. But considering that our city of Florence, the daughter and creature of Rome, was rising, and had great things before her, whilst Rome was declining, it seemed to me fitting to collect in this volume and new chronicle all the deeds and beginnings of the city of Florence, in so far as it has been possible for me to

255

find and gather them together, and to follow the doings of the Florentines in detail, and the other notable things of the universe in brief, as long as it shall be God's pleasure; in hope of which, rather than in my own poor learning, I undertook, by his grace, the said enterprise; and thus in the year 1300, having returned from Rome, I began to compile this book, in reverence to God and the blessed John, and in commendation of our city of Florence.

§ 37.—*How Count Guido of Flanders and two sons of his surrendered to* **1300** *a.d.* *the king of France, and how they were deceived and cast into prison.*

§ 38.—*How the parties of the Blacks and Whites first began in the city of Pistoia.*

1300 a.d.

In these times the city of Pistoia being in happy and great and good estate, among the other citizens there was one family very noble and puissant, not however of very ancient lineage, which was called the Cancellieri, born of one Ser Cancelliere, which was a merchant, and gained much wealth, and by his two wives had many sons, which by reason of their riches all became knights, and men of worth and substance, and from them were born many sons and grandsons, so that at this time they numbered more than 100 men in arms, rich and puissant and of many affairs, so that not only were they the leading citizens of Pistoia, but they were among the most puissant families of Tuscany. There arose among them through their exceeding prosperity, and through the suggestion of the devil, contempt and enmity, between them which were born of one wife against them which were born of the other; and the one part took the name of the Black Cancellieri, and the other of the Whites, and this grew until they fought together, but it was not any very great affair. And one of those on the side of the White Cancellieri having been wounded, they on the side of the Black Cancellieri, to the end they might be at peace and concord with them, sent him which had done the injury and handed him over to the mercy of them which had received it, that they should take amends and vengeance for it at their will; they on the side of the White Cancellieri, ungrateful and proud, having neither pity nor love, cut off the hand of him which had been commended to their mercy on a horse manger. By which sinful beginning, not only was the house of the Cancellieri divided, but many violent deaths arose therefrom, and all the city of Pistoia was divided, for some held with one part and some with the other, and they called themselves the Whites and the Blacks, forgetting among themselves the Guelf and Ghibelline parties; and many civil strifes and much peril and loss of life arose therefrom in Pistoia; and not only in Pistoia, but afterwards the city of Florence and all Italy was contaminated by the said parties, as hereafter we shall be able to understand and know. The Florentines, fearing lest the said factions should stir up rebellion in the city to the hurt of the Guelf party, interposed to bring about an atonement between them, and took the lordship of the city, and brought both parties of the Cancellieri from

257

Pistoia, and set them under bounds at Florence. The Black party were kept in the house of the Frescobaldi in Oltrarno, and the White party in the house of the Cerchi in Garbo, through kinship which there was between them. But like as one sick sheep infects all the flock, thus this accursed seed which came from Pistoia, being in Florence corrupted all the Florentines, and first divided all the races and families of the nobles, one part thereof holding to and favouring one side, and the other the other, and afterwards all the popolari. For the which cause and beginning of strife not only were the Cancellieri not reconciled together by the Florentines, but the Florentines by them were divided and broken up, increasing from bad to worse, as our treatise will hereafter make manifest.

§ 39.—*How the city of Florence was divided and brought to shame by the said White and Black parties.*

1300 a.d.

In the said time, our city of Florence was in the greatest and happiest state which had ever been since it was rebuilt, or before, alike in greatness and power and in number of people, forasmuch as there were more than 30,000 citizens in the city, and more than 70,000 men capable of arms in the country within her territory; and she was great in nobility of good knights, and in free populace, and in riches, ruling over the greater part of Tuscany; whereupon the sin of ingratitude, with the instigation of the enemy of the human race, brought forth from the said prosperity pride and corruption, which put an end to the feasts and joyaunce of the Florentines. For hitherto they had been living in many delights and dainties, and in tranquillity and with continual banquets; and every year throughout almost all the city on the first day of May, there were bands and companies of men and of women, with sports and dances. But now it came to pass that through envy there arose factions among the citizens; and one of the chief and greatest began in the sesto of offence, to wit of Porte San Piero, between the house of the Cerchi, and the Donati; on the one side through envy, and on the other through rude ungraciousness. The head of the family of the Cerchi was one M. Vieri dei Cerchi, and he and those of his house were of great affairs, and powerful, and with great kinsfolk, and were very rich merchants, so that their

258

company was among the largest in the world; these were luxurious, inoffensive, uncultured and ungracious, like folk come in a short time to great estate and power. The head of the family of the **Cf. Purg. xxiv. 22.** Donati was M. Corso Donati, and he and those of his house were gentlemen and warriors, and of no superabundant riches, but were called by a gibe the Malefami. Neighbours they were in Florence and in the country, and while the one set was envious the other stood on their boorish dignity, so that there arose from the clash a fierce scorn between them, which was greatly inflamed by the ill seed of the White and Black parties from Pistoia, as we made mention in the last chapter. And the said Cerchi were the heads of the White party in Florence, and with them held almost all the house of the Adimari, save the branch of the Cavicciuli; all the house of the Abati, which was then very powerful, and part of them were Guelf and part were Ghibelline; a great part of the Tosinghi, specially the branch of Baschiera; part of the house of the Bardi, and part of the Rossi, and likewise some of the Frescobaldi, and part of the Nerli and of the Mannelli, and all the Mozzi, which then were very powerful in riches and in estate; all those of the house of the Scali, and the greater part of the Gherardini, all the Malispini, and a great part of the Bostichi and Giandonati, of the Pigli, and of the Vecchietti and **Par. xv., xvi.** Arrigucci, and almost all the Cavalcanti, which were a great and powerful house, and all the Falconieri which were a powerful house of the people. And with them took part many houses and families of popolani, and lesser craftsmen, and all the Ghibelline magnates and popolani; and by reason of the great following which the Cerchi had, the government of the city was almost all in their power. On the side of the Blacks were all they of the house of the Pazzi, who may be counted with the Donati as the chiefs, and all the Visdomini and all the Manieri and Bagnesi, and all the Tornaquinci, and the Spini and the Bondelmonti, and the Gianfigliazzi, Agli, and Brunelleschi, and Cavicciuli, and the other part of the Tosinghi; all the part that was left of all the Guelf houses named above, for those which were not with the Whites held on the contrary with the Blacks. And thus from the said two parties all the city of Florence and its territory was divided and contaminated. For the which cause, the Guelf party, fearing lest the said parties should be turned to account by the Ghibellines, sent to the court to Pope Boniface, that he might use some remedy. For the which thing the said Pope sent for M. Vieri de' Cerchi, and when he came before him, he prayed him to make peace with M. Corso Donati and with his party, referring their differences to him; and he promised him to put him and his followers into great and good estate, and to grant him such spiritual favours as he might ask of him. M. Vieri, albeit he was in other things a sage knight, in this was but little sage, and was too obstinate and capricious, insomuch that he would grant nought of the Pope's request; saying that he was at war with no man; wherefore he returned to Florence, and the Pope was moved with indignation against him and against his party. It came to pass a little while after that certain both of one party and of the other were riding through the city armed and on their guard, and with the party of the young Cerchi was Baldinaccio of the Adimari, and Baschiera of the Tosinghi, and Naldo of the Gherardini, and Giovanni Giacotti Malispini, with their followers, more than thirty on horseback; and with the young Donati were certain of the Pazzi and of the Spini, and others of their company. On the evening of the first of May, in the year 1300, while they were watching a dance of ladies which was going forward on the piazza of Santa Trinita, one party began to scoff at the other, and to urge their horses one against the other, whence arose a great conflict and confusion, and many were wounded, and, as ill-luck would have it, Ricoverino, son of M. Ricovero of the Cerchi, had his nose cut off his face; and through the said scuffle that evening all the city was moved with apprehension and flew to arms. This was the beginning of the dissensions and divisions in the city of Florence and in the Guelf party, whence many ills and perils followed on afterwards, as in due time we shall make mention. And for this cause we have narrated thus extensively the origin of this beginning of the accursed White and Black parties, for the great and evil consequences which followed to the Guelf party, and to the Ghibellines, and to all the city of Florence, and also to all Italy; and like as the death of M. Bondelmonte the elder was the beginning of the Guelf and Ghibelline parties, so this was the beginning of the great ruin of the Guelf party and of our city. And note, that the year **1299 a.d.** before these things came to pass, the houses of the commonwealth were built, which began at the foot of the old bridge over the Arno, and extended towards the fortress of Altafronte, and to do this they raised the piles at the

260

foot of the bridge, and they had of necessity to move the statue of Mars; and whereas at the first it looked towards the east, it was turned towards the north, wherefore, because of the augury of old, folk said: "May it please God that there come not great changes therefrom to our city."

§ 40.—*How the Cardinal d'Acquasparta came as legate from the Pope to make peace in Florence, and could not do it.*
1300 a.d.

By reason of the aforesaid events and the factions of the White and Black parties, the captains of the Guelf party and their council were fearful lest through the said divisions and strifes the Ghibelline party might rise to more power in Florence, which under the plea of good government already seemed likely; and many Ghibellines held to be good men were beginning to be set in office; and moreover those which held with the Black party, to recover their estate, sent ambassadors to the court to Pope Boniface to pray him, for the good of the city and for the party of the Church, to take some action. For the which thing straightway the Pope appointed as legate to follow up this **Par. xii. 124.** matter Brother Matteo d'Acquasparta, his cardinal bishop of Porto, of the Order of the Minor Friars, and sent him to Florence, which came there in the month of June following, in the said year 1300, and was received with great honour by the Florentines. And when he had taken some repose in Florence, he craved jurisdiction from the commonwealth to reconcile the Florentines together; and to the end he might take away the said White and Black parties he desired to reform the city, and to throw the offices open again; and those which were of one part and of the other which were worthy to be priors, their names were to be put into a bag together, in each of the sesti, and were to be drawn thence every two months, as chance would have it; forasmuch as through the ill-will which had arisen from the factions and divisions, there was never an election of priors by the colleges of Consuls of the Arts but that almost all the city was moved to uproar, and at times with great preparation of arms. They of the White party which were at the head of the government of the city, through fear of losing their estate, and of being deceived by the Pope and the legate by means of the said reformation, took the worse counsel, and would not

261

yield obedience; for the which thing the said legate was offended, and returned to court, and left the city of Florence excommunicate and under interdict.

§ 41.—*Concerning the evils and dangers which followed afterwards to our city.* **1300 a.d.**

When the legate was departed from Florence the city remained in great turmoil and in evil state. It came to pass in the month of December following that M. Corso Donati went with his followers, and they of the house of the Cerchi with their followers, to the burial of a lady of the house of Frescobaldi; and when the two parties came face to face, they were minded to assault one another, wherefore all the folk which were at the burial rose in uproar; and thus every one returned in flight to his own house, and all the city flew to arms, and each of the parties gathered a great assembly at their house. M. Gentile dei **Sonnet xxxii. 1. Vita Nuova 3: 97-100; 24: 19, 45; 25: 111-113; 31: 21-24; 33: 4; De Vulg. El. i. 13: 37; ii. 6: 68; 12: 16, 62.** Cerchi, Guido Cavalcanti, Baldinaccio and Corso of the Adimari, Baschiera della Tosa, and Naldo of the Gherardini, with their companions and followers on horse and on foot, went in haste to Porte San Piero to the house of the Donati, and not finding them at Porte San Piero, hastened to San Piero Maggiore, where was M. Corso with his companions and assembly, and by them they were stoutly resisted and driven back and wounded, to the shame and dishonour of the Cerchi and of their followers; and for this they were condemned, both the one party and the other, by the commonwealth. A little while after, certain of the Cerchi were in the country at Nepozzano and Pugliano at their country homes and farms; and as they were returning to Florence, they of the house of the Donati, being assembled with their friends at Remole, opposed their path, and there were wounds and assaults both on one side and on the other; for the which cause both one side and the other were accused and condemned for the assemblage and assaults; and the greater part of those of the house of the Donati, not being able to pay their fine, chose imprisonment, and were put under confinement. The Cerchi desired to follow their example, for M. Torrigiano dei Cerchi had said: "They shall not overcome us in this wise, as they did the Tedaldini, eating them up by fines"; so he induced his companions to choose imprisonment, against the will of M. Vieri dei Cerchi and of the other wise men of his house, which knew the disposition and wantonness of their youths; and it came to pass that a certain accursed Ser Neri degli Abati, overseer of that prison, eating with them, set before them a present of a poisoned black-pudding, whereof they ate; whence in a little while, after two days, two of the White and two of the Black Cerchi died, and Pigello Portinari and Ferraino dei Bronci, and for this no vengeance was taken.

§ 42.—*Of the same.*
1300 a.d.

The city of Florence, being in such heat and dangers from strifes and enmities, whence very often the city was in uproar and at arms, M. Corso Donati, the Spini, the Pazzi, and some of the Tosinghi and Cavicciuli, and their followers, both magnates and popolani of their faction of the Black party, with the captains of the Guelf party, which were then of their mind and purpose, assembled in the church of Santa Trinita, and there took counsel and oath together to send ambassadors to the court to Pope Boniface, to the end he might invite some prince of the house of France, which should restore them to their estate, and abase the Popolo and the White party, and for this end to spend to their utmost power; and thus they did, wherefore the news spreading through the city through some report, the commonwealth and the people were much troubled, and inquisition was made by the magistrates; wherefore M. Corso Donati, which was leader in the matter, was condemned in goods and in person; and the other leaders thereof, in more than 20,000 pounds; and they paid them. And this done, there were banished and set under bounds Sinibaldi, brother of M. Corso, and some of his family, and M. Rosso, and M. Rossellino della Tosa, and others their companions; and M. Giacchinotto and M. Pazzino dei Pazzi, and some of the younger members of their families, and M. Geri Spini and some of his family, to the village of the Pieve. And to still all anxiety the people sent the chiefs of the other party out of the city and placed them under bounds at Serrezzano; to wit, M. Gentile, and M. Torrigiano and Carbone of the Cerchi, and some of their companions, Baschiera della Tosa and some of his family, Baldinaccio degli Adimari and some of his family, Naldo dei Gherardini and some of his family, Guido Cavalcanti and some of his family, and Giovanni Giacotti Malespini. But this party abode less time under bounds, forasmuch as they were recalled by reason of the unhealthiness of the place, and Guido Cavalcanti returned thence sick, whence he **Inf. x. 58-69, 110, 111.** died; and he was a great loss, seeing that he was a philosopher and a man accomplished in many things, save only that he was too sensitive and passionate. In such fashion was our city guided in the storm.

§ 43.—*How Pope Boniface sent into France for M. Charles of Valois.*
1300 a.d.

When the legate, Brother Matteo d'Acquasparta, had returned to the papal court, he informed Pope Boniface of the evil and uncertain condition of the city of Florence; and afterwards, by reason of the things which came to pass after the departure of the legate, as we have said, and by reason of the importunity and free expenditure of the captains of the Guelf party, and of the aforesaid exiles which were at the village of the Pieve hard by the court, and of M. Geri Spini (for he and his company were merchants for Pope Boniface and his general advisers), it came to pass that by their zeal and industry, and by that of M. Corso Donati, who followed the court wheresoever it went, the said Pope Boniface took counsel to send for M. Charles of Valois, brother of the king of France, with a double purpose; principally for the aid of King Charles in his Sicilian war, giving the king of France and the said M. Charles to understand that he would cause him to be elected Emperor of the Romans, and confirm the election, or at the least by the authority of the Pope and of Holy Church would make him imperial lieutenant for the Church in virtue of the rights of the Church when the Empire is vacant; and beyond this he gave him the title of Peacemaker in Tuscany, to the end he might use all his force to bring Florence to his purpose. And when he sent his legate into France for the said M. Charles, the said M. Charles by the will of the king, his brother, came, as we shall hereafter make mention, in the hope of being Emperor, because of the promises of the Pope, as we have said.

264

§ 44.—*How the Guelfs were driven from Agobbio, and how they* **1301 a.d.** *afterwards recovered the city and drove the Ghibellines thence.*

§ 45.—*How the Black party were driven out of Pistoia.*

1301 a.d.

Inf. xxiv. 143.

In the year of Christ 1301, in the month of May, the White party in Pistoia, with the aid and favour of the Whites which were governing the city of Florence, drove thence the Black party and destroyed their houses, palaces and possessions, and among others a strong and rich possession of palaces and towers which pertained to the Black Cancellieri, which was called Damiata.

§ 46.—*How the Interminelli and their followers were driven out of* **1301 a.d.** *Lucca.* § 47.—*How the Guelf refugees from Genoa were peaceably restored.* § 48.—*How a comet appeared in the heavens.*

§ 49.—*How M. Charles of Valois of France came to Pope Boniface, and afterwards came to Florence and drove out the White party.*

1301 a.d.

In the said year 1301, in the month of September, there came to the city of Alagna, in Campagna, where was Pope Boniface with his court, Charles, count of Valois, brother of the king of France, with many counts and barons, and with 500 French horsemen in his company, having taken the way from Lucca to Alagna without entering into Florence for lack of trust therein; which M. Charles was received with honour by the Pope and his cardinals; and there came to Alagna King Charles and his sons to speak with him and to do him honour; and the Pope made him count of Romagna. And after they had taken counsel and he had arranged with the Pope and with King Charles the expedition into Sicily in the following spring, which was the chief reason why he was come from France, the Pope, not forgetting the anger he had felt against the White party in Florence, and desirous that Charles should not pass the winter in vain, gave him the title of Peacemaker in Florence for the annoyance of the Guelfs in Florence, and ordained that he should return to the city of Florence. And thus he did, with his followers and with many others, Florentines, Tuscans, and Romagnese, refugees, and under bounds from their cities, because they were of the party of the Black Guelfs. And when he was come to Siena, and then to Staggia, they which governed the city of Florence, being fearful of his coming, held long counsel whether to allow him to enter the city or no. And they sent ambassadors to him, and he made answer with fair and friendly words, saying that he was come for their good and well-being, and to make peace among them; for the which thing they which ruled the city (who, albeit they were of the White party, called themselves and desired to remain Guelf) determined to allow him to enter. And thus, on the day of All Saints, 1301, M. Charles entered into Florence with **Purg. xx. 70-78.** his followers unarmed, and the Florentines did him great honour, coming to meet him in procession with many jousters bearing standards, and horses draped in silk. And when he had reposed himself and sojourned some days in Florence, he craved from the commonwealth the lordship and charge of the city, and authority to make peace among the Guelfs. And this was assented to by the commonwealth, on the 5th day of November, in the church of Santa Maria Novella, where were assembled the Podestà, and captain, and priors, and all the councillors and the bishop, and all the good people of Florence; and when his demand had been made, counsel and deliberation were held thereupon, and the lordship and charge of the city was remitted to him. And M. Charles, after his secretary had set the matter forth, with his own mouth accepted it and swore to it, and, as the king's son, promised to preserve the city in peaceful and good state; and I, the writer, was present at these things. And straightway the contrary was done by him and by his followers, for, by the counsel of M. Musciatto Franzesi, which was come from France as his guide, and by agreement with the Black Guelfs, he caused his followers to take arms, even before he had returned to his house; for he abode in the house of the Frescobaldi, in Oltrarno. Wherefore, when the citizens saw this new sight of his horsemen in arms, the city was all thrown into suspicion and alarm, and both magnates and popolani took arms, each one in the house of his friends as best he might, barricading the city in divers parts. But in the house of the Priors but few assembled, and the people was as good as without a head, for the priors and they which ruled the commonwealth saw that they were

266

betrayed and deceived. In the midst of this tumult, M. Corso de' Donati, which was banished as a rebel, came that same day from Peretola to Florence by agreement, with some following of certain of his friends and foot-soldiers; and when the priors and the Cerchi, his enemies, heard of his coming, M. Schiatta de' Cancellieri, which was captain of 300 mercenary horsemen for the commonwealth of Florence, came to them and offered to go against the said M. Corso to take him and to punish him; but M. Vieri, head of the Cerchi, would not consent thereto, saying, "Let him come," confiding in the vain hope that the people would punish him. Wherefore the said M. Corso entered into the suburbs of the city, and finding the gates of the old circle shut, and not being able to enter, he came to the postern of the Pinti, which was by the side of San Piero Maggiore, between his houses and those of the Uccellini, and finding that shut, he began to beat it down, and in like manner did his friends within, so that without difficulty it was broken down. And when he had entered in he stood in array upon the piazza of San Piero Maggiore, and folk were added to him, with following of his friends, crying, "Long live M. Corso!" and "Long live the baron!" to wit, M. Corso himself, for so they named him; and he, seeing his forces and followers to have increased, the first thing that he did was to go to the prisons of the commonwealth, which were in the houses of the Bastari, in the street of the palace, and these he opened by force, and set the prisoners free; and this done, he did the like at the palace of the Podestà, and then went on to the Priors, causing them for fear to lay down the government and return to their homes. And during all this destruction of the city M. Charles of Valois and his people gave no counsel nor help, nor did he keep the oath and promise made by him. Wherefore the tyrants and malefactors and banished men which were in the city took courage, and the city being unguarded and without government, they began to rob the shops and places of merchandise and the houses which pertained to the White party, or to any one that had not the power to resist, slaying and wounding many persons, good men of the White party. And this plague endured in the city for five days continually, to the great ruin of the city. And afterwards it continued in the country, the troopers going on robbing and burning houses for more than eight days, whereby a great number of beautiful and rich possessions were destroyed and

267

burned. And when the said destruction and burning was ended, M. Charles and his council reconstituted the city and elected a government of Priors of the popolani of the Black party. And in that same month of November there came to Florence the aforesaid legate of the Pope, Cardinal Matteo d'Acquasparta, to make peace among the citizens; and he reconciled the houses of the Cerchi and Adimari and their followers of the White party, and the Donati and Pazzi and their followers of the Black party, arranging marriages between them; and when he desired to divide the offices among them, they of the Black party with the forces of M. Charles would not allow it, wherefore the legate was troubled, and returned to court, leaving the city under an interdict. And the said peace endured but little, for it came to pass on the ensuing day of the feast of the Nativity, when M. Niccola, of the White Cerchi, was on his way to his farm and mills with his company on horseback, as they were passing through the piazza of Santa Croce, where preaching was going on, Simone, son of M. Corso Donati, which was sister's son to the said M. Niccola, urged and prompted to evil-doing, followed the said M. Niccola with his companions and troopers on horseback; and when he came up with him at the Ponte ad Affrico, he assailed him in combat; wherefore the said M. Niccola, without fault or cause, not being on his guard against his said nephew Simone, was slain and dragged from his horse. But, as it pleased God, the punishment was prepared for the sin, for the said Simone being struck in the side by the said M. Niccola, died that same night; wherefore, albeit it was a just judgment, yet it was held as a great loss, forasmuch as the said Simone was the most finished and accomplished youth of Florence, and would have come to greater honour and state, and was all the hope of his father, M. Corso; which, after his joyous return and victory, had, in brief space, a sorrowful beginning of his future downfall. And shortly after this time the city of Florence, not being able to rest by reason of its being big with the poison of the factions of White and Black, must needs bring forth a woeful catastrophe; wherefore it **1302 a.d.** came to pass in the following April, by the scheming and plotting of the Blacks, one of M. Charles' barons, which was called Pierre Ferrand of Languedoc, fostered a plot with them of the house of Cerchi, and with Baldinaccio of the Adimari, and Baschiera of the Tosinghi, and Naldo Gherardini, and others of their followers of the White party, as though, under great promise of moneys, he should go about, with his retinue and friends, to restore them to their estate and betray M. Charles; concerning which letters were written or forged with their seals, which, by the said M. Pierre Ferrand, as had been arranged, were then carried to M. Charles. For which thing the said leaders of the White party, to wit, all of the house of the White Cerchi of Porte San Piero, Baldinaccio and Corso of the Adimari, with almost all the Bellincioni branch, Naldo of the Gherardini, with his branch of the house, Baschiera of the Tosinghi, with his branch of the said house, some of the house of the Cavalcanti, Giovanni Giacotto Malispini and his allies, were cited; but they did not appear, either for fear of the wrong deed they had committed, or for fear of losing their persons by reason of the said treachery; but they departed from the city, in company with their [Ghibelline] adversaries; some going to Pisa, and some to Arezzo and Pistoia, consorting with the Ghibellines and the enemies of the Florentines. For the which thing they were condemned by M. Charles as rebels, and their palaces and goods in the city and in the country destroyed; and the like with many of their followers, both magnates and popolani. And after this fashion was abased and driven away the ungrateful and proud party of the Whites, in company of many Ghibellines of Florence, by M. Charles of Valois of France, by commission of Pope Boniface, on the 4th day of April, 1302, whence there came to our city of Florence much ruin and many perils, as hereafter, in due time, we shall, as we read on, be able to understand.

§ 50.—*How M. Charles of Valois passed into Sicily to make war for* **1302 a.d.** *King Charles, and made a shameful peace.* § 51.—*How the band of Roumania was formed.* § 52.—*How the Florentines and Lucchese marched upon the city of Pistoia, and how they took the castle of Serravalle by siege.* § 53.—*How the Florentines took the castle of Piantrevigne and many other castles that the Whites had caused to rebel.* § 54.—*How the island of Ischia belched out a marvellous fire.* § 55.—*How the common people of Bruges rebelled against the king of France and slew the French.* § 56.—*Of the great and disastrous rout of the French by the Flemings at Courtray.* § 57.—*Of what lineage were the present counts and lords of Flanders.* § 58.—*How the king of France reassembled his host, and with all his forces attacked the Flemings, and returned to France with little honour.*

§ 59.—*How Folcieri da Calvoli, Podestà of Florence, caused certain citizens of the White party to be beheaded.*

1302 a.d.

Purg. xiv. 58-66.

In the said year 1302, Folcieri da Calvoli of Romagna, a fierce and cruel man, had been made Podestà of Florence, by the influence of the leaders of the Black party. Now the said leaders lived in great trepidation, forasmuch as the White and Ghibelline party was very powerful in Florence, and the exiles were plotting every day in treaty with their friends which had remained in Florence. Wherefore the said Folcieri suddenly caused certain citizens of the White party and Ghibellines to be taken; which were, M. Betto Gherardini, and Masino de' Cavalcanti, and Donato and Tegghia his brother, of the Finiguerra da Sammartino, and Nuccio Coderini de' Galigai, which was but half-witted, and Tignoso de' Macci; and at the petition of M. Musciatto Franzesi, which was among the lords of the city, there were to have been taken certain heads of the house of the Abati his enemies, but hearing this they fled and departed from Florence, and never afterwards were citizens thereof. And a certain sexton of the Calze was among the prisoners. They were charged with plotting treachery in the city with the exiled Whites; and whether guilty or not, were made to confess under torture that they were going to betray the city, and to give up certain gates to the Whites and Ghibellines; but the said Tignoso de' Macci, through weight of flesh, died under the cord. All the other aforesaid prisoners he judged, and caused them to be beheaded, and all of the house of the Abati he condemned as rebels, and destroyed their goods, whence the city was greatly disturbed, and there followed many evils and scandals. And in the said year there was much scarcity of victuals, and grain was sold in Florence at twenty-two shillings the bushel, reckoning fifty-one shillings to a golden florin.

§ 60.—*How the White party and the Ghibelline refugees from Florence came to Puliciano and departed thence in discomfiture.*

1302 a.d.

In the said year, in the month of March, the Ghibelline and White

270

refugees from Florence, with the forces of the Bolognese whose government was of the White party, and with the aid of the Ghibellines of Romagna and of the Ubaldini, came to Mugello with 800 horse and 6,000 foot, whereof Scarpetta degli Ordilaffi of Forlì was captain. And they took the village and stronghold of Puliciano without opposition, and besieged a fortress which was there held by the Florentines, thinking there to make a great head, and gather Mugello under their rule, and afterwards to extend their forces as far as the city of Florence. When the tidings come to Florence, immediately they rode to Mugello, gentle and simple, with all the forces of the city; and when they were come to the village, and the Lucchese and other friends were come also, they sallied forth in array and order against the enemy; and when the horsemen of Bologna heard of the sudden coming of the Florentines, and found themselves deceived by the White refugees from Florence, which had given them to understand that the Florentines for fear of their friends which remained within the city would not venture to sally forth from the city, they held themselves to be betrayed, and in great fear without any order they departed from Puliciano of Mugello, and came to Bologna; wherefore the White and Ghibelline refugees were routed and dispersed, and departed by night without stroke of sword as if defeated, leaving all their harness, and many of them threw away their arms, and some of the best of them were slain, or taken by certain scouts which were sent on in advance. Among the other notable and honourable citizens and ancient Guelfs which had become Whites, there was taken M. Donato Alberti, the judge, and Nanni de' Ruffoli of the Porte del Vescovo. After Nanni had been taken, he was slain by one of the Tosinghi; and Donato Alberti had his head cut off, by that same law which he had made and introduced into the Ordinances of Justice, when he was ruling and was prior. And with the said M. Donato Alberti were taken prisoner and beheaded two of the Caponsacchi, and one of the Scogliari, and Lapo di Cipriani, and Nerlo degli Adimari, and about ten others of little account; by reason of which rout the White and the Ghibelline refugees were much cast down.

§ 61.—*Incident, relating how M. Maffeo Visconti was driven from Milan.*
1302 a.d.

In the said year 1302, on the 16th day of June, M. Maffeo Visconti, captain of Milan, was driven from his lordship; and this was the cause: he and his sons desired to govern Milan entirely, and to give no share of honour to M. Piero Visconti, and to others his kinsmen, and to other cattani and feudatories. For the which cause scandal arose in Milan, and the lords della Torre, with the forces of the patriarch of Aquilea, came with a great host against Milan, and with them M. Alberto Scotti da Piacenza, and Count Filippone da Pavia, and M. Antonio da Foseraco of Lodi. M. Maffeo sallied forth against them, but because of the strife which he had with his kinsmen, he was ill-supported, and had not sufficient power against his enemies; wherefore M. Alberto Scotti undertook the office of mediator to make peace, and deceived and betrayed M. Maffeo, who trusted himself to him; for he deposed him from the office of captain, wherefore M. Maffeo for shame would not return to Milan; but the lords della Torre were restored to Milan without a battle, and M. Mosca and M. Guidetto di M. Nappo della Torre remained lords of Milan. And M. Mosca dying a little while after, the said M. Guidetto caused himself to be proclaimed captain of Milan, and ruled harshly, and was much dreaded and feared, and so persecuted the said M. Maffeo and his sons that he brought them well nigh to nought, and they were fain to go begging through many places and countries; and in the end for their security they took refuge in a little castle in the territory of Ferrara, which pertained to the marquises of Este, their kinsfolk, inasmuch as Galeasso, son to Maffeo, had for wife the sister of the marquis. And **Purg. viii. 73-75.** when M. Guidetto della Torre, which was captain of Milan, and his enemy heard this, he desired news of him and of his state, and said to a wise and clever jongleur: "If thou desirest to gain a palfrey and a mantle of vair, go to the place where M. Maffeo Visconti abides, and spy out his state." And in mockery of him he said: "When thou takest leave of him, ask him two questions: first, ask him how he fares and what manner of life is his; secondly, when he thinks to return to Milan." The minstrel departed and came to M. Maffeo, and found him very meanly furnished, compared with his former state; and on departing from him, he asked his aid in getting a palfrey and a mantle of vair; and he answered, he would aid him gladly, but he might not have them from him, for he had none such. Then he said: "It is

272

not from you that I would have them, but answer me two questions which I shall put to you"; and he told the two questions wherewith he had been charged. The wise man understood from whom they came, and straightway made answer very wisely. To the first he said: "Methinks I fare well, forasmuch as I know how to live after the times"; to the second he answered and said: "Thou shalt say to thy lord, M. Guidetto, that when the measure of his sins is greater than mine, I will return to Milan." And when the jongleur was come back to M. Guidetto, and had brought the answer, he said: "Aye, thou hast earned the palfrey and the mantle, for those are the words of none other than the wise M. Maffeo."

§ 62.—*How there arose strife and enmity between Pope Boniface and King Philip of France.*

1302 a.d.

Cf. Purg. xxxii. 148-160.

In the said time, albeit some while before the defeat of Courtray, the king of France had become angered against Pope Boniface, by reason of the promise which the said Pope had made to the king, and to M. Charles of Valois, his brother, to make him Emperor, when he sent for him, as afore we made mention; which thing he did not fulfil, be the cause what it might. Nay, rather in the same year he had confirmed as **Cf. Purg. vi. 97-117.** king of the Romans Albert of Austria, son of King Rudolf, for the which thing the king of France held himself to be greatly deceived and betrayed by him, and in his wrath he entertained and did honour to Stefano della Colonna, his enemy, which was come to France on hearing of the discord which had arisen; and the king to the best of his power favoured him and his followers. And beyond this, the king caused the bishop of Pamiers, in the district of Carcassone, to be taken prisoner on charge of being a Paterine; and he spent the revenues of every vacant bishopric, and would confer the investitures himself. Wherefore Pope Boniface, which was proud and disdainful, and bold in doing all great things, of high purposes and powerful, as he was and as he held himself to be, beholding these outrages on the part of the king, added indignation to ill-will, and became wholly an enemy to the king of France. And at first, to establish his rights, he caused all the great prelates of France

273

to be invited to his court; but the king of France opposed them, and would not let them go, wherefore the Pope was the more greatly incensed against the king, and would have it, according to his privilege and decrees, that the king of France, like other Christian princes, ought to acknowledge the temporal as well as the spiritual sovereignty of the Apostolic Chair; and for this he sent into France as his legate a Roman priest, archdeacon of Narbonne, that he might protest against and admonish the king under pain of excommunication to comply thereto, and acknowledge him; and if he would not do this, he was to excommunicate him and leave him under an interdict. And when the said legate came to the city of Paris, the king would not allow him to publish his letters and privileges, nay rather they were taken from him by the king's people, and he himself was dismissed from the realm. And when the said papal letters came before the king and his barons in the temple, the Count d'Artois, which was then living, threw them into the fire and burnt them in despite, whence great judgment came upon him; and the king ordered that all the entrances to his kingdom should be guarded, so that no message nor letter from the Pope should enter into France. When Pope Boniface heard this, he pronounced sentence of excommunication against the said Philip, king of France; and the king of France to justify himself, and to make his appeal, summoned in Paris a great council of clerics and prelates and of all his barons, excusing himself, and bringing many charges against Pope Boniface of heresy, and simony, and murders, and other base crimes, by reason whereof he ought to be deposed from the papacy. But the abbot of Citeaux would not consent to the appeal, rather he departed, and returned into Burgundy in despite of the king of France. In such wise began the strife between Pope Boniface and the king of France, which had afterwards so ill an end; whence afterwards arose great strife between them, and much evil followed thereupon, as hereafter we shall make mention.

In these times there came to pass a very notable thing in Florence, for Pope Boniface having presented to the commonwealth of Florence a fine young lion, which was confined by a chain in the court of the palace of the Priors, there came in thither an ass laden with wood, which when it saw the said lion, either through the fear he had of him or through a miracle, straightway attacked the lion fiercely, and so struck him with his hoofs that he died, notwithstanding the help of many men which were there present. This was held for a sign of great changes to come, and such like, which certainly came to pass to our city in these times. But certain of the learned said that the prophecy of the Sibyl was fulfilled where she said: "When the tame beast shall slay the king of beasts, then will begin the destruction of the Church"; and this was shortly made manifest in Pope Boniface himself, as will be found in the chapter following.

§ 63.—*How the king of France caused Pope Boniface to be seized in Anagna by Sciarra della Colonna, whence the said Pope died a few days afterwards.*

1303 a.d.

Purg. xx. 85-90.

After the said strife had arisen between Pope Boniface and King Philip of France, each one sought to abase the other by every method and guise that was possible: the Pope sought to oppress the king of France with excommunications and by other means to deprive him of the kingdom; and with this he favoured the Flemings, his rebellious subjects, and entered into negotiations with King Albert of Germany, encouraging him to come to Rome for the Imperial benediction, and to cause the Kingdom to be taken from King Charles, his kinsman, and to stir up war against the king of France on the borders of his realm on the side of Germany. The king of France, on the other hand, was not asleep, but with great caution, and by the counsel of Stefano della Colonna and of other sage Italians, and men of his own realm, sent one M. William of Nogaret of Provence, a wise and crafty cleric, with M. Musciatto Franzesi, into Tuscany, furnished with much ready money, and with drafts on the company of the Peruzzi (which were then his merchants) for as much money as might be needed; the Peruzzi not knowing wherefore. And when they were come to the fortress of Staggia, which pertained to the said M. Musciatto, they abode there long time, sending ambassadors and messages and letters; and they caused people to come to them in secret, giving out openly that they were there to treat concerning peace between the Pope and the king of France, and that for this cause they had brought the said money; and under this colour they conducted secret negotiations to take Pope Boniface prisoner in Anagna, spending thereupon much money,

275

corrupting the barons of the country and the citizens of Anagna; and as it had been purposed, so it came to pass; for Pope Boniface being with his cardinals, and with all the court, in the city of Anagna, in Campagna, where he had been born, and was at home, not thinking or knowing of this plot, nor being on his guard, or if he heard anything of it, through his great courage not heeding it, or perhaps, as it pleased God, by reason of his great sins,—in the month of September, 1303, Sciarra della Colonna, with his mounted followers, to the number of 300, and many of his friends on foot, paid by money of the French king, with troops of the lords of Ceccano and of Supino, and of other barons of the Campagna, and of the sons of M. Maffio d'Anagna, and, it is said, with the consent of some of the cardinals which were in the plot, one morning early entered into Anagna, with the ensigns and standards of the king of France, crying: "Death to Pope Boniface! Long life to the king of France!" And they rode through the city without any hindrance, or rather, well-nigh all the ungrateful people of Anagna followed the standards and the rebellion; and when they came to the Papal Palace, they entered without opposition and took the palace, forasmuch as the present assault was not expected by the Pope and his retainers, and they were not upon their guard. Pope Boniface—hearing the uproar, and seeing himself forsaken by all his cardinals, which were fled and in hiding (whether through fear or through set malice), and by the most part of his servants, and seeing that his enemies had taken the city and the palace where he was—gave himself up for lost, but like the high-spirited and valorous man he was, he said: "Since, like Jesus Christ, I am willing to be taken and needs must die by treachery, at the least I desire to die as Pope"; and straightway he caused himself to be robed in the mantle of S. Peter, and with the crown of Constantine on his head, and with the keys and the cross in his hand, he seated himself upon the papal chair. And when Sciarra and the others, his enemies, came to him, they mocked at him with vile words, and arrested him and his household which had remained with him; among the others, M. William of Nogaret scorned him, which had conducted the negotiations for the king of France, whereby he had been taken, and threatened him, saying that he would take him bound to Lyons on the Rhone, and there in a general council would cause him to be deposed and condemned. The high-spirited

276

Pope answered him, that he was well pleased to be condemned and deposed by Paterines such as he, whose father and mother had been burnt as Paterines; whereat M. William was confounded and put to shame. But afterwards, as it pleased God, to preserve the holy dignity of the Popes, no man dared to touch him, nor were they pleased to lay hands on him, but they left him robed under gentle ward, and were minded to rob the treasure of the Pope and of the Church. In this pain, shame and torment the great Pope Boniface abode prisoner among his enemies for three days; but, like as Christ rose on the third day, so it pleased Him that Pope Boniface should be set free; for without entreaty or other effort, save the Divine aid, the people of Anagna beholding their error, and issuing from their blind ingratitude, suddenly rose in arms, crying: "Long live the Pope and his household, and death to the traitors"; and running through the city they drove out Sciarra della Colonna and his followers, with loss to them of prisoners and slain, and freed the Pope and his household. Pope Boniface, seeing himself free, and his enemies driven away, did not therefore rejoice in any wise, forasmuch as the pain of his adversity had so entered into his heart and clotted there; wherefore he departed straightway from Anagna with all his court, and came to Rome to S. Peter's to hold a council, purposing to take the heaviest vengeance for his injury and that of Holy Church against the king of France, and whosoever had offended him; but, as it pleased God, the grief which had hardened in the heart of Pope Boniface, by reason of the injury which he had received, produced in him, after he was come to Rome, a strange malady so that he gnawed at himself as if he were mad, and in this state he passed from this life **Inf. xix. 52-57.** on the 12th day of October in the year of Christ 1303, and in the church of S. Peter, near the entrance of the doors, in a rich chapel which was built in his lifetime, he was honourably buried.

§ 64.—*We will further tell of the ways of Pope Boniface.*

This Pope Boniface was very wise both in learning and in natural wit, and a man very cautious and experienced, and of great knowledge and memory; very haughty he was, and proud, and cruel towards his enemies and adversaries, and was of a great heart, and much feared by all people; and he exalted and increased greatly the estate and the rights of Holy Church, and he commissioned M. Guglielmo da Bergamo and M. Ricciardi of Siena, who were cardinals, and M. Dino Rosoni of Mugello, all of them supreme masters in laws and in decretals, together with himself, for he too was a great master in divinity and in decretals, to draw up the Sixth Book of the Decretals, which is as it were the light of all the laws and the decretals. A man of large schemes was he, and liberal to folk which pleased him, and which were worthy, very desirous of worldly pomp according to his estate, and very desirous of wealth, not scrupulous, nor having very great or strict conscience **Par. xxx. 148.** about every gain, to enrich the Church and his nephews. He made many of his friends and confidants cardinals in his time, among others two very young nephews, and his uncle, his mother's brother; and twenty of his relations and friends of the little city of Anagna, bishops and archbishops of rich benefices; and to another of his nephews and his sons, which were counts, as we afore made mention, to them he left almost unbounded riches; and after the death of Pope Boniface, their uncle, they were bold and valiant in war, doing vengeance upon all their neighbours and enemies, which had betrayed and injured Pope Boniface, spending largely, and keeping at their own cost 300 good Catalan horsemen, by force of which they subdued almost all the Campagna and the district of Rome. And if Pope Boniface, while he was alive, had believed that they could be thus bold in arms and valorous in war, certainly he would have made them kings or great lords. And note, that when Pope Boniface was taken prisoner, tidings thereof were sent to the king of France by many couriers in a few days, through great joy; and when the first couriers arrived at Sion, beyond the mountain of Brieg [Sion under Brieg], the bishop of Sion, which then was a man of pure and holy life, when he heard the news was, as it were, amazed, and abode some while in silent contemplation, by reason of the wonderment which took him at the capture of the Pope; and coming to himself he said aloud, in the presence of many good folk: "The king of France will rejoice greatly on hearing these tidings, but I have it by Divine inspiration, that for this sin he is judged by God, and that great and strange perils and adversities, with shame to him and his lineage, will overtake him very swiftly, and he and his sons will be cast out from the inheritance of the realm." And this we learned a little while after, when we passed by Sion, from persons worthy of belief, which were present to hear. Which sentence was a prophecy in all its parts, as afterwards the truth will show, in due time, when we narrate the doings of the said king of France and of his sons. And the judgment of God is not to be marvelled at; for, albeit Pope Boniface was more worldly than was fitting to his dignity, and had done many things displeasing to God, God caused him to be punished after the fashion that we have said, and afterwards He punished the offender against him, not so much for the injury against the person of Pope Boniface, as for the sin committed against the Divine Majesty, whose countenance he represented on earth. We will leave this matter, which is now ended, and will turn back somewhat to relate of the doings of Florence and of Tuscany, which were very great in those times.

§ 65.—*How the Florentines had the castle of Montale, and how they* **1303 a.d.** *marched upon Pistoia together with the Lucchese.* § 66.—*How Benedict XI. was elected Pope.*

§ 67.—*How King Edward of England recovered Gascony and defeated the Scots.* **1303 a.d.**

In this year Edward, king of England, made peace with King Philip of France, and recovered Gascony, doing homage to him therefor; and to this the king of France consented, by reason of the contest which he had with the Church after the capture which he had made of Pope Boniface, and by reason of the war in Flanders, to the intent the said **Par. xix. 121-123.** king of England might not be against him. And in this same year, the said King Edward being ill, the Scots marched into England, for which cause the king had himself borne in a litter, and went out with the host against the Scots, and defeated them, and became lord over all the lands of Scotland, save only the marshes and rugged mountains, wherein the rebel Scots had taken refuge

279

with their king, which was named Robert Bruce, which, from lowly birth, had risen to be king.

§ 68.—*How there were in Florence great changes and civic battles through desire that the accounts of the commonwealth should be examined.*

1303 a.d.

In the said year 1303, in the month of February, the Florentines were in great discord among themselves, by reason that M. Corso Donati did not consider that he was so great in the commonwealth as he desired, and thought himself worthy to be; and the other magnates and powerful popolani of his Black party had gotten more authority in the commonwealth than seemed to him good; and being already at enmity with them, either through pride, or through envy, or through desire of lordship, he made a new faction, leaguing himself with the Cavalcanti, whereof the most part were Whites, saying that he desired that the public accounts of those which had held office, and had administered the monies of the commonwealth, should be examined; and they made their head M. Lottieri, bishop of Florence, which was of the family of the Tosa of the White branch, with certain magnates, against the priors and the people; and there was fighting in the city in many places and for many days, and they set engines in many towers and strongholds of the city after the ancient manner, which should hurl missiles and shoot at each other; and upon the towers of the Bishop's Palace they raised a mangonel directed against his enemies hard by. The priors strengthened themselves with people and men-at-arms of the city and of the country, and boldly defended the palace, for many assaults and attacks were made upon them; and the house of the Gherardini held with the people, with a great following of their friends from the country; and likewise the house of the Pazzi, and of the Spini and M. Tegghiaio Frescobaldi with his branch of the family, which were a great aid to the people; and M. Lotteringo de' Gherardini was slain by an arrow in a battle which was fought in Porte Sante Marie. Other houses of the magnates did not hold with the people, but some were with the bishop and with M. Corso, and some which liked him not stood apart from the strife. For the which dissension and civil fighting much evil was committed in the city and in the country, of murders, and burnings, and robberies, as in a city ungoverned and disordered, without any rule from the government, save that each should do all possible harm to the other; and the city was all full of refugees, and strangers, and folk from the country, each house with its own following; and the city would have utterly destroyed itself had not the Lucchese come to Florence at the request of the commonwealth, with great number of foot and horse; who took in hand the matter, and the guardianship of the city, and general authority was of necessity given to them, so that for sixteen days they freely ruled the city, issuing a proclamation on their own authority. And when the proclamation was made throughout the city in the name of the commonwealth of Lucca, it seemed evil to many Florentines, and a great outrage and wrong; wherefore one Ponciardo de' Ponci di Vacchereccia struck the herald from Lucca in the face with his sword while he was reading the proclamation, for which cause afterwards they sent forth no more proclamations in their own name; but so wrought that at last they quieted the uproar and caused each party to lay down arms, and restored the city to quiet, calling for new priors to promote peace, the people remaining in its estate and liberty; and they inflicted no punishment for misdeeds committed, but whoever had suffered wrong had to bear his loss. And in addition to the said plague there was great famine that year, and grain was worth more than twenty-six shillings the bushel, level measure, of fifty-two shillings to the golden florin; and if it had not been that the commonwealth and the rulers in the city had made provision beforehand, and had caused to be brought by the hand of the Genoese from Sicily and from Apulia full 26,000 bushels of grain, the citizens and the country people could not have escaped from famine: and this traffic in grain was, with others, one of the causes why they desired to examine the accounts of the commonwealth, by reason of all the money which was passing; and certain, whether rightly or wrongly, were spoken evil of and blamed thereanent. And this adversity and peril of our city was not without the judgment of God, by reason of many sins committed through the pride and envy and avarice of our then living citizens, which were then ruling the city, and alike of the rebels therein, as of those which were governing, for they were great sinners, nor was this the end thereof, as hereafter in due time may be seen.

§ 69.—*How the Pope sent into Florence as legate the Cardinal da Prato to make*

281

peace, and how he departed thence in shame and confusion.
1303 a.d.

During the said discord among the Florentines, Pope Benedict, with good intent, sent to Florence the Cardinal da Prato as legate to set the Florentines at peace one with another, and likewise with their exiles and all the province of Tuscany; and he came to Florence, on the tenth day of the month of March, 1303, and was received by the Florentines with great honour and with great reverence, as by men who felt themselves to be divided and in evil state; and those which had the disposition and desire to live rightly, loved peace and concord, and it was the contrary with the others. This Cardinal Niccolo, of the city of Prato, was a preaching friar, very wise in learning, and of natural intelligence, subtle and sagacious, and cautious, and very experienced; and by descent he was of the Ghibellines, and it was afterwards seen that he favoured them greatly; albeit at the first he showed good and impartial intentions. When he was in Florence, in a public sermon and discourse in the piazza of San Giovanni, he showed forth his privileges as legate, and made manifest his intention, by command of the Pope, of setting the Florentines at peace one with another. The good popolani which ruled the city, seeing themselves in evil estate by reason of the disturbances and riots and strifes, brought about in those times by the magnates against the people to abase and undo them, took part with the cardinal in the desire for peace; and by way of reconstruction of the Occasional Councils, they gave him full and free right to set the citizens at peace one with another within the city, and with their exiles without, and to appoint the priors and gonfaloniers and rulers of the city at his pleasure. And this done, he gave his mind to making peace among the citizens, and renewed the order of the nineteen gonfaloniers of the companies after the fashion of the ancient Popolo of old, and he summoned the gonfaloniers and gave them the banners after the fashion and devices that still are, save that they bore not the label of the arms of the king in chief. And by reason of these reforms of the cardinal the people were much heartened and strengthened, and the magnates were brought low, so that they never ceased trying to bring about changes and to hinder the cardinal to the end they might disturb the peace, that the

Whites and the Ghibellines might not have state nor power to return to Florence, and that they themselves might enjoy their goods which had been confiscated as of rebels, both in the city and in the country. For all this the cardinal did not cease from pursuing peace, with the aid and favour of the people, and he caused twelve plenipotentiaries of the exiles to come into Florence, two for **Cf. Epistola i.** each sesto, one from amongst the chief Whites and one Ghibelline; and he had them to sojourn in the Borgo di San Niccolo, and the legate sojourned in the palaces of the Mozzi of S. Gregorio, and often he had them to take counsel with the leaders of the Guelfs and of the Blacks in Florence to find out means and security of peace, and to order alliances between the exiles, and the nobles within. In these negotiations it seemed to the powerful Guelfs and Blacks that the cardinal was too much supporting the side of the Whites and of the Ghibellines, and they took counsel subtly to the end they might disturb the negotiations, to send a counterfeit letter, with the seal of the cardinal, to Bologna and into Romagna, to his friends the Ghibellines and the Whites, that they should, without any hindrance or delay, come to Florence with men in arms on horse and on foot to his aid; and some say withal that it was true that the cardinal sent it; wherefore some of those people came as far as Trespiano and some to Mugello. By which coming there arose in Florence great murmuring and ill-feeling, and the legate was much blamed and reproached therefor; and he, whether he were guilty or no, denied it to the people. Through which ill-feeling, and also through fear of suffering harm, the twelve White and Ghibelline plenipotentiaries departed from Florence and came to Arezzo, and the people which had come to the legate, by his command returned to Bologna and to Romagna, and the ill-will was somewhat quieted in Florence. Those which were ruling the city counselled the cardinal that, to avoid suspicion, he should go to Prato, and should reconcile the citizens thereof among themselves, and likewise the Pistoians, and in the meanwhile in Florence a way might be found of making general peace with the exiles. The cardinal, not being able to do otherwise, did this, and, whether in good faith or no, went to Prato and requested the inhabitants to trust in him, and he would reconcile them. Now the leaders of the Black party and of the Guelfs of Florence marked the ways of the cardinal, how that he greatly favoured the

283

Ghibellines and Whites and would fain restore them to Florence, and saw likewise that the people followed him; wherefore they feared it might turn out perilous to the Guelf party, and ordained with the Guazzalotti of Prato, a powerful house of the Black party, and strong Guelfs, to bring to pass in Prato a schism and riot against the cardinal, and to raise a tumult in the city; wherefore the cardinal, seeing the inhabitants of Prato to be ill-disposed, and fearing for his person, departed from Prato, and excommunicated the inhabitants, and laid the city under interdict, and came to Florence, and proclaimed war against Prato, and offered remission of sins and of penalties to whosoever would march against Prato; and many citizens prepared to go thither on horse and on foot, folk that were, in faith, more Ghibelline than Guelf, and they went as far as Campi. In this assembling of the host much folk gathered in Florence of folk from the country and foreigners, and the fear and jealousy of the Guelfs began to increase; wherefore many which at the first had held with the cardinal, changed their purpose through the turbulence which they observed; and the magnates of the Black party, and likewise they which were temporising with the cardinal, furnished themselves with arms and with men, and the city was all in disorder, and they were ready to fight one another. The cardinal legate, seeing that he could not carry out his purpose of leading an army against Prato, and that the city of Florence was disposed to civil strife, and that of those which had held with him, some were now against him, became fearful and uneasy, and suddenly departed from Florence on the 4th day of June, 1304, saying to the Florentines: "Seeing that ye desire to be at war and **Cf. Inf. x. 79-81.** under a curse, and do not desire to hear or to obey the messenger of the vicar of God, or to have rest or peace among yourselves, abide with the curse of God and of Holy Church"; thus he excommunicated the citizens, and left the city under an interdict, whence it was held, that by this curse, whether just or unjust, there fell judgment and great peril on our city through the adversities and perils which came to pass therein but a short time after, as hereafter we shall make mention.

§ 70.—*How the bridge of Carraia fell, and how many people died there.*
1304 a.d.

In this same time that the Cardinal da Prato was in Florence, and was beloved by the people and by the citizens, who hoped that he might set them at peace one with another, on the first day of May, 1304, just as in the good old times of the tranquil and good estate of Florence, it had been the custom for companies and bands of pleasure-makers to go through the city rejoicing and making merry, so now again they assembled and met in divers parts of the city; and one district vied with the other which could invent and do the best. Among others, as of old was the custom, they of Borgo San Friano were wont to devise the newest and most varied pastimes; and they sent forth a proclamation that whosoever desired news of the other world should come on the 1st day of May upon the Carraia Bridge, and beside the Arno; and they erected upon the Arno a stage upon boats and vessels, and thereupon they made the similitude and figure of hell, with fires and other pains and sufferings, with men disguised as demons, horrible to behold, and others which had the appearance of naked souls, which **Cf. Inf. vi. 36.** seemed to be persons, and they were putting them to the said divers torments, with loud cries, and shrieks, and tumult, which seemed hateful and fearful to hear and to see; and by reason of this new pastime there came many citizens to look on, and the Carraia Bridge, which then was of wood from pile to pile, was so burdened with people that it gave way in many places, and fell with the people which were upon it, wherefore many were killed and drowned, and many were maimed; so that the pastime from sport became earnest, and, as the proclamation had said, many by death went to learn news of the other world, with great lamentation and sorrow to all the city, for each one believed he must have lost his son or his brother there; and this was a sign of future ill, which in a short time should come to our city through the exceeding wickedness of the citizens, as hereafter we shall make mention.

§ 71.—*How Florence was set on fire, and a great part of the city burnt.*
1304 a.d.

When the Cardinal da Prato had departed from Florence after the manner aforesaid, the city was left in evil state and in great confusion; for there was the party which held with the cardinal, whereof were leaders the Cavalcanti and the Gherardini, the Pulci and the White Cerchi of the Garbo,

285

which were merchants of Pope Benedict, with a following of many houses of the people, (which feared the magnates might break up the Popolo if they got the government), from among the leading houses and families of the popolani of Florence, such as the Magalotti, and Mancini, Peruzzi, Antellesi, and Baroncelli, and Acciaiuoli, and Alberti, Strozzi, Ricci, and Albizzi, and many others; and they were well provided with foot-soldiers and with men-at-arms. On the contrary part, to wit, the Blacks, the leaders were M. Rosso della Tosa, with his branch of Blacks, M. Pazzino de' Pazzi, with all his family, the part of the Adimari which were called the Cavicciuli, and M. Geri Spini, with his kin, and M. Betto Brunelleschi; M. Corso Donati stood neutral, forasmuch as he was ill with the gout, and because he was angered with these leaders of the Black party; and almost all the other magnates held aloof, and the popolani also, save the Medici and the Giugni, which held strongly with the Blacks. And the fighting began between the White Cerchi and the Giugni at their houses at the Garbo, and they fought there by day and by night. In the end, the Cerchi defended themselves with the aid of the Cavalcanti and Antellesi, and the force of the Cavalcanti and Gherardini so increased that with their followers they rode through the city as far as the Mercato Vecchio, and from Orto San Michele as far as the piazza of S. Giovanni, without any opposition or hindrance whatever, because their forces increased both in the city and in the country; forasmuch as the greater part of the people followed them, and the Ghibellines sided with them; and they of Volognano and their friends were coming to their aid with more than 1,000 foot-soldiers; and were already at Bisarno; and certainly on that day they would have conquered the city and driven out thence the aforesaid leaders of the Blacks and Guelfs, whom they held as their enemies (forasmuch as it was said that they had caused M. Betto Gherardini to be beheaded, and Masino Cavalcanti and the others, as we before made mention), save that when they were flourishing and victorious in several parts of the city where they were fighting against their enemies, it came to pass, as it pleased God, either to avoid worse ill, or that He permitted it to punish the sins of the Florentines, that one, Ser Neri Abati, a clerk and prior of San Piero Scheraggio, a worldly and dissolute man, and a rebel against and enemy of his associates, of purpose set fire first to the house of his associates in

286

Orto San Michele, and then to the Florentine Calimala at the house of the Caponsacchi, near to the entrance of the Mercato Vecchio. And the accursed fire was so furious **Cf. Par. xvi. 121, 122.** and impetuous, fanned by the north wind, which was blowing strongly, that on that day were burnt the houses of the Abati, and of the Macci, and all the loggia of Orto San Michele, and the houses of the Amieri, and Toschi, and Cipriani, and Lamberti, and Bachini, and Buiamonti, and all Calimala, and the houses of the Cavalcanti, and all around the Mercato Nuovo and S. Cecilia, and all the street of Porte Sante Marie as far as the Ponte Vecchio, and Vacchereccia, and behind San Piero Scheraggio, and the houses of the Gherardini, and of the Pulci and Amidei and Lucardesi, and all the neighbourhood of the said places, almost to the Arno; and, in short, all the marrow and yolk and the most precious places of the city of Florence were burnt, and the number of the palaces and towers and houses was more than 1,700. The loss of stores, and of treasure, and of merchandise was infinite, forasmuch as in those places were almost all the merchandise and precious things of Florence, and that which was not burnt was robbed by highwaymen as it was being carried away, the city being continually at war in divers places, wherefore many companies, and clans, and families were ruined and brought to poverty by the said fires and robberies. This plague came upon our city of Florence on the 10th day of June, in the year of Christ 1304; and for this cause the leaders of that faction the Cavalcanti, which were among the most powerful houses in Florence, both in retainers, and in possessions, and in goods, and the Gherardini, among the greatest in the country, their houses and those of their followers being burnt down, lost their vigour and estate, and were driven out of Florence as rebels, and their enemies recovered their estate, and became lords over the city. And then it was verily believed that the magnates would set aside the Ordinances of Justice of the Popolo, and this they would have done if it had not been that through their factions they were themselves at variance one with another, and each party sided with the people to the end they might not lose their estate. We must now go on to tell of the other events which were in many parts in these times, forasmuch as there arose thence further adverse fortune to our city of Florence.

§ 72.—*How the Whites and Ghibellines came to the gates of Florence, and*

departed thence in discomfiture.
1304 a.d.

When the Cardinal da Prato had returned to the Pope, which was at Perugia with his court, he made many complaints against them which were ruling the city of Florence, and accused them before the Pope and the college of cardinals of many crimes and faults, showing them to be sinful men and enemies of God and of Holy Church, and recounting the dishonour and treachery which they had done to Holy Church when he had desired to restore them to good and peaceful estate; for the which thing the Pope and his cardinals were greatly moved with anger against the Florentines, and by the counsel of the said Cardinal da Prato the Pope cited twelve of the chief leaders of the Guelf party and of the Blacks which were in Florence, which were directing all the state of the city, the names whereof were these: M. Corso Donati, M. Rosso della Tosa, M. Pazzino de' Pazzi, M. Geri Spini, M. Betto Brunelleschi. And they were to appear before him under pain of excommunication and deprivation of all their goods; which straightway came obediently thither with a great company of their friends and followers in great state, for they were more than 150 on horseback, to defend themselves before the Pope against the charges which the Cardinal da Prato had made against them. And in this summons and citation of so many leaders of Florence, the Cardinal da Prato cunningly planned a great treachery against the Florentines, straightway sending letters to Pisa, and to Bologna, and to Romagna, to Arezzo, to Pistoia, and to all the leaders of the Ghibelline and White party in Tuscany and in Romagna, that they should assemble with all their forces and those of their friends on foot and on horse, and on a day named should come in arms to the city of Florence, and take the city, and drive out thence the Blacks and those which had been against him, saying that this was by the knowledge and will of the Pope (the which thing was a great falsehood and lie, forasmuch as the Pope knew nothing thereof), and encouraging each one to come securely, forasmuch as the city was weak, and open in many places; and saying that he of his zeal had summoned and caused to appear at the court all the leaders of the Black party, and that within the city there was a large party which would welcome them and would surrender the city to them; and that they should gather together and come secretly and quickly. And when they had received these letters, they rejoiced greatly, and, being encouraged by the favour of the Pope, each one furnished himself according to his power, and moved towards Florence on the day appointed. And two days before, through their great eagerness, the Pisans, with their troops and with all the Florentines which were in Pisa, to the number of 400 horsemen, whereof Count Fazio was captain, came as far as the stronghold of Marti; and all the other assembly of Whites and Ghibellines came towards Florence after so secret a fashion that they were at Lastra above Montughi, to the number of 1,600 horse and 9,000 foot, ere the most could believe it in Florence, forasmuch as they had not allowed any messenger which should announce their coming to find his way to Florence; and if they had descended upon the city one day sooner, without doubt they would have had the city, forasmuch as there was no preparation, nor store of arms, nor defence. But they abode that night at Lastra and at Trespiano, extending as far as Fontebuona, awaiting M. Tolosata degli Uberti, captain of Pistoia, which was taking the way across the mountains with 300 horse, Pistoian and mercenary, and with many on foot; and in the morning, seeing that he did not come, the Florentine refugees determined to come to the city, thinking to have it without stroke of sword, and this they did, leaving the Bolognese at Lastra, which, by reason of their cowardice, or perhaps because of the Guelfs which were among them, were not in favour of the enterprise; so the rest came on, and entered into the suburb of San Gallo without any hindrance, for at that time the city had not the circles of the new walls, nor the moats, and the old walls were open and broken down in many places. And when they had entered into the suburbs, they broke down a wooden palisade with a gate leading into the suburb, which was abandoned by our citizens without defence; and the Aretines carried off the bolt of the said gate, and in contempt of the Florentines took it to Arezzo, and set it in their chief church of San Donato. And when the said enemies were come down through the suburbs towards the city, they assembled at Cafaggio, by the side of the Servi, and they were more than 1,200 horsemen, and common folks in numbers, with many folk from the country following them, and with Ghibellines and Whites from within, which had come out to their aid. Now this was ill advised on their part, as we shall tell hereafter, for they had stationed themselves in a place without water; for if they had taken up their stand on the piazza of Santa Croce, they would have had the river and water for themselves and for their horses, and the Città Rossa round about, without the old walls, all which was so built with houses as to accommodate an army in safety were it never so large; but to whom God wills ill, from him He takes all wit and judgment. When, on the evening before, the tidings were brought to Florence, there was great fear and suspicion of treachery, and the city was on guard all night; but by reason of fear some went this way, some that, all at random, each one removing his goods. And of a truth it was said that the greatest and best houses in Florence, of magnates, and popolani, and Guelfs, knew of this purpose, and had promised to surrender the city; but hearing of the great force of the Ghibellines of Tuscany and the enemies of our commonwealth which were come with our exiles, they feared greatly for themselves, and that they should be driven away and robbed, and so they changed their purpose, and looked to defend the city together with the rest. Certain of our exiled leaders, with part of their followers, departed from Cafaggio from the army, and came to the gate of the Spadari, and this they attacked and conquered, and entered in together with their banners as far as the piazza of S. Giovanni; and if the larger force which was in Cafaggio had then come towards the city, and attacked some other gate, they would certainly not have been resisted. In the piazza of S. Giovanni were assembled all the valiant men and Guelfs which were giving themselves to the defence of the city, not, however, in great numbers (perhaps 200 horse and 500 foot), and with the aid of large crossbows they drove back the enemy without the gate, with the loss of some taken and slain. The news went to Lastra to the Bolognese by their spies, reporting that their side had been routed and discomfited, and straightway, without learning the certainty thereof, for it was not true, they departed in flight as best they could, and when they met M. Tolosato with his followers in Mugello, which was advancing with full knowledge of the truth, he would have retained them and caused them to turn back; but this he could not bring about, neither through entreaties nor threats. They of the main body in Cafaggio, when they heard the news from Lastra how the Bolognese had departed in confusion, as it pleased God,

290

straightway took fear, and through the discomfort of continuing in array until after noon in the burning sun,—the heat being great, and not having sufficiency of water for themselves and for their horses,—began to disperse and to depart in flight, throwing away their arms without assault or pursuit of the citizens, forasmuch as they scarce followed after them at all, save certain troopers of their own free will. And thus many of the enemy died, either by the sword or from exhaustion, and were robbed of arms and of horses; and certain of the prisoners were hanged in the piazza of San Gallo and along the road, on the trees. But verily it was said that, notwithstanding the departure of the Bolognese, if they had stood firm until the coming of M. Tolosato, which they could assuredly have done by reason of the small number of horse which were defending Florence, they would yet have gained the city. But it seemed to be the work and will of God that they should be bewitched, to the end our city of Florence might not be wholly laid waste, sacked, and destroyed. This unforeseen victory and escape of the city of Florence was on S. Margaret's Day, the 20th of the month of July, the year of Christ 1304. We have made such an extensive record, forasmuch as we were there present, and by reason of the great risk and peril from which God saved the city of Florence, and to the end our descendants may take therefrom example and warning.

§ 73.—*How the Aretines recovered the castle of Laterino which the* **1304 a.d.** *Florentines held.* § 74.—*Of certain further things which came to pass in Florence in the said times.* § 75.—*How the Florentines went out against and took the strongholds of the Stinche and Montecalvi which were held by the Whites.* § 76.—*Returns back somewhat to* tell **1303 a.d.** *of the story of the Flemings.* § 77.—*How Guy of Flanders was routed and seized, with his armada, by the admiral of the king of France.* **1304 a.d.** § 78.—*How the king of France defeated the Flemings at Mons-en-Puelle.* § 79.—*How, shortly after the defeat of Mons-en-Puelle, the Flemings returned to the conflict with the king of France and gained a favourable peace.*

§ 80.—*How Pope Benedict died; and of the new election of Pope Clement V.* **1304 a.d.**

In the year of Christ 1304, on the 27th day of the month July, Pope Benedict died in the city of Perugia, it was said by poison; for when he was eating at his table, there came to him a young man veiled and attired in the garb of a woman, as a serving sister of the nuns of S. Petronella, in Perugia, with a silver basin wherein were many fine ripe figs, and he presented them to the Pope from his devout servant, the abbess of that nunnery. The Pope received them with great pleasure, and forasmuch as he was fond of them, and without any one tasting thereof beforehand, seeing that they were presented by a woman, he ate many thereof, whereat he straightway fell ill, and in a few days died, and was buried with great honour at the Preaching Friars (for he was of that Order), in San Ercolano, of Perugia. This was a good man, and virtuous and just, and of holy and religious life, and desirous to do right in all things; and through the envy of certain of his brother cardinals, it was said, they compassed his death after the said manner; wherefore God recompensed them, if they were guilty thereof, in a short time, by a very just and open vengeance, as will be shown hereafter. For after the death of the said Pope there arose a schism and a great discord among the college of cardinals in electing the Pope; and by reason of their differences they were divided into two almost equal parties; the head of the one was M. Matteo Rosso, of the Orsini, with M. Francesco Guatani, nephew that was of Pope Boniface; and the leaders of the other were M. **Epistola viii.** Napoleone, of the Orsini dal Monte, and the Cardinal da Prato, which hoped to restore their kinsfolk and friends, the Colonnesi, to their estate, and were friends of the king of France, and leaned towards the Ghibelline side. And when they had been shut up for a period of more than nine months, and were pressed by the Perugians to nominate a Pope, and could not come to an agreement, at last the Cardinal da Prato, finding himself in a secret place with the Cardinal Francesco, of the Guatani, said to him, "We are doing great harm and injury to **1305 a.d.** the Church by not choosing a Pope." And M. Francesco said, "It does not lie with me." And the other replied, "If I could find a good way of escape, wouldst thou be content?" He made answer that he would; and thus conversing together they came to this agreement, by the industry and sagacity of the Cardinal da Prato, who, treating with the said M. Francesco Guatani, gave him his choice; for it was determined that the one party, to avoid all suspicion, should choose three men from beyond the Alps suitable for the papacy, whomsoever it pleased them, and the other party, within forty days, should take one of the three, whichever they pleased, and that he should be Pope. The party of M. Francesco Guatani preferred to make the first choice, thinking thus to have the advantage, and he elected three archbishops from beyond the Alps, made and created by Pope Boniface, his uncle, which were his great friends and confidants, and enemies of the king of France, their adversary, trusting that whichever the other party might take they would have a Pope after their mind, and a friend. Among these three the archbishop of Bordeaux was the one in whom they most trusted. The wise and far-seeing Cardinal da Prato thought that their purpose would be better carried out by taking M. Raimond de Goth, archbishop of Bordeaux, than by taking either of the others; albeit he had been appointed by Pope Boniface, and was no friend of the king of France, by reason of injuries done to his kinsfolk in the war of Gascony by M. Charles of Valois; but knowing him to be a man desirous of honour and lordship, and that he was a Gascon, who are by nature covetous, and that he might easily make peace with the king of France, they secretly took counsel, and he and his party in the college took an oath, and having confirmed with the other part of the college the documents and papers concerning the said agreements and pacts, by his letters, and those of the other cardinals of his party, they wrote to the king of France, and enclosed under their seals the pacts and agreements and commissions between themselves and the other part of the college, and by faithful and good couriers ordered by means of their merchants (the other party knowing nothing of this), they sent from Perugia to Paris in eleven days, admonishing and praying the king of France by the tenor of their letters, that if he wished to recover his estate in Holy Church and relieve his friends, the Colonnesi, he should turn his foe into a friend, to wit M. Raimond de Goth, archbishop of Bordeaux, one of the three chosen and most trusted by the other party; seeking and stipulating with him for liberal terms for himself and for his friends, forasmuch as to his hands was committed the election of the one of those three, whichever he pleased. The king of France having received the said letters and commissions, rejoiced greatly, and was eager for the undertaking. First of all he sent friendly letters by messengers into Gascony to M. Raimond de Goth, archbishop of Bordeaux, that he should come to meet him, for he desired to speak with him; and within the next six days the king came in person with a small company, to a secret conference with the said archbishop of Bordeaux in a forest, at an abbey in the district of S. Jean d'Angelus, and when they had heard mass together and sworn faith upon the altar, the king parleyed with him with good words to reconcile him with M. Charles; and then he said thus to him, "Behold, archbishop, I have in my hand the power to make thee Pope if I will, and for this cause am come to thee; and, therefore, if thou wilt promise to grant me six favours which I shall ask of thee, I will do thee this honour, and to the end thou mayest be assured that I have this power,"—he drew forth and showed him the letters and commissions from both one part of the college and the other. The Gascon, coveting the papal dignity, and seeing thus suddenly how with the king lay the power of making him Pope, as it were stupefied with joy, threw himself at his feet, and said, "My lord, now I know that thou lovest me more than any other man, and wouldst return me good for evil; thou hast to command and I to obey, and always it shall be so ordered." The king lifted him up and kissed him on the mouth, and then said to him, "The six special graces that I ask of thee are these: the first, that thou wilt reconcile me perfectly with the Church, and procure my pardon for my misdeed which I committed in the capture of Pope Boniface. The second, that thou wilt recommunicate me and my followers. The third article, that thou wilt grant me all the tithes of the realm for five years, in aid of my expenses which I have incurred for the war in Flanders. The fourth, that thou wilt promise to destroy and annul the memory of Pope Boniface. The fifth, that thou wilt restore the honour of the cardinalate to M. Jacopo and M. Piero della Colonna, and restore them to their estate, and together with them wilt make certain of my friends cardinals. The sixth grace and promise I reserve till due time and place, for it is secret and great." The archbishop promised everything on oath upon the body of Christ, and, furthermore, gave him as hostages his brother and two of his nephews; and the king swore to him and promised that he should be elected Pope. And this done, with great love and joy they parted, and the king returned to Paris, taking with him the said hostages under cover of love and of reconciling them with M. Charles; and straightway he wrote in answer to the Cardinal da Prato and to the others of his party, telling what he had done, and that they might safely elect as Pope M. Raimond de Goth, archbishop of Bordeaux, as a trustworthy and sure friend. And as it pleased God, the matter was so urgently pressed that in thirty-five days the answer to the said mandate was come back to Perugia with great secrecy. And when the Cardinal da Prato had received the said answer, he showed it secretly to his party, and craftily summoned the other party, when it should please them to assemble together, forasmuch as they desired to observe the agreement, and so it was immediately done. And when the said parties were gathered together, and it was necessary to ratify and confirm the order of the said compacts with authenticated papers and oaths, it was solemnly done. And then the said Cardinal da Prato wisely cited an authority from Holy Scripture which was fitting to the occasion, and by the authority committed to him after the said manner, he elected as Pope the aforesaid M. Raimond de Goth, archbishop of Bordeaux; and this was accepted and confirmed with great joy by both parties, and they sang with a loud voice "Te Deum Laudamus," etc., the party of Pope Boniface not knowing of the deceit and fraud which had been carried out, rather believing that they had as Pope that man in whom they most trusted; and when the announcements of the election came abroad, there was great strife and disturbance between their families, forasmuch as each said that he was the friend of their party. And this done, and the cardinals being come forth from their confinement, it was straightway determined to send him the election and decree across the mountains where he was. This election took place on the 5th day of **Inf. xix. 82-87. Par. xvii. 82. xxvii. 58, 9. xxx. 142-148.** June in the year of Christ 1305, when the apostolic chair had been vacant ten months and twenty-eight days. We have made so long a record of this election of the Pope, by reason of the subtle and fine deceit which took place, and for its bearing on the future, forasmuch as great things followed thereupon, as hereafter we shall relate, during the time of his papacy and of his successor. And this election was the cause whereby the papacy reverted to foreigners, and the court went beyond the mountains, so that for the sin committed by the Italian cardinals in the death of Pope Benedict, if they were guilty thereof, and in the fraudulent election, they were well punished by the Gascons, as we shall tell hereafter.

§ 81.—*Of the coronation of Pope Clement V. and of the cardinals* **1305 a.d.**

295

which he made. § 82.—*How the Florentines and the Lucchese besieged and took the city of Pistoia.* § 83.—*How the cities of Modena and of Reggio rebelled against the marquis of Este, and how the Whites and the Ghibellines were driven out of Bologna.*

§ 84.—*How there arose in Lombardy one Fra Dolcino with a great company of heretics, and how they were burnt.*

1305 a.d.
Inf. xxviii. 55-60.

In the said year 1305, in the territory of Novara in Lombardy, there was one Frate Dolcino, which was not a brother of any regular Order, but as it were a monk outside the Orders, and he rose up and led astray a great company of heretics, men and women of the country and of the mountains, of small account; and the said Fra Dolcino taught and preached that he was a true apostle of Christ, and that everything ought to be held lovingly in common, and women also were to be in common, and there was no sin in so using them. And many other foul articles of heresy he preached, and maintained that the Pope and cardinals and the other rulers of Holy Church did not observe their duty nor the evangelic life; and that he ought to be made Pope. And he, with a following of more than 3,000 men and women, abode in the mountains, living in common after the manner of beasts; and when they wanted victuals they took and robbed wherever they could find any; and thus he reigned for two years. At last those which followed the said dissolute life, becoming weary of it, his sect diminished much, and through want of victuals and by reason of the snow he was taken by the Navarese and burnt, with Margaret his companion, and with many other men and women which with him had been led astray.

§ 85.—*How Pope Clement sent as legate into Italy Cardinal Napoleone* **1306 a.d.** *of the Orsini, and how he was ill received.* § 86.—*How the Florentines besieged and took the strong castle of Montaccianico and dismantled it, and caused Scarperia to be built.* § 87.—*How the Florentines strengthened the Popolo, and chose the first executor of the Ordinances of Justice.*

§ 88.—*Of the great war which was begun against the marquis of Ferrara, and how he died.*

1306 a.d.

Inf. xii. 112; xviii. 55-57. Purg. v. 73-78. xx. 79-81. De Vulg. El. I. 12: 38; II. 6: 42-44.

In the said year 1306, the Veronese, Mantuans, and Brescians made a league together, and declared a great war against the Marquis Azzo of Este, which was lord of Ferrara, because they feared that he was desirous to be lord over Lombardy, forasmuch as he had taken to wife a daughter of King Charles; and they overran his places and took from him some of his strongholds. But the year after, when he had gathered his forces, with the aid of the Piedmontese and of King Charles, he made a great expedition against them, and overran their places and did them much hurt. But a little time after the said marquis fell sick, and died in great pain and misery; and he had been the gayest and most redoubted and powerful tyrant in Lombardy, and he left no son of lawful wedlock, and his lands and lordship became a cause of great strife between his brothers and nephews, and one of his bastard sons, which was named Francis, whom the Venetians greatly favoured because he was born in Venice; and much strife and war followed therefrom with hurt to the Venetians, as hereafter in due time we shall make mention.

§ 89.—*How M. Napoleone Orsini, the legate, came to Arezzo; and of* **1306 a.d.**

1307 a.d.

Purg. vii. 132. *the expedition which the Florentines made against Gargosa.* § 90.—*How the good King Edward of England died.* § 91.—*How the king of France went to Poitiers to Pope Clement, to cause the memory of Pope Boniface to be condemned.*

§ 92.—*How and after what fashion was destroyed the Order and mansion of the Temple of Jerusalem by the machinations of the king of France.*

1307 a.d.

Purg. xx. 91-93.

In the said year 1307, before the king of France departed from the court of Poitiers, he accused and denounced to the Pope, incited thereto by his officers and by desire of gain, the master and the Order of the Temple, charging them with certain crimes and errors, whereof as the king had been

297

informed the Templars were guilty. The first movement came from a prior of the said Order, of Monfaucon in the region of Toulouse, a man of evil life and a heretic, and for his faults condemned to perpetual imprisonment in Paris by the grand master. And finding himself in prison with one Noffo Dei, of our city of Florence, a man full of all vices, these two men, despairing of any salvation, evilly and maliciously invented the said false accusation in hope of gain, and of being set free from prison by aid of the king. But each of them a little while after came to a bad end; forasmuch as Noffo was hanged and the prior stabbed. To the end they might move the king to seek his gain, they brought the accusation before his officers, and the officers brought it before the king; wherefore the king was moved by his avarice, and made secret arrangements with the Pope and caused him to promise to destroy the Order of the Templars, laying to their charge many articles of heresy; but it is said that it was more in hope of extracting great sums of money from them, and by reason of offence taken against the master of the Temple and the Order. The Pope, to be rid of the king of France, by reason of the request which he had made that he would condemn Pope Boniface, as we have before said, whether rightly or wrongly, to please the king promised that he would do this; and when the king had departed, on a day named in his letters, he caused all the Templars to be seized throughout the whole world, and all their churches and mansions and possessions, which were almost innumerable in power and in riches, to be sequestered; and all those in the realm of France the king caused to be occupied by his court, and at Paris the master of the Temple was taken, which was named Jacques of the lords of Molay in Burgundy, with sixty knights, friars and gentlemen; and they were charged with certain articles of heresy, and certain vile sins against nature which they were said to practise among themselves; and that at their profession they swore to support the Order right or wrong, and that their worship was idolatrous, and that they spat upon the cross, and that when their master was consecrated it was secretly and in private, and none knew the manner; and alleging that their predecessors had caused the Holy Land to be lost by treachery, and King Louis and his followers to be taken at Monsura. And when sundry proofs had been given by the king of the truth of these charges, he had them tortured with divers tortures that they might

298

confess, and it was found that they would not confess nor acknowledge anything. And after keeping them a long time in prison in great misery, and not knowing how to put an end to their trial, at last outside Paris at S. Antoine (and the **1310 a.d.** like was also done at Senlis in France) in a great park enclosed by wood, fifty-six of the said Templars were bound each one to a stake, and they began to set fire to their feet and legs little by little, admonishing them one after the other that whosoever of them would acknowledge the error and sins wherewith they were charged might escape; and during this martyrdom, exhorted by their kinsfolk and friends to confess, and not to allow themselves to be thus vilely slain and destroyed, yet would not one of them confess, but with weeping and cries they defended themselves as being innocent and faithful Christians, calling upon Christ and S. Mary and the other saints; and by the said martyrdom all burning to ashes they ended their lives. And the master was reserved, and the brother of the dauphin of Auvergne, and Brother Hugh of Peraud, and another of the leaders of the Order, which had been officers and treasurers of the king of France, and they were brought to Poitiers before the Pope, the king of France being present, and they were promised forgiveness if they would acknowledge their error and sin, and it is said that they confessed something thereof; and when they had returned to Paris there came thither two cardinal legates to give sentence and condemn the Order upon the said confession, and to impose some discipline upon the said master and his companions; and when they had mounted a great scaffold, opposite the church of Nôtre Dame, and had read the indictment, the said master of the Temple rose to his feet, demanding to be heard; and when silence was proclaimed, he denied that ever such heresies and sins as they had been charged with had been true, and maintained that the rule of their Order had been holy and just and catholic, but that he certainly was worthy of death, and would endure it in peace, forasmuch as through fear of torture and by the persuasions of the Pope and of the king, he had by deceit been persuaded to confess some part thereof. And the discourse having been broken off, and the sentence not having been fully delivered, the cardinals and the other prelates departed from that place. And having held counsel with the king, the said master and his companions, in the Isle de Paris and before the hall of the king, were put to martyrdom after the same manner as the rest of their brethren, the master burning slowly to death and continually repeating that the Order and their religion was catholic and righteous, and commending himself to God and S. Mary; and likewise did the brother of the dauphin. Brother Hugh of Peraud, and the other, through fear of martyrdom, confessed and confirmed that which they had said before the Pope and the king, and they escaped, but afterwards they died miserably. And by many it was said that they were slain and destroyed wrongly and wickedly, and to the end their property might be seized, which afterwards was granted in privilege by the Pope to the Order of the Hospitallers, but they were required to recover and redeem it from the king of France and the other princes and lords, and that with so great a sum that, with the interest to be paid thereupon, the Order of the Hospitallers was, and is, poorer than it was before in its property; or perhaps God brought this about by miracle to show how things were. And the king of France and his sons had afterwards much shame and adversity, both because of this sin and of the capture of Pope Boniface, as hereafter shall be related. And note, that the night after the said master and his companion had been martyred, their ashes and bones were collected as sacred relics by friars and other religious persons, and carried away to holy places. In this manner was destroyed and brought to nought the rich and powerful Order of the Temple at Jerusalem, in the year of Christ 1310. We will now leave the doings in France and return to our doings in Italy.

§ 93.—*Of events and defeats which came to pass in Romagna and in* **1307 a.d.** **1308 a.d.** *Lombardy.* § 94.—*Of the death of King Albert of Germany.* § 95.—*How the Podestà of Florence fled with the Hercules seal of the commonwealth.*

§ 96.—*How Corso Donati, the great and noble citizen of Florence, died.* **1308 a.d.**

In the said year 1308, there being in the city of Florence increasing strife between the nobles and the powerful popolani of the Black party which were ruling the city, by reason of rivalry for state and lordship, which began at the time of the tumult when they demanded to see the accounts, as we have before made mention; this jealous disposition must needs bring forth sorrowful consequences, because from the sins of pride and envy and avarice, and other vices which reigned among them, they were divided into factions; and the leader of one faction was M. Corso de' Donati, with a following of some nobles, and of certain popolani, among others them of the house of Bordoni; and of the other party were leaders M. Rosso della Tosa, M. Geri Spini, and M. Pazzino dei Pazzi, and M. Betto Brunelleschi, with their allies, and with the Cavicciuli, and with many houses of magnates and popolani, and the greater part of the good people of the city, which had the offices and the government of the city, and of the people. M. Corso and his followers believed themselves to have been ill-treated with regard to offices and honours, whereof they held themselves to be more worthy, forasmuch as they had been the principal restorers of the Blacks to their estate, and had driven out the Whites; but by the other party it was said that M. Corso desired to be lord over the city with no equal. But whatever may have been the truth or the cause, his aforesaid opponents and they which ruled the city had hated and greatly feared him, ever since he had allied himself by marriage to Uguccione della Faggiuola, a Ghibelline, and hostile to the Florentines; and also they feared him because of his ambition and power and following, being uncertain whether he would not take their state from them, and drive them from the city, and above all, because they found that the said M. Corso had made a league and covenant with the said Uguccione della Faggiuola, his father-in-law, and had sent for him and his aid. For the which thing, in great jealousy, the city suddenly rose in an uproar, and the priors caused the bells to be sounded, and the people and the nobles, on horse and on foot, flew to arms, and the Catalan troops with the king's marshal, which were at the service of them which ruled the city. And straightway, as had been ordained by the aforesaid leaders, an inquisition or accusation was given to the Podestà, to wit, to M. Piero della Branca d'Agobbio, against the said M. Corso, charging him with wishing to betray the people, and to overturn the city, by bringing thither Uguccione della Faggiuola with the Ghibellines and enemies of the commonwealth. And he was first cited to appear, and then proclamation was made against him, and then he was condemned; in less than an hour, without giving any longer time for his trial, M. Corso was condemned as a rebel and traitor to his commonwealth, and straightway the priors set forth with the standard of justice, and the Podestà, captain and executioner, with their retainers and with the standard-bearers of the companies, with the people in arms, and the troops on horse, amid the acclamations of the people, to go to the house where dwelt M. Corso at San Piero Maggiore, to carry out the sentence. When M. Corso, having heard of the attack against him (or, as some said, in order to strengthen himself to carry out his purpose, for he was expecting Uguccione della Faggiuola with a great following which was already come to Remole), had barricaded himself in the road of San Piero Maggiore, at the foot of the towers of Cicino, and in Torcicoda, and at the entrance of the way which goes towards the Stinche, and at the way of San Brocolo, with strong barricades, and with much folk, his kinsmen and friends, in arms and with crossbows, enclosed within the barricade, and at his service. The people began to attack the said barricades in divers places, and M. Corso and his friends to defend them boldly; and the battle endured the greater part of the day, and was so strong that, with all the power of the people, if the reinforcements of Uguccione's followers and the other friends from the country invited by M. Corso had joined him in time, the people of Florence would have had enough to do that day; because, albeit they were many, yet were they ill-ordered and not well agreed, forasmuch as to part of them the attack was not pleasing. But when Uguccione's followers heard how M. Corso was attacked by the people, they turned back, and the citizens which were within the barricade began to depart, so that he remained very scant of followers, and certain of the people broke down the wall of the orchard over against the Stinche, and entered in with a great company of men in arms. When M. Corso and his followers saw this, and that the aid of Uguccione and of his other friends was belated and had failed them, he abandoned the houses, and fled out of the city, the which houses were straightway plundered and destroyed by the people, and M. Corso and his followers were pursued by certain citizens on horse and by certain Catalans, sent expressly to take him. And Gherardo Bordoni was overtaken by Boccaccio Cavicciuli, at the Affrico, and slain, and his hand was cut off and taken to the street of the Adimari, and nailed to the door of M. Tedici degli Adimari, his associate, by reason of enmity between them. M. Corso, departing quite alone, was overtaken and captured near Rovezzano by certain Catalans on horse, and as they were taking him prisoner to Florence, when they were hard by San Salvi, he prayed them to let him go free, promising them much money if they would let him escape, but they held to their purpose of taking him to Florence, as had been commanded them by their lords; then M. Corso, in fear of coming into the hands of his enemies, and of being brought to justice by the people, being much afflicted with gout in his hands and feet, let himself fall from his horse. The said Catalans seeing him on the **Purg. xxiv. 81-87.** ground, one of them gave him a thrust with his lance in the throat, which was a mortal blow, and then left him there for dead; the monks of the said convent carried him into the abbey, and some said that before he died he gave himself into their hands as a penitent, and some said that they found him dead; and the next morning he was buried in San Salvi with little honour and but few present, for fear of the commonwealth. This M. Corso Donati was among the most sage, and was a valiant cavalier, and the finest speaker, and most skilled, and of the greatest renown and of the greatest courage and enterprise of any one of his time in Italy, and a handsome and gracious cavalier in his person; but he was very worldly, and in his time caused many conspiracies and scandals in Florence to gain state and lordship; and for this cause have we made so long a treatise concerning his end, forasmuch as it was of great moment to our city, and after his death many things followed thereupon, as may be understood by the intelligent, to the end he may be an example to those which come after.

§ 97.—*How the church of the Lateran at Rome was burned.* § 98.—*How* **1308 a.d.** *the magnates of Samminiato destroyed their Popolo.* § 99.—*How the Tarlati were expelled from Arezzo, and the Guelfs restored.* § 100.—*How the Ubaldini returned to submission to the commonwealth of Florence.*

§ 101.—*After what manner Henry, count of Luxemburg, was elected emperor of Rome.*

1308 a.d.

In the said year 1308, the King Albert of Germany being dead, as we afore said, by the which death the Empire was left vacant, the electors of Germany were at great discord among themselves concerning the election; and when the king of France heard of the said vacancy, he thought within himself that now his purpose would be carried out with little difficulty, by reason of the sixth promise which Pope Clement had secretly made to him when he promised to make him Pope, as we afore made mention; and he assembled his secret council with M. Charles of Valois, his brother, and there he revealed his intention, and the long desire which he had had that the Church of Rome should elect as king of the Romans M. Charles of Valois, even while Albert, king of Germany, was living, by means of his forces and power and money, and with the aid of the Pope and the Church; for at other times of old the election had passed from the Greeks to the French, and from the French to the Italians, and from the Italians to the Germans. And now much more ought it to come to pass, seeing the Empire was vacant, and especially by reason of the said promise and oath, which Pope Clement had made to him when he had made him Pope. And he revealed all the secret covenant with him, and this done, he asked their counsel and made them swear secrecy. To this enterprise the king was encouraged by all his counsellors, and that to this end he should use all the power of the crown and of his realm, so that it might be brought about, alike for the honour of M. Charles of Valois, who was worthy thereof, and that the honour and dignity of the Empire might return to the French, as it had of old pertained long time to their forefathers, Charles the Great and his successors. And when the king and M. Charles heard the encouragement and good-will of his council, they rejoiced greatly, and took counsel that without delay the king and M. Charles, with a great force of barons and knights in arms, should go to Avignon to the Pope, before the Germans should have made any other election, showing and giving out that his going was concerning the petition against the memory of Pope Boniface; and that when the king came to the court, he should require from the Pope the sixth and secret promise,—to wit, the election and confirmation as Emperor of Rome of M. Charles of Valois; and he being so strong in followers, no cardinal nor any one else, not even the Pope, would dare to refuse him. And this ordered, the barons and knights were commanded to provide themselves with arms and with horses to bear the king company on his journey to Avignon; and they of the signiory of Provence were to make ready, and should number more than 6,000 knights in arms. But as it pleased God, who willed not that the Church of Rome should be wholly subject to the house of France, these preparations of the king and his purpose were secretly made known to the Pope by one of the privy council of the king of France. The Pope, fearing the coming of the king with so great a force, remembering the promise he had made, and perceiving that it was most contrary to the liberty of the Church, held secret counsel with M. d'Ostia, Cardinal da Prato alone, forasmuch as they were already indignant with the king of France, by reason of his inordinate demands, and because, if the Church had condemned the memory of Pope Boniface, that which he had done would have been made null and void, and the Cardinal da Prato had been made cardinal by Boniface with certain others, as we have said in another place. The said cardinal, hearing that which the Pope had learned of the purpose and of the coming of the king of France, spake thus: "Holy Father, here there is but one remedy, to wit, before the king makes his request of thee, thou must secretly and carefully arrange with the princes of Germany that they complete the election to the Empire." This counsel pleased the Pope, but he said: "Whom do we will to be Emperor?" Then the cardinal, with much foresight, not only to secure the liberty of the Church, but to advance his own interests and those of his Ghibelline party, which he would fain exalt in Italy, said: "I hear that the count of Luxemburg is to-day the best man in Germany, and the most loyal and bold, and the most catholic; and I do not doubt, if by thy means he comes to this dignity, that he will be faithful and obedient to thee and to Holy Church, and a man who will come to great things." The Pope was pleased with the good report which he heard of him, and said: "How can this election be brought about by us secretly, sending letters under our seal, unknown to the college of our brother cardinals?" The cardinal made answer: "Write thy letters to him and to the electors under a small and secret seal, and I will write to them in my letters more fully concerning thy purpose, and I will send them by my servant"; and so it was done. And as it pleased God, when the messengers were come into Germany, and had presented the letters, in eight days the princes of Germany were assembled at Middleburg, and there without dissent they elected as king of the Romans Henry, count of Luxemburg; and this was from the industry and activity of the said cardinal which wrote these words among others to the princes: "See that ye are united in this matter, and without delay; if not, I believe that the election and the lordship of the Empire will return to the

305

French." This done, the election was straightway made public in France and at the papal court; and the king of France, not knowing the manner thereof, and making preparations to go to the court, held himself deceived, and was never afterwards a friend of the said Pope.

§ 102.—*How Henry the Emperor was confirmed by the Pope.*
1308 a.d.

In the said year, after Henry of Luxemburg had been elected king of the Romans, he sent for his confirmation to Avignon to the court of Pope Clement the count of Savoy, his kinsman, and M. Guy of Namûrs, brother of the count of Flanders, his cousin, which were honourably received by the Pope and by the cardinals; and in the month of April, 1308, the said Henry was confirmed as Emperor by the Pope, and it was ordained that the Cardinal dal Fiesco and the Cardinal da Prato should be legates in Italy, and should bear him company when he should have crossed the mountains, commanding in the Church's name that he should be obeyed by all. Immediately when his ambassadors had returned with the Pope's confirmation, he went to Aix-la-Chapelle in Germany with all the barons and prelates of Germany, and there were there the duke of Brabant, and the count of Flanders, and the count of Hainault, and more barons of France; and at Aix, by the archbishop of Cologne, he was with honour and without any opposition crowned with the first crown, on the day of the Epiphany, 1308, as king of the Romans.

§ 103.—*How the Venetians took the city of Ferrara and then lost it again.* § 104.—*How the master of the Hospital took the island of Rhodes.* § 105.—*How the king of Aragon prepared an expedition against Sardinia.* § 106.—*How the Guelfs were expelled from Prato, and then were reinstated.* § 107.—*How the Tarlati returned to Arezzo and expelled the Guelfs therefrom.* § 108.—*How King Charles II. died.* § 109.—*Of the signs that appeared in the air.* § 110.—*How the Florentines renewed war with Arezzo.* § 111.—*How the Lucchese would have destroyed Pistoia, and the Florentines opposed them.*

§ 112.—*How Robert was crowned king over the kingdom of Sicily and Apulia.*
1309 a.d.

In the month of June of the year 1309, Duke Robert, now King Charles' eldest son, went by sea from Naples to Provence, to the court, with a great fleet of galleys, and a great company, and was crowned king of **Par. viii. 76-84.** Sicily and of Apulia by Pope Clement, on S. Mary's Day in September of the said year, and was entirely acquitted of the loan which the Church had made to his father and grandfather for the war in Sicily, which is said to have been more than 300,000 ounces of gold. In the said year and month the Guelfs were driven out of Amelia by the forces of the Colonnesi.

§ 113.—*How they of Ancona were discomfited by Count Frederick.*
§ 114.—*How M. Ubizzino Spinoli was driven out of Genoa and defeated.*
§ 115.—*How the Venetians were defeated at Ferrara.* § 116.—*Of the war between them of Volterra and them of Sangimignano.* § 117.—*How the Orsini of Rome were defeated by the Colonnesi.* § 118.—*How the folk of Arezzo were defeated by the marshal of the Florentines.* § 119.—*How the Florentines marched upon Arezzo.*

§ 120.—*How the ambassadors of Henry, king of the Romans, came to Florence.*
1310 a.d.

In the said year, on the 3rd day of July, there came to Florence M. Louis of Savoy, senator elect of Rome, with two clerics, prelates of Germany, and M. Simone Filippi of Pistoia, ambassadors from the Emperor, requiring the commonwealth of Florence to prepare to do honour to his coronation, and to send their ambassadors to him to Lausanne; and they required and commanded that the expedition which had been sent against Arezzo should be withdrawn. A great and fine council was held by the Florentines, wherein the ambassadors discreetly set forth their embassy. M. Betto Brunelleschi was called upon to respond for the commonwealth, which at the first made answer with proud and unfitting words, wherefor he was afterwards blamed by the wise; then answer was discreetly made, and courteously, by M. Ugolino Tornaquinci, whereon they departed, well content, on the 12th day of July, and went to the host of the Florentines to Arezzo, and made the like command that the host should depart, which did not therefore depart. The said ambassadors abode in Arezzo, very wrathful against the Florentines.

§ 121.—*Of wondrous folk that went their way through Italy beating* **1310 a.d.** *themselves.*

END OF SELECTIONS FROM BOOK VIII.

BOOK IX.

Here begins the Ninth Book. How Henry, count of Luxemburg, was made Emperor.

§ 1.—Henry, count of Luxemburg, reigned four years and seven months **1310 a.d.** and eighteen days from his first coronation to his end. He was wise and just and gracious, valiant and firm in arms, virtuous and catholic; and albeit of low estate according to his lineage, he was great-hearted, feared and redoubted; and if he had lived longer he would have done the greatest things. This man was elected emperor **Par. xvii. 82, xxx. 133-138. Epistolæ v. vi. vii.** after the manner aforesaid, and immediately when he had received confirmation from the Pope he caused himself to be crowned king in Germany; and afterwards he pacified all the disputes between the barons of Germany, and purposed earnestly to come to Rome for the imperial crown, and to pacify Italy from the divers discords and wars which were therein, and then to carry out the expedition over seas to recover the Holy Land, if God had granted it to him. Whilst he abode in Germany to pacify the barons, and to provide himself with money and with followers before crossing the mountains, Wenceslas, king of Bohemia, died, and left no male heir, but only two daughters, the one already wife of the duke of Carinthia, and the other, by the counsel of his barons, Henry gave to wife to John, his son, whom he crowned king of Bohemia, and left him in his place in Germany.

In the said year 1310, the Emperor came to Lausanne with few followers, awaiting his forces, and the embassies from the cities of Italy, and there abode many months. When the Florentines heard this they took counsel to send him a rich embassage, and likewise the Lucchese, and the Sienese, and the other cities of the Tuscan league; and the ambassadors were actually chosen, and the stuffs for their robes prepared, that they might be honourably arrayed. Yet this journey was abandoned by reason of certain Guelf magnates of Florence, which feared lest under pretence of peace the Emperor might restore the banished Ghibellines to Florence, and make them lords thereof; wherefore suspicion arose, and afterwards indignation, whence followed great peril to all Italy, forasmuch as when the ambassadors from Rome, and they of Pisa and of the other cities were come to Lausanne in Savoy, the Emperor asked why the Florentines were not there. Then answer was made to the lord by the ambassadors of the refugees from Florence, that it was because they were afraid of him. Then said the Emperor: "They have done ill, forasmuch as our desire was to have all the Florentines, and not only a faction, for our faithful subjects, and to make that city our treasure and archive house, and the loftiest of our empire." And it was known of a surety by folk which were near to him, that up to that time he had purposed with pure intent to maintain them which were ruling Florence in their estate, which intent the refugees greatly dreaded. But henceforth, by reason of this anger, or through evil report of his ambassadors which came to Florence, and of the Ghibellines and Pisans, he gave his mind the other way. Wherefore, in the following August, the Florentines, being alarmed, raised 1,000 citizen cavalry, and began to provide themselves with soldiers and with money, and to make a league with King Robert, and with many cities of Tuscany and of Lombardy, to oppose the coming and the coronation of the Emperor; and the Pisans, to the end that he might cross the Alps, sent him 70,000 golden florins, and promised him as many more when he should be come to Pisa; and with this aid he set forth from Lausanne, forasmuch as he was not himself a lord rich in money.

§ 8.—*How King Robert came to Florence as he returned from his coronation.*
1310 a.d.

In the said year 1310, on the 30th day of September, King Robert came to Florence on his way back from his coronation at Avignon, where was the Pope's court; he abode in the house of the Peruzzi dal Parlagio [of the Forum], and the Florentines did him much honour, and held jousts, and gave him large presents of money, and he abode in Florence until the 24th day of October, to reconcile the Guelfs together, which were divided into factions among themselves, and to treat of warding off the Emperor. He could do but little in reconciling them; so much had error increased among them, as before has been narrated.

§ 9.—*How the Emperor Henry passed into Italy and gained the city of Milan.* **1310 a.d.**

In the year 1310, at the end of September, the Emperor departed from Lausanne with his followers, and crossed the mountains of M. Cenis, and at the beginning of October he came to Turin in Piedmont: afterwards he came to the city of Asti, the 10th day of October. By **Johannes de Virgilio. Carmen v. 26.** the people of Asti he was peaceably received as lord, and they went out to meet him, with rejoicing and a great procession, and he pacified all the disputes among the people of Asti. In Asti he awaited his followers, and before he departed he had nigh upon 2,000 horse from beyond the mountains. In Asti he abode more than two months, forasmuch as at that time M. Guidetto della Torre was ruler in Milan, a man of great wit and power, which had, between soldiers and citizens, more than 2,000 cavalry, and by his force and tyranny he kept out of Milan the Visconti and their Ghibelline party, and also his associate, the archbishop, with many other Guelfs. This M. Guidetto was in league with the Florentines and with the other Guelfs of Tuscany and of Lombardy, and opposed the coming of the Emperor, and would have succeeded if it had not been that his own associates with their following led the Emperor to make for Milan, by the counsel of the cardinal of Fiesco, the Pope's legate. M. Guidetto, not being able to provide against everything, consented to his coming, against his will; and thus the Emperor entered into Milan on the vigil of the Feast of the Nativity, and on the Day of the Epiphany, the 6th of January, he was crowned in S. Ambrogio by the archbishop of Milan, with the second crown

311

of iron, with great honour, both he and his wife. [And the said crown is in Milan, and is of fine tempered steel as for a sword, made in the form of a wreath of laurel, wherein rich and precious stones were inlaid, after the fashion of the Cæsars which were crowned with laurel in their triumphs and victories; and it is made of steel by way of a figure and similitude, for like as steel and iron surpass all other metals, so the Cæsars, triumphing by the force of the Romans and Italians, which then were all called Romans, surpassed and subdued to the Empire of Rome all the nations of the earth.] And at the said coronation were ambassadors from well-nigh all the cities of Italy save Florence and those of their league. And whilst he abode in Milan he caused all the Milanese to be at peace one with another, and restored M. Maffeo Visconti and his party, and the archbishop and his party, and in general every man who was in banishment. And well-nigh all the cities and lords of Lombardy came to do his bidding, and to give him great quantity of money; and he sent his vicar into all the cities save into Bologna and Padua, which were against him, and were with the league of the Florentines.

§ 10.—*How the Florentines enclosed the new circle of the city with moats.*
1310 a.d.

In the said year, on S. Andrew's Day, the Florentines, through fear of the coming of the Emperor, took counsel to enclose the city with moats from the Porta San Gallo as far as the Porta Santo Ambrogio, which is **Cf. Epist. vi.** called La Croce a Gorgo, and then as far as the river Arno; and then from the Porta San Gallo to the Porta dal Prato d'Ognissanti, where the walls were already founded, they were raised eight cubits higher. And this work was done quickly and in short time, which thing was assuredly afterwards the salvation of the city of Florence, as hereafter shall be narrated; inasmuch as theretofore the city had been all exposed and the old walls in great measure pulled down and sold to the neighbouring inhabitants, to enlarge the old city, and to enclose the suburbs and the new additions.

§ 11.—*How the della Torre were driven out of Milan.*
1310 a.d.

In the said year, on the 11th day of the month of February, M.

Guidetto della Torre, seeing himself cast out from the lordship of Milan, and Maffeo Visconti and his other enemies much in favour with the Emperor, thought to cause the city of Milan to rebel against the Emperor, seeing that he had with him but few horse, forasmuch as they were gone away and dispersed throughout the cities of Lombardy; and this would have come to pass, if it had not been that Matteo Visconti very wisely warned the Emperor thereof, and his marshal, and the count of Savoy. For the which thing the city rose in arms and uproar, and there was some fighting. Now there were who said that M. Maffeo Visconti by his wit and sagacity deceived him to the end he might bring him under the Emperor's suspicion, coming to him secretly, and complaining of the lordship of the Emperor and of the Germans, making as though he would better love the freedom of Milan than such lordship; and saying to him that he would rather have him for lord than the Emperor, and that he and his followers would give him all aid and assistance in driving out the Emperor. To which proposal M. Guidetto gave heed, trusting in his former enemy, through desire of recovering his state and lordship; or perhaps it was for his sins, of which he had many, and was the answer of Maffeo coming true, which he had made to him through the mouth of the jongleur, as we related before. M. Maffeo under the said promise betrayed him, and revealed all to the Emperor and to his council; and this we believe of a surety, because of what we heard thereof afterwards from wise Lombards which were then in Milan. And for this cause M. Guidetto della Torre was called upon to defend himself, who did not appear, but departed with his followers from Milan, asserting that he was not guilty of treachery, but that his enemies had charged him therewith to bring him to nought and drive him out of Milan. But the most believe that he was in fault, forasmuch as he was in league with the Florentines and the Bolognese, and with other Guelf cities, and it was said that he was to receive much money therefor from the Florentines and their league. But whatever might have been the cause, the said intrigues made the city of Cremona immediately rebel against the Emperor, on the 20th day of February, and this rebellion and others in Lombardy were of a surety brought about by the zeal and the spending of the Florentines, to give the Emperor so much to do in Lombardy that he would not be able to come into Tuscany. At this time the

313

Ghibellines of Brescia drave out the Guelfs, and this likewise came to pass to those of Parma; for the which thing the Emperor sent his vicar and followers into Brescia, and caused peace to be made, and the Guelfs to return to the city, which a short time afterwards finding themselves strong in the city, and seeing that Cremona had rebelled, and being encouraged by the Florentines and the Bolognese with monies and large promises, drave out the Ghibellines from Brescia, and altogether rebelled against the Emperor, and prepared to make war against him.

§ 12.—*How there was great scarcity in Florence, and concerning other events.*
1310 a.d.

In the said year 1310, from December to the following May, there was the greatest scarcity in Florence, for a bushel of grain cost half a golden florin, and was all mixed with buck-wheat. And the arts and trade had never been worse in Florence than during this time, and the expenses of the commonwealth were very great, and there was much ill-will and fear concerning the coming of the Emperor. At that time, at the end of February, the Donati slew M. Betto Brunelleschi, and a little while after the said Donati and their kinsfolk and friends assembled at San Salvi and disinterred M. Corso Donati, and made great lamentation, and held a service as if he were only just dead, showing that by the death of M. Betto vengeance had been done, and that he had been the counsellor of M. Corso's death, wherefore all the city was as it were moved to tumult.

§ 13.—*How the relics of St. Barnabas came to Florence.* **1311 a.d.**

§ 14.—*How the Emperor besieged Cremona, and his people took Vicenza.*
1311 a.d.

In the said year, the 12th day of the month of April, the Emperor was besieging Cremona with an host, and he sent the bishop of Geneva, his cousin, with 300 horsemen from beyond the mountains, and with the force of M. Cane della Scala of Verona, and suddenly took the city of **Par. xvii. 76-93. Epistola x. Quest. de Acqua et Terra. § 24.—Cf. Inf. i. 100-111. Purg. xxxiii. 40-45.** Vicenza from the Paduans, and they which were of Padua in the fortress, through fear, without defending themselves,

314

abandoned the fortress, the which loss caused great dismay to the Paduans, and to all their allies; for the which thing, a little while after, the Paduans were reconciled to the Emperor, and gave him the lordship of Padua, and 100,000 golden florins in divers payments, and they received his vicar. The said bishop of Geneva went afterwards to Venice, and craved aid for the Emperor of the Venetians. The Venetians did him great honour, and gave him to buy precious stones for his crown 1,000 pounds of Venetian grossi; and in Venice from these monies and with others was made the crown, and the imperial throne, very rich and magnificent, the throne of silver gilt, and the crown with many precious stones.

§ 15.—*How the Emperor took the city of Cremona.*
1311 a.d.

In 1311, on the 20th of April, the Emperor being with his army at Cremona, the city being much straitened, forasmuch as they were ill-provided by reason of their sudden rebellion, they surrendered the city to the Emperor's mercy, through the negotiations of the archbishop of Ravenna; and he received them and pardoned them, and caused the walls and all the fortresses of the city to be destroyed, and laid a heavy fine upon them. And when he had taken Cremona, immediately he went with his army against the city of Brescia on the 14th day of May, and there he found himself with larger forces, and more numerous and better cavaliers than he had ever had, for of a truth there were there more than 6,000 good horsemen; 4,000 and more Germans, and Frenchmen, and Burgundians, and men of birth; and the rest Italians. For after he had taken Milan and then Cremona, many great lords of Germany and of France came into his service, some for pay, and many for love. And verily if he had abandoned the enterprise of the siege of Brescia, and had come into Tuscany, he would have quietly secured Bologna, Florence, and Lucca and Siena, and afterwards Rome, and the Kingdom of Apulia, and all the lands against him, forasmuch as they were not furnished nor provided, and the minds of the people were much at variance, forasmuch as the said Emperor was held to be the most just and benign sovereign. It pleased God that he should abide at Brescia, the which siege cost him much both in people and in power, by reason of the great destruction both by

315

death and pestilence, as hereafter I shall make mention.

§ 16.—*How the Florentines, by reason of the Emperor's coming, recalled from banishment all the Guelfs.*

1311 a.d.

In the said year, on the 26th day of April, the Florentines having heard how Vicenza and Cremona had surrendered to the Emperor, and how he was going to the siege of Brescia, in order to strengthen themselves put forth express decree and ordinance, and recalled from banishment all the Guelf citizens and country people under what sentence soever they had been banished, on their paying a certain small toll; and they made many leagues both in the city and in the country, and with the other Guelf cities of Tuscany.

§ 17.—*How the Florentines, with all the Guelf cities of Tuscany, made a league together against the Emperor.*

1311 a.d.

In the said year 1311, on the 1st day of June, the Florentines, the Bolognese, the Lucchese, the Sienese, the Pistoians, and they of Volterra, and all the other Guelf cities of Tuscany held a parliament, and concluded a league together, and a union of knights, and swore together to defend one another and oppose the Emperor. And afterwards, on the 26th day of June, the Florentines sent the king's marshal with 400 Catalan soldiers which were in their pay, for the defence of Bologna, and to oppose the Emperor if he should advance from that quarter; and in like manner the Sienese and Lucchese sent troops, and they abode there many months in Bologna and in Romagna in the service of King Robert.

§ 18.—*How King Robert caused the Ghibellines of Romagna to be taken* **1311 a.d.** *by craft.* § 19.—*How the Pope's marquis took Fano and Pesaro.*

§ 20.—*How the Emperor Henry took the city of Brescia by siege.*

1311 a.d.
Epistola vii.

In the said year 1311, the Emperor being with his army before Brescia, there were many assaults made, wherein much people died both within and without the city, among which was slain in an assault, by an arrow from a large crossbow, M. Waleran of Luxemburg, brother in blood and marshal of the Emperor, and many other barons, good knights; whence came great fear to all the host. And encouraged by this, the Brescians sallied forth ofttimes to attack the host, and in the month of June some of them were routed and discomfited, and forty of them were taken prisoners of the chief of the city, and fully 200 slain, among which prisoners was M. Tebaldo Brusciati, which was leader of the people within the city, a man of great valour, which had been a friend of the Emperor, who had restored him to Brescia when the Guelfs had been driven out: wherefore the Emperor caused him to be drawn asunder by four horses as a traitor, and many others he caused to be beheaded, whereby the power of the Brescians was much enfeebled; but for all that they within the city did not abandon the defence of the city. In that siege the air was corrupted by the stench of the horses and the long sojourn of the camp, wherefore there arose much sickness both within and without, and a great part of them from beyond the mountains fell sick, and many great barons died there, and some departed by reason of sickness, and afterwards died thereof on the road. Among the others died there the valiant M. Guy of Namûrs, brother of the count of Flanders, which was leader of the Flemings at the rout of Courtray, a man of great worth and renown; for which cause most part of the host counselled the Emperor that he should depart. He holding the needs within the city to be yet greater, alike from sickness and death, and from lack of victuals, determined not to depart till he should have taken the city. They of Brescia, as food was failing them, by the hand of the cardinal of Fiesco surrendered themselves to the mercy of the Emperor, on the 16th day of September, in the said year. Who, when he had gotten the city, caused all the walls and strongholds to be destroyed, and exacted a fine of 70,000 golden florins. Thus with great difficulty, after much time, he gained the city by reason of their evil estate; and 100 of the best men

317

of the city, both magnates and popolari, he sent into banishment, confining them within bounds in divers places. When he had departed from Brescia, with great loss and hurt, seeing that not a fourth part of his people were left to him, and of these a great part were sick, he held his parliament in Cremona. There, by the influence and encouragement of the Pisans and of the Ghibellines and Whites of Tuscany, he determined to come to Genoa, and there re-establish his state, and in Milan he left as vicar and captain M. Maffeo Visconti; and in Verona, M. Cane della Scala; and in Mantua, M. Passerino de' Bonaposi; and in Parma, M. Ghiberto da Correggia; and all the other cities of Lombardy in like manner he left under tyrants, not being able to do otherwise, through his evil estate, and from each one he received much money, and invested them with the privileges of the said lordships.

§ 21.—*How the Florentines and Lucchese strengthened the frontiers by* **1311 a.d.** *reason of the Emperor's coming.*

§ 22.—*How Pope Clement sent legates to crown the Emperor Henry.*

1311 a.d.

Par. xvii. 82.

In the year of Christ 1311, Pope Clement, at the request of the Emperor, not being able to come in person to Rome to crown him, by reason of the council which had been summoned, sent the bishop of Ostia, Cardinal da Prato, as legate, with power to act as if he had been the Pope in person; and he was with him in Genoa in the month of October; and the said Pope sent as legate into Hungary Cardinal Gentile da Montefiore to crown Carlo Rimberto, son that was of Charles Martel and nephew of King Robert, as king over the realm of Hungary, and to give him the aid and favour of the Church. And this the said cardinal did, and abode long time in Hungary, until the said Carlo had conquered almost all the country, and he had crowned him in peace. And on the return of the said cardinal to Italy, he received commandment from the Pope to bring to him across the mountains all the Church treasure which was in Rome and in the other cities pertaining to the Holy See, and this he brought as far as the city of Lucca. Beyond that he could not bring it, neither by land nor by sea, because the coasts of Genoa, both land and sea, were all in commotion of war through the Guelf and

Ghibelline parties, by reason of the Emperor's coming. He left it in Lucca in the sacristy of San Friano, which treasure was afterwards robbed by the Ghibellines; as hereafter we shall make mention.

§ 23.—*How Pope Clement summoned a council at Vienne in Burgundy, and* **1311 a.d.** *canonised S. Louis, son of King Charles.* § 24.—*How the Emperor Henry came into the city of Genoa.* § 25.—*How an imperial vicar came to Arezzo.*

§ 26.—*How the ambassadors from the Emperor came to Florence, and were driven thence.*
1311 a.d.

In the said year, and month of October, there came to Florence M. Pandolfo Savelli, of Rome, and other clerks as ambassadors from the Emperor. When they were come to Lastra, above Montughi, the priors of Florence sent them word not to enter into Florence, but to depart. The said ambassadors, not being willing to depart, were robbed by Florentine highwaymen, with the secret consent of the priors; and fleeing in peril of their lives, they departed by the way of Mugello to Arezzo, and afterwards from Arezzo summoned all the nobles and lords and the commonwealths of Tuscany to prepare themselves to come to the Emperor's coronation at Rome.

§ 27.—*How the Florentines sent their troops to Lunigiana to oppose* **1311 a.d.** *the passage of the Emperor.*

§ 28.—*How the empress died in Genoa.*
1311 a.d.

In the said year, in the month of November, there died in Genoa the empress, wife of the Emperor, which was held to be a holy and good woman, and was daughter of the duke of Brabant; and was buried in the Minor Friars with great honour.

§ 29.—*How the Emperor put the Florentines under the ban of the Empire.*
1311 a.d.

In the said year and month the Emperor issued a proclamation from Genoa against the Florentines that, if within forty days they did not send him

319

twelve good men with a plenipotentiary and full promise to obey him, he would condemn their goods and persons to be forfeit, wherever found. The commonwealth of Florence did not send any messengers, but all the Florentine merchants which were in Genoa received orders to depart thence, and this they did; and after that, all merchandise which was found in Genoa in the name of the Florentines was seized by the court of the Emperor.

§ 30.—*Of the scandal which was in Florence among the wool-workers.* **1311 a.d.**

§ 31.—*How King Robert sent men to Florence to oppose the Emperor.*

§ 32.—*How the city of Brescia rebelled against the Emperor.*

1311 a.d.

In the said year, in the end of December, the Guelfs of Brescia re-entered the city to cause it to rebel against the Emperor. Thither rode M. Cane della Scala with his forces, and drave them out thence with great loss. And in the said month of December M. Ghiberto da Correggia, which was holding Parma, rebelled against the lordship of the Emperor, as likewise did they of Reggio; and the Florentines and the rest of the league of the Guelfs of Tuscany sent aid to them of man and horse.

§ 33.—*How there was great tumult in Florence by reason of the death of M. Pazzino de' Pazzi.*

§ 34.—*How the city of Cremona rebelled against the Emperor.*

1311 a.d.

In the said year 1311, on the 10th day of the said month of January, the Cremonese rebelled against the lordship of the Emperor, and drave out his people and his vicar, and this was through the suggestion of the Florentines, which still had their ambassador there to treat of this, promising to the Cremonese much aid in money and in people; but the promise was ill fulfilled to them by the Florentines.

§ 35.—*How the marshal of the Emperor came to Pisa, and began war with the Florentines.*

1311 a.d.

In the said year, on the 11th of January, Henry of Namûrs, brother of

320

Count Robert of Flanders, marshal of the Emperor, came by sea to Pisa with but small following, and two days after sallied forth from Pisa with his men, and took station this side Pontadera, and all the goods of the Florentines which were coming from Pisa he caused to be captured and taken back to Pisa; whence the Florentines had great loss. For this cause the Florentines sent foot and horse to Samminiato and the frontier there.

§ 36.—*How the Paduans rebelled against the lordship of the Emperor.*
1311 a.d.

In the said year, on the 15th of February, the Paduans, with the help of the Florentines and of the Bolognese, rebelled against the lordship of the Emperor, and drave out his vicar and his followers; and tumultuously slew M. Guglielmo Novello, their fellow-citizen and chief leader of the Ghibelline party in Padua.

§ 37.—*How the Emperor Henry came to the city of Pisa.* § 38.—*How they of Spoleto were defeated by the Perugians.*

§ 39.—*Of the gathering together made by King Robert and the league of Tuscany at Rome to oppose the coronation of the Emperor Henry.*
1312 a.d.

In the year 1312, in the month of April, when King Robert heard of the preparation which the king of Germany was making in Pisa, to come to Rome to be crowned, he sent forward to Rome, at the request and with the support of the Orsini, M. John, his brother, with 600 Catalan and Apulian horsemen, and they came to Rome the 16th day of April; and he sent to the Florentines and Lucchese and Sienese, and to the other cities of Tuscany which were in league with him, to send their forces there; wherefore there went forth from Florence on the 9th day of May, 1312, a troop of 200 horsemen of the best citizens, and the marshal of King Robert which was in their pay, with 300 Catalan horse and 1,000 foot, very fine soldiers; and the royal standard was borne by M. Berto di M. Pazzino dei Pazzi, a valiant and wise young knight, which died at Rome in the service of the king and of the commonwealth of Florence. And from Lucca there went 300 horse and 1,000 foot, and of Sienese 200 horse and 600 foot, and many other cities of

Tuscany and of the Roman state sent men thither. Which all were in Rome on the 21st day of May, 1312, to oppose the coronation of the Emperor; and with the force of the said Orsini, of Rome, and of their followers they took the Capitol, and drave out thence by force M. Louis, of Savoy, the senator; and they took the towers and fortresses at the foot of the Capitol, above the market, and fortified Hadrian's Castle, called S. Angelo, and the church and palaces of S. Peter; and thus they had the lordship and rule over more than the half of Rome, and that, too, the most populous; and all the Transtiberine district. The Colonnesi and their following, which took the side of the Emperor, held the Lateran, Santa Maria Maggiore, the Coliseum, Santa Maria Ritonda, the Milizie, and Santa Savina; and thus each party was defended by bars and bolts in great strongholds. And as the people of Florence abode there, on S. John Baptist's Day, their principal feast, **Cf. Par. xvi. 42.** they ran the races in Rome for their cloth of crimson samite, as they were wont to do on the said day in Florence.

§ 40.—*How the Emperor Henry departed from Pisa and came to Rome.*
1312 a.d.

In the said year, on the 23rd day of April, the king of Germany departed from Pisa with his people to the number of 2,000 horse and more, and took the way of the Maremma, and then by the country of Siena, and by that of Orvieto, without sojourning, and without any hindrance he came to Viterbo, and had it without opposition, forasmuch as it pertained to the lordship of the Colonnas. And as he passed through the territory of Orvieto, the Filippeschi of Orvieto, with their following of Ghibellines, began a strife within the city against **Cf. Purg. vi. 107.** the Monaldeschi and the other Guelfs of Orvieto, to give the city to the Emperor. The Guelfs, being strong and well-armed, fought vigorously before the Ghibellines could gain the aid of the Emperor's troops, and overcame them, and drave them out of the city with many slain and captured. Then the king of Germany abode many days at Viterbo, not being able to gain admittance by the gate of S. Piero of Rome; and the Emilian Bridge over the Tiber being fortified and guarded by the forces of the Orsini, at last he departed from Viterbo, and stayed at Monte Malo; and afterwards by the forces of his **Cf. Par. xv. 109-111.** followers

322

from without, and those of the Colonnesi and their party within, he assailed the fortresses and strongholds of the Emilian Bridge, and by strength overcame them, and thus he entered into Rome on the 7th day of May, and came to Santa Savina to sojourn.

§ 41.—*How M. Galeasso Visconti of Milan took the city of Piacenza.* **1312 a.d.** § 42.—*How the Florentines drave away the Pisans in discomfiture from Cerretello.*

§ 43.—*How Henry of Luxemburg was crowned Emperor at Rome.*
1312 a.d.

In the said year, whilst the king of the Romans abode long time in Rome, till he might come by force to the church of S. Peter to be crowned, his followers had many battles with the opposing forces of King Robert and the Tuscans, and overcame them by force and regained the Capitol, and the fortresses above the market, and the towers of S. Mark. And verily it seems as if he would have been victorious in large measure in the strife, save that on one day, the 26th day of May, when in a great battle, the bishop of Liège, with many barons of Germany, having forced the lines, was traversing the city well-nigh to the bridge of S. Angelo, King Robert's followers, with the Florentines, departed from the Campo di Fiore by crossways, and attacked the enemy in the flank, and pursued and broke them up; and more than 250 horsemen were either slain or taken prisoner, among which the said bishop of Liège was taken; and whilst a knight was bringing him behind him disarmed on his horse to M. John, brother of King Robert, a Catalan, whose brother had been slain in this pursuit, thrust at him in the back with his sword; wherefore, when he came to the castle of S. Angelo, in a short time he died; and this was a heavy loss, forasmuch as he was a lord of great valour and of great authority. By reason of the said loss and discomfiture, King Robert's followers and their men increased greatly in vigour and audacity, and those of the king of Germany the contrary. When he perceived that these conflicts did not make for his good, and that he was losing his men and his honour, having first sent to the Pope to ask that his cardinals might crown him in whatever church of Rome might please them, he determined to have himself crowned in S. John Lateran; and there was he crowned by the bishop of Ostia, Cardinal da Prato, and by M. Luca dal Fiesco, and M. Arnaldo

Guasconi, cardinals, the day of S. Peter in Vincola, the 1st of August, 1312, with great honour from those people which were with him, and from those Romans which were on his side. And the Emperor Henry having been crowned, a few days after he departed to Tivoli to sojourn there, and left Rome barricaded and in evil state, and each party kept its streets and strongholds fortified and guarded. And when the coronation was over, there departed of his barons, the duke of Bavaria and his people, and other lords of Germany, which had served him, so that he remained with but few foreigners.

§ 44.—*How the Emperor departed from Rome to go into Tuscany.*
1312 a.d.

Then the Emperor departed from Tivoli, and came with his people to Todi, and was received honourably by the inhabitants, and as their lord, forasmuch as they took his part. The Florentines and the other Tuscans, hearing that the Emperor had departed from Rome and was taking his way towards Tuscany, straightway sent for their troops which were at Rome, to the end they might be stronger against his coming. And when the said troops had returned, the Florentines and the other cities of Tuscany garrisoned their fortresses with horsemen and with soldiers, to resist the coming of the Emperor, fearing greatly his forces, and confining more straitly the Ghibellines and others which were suspected; and the Florentines increased the number of their horsemen to 1,300, and of soldiers they had with the marshal and with others 700, so that they had about 2,000 horsemen; and every other town and city of Tuscany in the league of King Robert and of the Guelf party, had strengthened itself with soldiers for fear of the Emperor.

§ 45.—*How the Emperor came to the city of Arezzo, and afterwards how he came towards the city of Florence.*
1312 a.d.

In the said month of August, in 1312, the Emperor departed from Todi and passed through the region of Perugia, destroying and burning, and his people took by force Castiglione of Chiusi on the lake, and from there he came to Cortona, and then to Arezzo, and was received by the Aretines with great honour. And in Arezzo he assembled his army to come against the city of Florence, and suddenly he departed from Arezzo and entered into the territory of Florence on the 12th day of September, and there was straightway surrendered to him the fortress of Caposelvole upon the Ambra which pertained to the Florentines. And then he pitched his camp before the fortress of Montevarchi, which was well furnished with soldiers, both horse and foot, and with victuals; against it he ordered many assaults, and caused the moats to be emptied of water, and filled up with earth. They within the city, seeing that they were so hotly assailed, and that the city had low walls, and that the horsemen of the Emperor fighting on foot, and mounting the walls on ladders, did not fear the arrows nor the stones which were thrown down, were greatly dismayed, and believing that the Florentines would not succour them, surrendered themselves on the third day to the Emperor. And when he had taken Montevarchi, without delay he came with his host to the fortress of Sangiovanni, which in like manner surrendered itself to him, and he took there seventy Catalan horsemen, in the service of the Florentines: and thus without hindrance he came to the village of Fegghine.

§ 46.—*How the Florentines were well-nigh discomfited at the fortress of Ancisa by the army of the Emperor.*

1312 a.d.

When the Florentines heard that the Emperor had departed from Arezzo, immediately the people and horsemen of Florence, without awaiting other aid, rode to the fortress of Ancisa upon the Arno, and they were about 1,800 horse and many foot, and at Ancisa they encamped to hold the pass against the Emperor. And when he heard this, he came with his army to the plain of Ancisa upon the island of Arno which is called Il Mezzule, and challenged the Florentines to battle. The Florentines, knowing themselves to be in number of their horsemen not much superior to those of the Emperor, and being without a captain, did not desire to try the fortune of battle, believing that they could hinder the Emperor by reason of the difficult pass, so that he could not get through to Florence. The Emperor seeing that the Florentines were not willing to fight, by counsel of the wise men of war, refugees from Florence, took the way of the hill above Ancisa, and by narrow and difficult ways passed the fortress and came out on the side towards Florence. The host of the Florentines perceiving his movements, and fearing lest he should come to the city of Florence, some part of them with the king's marshal and his troops departed from Ancisa, to be before him in the way. The count of Savoy, and M. Henry of Flanders, which were come before to take the pass, vigorously attacked them which were at the frontier under Montelfi, and with the advantage which they had of the hill, they put them to flight and discomfiture, and some pursued them as far as the village of Ancisa. The rout of the Florentines was more through the dismay caused by the sudden assault, than by loss of men; for among them all there were not twenty-five horsemen slain, and less than one hundred footmen; and well-nigh all the foreigners which came in pursuit of them as far as the village were slain. Nevertheless, the followers of the Emperor remained victorious in the combat, and the Florentines were filled with fear; and the Emperor spent that night two miles this side of Ancisa on the way to Florence. The Florentines remained in the fortress of Ancisa, as it were besieged and with but little provision of victuals, so that, if the Emperor had been constant to the siege, the Florentines which were at Ancisa would have been well-nigh all slain or taken. But as it pleased God, the Emperor resolved that night to go direct to the city of Florence, believing that he should take it without opposition; and he left the host of the Florentines behind at Ancisa, seeing that they were in a state of siege, and in much fear, and in great disorder.

§ 47.—*How the Emperor Henry encamped with his host before the city of Florence.*

1312 a.d.

And thus the day following, the 19th day of September, 1312, the Emperor came with his host to the city of Florence, his followers setting fire to everything they came across; and thus he crossed the river Arno, over against where the Mensola enters it, and abode at the monastery of Santo Salvi, with perhaps 1,000 horsemen. The rest of his followers remained in Valdarno, and part at Todi, which came to him afterwards; and as they came through the region of Perugia, they were assailed by the Perugians, and defended themselves against them, and passed on with loss and shame to the

326

Perugians. And the Emperor came thither so suddenly that the most part of the Florentines could not believe that he was there in person; and they were so dismayed and fearful about their horsemen which were left at Ancisa well-nigh discomfited, that if the Emperor and his followers, upon their sudden coming had advanced to the gates, they would have found them open and ill-guarded; and it is thought by most that the city would have been taken. The Florentines, however, beholding the burning of the houses along the way, called the people to arms by sound of bell, and with the standards of their companies they came to the piazza of the Priors, and the bishop of Florence armed himself, with the horses belonging to the clergy, and hastened to defend the Porta Santo Ambrogio and the moats; and all the people on foot were with him; and they barred the gates, and ordered the standard-bearers and their people, at their posts along the moats, to guard the city by day and by night. And within the city on that side they pitched a camp with pavilions, tents, and booths, to the intent the guard might be stronger, and made palisades along the moats of all kinds of wood, with portcullises, in a very short time. And thus abode the Florentines in great fear for two days, for their horsemen and their army were returning from Ancisa by divers ways by the vale of Robbiano, and from Santa Maria in Pianeta a Montebuoni [Impruneta] in the night season. When they came to Florence, the city was reassured; and the Lucchese sent thither in aid and defence of the city 600 horse and 3,000 foot, and the Sienese 600 horse and 2,000 foot, and they of Pistoia 100 horse and 500 foot, and they of Prato 50 horse and 400 foot, and they of Volterra 100 horse and 300 foot, and Colle and Sangimignagno and Samminiato each 50 horse and 200 foot, the Bolognese 400 horse and 1,000 foot; from Romagna there came, what with Rimini and Ravenna and Faenza and Cesena and the other Guelf cities, 300 horse and 1,500 foot, and from Agobbio 100 horse, and from the city of Castello 50 horse. From Perugia there came no aid, by reason of the war which they had with Todi and Spoleto. And thus within eight days of the siege being declared by the Emperor, the Florentines with their allies were more than 4,000 horse, and foot without number. The Emperor had 1,800 horsemen, whereof 800 were foreigners and 1,000 Italians, from Rome, from the March, from the Duchy, from Arezzo, and **Purg. vi. 111.** from Romagna, and from the Counts Guidi, and them of Santafiore, and the Florentine refugees; and much people on foot, forasmuch as the country people of the region which he was occupying, all followed his camp. And that year was the most fertile and fruitful in all food which had been for thirty years past. The Emperor abode at the siege until the last day of the month of October, laying the whole country waste towards the eastern side, and did great hurt to the Florentines without any attack upon the city, being in hopes of gaining it by agreement; and even if he had attacked it, it was so well furnished with horsemen, that there would have been two or more defending the city for every one without, and of foot four to one; and the Florentines were in such good heart that the most part went about unarmed, and they kept all the other gates open, save the one on that side; and the merchandise came in and went out as if there had been no war. As to the Florentines sallying forth to battle, either by reason of cowardice or of prudence in war, or because they had no leader, they would in no wise trust to the fortune of the combat, albeit they had greatly the advantage, had they but had a good captain, and been more united among themselves. Certainly they rode out to Cerretello, whither the Pisans had marched with their army, and they forced them to withdraw from it again, as though defeated, in the month of October. The Emperor lay sick many days at San Salvi, and perceiving that he could not gain the city by agreement, and that the Florentines would not give battle, he departed, not yet recovered. [And whilst he was still at San Salvi, the count of Savoy was discoursing with the abbot and certain monks of that place, concerning the Emperor, how he had heard from his astrologers or by some other revelation, that he was to conquer as far as to the world's end; then said the abbot smiling: "The prophecy is fulfilled, for hard by where you are dwelling, there is a road which has no exit, which is called the World's End"; wherefore the count and the other barons which heard this were confounded in their vain hope: and for this reason, wise men ought not to put faith in any prophecy or sayings of astrologers, for they are lies and have a double meaning.]

§ 48.—*How the Emperor abandoned the siege, and departed from San Salvi, and came to San Casciano, and then to Poggibonizzi.*

1312 a.d.

The Emperor with his host departed on the night before All Saints, and having burnt his camp, he passed the Arno by the way which he came, and encamped on the plain of Ema, three miles from the city. On his going the Florentines did not sally forth from the city by night, but they sounded the bells and all men stood to arms; and for this cause, as was afterwards known, the followers of the Emperor were in great trepidation about their departure, lest they should be attacked by night either in front or in rear by the Florentines. The morning following, a part of the Florentines went to the hill of Santa Margherita above the camp of the Emperor, and by way of skirmishes they made many assaults upon them, in the which they had the worse; and having tarried there three days in shame, he departed and came with his host to the village of San Casciano, eight miles from the city; wherefore the Florentines caused a trench to be dug round the increase of the sesto of Oltrarno outside the ancient walls, on the first of December, 1312. And the Emperor being at San Casciano, the Pisans came thither to his aid with full 500 horse and 3,000 foot, and 1,000 archers of Genoa, and they arrived the 20th day of November. At San Casciano he abode until the 6th day of January, without making any attack upon the Florentines save incursions, and laying waste, and burning houses in the region; and he took many strongholds of the country; nor did the Florentines therefore sally forth to battle, save in incursions and skirmishes, wherein now one party and now the other suffered loss, not worthy of much mention, save that at one encounter, at Cerbaia in the Val di Pesa our troops were routed by the Germans, and one of the Spini was there slain, and one of the Bostichi, and one of the Guadagni, because of their boldness at that place; for they were of a company of volunteers, with a captain, their banner bearing a red stripe on a green field, and they called themselves the Cavaliers of the Stripe, of the most famous young men of Florence, and they did many feats of arms. But during this time, the Florentines parted from a great number of their allies and let them go; and the Emperor himself had not many followers; and by reason of his long sojourn and by the discomfort of the cold, there began in the camp at San Casciano to be great sickness and mortality among the people, which greatly infected the country, and reached as far as to Florence; for the which cause the Emperor departed with his host from San Casciano and came to Poggibonizzi, and took the strongholds of Barberino and of San Donato in Poggio, and many other fortresses; at Poggibonizzi he restored the fortress upon the hill, as of old it was wont to be, and gave it the name of the Imperial Fortress. There he abode until the 6th day of March, and during that sojourn he was in great need of provision, and suffered much want, he and all his host, forasmuch as the Sienese on the one side, and the Florentines on the other, between them had closed the roads, and 300 soldiers of King Robert were in Colle di Valdelsa, and harassed them continually; and 200 of the Emperor's horsemen, as they were returning from Casole, were defeated by the king's horsemen which were in Colle, on the 14th day of February, 1312. And on the other side, the marshal with the soldiers of Florence, harassed him in Sangimignagno, so that the state of the Emperor was much diminished, and there scarce remained to him 1,000 horse, forasmuch as M. Robert of Flanders had departed with his followers, and the Florentines took him in flank at Castelfiorentino, and a great part of his men were slain or taken, and he fled with a few, albeit he had held the field well, and had given them which attacked him much to do, which were four to his one, and were much shamed thereby.

§ 49.—*How the Emperor departed from Poggibonizzi and returned to Pisa, and issued many bans against the Florentines.*

1313 a.d.

Thus the Emperor perceived himself to be brought low in men and in victuals, and also in money, so that nought was left to him to spend, save only that ambassadors from King Frederick of Sicily, which landed at Pisa, and came to him to Poggibonizzi to make a league with him against King Robert, gave him 20,000 golden pistoles. When he had paid his debts with these, he departed from Poggibonizzi, and without halting came to Pisa, on the 9th day of March, 1312, in very evil plight, both he and his followers; but the Emperor Henry had this supreme virtue in him, that never in adversity was he as one cast down, nor in prosperity was he vainglorious. When the Emperor had returned to Pisa he proclaimed a great and weighty sentence against the Florentines, taking from them all jurisdiction and honours, disqualifying all the judges and notaries, and condemning the commonwealth of Florence to pay 100,000 marks of silver; and many citizens, both magnates and popolani who were in the government of Florence, he condemned in their money, and persons, and goods; and the Florentines were not to coin money in gold or in silver; and he granted to M. Ubizzino Spinoli of Genoa and to the marquis of Montferrat, the privilege of coining florins counterfeited after the impression of those of the Florentines; the which thing, by wise men, was charged against him as a great fault and sin, for however indignant and wrathful he might be against the Florentines, he ought never to have granted a privilege to coin false florins.

§ 50.—*How the Emperor condemned King Robert.*
1313 a.d.

Against King Robert he likewise proclaimed a heavy sentence, declaring his realm of Apulia and the county of Provence to be forfeit, and himself and his heirs to be condemned in their persons as traitors against the Empire; which sentence was afterwards declared null and void by Pope John XXII. And while the Emperor was in Pisa, M. Henry of Flanders, his marshal, rode to Versilia and Lunigiana with 800 horse and 6,000 foot, and took Pietrasanta by force on the 28th day of March, 1313. The Lucchese, which were at Camaiore with the forces of the Florentines, did not venture to oppose him, but returned to Lucca; and Serrezzano, which was held by the Lucchese, surrendered to the Marquises Malispini, who held with the Emperor.

§ 51.—*How the Emperor made ready to enter into the Kingdom against King Robert, and departed from Pisa.*
1313 a.d.

This done, the Emperor took counsel not to encounter the Florentines and the other Tuscans (whereby he had little bettered his state, but rather made it worse), but to bring matters to a head, and to march against King Robert with all his force and take the Kingdom from him; and if he had done this, it was believed that he would have been master of all Italy; and certainly this would have come to pass, if God had not averted it, as we shall make mention. He made a league with King Frederick, who held the island of Sicily, and with the Genoese, and ordained that each one, on the day named, should put to sea with a large fleet of armed galleys; he sent into Germany and into Lombardy for fresh troops, and made the like demands on all his subjects, and on the Ghibellines of Italy. During this sojourn in Pisa, he collected much money, and without sleeping, caused his marshal continually to make war against Lucca and Samminiato, though he made but little progress. In the summer of 1313, which he passed in Pisa, after his forces were come to him, he numbered more than 2,500 foreign horsemen, for the most part Germans, and of Italians fully 1,500 horsemen. The Genoese armed at his request seventy galleys, whereof M. Lamba d'Oria was admiral, and he came with the said navy to the port of Pisa, and parleyed with the Emperor; afterwards he departed towards the kingdom to the island of Ponzo. King Frederick armed fifty galleys, and on the day named, the 5th of August, 1313, the Emperor departed from Pisa; and the same day it came to pass that King Frederick departed from Messina with his army, and with 1,000 horse, encamped in Calabria, and took the city of Reggio, and many other cities.

§ 52.—*How the Emperor Henry died at Bonconvento, in the country of Siena.* **1313 a.d.**

When the Emperor had departed from Pisa he crossed the Elsa, and attacked Castelfiorentino, and could not take it; he went on through Poggibonizzi and Colle, as far as Siena alongside the gates. In Siena there were many folk of war, and certain Florentine horsemen sallied forth from the Cammollia Gate to skirmish, and were worsted and driven back into the city; and Siena was in great fear; and the Emperor passed by the city and encamped at Montaperti upon the Arbia; there he began to be sick, albeit his sickness had made itself felt even from his departure from Pisa; but because he would not fail to depart on the day named, he set forth on his journey. Then he went to the plain of Filetta, to bathe in the baths of Macereto, and from there he went to the village of Bonconvento, twelve miles beyond Siena. There he grew rapidly worse, and, as it pleased God, he passed from this life on the day of S. Bartholomew, the 24th day of August, 1313.

§ 53.—*Relates how, when the Emperor was dead, his host was divided, and the*

barons carried his body to the city of Pisa.
1313 a.d.

When the Emperor Henry was dead, his host, and the Pisans, and all his friends were in great grief thereat, and the Florentines, Sienese and Lucchese and they of their league rejoiced greatly. And when he was dead, straightway the Aretines and the other Ghibellines from the March and from Romagna departed from the host at Bonconvento, wherein were great numbers of people, both on horse and on foot. His barons and the Pisan cavalry, with their followers, without delay passed through the Maremma with his body, and brought it to Pisa; there, with great sorrow and also with great honour, they buried it in their cathedral. This was the end of the Emperor Henry. And let not the reader marvel, that his story has been continued by us without recounting other things and events in Italy and in other provinces and realms; for two reasons, one, because all Christians and also Greeks and Saracens were intent upon his doings and fortunes, and therefore but few notable things came to pass in any other place; the other, that by reason of the divers and manifold great fortunes which he met withal in the short time that he lived, it is verily believed by the wise, that if death had not come so early to a lord of such valour and of such great undertakings as he was, he would have conquered the Kingdom, and taken it from King Robert, who had made but little preparation for its defence. Rather was it said by many, that King Robert would not have awaited him, but would have gone by sea to Provence; and after he had conquered the Kingdom as he purposed, it **Par. xxx. 133-138.** would have been very easy for him to conquer all Italy and many of the other provinces.

§ 54.—*How Frederick, the said king of Sicily, came by sea to the city of Pisa.*
§ 55.—*How the Count Filipponi of Pavia was defeated at Piacenza.*
§ 56.—*How the Florentines gave the lordship of Florence to King Robert for five years.*
1313 a.d.

In the said year 1313, whilst the Emperor was yet alive, the Florentines finding themselves in evil case, alike from the forces of the

333

Emperor and of their own exiles, and also having dissensions among themselves from the factions which had arisen as to the filling of the magistracies, they gave themselves to King Robert for five years, and then afterwards they renewed it for three, and thus for eight years King Robert had the lordship over them, sending them a vicar every six months, and the first was M. Giacomo di Cantelmo of Provence, who came to Florence in the month of June, 1313. And the Lucchese and the Pistoians and the men of Prato did the like, in giving the lordship to King Robert. And of a surety this was the salvation of the Florentines, for by reason of the great divisions among the Guelfs, if there had not been this device of the lordship of King Robert they would have been torn to pieces and destroyed by each other, and one side or the other cast out.

§ 57.—*How the Spinoli were expelled from Genoa.* § 58.—*How **1313 a.d.*** *Uguccione da Faggiuola, lord of Pisa, made great war against the Lucchese, so that they restored the Ghibelline refugees to Lucca under enforced terms of peace.*

§ 59.—*Of the death of Pope Clement.*
1314 a.d.

In the year 1314, on the 20th day of April, Pope Clement died; he was on his way to Bordeaux, in Gascony, and when he had passed the Rhone at Roquemaure, in Provence, he fell sick and died. This was a man very greedy of money, and a simoniac, which sold in his court every **Inf. xix. 82-87. Par. xvii. 82, xxvii. 58-60, xxx. 142-148. Epist. v. 10: 167, 168.** benefice for money, and was licentious; for it was openly said that he had as mistress the countess of Perigord, a most beautiful lady, daughter of the count of Foix. And he bequeathed to his nephews and family immense and boundless treasure; and it was said that while the said Pope was yet alive, one of his nephews, a cardinal, died, whom he greatly loved; and he constrained a great master of necromancy to tell him what had become of his nephew's soul. The said master having wrought his arts, caused a chaplain of the Pope, a very courageous man, to be conducted by the demons, which had him to hell, and showed him visibly a palace wherein was a bed of glowing fire, and thereon was the soul of the said nephew which was dead, and they said to him that for his simony he was thus judged. And he saw in his vision another palace

334

being raised over against the first, which they told him was being prepared for Pope Clement. And the said chaplain brought back these tidings to the Pope, which was never afterwards glad, and he lived but a short time longer; and when he was dead, and his body had been left for the night in a church with many lights, his coffin caught fire and was burnt, and his body from the middle downwards.

§ 60.—*How Uguccione da Faggiuola with the Pisans took the city of Lucca and stole the treasure of the Church.* § 61.—*How M. Peter, brother of King Robert, came to Florence as lord.* § 62.—*How King Robert went with a great armament against Sicily, and besieged the city of Trapali.*

§ 63.—*How the Paduans were discomfited at Vicenza by M. Cane della Scala.*
1314 a.d.
Johannes de Virgilio. Carmen *v.* **28.**
Par. xvii. 76-93.

In the said year 1314, on the 18th day of September, the Paduans went in full force to Vicenza, and took the suburbs, and besieged the city; but M. Cane, lord of Verona, suddenly came to Vicenza, and with a few followers fought against the Paduans; and they being in disorder, trusting in themselves too much after having taken the suburbs, were discomfited, and many of them were slain and taken prisoner.

§ 64.—*How the Florentines made peace with the Aretines.* § 65.—*How a comet appeared in the heavens.*

§ 66.—*Of the death of Philip, king of France, and of his sons.*
1314 a.d.

In the said year 1314, in the month of November, the King Philip, king of France, which had reigned twenty-nine years, died by an ill-adventure; for, being at a chase, a wild boar ran between the legs **Par. xix. 118-120.** of the horse whereupon he was riding, and caused him to fall, and shortly after he died. He was one of the most comely men in the world, and of the tallest in person, and well proportioned in every limb; he was a wise man in himself, and good, after layman's fashion, but by reason of pleasure-seeking, especially in the chase, he did not devote **Purg. vii. 109, 110.** his powers to ruling his realm, but rather allowed them to be played upon by others, so that he was generally swayed by ill counsel, to which he lent a too ready credence; whence many perils came to his realm. He left three sons, Louis, king of Navarre; Philip, count of Poitou; and Charles, Count de la Marche. All these sons one after another in a short while became kings of France, one succeeding on the death of another. And a little while before King Philip, their father, died, there fell upon them great and shameful misfortune, for the wives of all three were found to be faithless; and each one of the husbands was among the most beauteous Christians in the world. The wife of King Louis was daughter of the duke of Burgundy. Louis, when he was king of France, caused her to be strangled with a towel, and then took to wife Queen Clemence, daughter, that was, of Charles **Cf. Par. ix. 1.** Martel, the son of Charles II., king of Apulia. The wives of the second and third sons were sisters, daughters of the count of Burgundy, and heiresses of the countess of Artois. Philip, count of Poitou, on his wife's denial of the charge, and because he loved her much, took her again as being good and beautiful; Charles, Count de la Marche, never would take his wife back, but kept her in prison. This misfortune, it was said, befell them as a miracle by reason of the sin which prevailed in that house of taking their kinswomen to wife, not regarding degrees, or perchance because of the sin committed by their father in taking Pope Boniface, as the bishop of Sion prophesied, as we have before narrated.

§ 67.—*Of the election which was made in Germany of two Emperors, one* **1314 a.d.**

1315 a.d. *the duke of Bavaria, and the other the duke of Austria.* § 68.—*How Uguccione, lord of Pisa, made great war against the neighbouring places.* § 69.—*How King Louis of France was crowned, and led an army against the Flemings, but gained nothing.*

§ 70.—*How Uguccione, lord of Lucca and of Pisa, laid siege to the castle of Montecatini.*

1315 a.d.

In the said year, Uguccione da Faggiuola, with his forces of German troops, being lord of all Pisa and of Lucca, having triumphed throughout all Tuscany, brought his host and laid siege to Montecatini, in Valdinievole, which was held by the Florentines after the loss of Lucca; and, albeit it was well furnished with good men, yet by means of the siege works it was greatly straitened, and in sore want of provisions. The Florentines sent into the Kingdom for M. Philip of Taranto, brother to King Robert, to oppose the fury of Uguccione, and of the Pisans, and of the Germans; and he came to Florence on the 11th of July with 500 horsemen in the pay of the Florentines, and with his son Charles, against the will of King Robert, who knew his brother to be more headstrong than wise, and also not very fortunate in battle, but rather the contrary; and if the Florentines had been willing to tarry longer, King Robert would have sent to Florence his son, the duke, with more order and more preparation, and a better following: but the haste of the Florentines, and the device of hostile fortune, made them desire only the prince, whence came to them thereafter much harm and loss of renown.

§ 71.—*How, when the prince of Taranto was come to Florence, the Florentines sallied forth with their army to succour Montecatini, and were defeated by Uguccione della Faggiuola.*

1315 a.d.
Johannes de Virgilio. Carmen *v.* 27.

When the prince of Taranto and his son were come to Florence, Uguccione, with all his forces from Pisa and from Lucca, and those of the bishop of Arezzo, and of the counts of Santafiore, and of all the Ghibellines of Tuscany and the exiles of Florence, with aid of the Lombards, under M. Maffeo Visconti and his sons, to the number of 2,500 and more horse, and a great number of foot, came to besiege the stronghold of Montecatini. The Florentines, in order to succour it, assembled a great host, and since they invited all their friends, there were there Bolognese, Sienese, men of Perugia and of the city of Castello, of Agobbio, and of Romagna, and of Pistoia, of Volterra, and of Prato, and of all the other Guelf and friendly cities of

337

Tuscany, to the number, with the followers of the prince and of M. Piero, of 3,200 horse and a very great number of foot; and they departed from Florence on the 6th day of August. And when the said host of the Florentines and of the prince was come to Valdinievole, over against that of Uguccione, many days they abode face to face with the torrent of the Nievole between them, and many assaults and skirmishes took place. The Florentines, with many captains and but little order, held their enemies for nought; Uguccione and his people held theirs in great fear, and for this cause they kept strict guard and wise generalship. Uguccione, receiving tidings that the Guelfs of the territory six miles around Lucca, at the instigation of the Florentines, were marching upon Lucca, and had already routed the escort and taken possession of the road whereby provisions were brought to his army, took counsel to withdraw from the siege; and by night he gathered his troops and burned his outworks, and came with his followers in battle array to the neutral ground on the plain commanded by both the two hosts, with the intention, if the prince and his host did not stretch out to intercept him, to march through and make for Pisa; and if they desired to fight, he would have the advantage of the field, and would risk the chances of battle. The prince and the Florentines and their host, perceiving this, when day broke left the camp, and moved their tents and baggage; and the prince being ill with ague, they showed but little foresight, nor kept good order in the troops, by reason of the sudden and unexpected breaking up of the camp, but they confronted the enemy, thinking to turn them to flight. Uguccione, perceiving that he could not avoid the battle, caused the outposts of the plain to be assailed (to wit, the Sienese and them of Colle and others,) by his forefighters, about 150 horse, whereof were captains with the imperial pennon, M. Giovanni Giacotti Malespini, a rebel against Florence, and Uguccione's son; and the Sienese and men of Colle were without resistance broken up and driven back as far as the troop of M. Piero, which was with the Florentine horse. There the said forefighters were checked and well-nigh all cut off and slain, and the said M. Giovanni was left there dead, and Uguccione's son, and their company; and the imperial pennon was cut down, with many good and brave folk.

§ 72.—*More about the said battle and defeat of the Florentines and of the prince.*

When the attack was begun, and Uguccione perceived how sorry a figure was made by the Sienese and the men of Colle when they fled by reason of the assault of his forefighters, he straightway caused the German troop to strike in, which were 800 horse and more; and they furiously attacked the camp and the said ill-ordered host, whereof by reason of the sudden movement a great part of the horse was not fully armed, and the foot so ill ordered, that when the Germans attacked them in flank, the javelin men let their missiles fall upon our own horse, and then took to flight. And this, among others was one great cause of the rout of the Florentine host, forasmuch as the said German troop pricking forward turned them to flight with little resistance save from the troop of M. Piero and of the Florentines, which endured long, but in the end were discomfited. In this battle there died M. Piero, brother of King Robert, and his body was never found; and M. Carlo, son of the prince, died there, and Count Charles of Battifolle, and M. Caroccio, and M. Brasco of Aragon, constables of the Florentines, men of great valour; and of Florence were left on the field some from well-nigh all the great houses and many magnates of the people, to the number of 114 cavaliers, between slain and prisoners; and, in like manner, of the best of Siena and Perugia and Bologna, and the other cities of Tuscany and of Romagna; in which battle there were slain 2,000 men in all, of horse and foot, and there were 1,500 prisoners. The prince fled with all the rest of his followers, some towards Pistoia and some towards Fucecchio and some by the Cerbaia; wherefore, since numbers were lost in the marshes of the Guisciana, many of the aforesaid slain were drowned without stroke of sword. This lamentable discomfiture was on the day of the beheading of S. John, the 29th day of August, 1315. After the said discomfiture, the stronghold of Montecatini surrendered to Uguccione, and the stronghold of Montesommano, which the Florentines held; and they which were within were allowed to go out safe and sound under conditions.

§ 73.—*How Vinci and Cerretoguidi rebelled against the Florentines.* § 74.—*How King Robert sent Count Novello into Florence as captain.* § 75.—*How Uguccione beheaded Banduccio Bonconti and his son, magnates of Pisa.* § 76.—*How the*

Florentines were divided into **1316 a.d.** *factions among themselves, and elected a Bargello.* § 77.—*How a part of the walls of Florence was built, and how bad coins were struck.* § 78.—*How Uguccione da Faggiuola was expelled from the lordship of Pisa and of Lucca, and how Castruccio at first had the lordship of Lucca.* § 79.—*How the count of Battifolle was vicar in Florence, and expelled the Bargello and changed the state of Florence.* § 80.—*Tells of a great famine and mortality beyond the mountains.*

§ 81.—*Of the election of Pope John XXII.*

1317 a.d.

Par. xxvii. 58. Epistola viii.

John XXII., born in Cahors, of base lineage, occupied the papal chair for 18 years 2 months and 26 days. He was elected on the 7th day of August, 1316, in Avignon by the cardinals, after a vacancy of two years, and after great discord among themselves, forasmuch as the Gascon cardinals, which were a large part of the college, desired the election of one of themselves, and the Italian and French and Provençal cardinals would not consent thereto, so much had they endured from the Gascon Pope. After long dispute, both one party and the other entrusted their votes to this Cahorsine, as a mediator, the Gascons believing that he would elect the cardinal of Bésiers, which was of their nation, or Cardinal Pelagrù. Who, with the consent of the other Italians and Provençals, and by the device of Cardinal Napoleone Orsini, head of the faction against the Gascons, gave the chair to himself, electing himself Pope after the manner ordained according to the Decretals. This man was a poor clerk, and his father was a cobbler, and he was brought up by the bishop of Arles, chancellor to King Charles II.; and by reason of his goodness and industry he came into favour with King Charles, who caused him to be educated at his charges, and then the king made him bishop of Frejus; and on the death of his master, the archbishop of Arles, to wit M. Piero da Ferriera, the chancellor, King Robert made him chancellor in his stead; and afterwards, of his care and sagacity, he sent letters as from King Robert to Pope Clement recommending himself, whereof the king, it was said, knew nothing at all, by reason of which letters he, the said bishop of Frejus, was promoted to be bishop of Avignon, and afterwards cardinal by reason of his wit and industry; wherefore King Robert, before he was made cardinal, was wroth with him, and took away the seal from him, forasmuch as he had sealed the said letters in his own favour to the said Pope Clement without his knowledge. This Pope John was crowned in Avignon on S. Mary's Day, the 8th day of September, 1316. Afterwards he was a great friend to King Robert, and he to him; and by his means he did great things, as hereafter shall be narrated. This Pope caused the Seventh Book of the Decretals to be completed which Pope Clement had begun, and set in order the solemnity and festival of the Sacrament of the Body of Christ, with great indulgences and pardons to whoso should be at celebration of the sacred offices, each hour, and he gave a general pardon of forty days to all Christians for every time that they made reverence when the priest repeated the name of Jesus Christ; this he did afterwards in the year 1318.

§ 82.—*How King Robert and the Florentines made peace with the Pisans and Lucchese.* § 83.—*How the Florentines recalled the bad money and issued the good money of the "new Guelf" mintage.* § 84.—*How King Robert sent his fleet to Sicily and did great damage.* § 85.—*How Ferrara rebelled against the Church.*

§ 86.—*How Uguccione da Faggiuola sought to re-enter Pisa, and what came of it in Pisa, and of the Marquis Spinetta.*
1317 a.d.

In the said year 1317, in the month of August, Uguccione da Faggiuola, with aid from M. Cane of Verona, came suddenly with much people, both horse and foot, into Lunigiana, supported by forces and letters of the Marquis Spinetta, who purposed to come to Pisa on the strength of certain negotiations which he had conducted in the city with men of his faction; which plot was discovered, and there was an outcry of the people, whereof Coscetto dal Colle of Pisa made himself the leader; and by the counsel of Count Gaddo they rushed in fury to the house of the Lanfranchi, which were in league with Uguccione, and slew four of the chief of the house; and others, together with their followers, they banished and set under bounds. When Uguccione perceived that he could not carry out his enterprise, he returned into Lombardy to Verona. Castruccio, lord of Lucca, and Uguccione's enemy, made a league with Count Gaddo and with the Pisans, and with aid of horsemen from them, he went with his host against the Marquis Spinetti, which had given Uguccione free passage, and took from him Fosdinuovo, a very strong castle, and Veruca and Buosi, and drave him from all his towns; and the said Spinetti fled with his family to M. Cane della Scala at Verona.

§ 87.—*How the Ghibelline party left Genoa.*

1317 a.d.

In the said year 1317, on the 15th day of September, the city of Genoa being under popular government, but the Grimaldi and the Fiescadori and their Guelf party being stronger than the d'Oria and their Ghibellines (on the one hand because King Robert favoured the Guelfs, and on the other hand because the Spinoli, which were of the Ghibelline party, and in exile from Genoa, were enemies of the d'Oria), certain of the house of the Grimaldi, by reason of enmity against the d'Oria, reinstated the Spinoli in Genoa, under pretence that they would abide under their command and that of the commonwealth. When they of the house of d'Oria and their friends perceived this, they feared greatly to be betrayed by the Guelfs and by the Grimaldi; and the city was all in arms and uproar; and the d'Oria not finding themselves powerful, by reason of the opposition of the Guelfs, and also of the Ghibelline Spinoli their enemies, concealed themselves and their friends, and showed no force of arms; by the which thing the Guelfs were encouraged and took up arms, and chose as captains of Genoa, M. Carlo dal Fiesco and M. Guasparre Grimaldi, on the 10th day of November, 1317. And when the Spinoli which were returned to Genoa saw that the city was come altogether to the Guelf party, and knew that this was through the care and industry of King Robert, straightway they agreed with the d'Oria and with their Ghibelline friends, and they all departed from the city together, on no other compulsion; whence afterwards ensued great scandal and war, as hereafter will be told, forasmuch as the said two houses of the d'Oria and the Spinola were the most powerful families of Italy on the side of the Ghibellines and the empire.

§ 88.—*How the Ghibellines of Lombardy besieged Cremona.*

§ 89.—*How M. Cane della Scala led an army against the Paduans, and took many castles from them.*

1317 a.d.

In the said year, in the month of December, the said M. Cane with his forces led his host against the Paduans, and took Monselici and Esti and a great part of their castles, and brought them so low that the following February, not being able to oppose him, they made peace according to M. Cane's pleasure, and promised to restore the Ghibellines to Padua; and this they did.

§ 90.—*How the exiles from Genoa with the force of the Ghibellines of Lombardy besieged Genoa.*

1318 a.d.

In the year 1318, when they of the houses of d'Oria and of Spinola with their following were in banishment from Genoa, and by reason of their power maintained themselves on the Riviera of Genoa on their estates, they sent ambassadors into Lombardy and made a treaty and league with M. Maffeo Visconti, captain of Milan, and with his sons **Cf. Convivio iv. 20: 38-41.** and with all the Lombard league which were Imperial and Ghibelline. For the which thing M. Marco Visconti, son of the said Maffeo, came from Lombardy with a great army of soldiers, Germans and Lombards, on horse and on foot, and with the said exiles from Genoa laid siege to the said city on the side of Co' di Fare and of the suburbs; and this was on the 25th day of March, 1318; and a few days after they of the house of d'Oria, with the aid of the others, led another army against the city of Albingano, on the Riviera of Genoa, and this they took, under conditions, in a few days. Afterwards, while the said host was still at Genoa, M. Edoardo d'Oria made a compact with the Abao [chief magistrate] of the people of Saona, and entered into the said city of Saona by night secretly, and straightway, with the aid of the Ghibellines of the city (for the greater part thereof were of the Imperial party), caused the said city to rebel against the commonwealth of Genoa in the month of April; for the which thing the forces of the exiles from Genoa increased greatly, so that well-nigh **Cf. Purg. iv. 25. Purg. iii. 49.** all the Western Riviera was under their lordship, save the strongholds of Monaco and Ventimiglia and the city of Noli; and in the Eastern Riviera they held Lerici.

343

§ 91.—*How the Ghibellines of Lombardy took Cremona.*

§ 92.—*How the exiles from Genoa took the suburbs of Prea.*

1318 a.d.

In the said year, at the end of May, the said exiles had besieged the city of Co' di Fare for two months, and it was bravely held by them within by means of a cunning device of ropes which kept the tower in communication with a vessel in the port of Genoa, and by this means they were supplied and provisioned in spite of all the host; wherefore the said exiles took counsel how they might dig and cut away the ground under the said tower. They within, fearing that it might fall, surrendered it on condition that their lives should be spared, and some said for money; and when they had returned into Genoa, they were condemned to death, and were cast down from a height. While the refugees were busied with the said siege, they continually attacked the suburbs of Prea, which are without the Oxen Gate; and fighting manfully, they took the place on the 25th day of June in the said year, whereby they advanced greatly, and the inhabitants of Genoa lost in like measure; for the host without increased, and gathered in the suburbs, and took the mountain of Peraldo and of S. Bernardo above Genoa, and surrounded the city; and above Bisagno they pitched another camp, so that the city was all besieged by land, and by sea it suffered great persecution from the galleys of Saona, and from the exiles, which had the lordship over the sea.

§ 93.—*How King Robert came by sea to succour Genoa.*

1318 a.d.

In the said year 1318, the Guelf party being thus besieged in Genoa by sea and by land, they sent their ambassadors to Naples to King Robert, who had been the cause of the whole disturbance in Genoa, that he should succour them and aid them without delay; and if he did not do this, they could not hold out, so straitened were they by the siege and by want of victuals. For the which thing King Robert straightway raised a great fleet of forty-seven transport vessels and twenty-five light galleys, and many other boats and craft laden with provisions; and he in person, with the prince of Taranto, and with M. John, prince of the Morea, his brothers, and with other

344

barons and with horsemen to the number of 1,200, departed from Naples on the 10th day of July, and came by sea, and entered into Genoa on the 21st day of July, 1318, and was honourably received by the citizens as their lord, and heartened the city, which could scarce hold out for lack of victuals. Immediately when the king was come to Genoa, the exiles broke up the camp which they had in Bisagno, and withdrew to the mountains of San Bernardo and of Peraldo, and to the suburbs of Prea towards the west.

§ 94.—*How the Genoese gave the lordship of Genoa to King Robert.*
1318 a.d.

In the said year, on the 27th day of July, the captains of Genoa and the Abao of the people, and the Podestà, in full parliament, renounced their jurisdiction and lordship, and with the consent of the people gave the lordship and care of the city and of the Riviera to Pope John and to King Robert for ten years, according to the constitutions of Genoa; and King Robert took it for the Pope and for himself, as one who had long desired it, thinking when he should have got the lordship of Genoa quietly in his hands, to be able to recover the island of Sicily, and overcome all his enemies; and it was for this purpose that, long ere this, he had stirred up revolution in the city, so as to drive thence the Spinoli and the d'Oria, forasmuch as ofttimes whilst they were lords of Genoa, they had opposed King Robert and King Charles, his father, and had helped them of Aragon which held the island of Sicily, as before we have made mention.

§ 95.—*Of the active war which the exiles of Genoa with the Lombards made against King Robert.*
1318 a.d.

The host without Genoa was not weakened by reason of King Robert's coming, but was largely increased by the aid of the lords of Lombardy, which held with the Imperial party; and they renewed their league with the emperor of Constantinople, and with King Frederick of Sicily, and with the marquis of Monferrat, and with Castruccio, lord of Lucca, and also secretly with the Pisans. And whilst they were at the siege, they were continually making strong and fierce assaults upon the city, hurling things against it from many engines, and attacking it in many places by day and by night—being men of great vigour—in such wise that King Robert with all his forces could gain nothing against them in any part. Rather by digging underground they undermined a great piece of the wall of Porta Santa Agnesa, and caused it to fall, and some of them entered by force into the city. Wherefore the king in person armed himself with all his followers, and they met one another with great vigour upon the ruined walls with swords in hand, but the great barons and knights of the king drove back their enemies with great loss both to one side and to the other, and they rebuilt the walls with great labour in a short time, working both day and night. The king and his followers being thus besieged and attacked in Genoa, sent for aid into Tuscany, and received it from many quarters: from the Florentines, 100 horse and 500 foot, all with lilies for their device, and the same number from Bologna, and likewise from Romagna, and from many other places, and they went to Genoa by sea by the way of Talamone; so that when his allies were come to him, the king was **Cf. Purg. xiii. 152.** supported in Genoa on the first day of November of the said year by more than 2,500 horse, and by footmen without number. Without were more than 1,500 horse, and the captain of the host was M. Marco Visconti of Milan, and they held the hill fortresses round about in such wise that the king could not go afield; and thus abode the said hosts in close war and skirmishes, hurling and shooting at one another all the said summer, and also the winter, forasmuch as neither one side nor the other could get the advantage. And thus abiding, M. Marco Visconti was so presumptuous as to request King Robert to fight with him in single combat, and whichever was victorious should be lord, which put the king into great scorn.

§ 96.—*How in the city of Siena there was a conspiracy, and uproar, and great changes followed thereupon.*

§ 97.—*How King Robert's followers discomfited the exiles from Genoa at the village of Sesto, and how they departed from the siege of the city.*

1318 a.d.

In the said year 1318, after that King Robert had been besieged in Genoa for more than six months, as already narrated, he bethought him that

346

he could not crush his enemies without unless he could land his army between the suburbs and Saona; and he raised a fleet of sixty galleys and transport vessels, and assembled 850 horse, and of foot full 15,000; and together with them were some Florentines and other Tuscans, and Bolognese and Romagnese; and they departed from Genoa on the 4th day of February, to bring the said people into the country around Sesto. And when the exiles and those without heard this, straightway they sent thither of their people on horse and on foot in great numbers to dispute the shore with King Robert's host, to the end the king's people might not come to land. Which people arrived on the 5th day of February, and with great travail, pushing empty casks before them, fought hand to hand with the enemy, the chief of them being Florentines and other Tuscans, which first descended from the galleys under the protection of the bowmen of the galleys which were by the shore; and by force of arms they landed, and broke up and discomfited the forces of the exiles upon the shore of Sesto, and many thereof were slain and taken prisoners; and they which escaped fled into the suburbs and to Saona, and the night following all the host **Johannes de Virgilio. Carmen v. 29.** which were in the suburbs and in the mountains of Paraldo and of San Bernardo departed and went towards Lombardy, and left all their baggage without having been pursued, forasmuch as the king would not that his people should follow after them because of the dangers of those mountains. Afterwards they of the city of Genoa recovered the suburbs of Prea and Co' di Fare and all the forts outside the city.

§ 98.—*How King Robert departed from Genoa and went to the papal* **1319 a.d.** *court in Provence.*

§ 99.—*How the exiles from Genoa with the Lombards returned to the siege of Genoa.*

1319 a.d.

In the said year 1319, when the exiles from Genoa heard of the departure of King Robert, they equipped in Saona twenty-eight galleys, whereof M. Conrad d'Oria was admiral, and they sent into Lombardy for aid, and assembled 1,000 and more horse, whereof the greater part were Germans, and a great number of common folk; and on the 27th day of July of the said year they returned with their army to Genoa, and set up their camp in Ponzevera, and on the 3rd day of August following they drew nigh to the city, attacking the suburbs in many places by land from the side of Bisagno; and the said galleys entered the port and strongly attacked the city, but gained nothing. And on the 7th day of August following there was a great battle in the plain of Bisagno between the exiles and those within the city, with great loss both to the one side and to the other, without either party having the honour of the victory, for those without retreated to the hill, and those within returned into the city; and afterwards they fought continually by day and by night against the city by sea and by land.

§ 100.—*How M. Cane della Scala took the suburbs of Padua.*
1319 a.d.

In the said year 1319, in August, M. Cane della Scala, with the exiles from Padua, whom the Paduans would not restore to the city according to the compact made by M. Cane, came with an army against Padua, with 2,000 horse and 10,000 foot, and took the suburbs, and set up there three camps in order the better to besiege it.

§ 101.—*How the Guelfs of Lombardy retook Cremona.* § 102.—*How M. Ugo dal Balzo was routed at Alessandria.* § 103.—*How the refugees from Genoa retook the suburbs of Genoa.* § 104.—*How the Ghibellines took Spoleto.* § 105.—*How the king of Tunis recovered his lordship.* § 106.—*How Castruccio, lord of Lucca, broke peace with the* **1320 a.d.** *Florentines, and began war against them again.* § 107.—*How folk of the refugees from Genoa were routed at Lerici.* § 108.—*How the Genoese took Bingane.* § 109.—*How the Pope and the Church invited M. Philip of Valois to come into Lombardy.* § 110.—*How M. Philip of Valois returned into France with shame, having gained nothing.* § 111.—*How Castruccio marched upon the Genoese Riviera.* § 112.—*How Frederick of Sicily sent his fleet of galleys to besiege Genoa.* § 113.—*How King Robert equipped his fleet of galleys to oppose that of the Sicilians, and what it accomplished.* § 114.—*Of the same.* § 115.—*How the Florentines forced Castruccio to return from the siege of Genoa.* § 116.—*Of the assaults which the exiles from Genoa and the Sicilians made upon the city, wherein they were worsted.* § 117.—*How the exiles from Genoa laid waste Chiaveri.* § 118.—*How the exiles from Genoa took Noli, and did divers acts of war.* § 119.—*How the king of Spain's brother was routed by the Saracens of*

Granada. § 120.—How the brothers of the Hospital defeated the Turks with their fleet at Rhodes.

§ 121.—How M. Cane della Scala being at the siege of Padua, was defeated by the Paduans and by the count of Görtz.
1320 a.d.

In the said year 1320, M. Cane della Scala, lord of Verona, had besieged the city of Padua with all his forces continually for more than a year, and having taken from that city well-nigh all its territory and strongholds, and having defeated them many times, had so crushed the city that it could hold out no longer, forasmuch as he had surrounded it entirely with ramparts occupied by his men, so that no provisions could enter therein. The said Paduans, well-nigh despairing of any escape, turned to the duke of Austria, king elect of the Romans, which sent to their succour the count of Görtz and the lord of Vals, with 500 steel-capped horsemen, and they suddenly, and as it were in secret, entered into Padua with these their followers. The said M. Cane, by reason of his great confidence and pride in his victories, and the great number of horse and of foot which were in his army, cared little for the Paduans, and by reason of the long siege, being too secure, had his troops in ill order. It came to pass that on the 25th day of August, 1320, the said count of Görtz, with his Friolese and Germans, and with the Paduans, sallied forth suddenly from the city, and vigorously assailed the host. M. Cane, with some of his ill-ordered horse, thinking to beat them back, gave battle, and by the count of Görtz and the Paduans was discomfited and unhorsed and wounded, and scarce came off with his life by the help of his followers, and escaped on a horse to Monselice; and his host was all routed, and many of his followers were slain or taken prisoners, and all their belongings lost; and thus by want of foresight the good fortune of this victorious tyrant changed to bad. At this siege of Padua died Uguccione della Faggiuola at Cittadella [al. In the city of Verona] of sickness, being come to aid M. Cane. He was the other great tyrant, which so persecuted the Florentines and Lucchese, as before we made mention.

§ 122.—How the count Gaddo, lord of Pisa, died; and how the count **1320 a.d.**
Nieri was made lord thereof. § 123.—How peace was made by the king of France with the

Flemings. § 124.—*How there was great dissension amongst them of the house of Flanders.* § 125.—*How the Ghibellines were expelled from Rieti.* § 126.—*How there was a great enrolling of armies by two emperors elect of Germany.* § 127.—*How the Marquis Spinetta allied himself with the Florentines against Castruccio, but it turned out to the shame of the Florentines.* § 128.—*How the offices were changed in Florence.* § 129.—*How the Marquis Cavalcabò, with the league of Tuscany, was routed in Lombardy.* § 130.—*How M. Galeasso of Milan had the city of Cremona.* § 131.—*How there was an eclipse of the sun, and the king of France died.* § 132.—*How the Bolognese expelled from Bologna Romeo de' Peppoli, the rich man, and his followers.* § 133.—*How the emperor of Constantinople had war with his sons.* § 134.—*How Frederick of Sicily was excommunicated, and how he had his son crowned over the kingdom.* § 135.—*How the Florentines sent to Frioli for horsemen.*

§ 136.—*Concerning the poet Dante Alighieri of Florence.*

1321 a.d.

In the said year 1321, in the month of July, Dante Alighieri, of Florence, died in the city of Ravenna, in Romagna, having returned from an embassy to Venice in the service of the lords of Polenta, with whom he was living; and in Ravenna, before the door of the chief church, he was buried with great honour, in the garb of a poet and of a great philosopher. He died in exile from the commonwealth of Florence, at the age of about fifty-six years. This Dante was a citizen of an honourable and ancient family in Florence, of the Porta San Piero, and our neighbour; and his exile from Florence was by reason that when M. Charles of Valois, of the House of France, came to Florence in the year 1301 and banished the White party, as has been afore mentioned at its due time, the said Dante was among the chief governors of our city, and pertained to that party, albeit he was a Guelf; and, therefore, for no other fault he was driven out and banished from Florence with the White party; and went to the university at Bologna, and afterwards at Paris, and in many parts of the world. This man was a great scholar in almost every branch of learning, albeit he was a layman; he was a great poet and philosopher, and a perfect rhetorician alike in prose and verse, a very noble orator in public speaking, supreme in rhyme, with the most polished **Inf. i. 87.** and beautiful style which in our language ever was up to his time and beyond it. In his youth he wrote the book of The New Life, of Love; and afterwards, when he was in exile, he wrote about twenty very excellent odes, treating of moral questions and of love; and he wrote three noble letters among others; one he sent to the government of Florence complaining of his undeserved exile; the second he sent to **Epistola vii.** the Emperor Henry when he was besieging Brescia, reproving him for his delay, almost in a prophetic strain; the third to the Italian **viii.** cardinals, at the time of the vacancy after the death of Pope Clement, praying them to unite in the election of an Italian Pope; all these in Latin in a lofty style, and with excellent purport and authorities, and much commended by men of wisdom and insight. And he wrote the Comedy, wherein, in polished verse, and with great and subtle questions, moral, natural, astrological, philosophical, and theological, with new and beautiful illustrations, comparisons, and poetry, he dealt and treated in 100 chapters or songs, of the existence and condition of Hell, Purgatory and Paradise as loftily as it were possible to treat of them, as in his said treatise may be seen and understood by whoso has subtle intellect. It is true that he in this Comedy delighted to denounce and to cry out after the manner of poets, perhaps in certain places more than was fitting; but may be his exile was the cause of this. He wrote also The Monarchy, in which he treated of the office of Pope and of Emperor. [And he began a commentary upon fourteen of his afore-named moral odes in the vulgar tongue which, in consequence of his death, is only completed as to three of them; the which commentary, judging by what can be seen of it, was turning out a lofty, beautiful, subtle, and very great work, adorned by lofty style and fine philosophical and astrological reasonings. Also he wrote a little book entitled, De Vulgari Eloquentia, of which he promises to write four books, but of these only two exist, perhaps on account of his untimely death; and here, in strong and ornate Latin and with beautiful reasonings, he reproves all the vernaculars of Italy.] This Dante, because of his knowledge, was **Cf. Canzone, 58-63.** somewhat haughty and reserved and disdainful, and after the fashion of a philosopher, careless of graces and not easy in his converse with laymen; but because of the lofty virtues and knowledge and worth of so great a citizen, it seems fitting to confer lasting memory upon him in this our chronicle, although, indeed, his noble works, left to us in writing, are the true testimony to him, and are an honourable report to our city.

END OF THE SELECTIONS FROM BOOK IX.

Grato e lontan digiuno
Tratto leggendo nel magno volume *** Soluto hai.

FOOTNOTES

[1] The complex and miserable history of Ugolino and Nino we have given only in its most essential portions. Even its connection with one of the most terrible and widely known passages in the *Inferno* cannot make it other than dreary, sordid, and unilluminating.

[2] The substance of this § is entirely drawn from Prof. Villari's recent work on Early Florentine History. "I Primi due Secoli della Storia di Firenze, Ricerche di Pasquale Villari." 2 vols., Florence, 1893, 1894. Price 8 fr. English translation by Madame Villari. "The Two First Centuries of Florentine History." Fisher Unwin. Price 2*s.* 6*d.* This work should be carefully studied in its entirety by all who desire to understand the constitutional history of Florence. N.B.—Some of our readers may be glad of the information that the modern scholar is Pasquale Villări (with short ă), and the mediæval chronicler Giovanni Villāni (with a long ā).

[3] If sense or frankness bold, if virtues' grace or gold,
If birth from noble source, could stay death in his course,
Frederick who here doth lie, would ne'er have come to die. Note on Corrected Text

Made in the USA
Columbia, SC
22 April 2022